BREATH AND BONES

BREATH
AND
BONES

SUSANN COKAL

UNBRIDLED
BOOKS

This little book treats of delicate subjects,
and has been sent to you only by request.
It is not intended for indiscriminate reading,
but for your own private information.

Unbridled Books
Denver, Colorado

Copyright © 2005 Susann Cokal

Library of Congress Cataloging-in-Publication Data

Cokal, Susann.
Breath and bones / Susann Cokal.
p. cm.
ISBN 1-932961-06-2 (alk. paper)
1. Artists' models—Fiction. 2. Women immigrants—Fiction.
3. Danish Americans—Fiction. I. Title.

PS3553.O43657B74 2005
813'.6—dc22

2005000016

1   3   5   7   9   10   8   6   4   2

Book Design by SH • CV

First Printing

To three generations of Familjeflickor—

TOVE RASMUSSEN
GUNVER HASSELBALCH
KRISHNA COKAL
GRY HASSELBALCH

Altid med de bedste hensigter.

Beauty like hers is genius.

DANTE GABRIEL ROSSETTI

PROLOGUE

Hygeia Springs, or Hygiene: 26.2 miles from the western (narrow gauge) rail terminus at Harmsway, with tracks presently being extended to the village itself. It is halfway up the mountain and so situated as to promote respiratory hygiene and health, with picturesque scenery on every side. The hospital building was erected at a cost of $80,000 and is not equaled by any other such institution in the West; thus for the last half-decade it has rivaled the nearby gold mines in its contributions to the region's prosperity. The visitor may enjoy the naturally carbonated spring waters or tour the small but none the less distinguished gallery of paintings, privately owned and free to the public on the first Monday of each month. Of several good hotels, the Celestial is the best.

FREDERICK E. SHEARER,
THE PACIFIC TOURIST, REVISED EDITION, 1892

The cemetery seemed to roll on for miles, its plinths and statues struggling through the folds of a hillside thinly dusted white. A strange situation for a house of art, the widow thought; but these graves, like the mine tailings on the mountain below or the crenellated fortress above, were nothing to her.

Two men met her at the fortress door. One was tall and raw and bony, with a disturbing stripe of pink scalp showing, as if he had been attacked by savages. His hands, also, were knotted with scar tissue, white ridges straining against the bones beneath. The other man, just slightly shorter, wore silken gloves, as if to say his own hands would do no more work on this earth; from his dark spectacles and blank expression, she surmised that he was blind. She did not ask their names, and they did not need to ask hers. She already knew the tall man, knew he was of her native country. She could speak as she wished, and he would translate.

"We are honored." The blind man spoke English, but quite clearly. "Thank you for traveling all this way."

"It was my husband's wish." She saw no need to pretend she was glad of it—though she was very glad finally to be unburdening herself of the crate and its contents. "Your drivers are opening the box now."

The taller man translated for the blind one, then turned back to her.

"Would you like to see where it will hang?" he asked, and she supposed she would.

There were four rooms to the gallery, each one feebly seeping light through narrow windows. The first two were crowded, with pictures hung nearly floor to ceiling and some of the frames knocking against each other.

The blind man served as guide. He remembered the placement of each picture and identified for her: "*Muses* by Holman Hunt . . . *Mother and Child* . . . Rossetti . . . the old Christiansborg Castle, painted by the Dane Christen Købke." He mispronounced that name, but she didn't bother to correct him.

In the third room, the style of the pictures changed; even the untrained visitor could see they were the work of a single artist, and one who preferred to paint the same subject several times: women with spears, women with masks, women with fishes' tails. Some of the canvases had been patch-worked, cut apart and resewn, with layers of paint crumbling off into colored dust at the seams. Every one of them featured a woman with flaming red hair and sharp, pale features—a woman the widow would rather not see here.

The blind man perhaps felt the same way, for he chose not to dwell on these pictures. "Figures from mythology," he merely said, and he unlocked the door to the fourth room, the one few visitors ever saw. The thin windows there were covered in velvet, making the room a tenebrous cave.

The widow hesitated. She had a mild dislike of the dark.

"This will be your painting's home," the tall man said, as the blind one felt his way inside.

"It is not my painting," she was quick to correct him. "My husband left it to your gallery in his will."

The tall man turned the screw for the gaslight. "And this is not my gallery. The owner lives up the mountain."

Light from the glass globes flared over the room and then subsided. Still the widow's eyes were dazzled. At first she saw only empty walls, and then something that made her raise the black handkerchief to her lips.

"*Er det—*"

"Yes," said her countryman. "It is."

It was a large cylinder with thick, slightly green glass walls. The ends of the cylinder were of glass, too, and the craftsmanship was so fine that the joinings were scarcely visible. But it was what the cylinder held inside that constituted the great wonder: the body of a woman, floating in a clear liquid, with a blue velvet gown and hair such a brilliant red that at first glance it appeared unnatural.

Again the blind man guessed the widow's thoughts. "She is real," he said. "True flesh, preserved in alcohol and other fluids. Go on, step closer and look."

The spectacle presented an irresistible lure; against a good part of her own will, the widow moved nearer. The corpse's hair and dress rippled faintly with the vibrations of her footsteps, while the scent of alcohol burned her nostrils. Up close, the body looked less alive; the flesh was a dead, arsenic white, and it, too, seemed to ripple. The face had lost some of its shape, as if the bones had turned to rubber; and most grotesque of all, the eyes were missing.

"Melted," the tall man whispered in their native tongue, when he saw where she was looking, "eaten away in the alcohol. But he"—gesturing toward the other man— "he doesn't know."

The blind man clearly did not understand. "Is she not beautiful?" he asked, with his face turned toward the coffin as if in all the world he could see this one thing. He touched the top of the glass curve with the gloved hand, and the widow had to swallow hard. She felt very hot in her silks.

"Too beautiful for the grave," the blind man went on, answering his own question. "Few scientists know this method of preservation; I learned it expressly for her. She was the last sight I saw before losing that faculty completely."

If she breathed, she would surely be ill. "But—"

"It was not a slow death, though it took us weeks to repair." The blind man spoke as if the death itself were of no importance. "If you look closely, you might see little wounds in her face and arms . . ."

She refused to look any closer. She heard the workmen approaching and felt a wave of relief that her duty here would soon be done. They came in stepping carefully, holding the immense canvas-wrapped picture removed from its crate.

The tall man gestured. "Against that wall."

"And be gentle," added the blind one.

The workmen propped it up, that artistic behemoth that had vexed her since the day her husband had bought it and proved that although he was willing to raise her to the state of matrimony, he could not shake off the hold of past fascination.

Travel had loosened the canvas wrapping until it now billowed like a sail. The workmen pulled it away to reveal the flat image of a woman, skin startlingly white, hair brilliantly red: an echo of the figure in the tube. Again the widow shuddered, and she looked away for what she thought would be the last time.

But what she saw was hardly more reassuring. The motion of so many feet and limbs had carried over into the cylinder, and the corpse inside was moving: the arms thrashing bonelessly, the hair storming around the eyeless face, and the lips parting as if to tell a story.

IMMACULATE HEART

She casts her best, she flings herself.
How often flings for nought, and yokes
Her heart to an icicle or whim . . .

COVENTRY PATMORE,
THE ANGEL IN THE HOUSE

Kapitel 1

. . . . .

This was our first glimpse of Denmark. Very flat it looked,—just out of water, and no more . . .

HELEN HUNT JACKSON,
GLIMPSES OF THREE COASTS

"D on't move," he said.

So Famke stifled her cough. She held her breath and tried to stay very, very still while the two frog-green eyes took her in. Up, down, and up again, a pencil tapped out her measure on the page, with a faint sound of scratching as he made refinements here or there.

Famke also had to repress the shivers, for it was cold in the room. She was wearing only the thinnest of summer chemises and was conscious that Albert could see everything beneath, right down to the triangle of red below her belly, which was as bright as the hair on her head. She felt exposed, proud and nervous in the way of a girl showing herself naked to a lover for the first time. But this was not the first time, and her companion was not pleased.

"Darling, do try to look alive," he murmured. "And graceful—or do you think nymphs are often hired for work on farms? It is more than positioning the bones, it's in the spirit, in the hands . . . like this"—he demonstrated— "see, darling, the *energy* and beauty flowing from my fingertips? You are a good mimic; now mimic me."

Famke tried to follow these latest instructions without, as he had previously enjoined, actually moving. She knew Albert didn't mean what he'd said, or not the unkind part of it; he always got grumpy just after starting work. In any event, he *had* found her on a farm, and she agreed that he had been a rescuer of sorts. So her arms remained in the air, fingers splayed in the sorcerous pose she'd kept this past hour, as the slow winter light changed from blue to gray and the bells of Our Savior's Church let the housewives know it was safe to step out to the shops.

Or perhaps she couldn't help moving just a little. Her arms ached and her lungs tickled, and she had to breathe, after all. All morning she'd been posing with hardly a word or a pause. A little sound broke from her nose.

"The devil!" Albert swore. In a better mood, he might have tossed in another "darling," but for now he knocked his sketchpad to the floor and strode off to stare moodily out the window.

At last Famke did let herself cough. She coughed a good, long time, to get all the tickles and scratches out of her lungs. When she was done she climbed down from the little platform and joined him at the window.

"Albert," she said, laying a tentative hand on his arm. She added, in English, "Sweetheart . . ."

He continued to sulk, so she looked out the window, too, and chewed a lip in thought. It was a pristine November day, sunlight dazzling on a full, thick blanket of snow that even the horses hadn't gone *tisse* over yet. Chimney smoke had only just begun to soot the rooftops, the trains were blocked by the snow on the rails, and in the narrow harbor chunks of ice were bumping against each other, like pieces of a giant jigsaw puzzle trying gently for a better fit. A draft leaked in through the warped panes and Famke, shivering, pressed herself against Albert's back.

She was somewhat pleased to find he was staring toward the ruin of the royal palace, now a white mound to the south. It was a mound they both knew well; one night a month or so ago, just after the fire that started in a garderobe had finally quenched itself in the harbor, the two of them had sneaked past the sentries and poked around the rubble for souvenirs. Famke had held a shuttered lantern while Albert dug out a nearly perfect silver tinderbox still filled with royal matches, something that he with his fondness for cheroots could put to far better use than she; and yet he presented it to her with a gallant flourish. It sat now on the icy mantel, polished to such a gloss that the three ladies carved on the top, whom Albert called the Graces, seemed to move with the light.

Albert spoke. "That ruin"—he pulled her up beside him and pointed, as if she couldn't see it for herself—"that was the first thing I saw when I woke this morning."

"Our first snowfalling," Famke agreed, but he didn't seem to hear.

"I said to myself, '*That* is my inspiration. *That* is what's been lacking in the work I came here to do . . . '"

"Your entryness," she elaborated, "to your Brothergood."

"Brotherhood." He adjusted the angle of her head, even though she wasn't posing now. "And yes, you are right. You," he said, looking at and yet beyond her, "will be Nimue, creating the ice cave in which you will make the noble Merlin a prisoner for time and all eternity. The enchantress baiting her trap. Eyes weaving spells—making this icy cell a crystal semblance of paradise . . ."

She strained to look especially magical. Albert often sounded to her like one of the priests who had visited the orphanage; their voices were full of poetry, but she had never been able to understand it, even in Danish.

He studied her critically and said, "Your figure is right, your eyes and your face. Your hair. And yet something is missing."

Famke dropped her last attempt at a pose. She hardly understood when Albert talked in this voice, with this passion and despair; he'd only just begun to teach her his language, and she was barely seventeen, hardly a scholar. She clutched her elbows and said, "Doesn't magic people feel cold?"

"*Cold*," Albert whispered. He was prone to repeating the last word that had stuck in his mind, as if there he'd find the revelation that would make him the most celebrated of the painterly association to which he aspired. "A paradise. Cold—ice!" And, perhaps giving up on some loftier endeavor, he kissed her.

Who would imagine paradise to be cold? Famke thought as Albert's lips oystered away at hers. To her the cold meant chilblains, a red nose, and extra pain in the lungs. Everyone had trouble keeping warm in a winter like this of 1884, and Albert for some reason insisted on living in a garret with a fireplace that would not draw. She didn't even have a full set of underwear on. But when she threw her arms around his neck and kissed him deep, she felt his warmth through the layers of his coat and waistcoat and shirt and undershirt, and sudden bright heat sprang into her cheeks, sweat to her brow. She broke into a fever so intense she might have swooned if she hadn't been caught by another fierce bout of coughing.

Albert released Famke and backed away, to look thoughtfully from her to the sketchpad. He was not particularly bothered by coughs, having come of age in one of England's coal towns where everybody hacked and suffered night sweats. He watched Famke with those green eyes, too big for their sockets but somehow always squinting, as she doubled over and coughed and coughed, till her face turned a bright beety red—she could feel it—and she developed an urgent need to visit the loo.

As she shuddered, Albert did nothing; but she expected no more. Only this watching, which was his work in life, just as posing for and waiting upon him and being watched had become hers. When she felt the coughing was done, she tried to smile apologetically with her swollen lips. At that, he reached into his sleeve and drew out a handkerchief.

When Famke took it and looked down, she saw another triangle marking her chemise—glistening, just beginning to soak into the delicate batiste, a fan of red droplets radiating out from the vee of her legs. It stretched nearly to the hem and her bare feet. If she could have turned any redder, her embarrassment and shame would have done it: The cough had brought a mist of blood from her lungs, and it had ruined her nymph's costume. She should get the chemise into cold water right now—but no, Albert had grabbed both her hands and was leading her back to the platform.

"That's it," he said excitedly. "That is it! Nimue was a *virgin* . . ." He pushed her hastily back into her former pose and added the pillows from their bed, arranging them at her feet. "Ice blocks," he murmured, and then: "She was a virgin, and she gave Merlin her love, and when he failed to return it, she used his own magic to cast a fearsome spell upon him."

Albert set Famke's shoulders and chin. "And her maiden's blood streaked the ice like flames." He looked at her pointedly, as if she could be expected to spray blood over the pillows on command. When that failed to happen, he continued thoughtfully, "Her blood wove a snare within the ice . . . Of course I cannot truly show that blood or where it came from, but I can suggest, in the shadows of the skirt . . ."

"I need to *tisse*," Famke bleated, but Albert stood on tiptoes to drop a little kiss at the corner of her eye. She held the pose.

Back at the easel, he dusted off the sketchpad with his hands. He took a long squinting look at Famke, then found half a charcoal pencil on the floor and began to draw. There was silence, except for the scratching of his pencil and the faint curses of the sailors in the harbor below.

Famke liked when Albert looked at her, even though now, as he plotted her against the stub of pencil or a longer brush, she knew he wasn't really seeing *her* at all: He was seeing his idea of this Nimue, a virginal nymph who lived in his mind but not in his bed. It was the same way as he saw the blood on Famke's chemise not as the sign of sickness but as a signal of beauty, something he called a symbol, unrelated to the coughs that plagued her.

Someone was coughing in the stairwell right now. A sailor, Famke guessed from the loud sound of it. She thought that the sailors who lived in Fru Strand's rooming house liked to look at her, too; but they looked differently. They saw the same things Albert saw, the same figure and eyes and hair, but even at her age she knew it didn't *mean* to them what it did to him. They were only boys, at the very beginning of their years at sea, renting a room for a week or two between voyages in much the same way as they rented girls for a night.

"Keep your arms up," Albert reminded her, and she brought her mind back into Nimue. *I am a magical nymph*, she told herself. *I am enslaving an ancient wizard. I do not wish to work on a farm again.*

Her raw lungs and full bladder only increased in discomfort, but she stood steadfast and focused on Albert's hands as they performed their infinitely delicate work, drawing her. He had beautiful fingers, long and bony, with a rainbow of paint always under the nails, and to Famke's mind they produced wonders. They had drawn her as an earthly Valkyrie, in a cloak made of swans' feathers (and nothing else); painted her as a nearly naked Gunnlod, the loveliest of the primordial Norse giants, watching over the three kettles of wisdom in a deep, deep cave (Albert seemed to be very fond of caves). And now this Nimue, a wizard's lover, who could be from icy Scandinavia but would be of great interest to the English critics who could make Albert's fortune. Famke had never heard of Merlin or of Nimue, but Albert was teaching her a great deal about the mythology of her people. He liked to set her lessons from the traveler's guidebooks scattered over the mantel.

"Maiden's blood," Albert said, repeating. He picked up a dry brush and ran it over the sketched Nimue. Famke watched from the corner of one wide eye as the charcoal lines blurred, and in blurring, came to a more vivid sense of life. It never failed to fascinate her, this transformation from paper and coal into human figure. *Her* figure.

She maintained the pose until, some minutes later, Albert opened a few tubes of paint and splotched a page with shades of weak blue and stark white, marking out the rhythm of color. It was clear there was to be a lot of ice, even in her gown.

With this, Albert nodded to her; she was through. Famke stepped off the little platform, looking askance at the pillows she'd been posing with; she and Albert did not have many, and she knew they wouldn't be sleeping with these until the painting was finished or abandoned. The pillows must keep their pose, too.

"What shall I call this one?" Albert asked conversationally as he mixed a thin, bright red. "*The Revenge of Nimue . . . The Ravishment of Merlin . . .*"

Famke took the chamberpot from under the bed and, at last, went to a corner to relieve herself. Albert could go on in this vein for hours, and he usually chose the most descriptive and least pronounceable title possible ("*The Violated Nimue, Enraged, Casting Spells Over Merlin's Prison*") for works he would eventually disown. Very little of Albert Castle's labor seemed to yield the results he desired, what he saw in his mind—a complete and wondrous world populated by celestial nymphs and robust goddesses, all with Famke's white skin and wild hair, demonstrating the myths of power and betrayal that had moved him ever since he opened his first book of poetry. He expected perfection and disappointed himself each time he picked up pencil or brush; and each time, the gesture grew in importance: His father had sworn to support Albert only up to his twenty-fifth birthday, which would come on the first day of April. If Albert did not manage to produce a saleable painting in that time, he would have to join his father's pencil-manufacturing company. But before any painting was half done, he deemed it unsatisfactory; he broke them all over his knee or tore them to bits, then took off at a run through the streets to purge his frustration.

Even now Albert picked up a heel of their morning bread and rubbed it over half the sketched page, erasing some mistake.

The one scrap that Famke had managed to preserve hung in a dark corner above their washtub, where he would be least tempted to destroy it. This was the first sketch he had ever made of her, and Famke looked up at it as she relieved herself: a farm girl, a tender of geese and pigs, with her cap pushed back on her head and a butterfly light in her eyes. Every detail was perfect; it was Famke exactly as she wished to see herself in those days, and it had taken him only an hour to complete.

For all their dissatisfactions, each of Albert's works was dense with that sort of detail and keen observation, labored over inch by inch. It was that labor that made their eventual destruction so heartbreaking to Famke. She once suggested that he sketch a rough outline first, to get an impression of the scene, but he reacted with horror: "Impressions are dangerous to a true artist," he said. "You speak like a Frenchwoman—you know, over there a man fills five or six canvases a day with *impressions*. The Brotherhood know that only in precise details is there truth. It is the difference between a tramp and a good workman—impressions are a passing pleasure; patience and industry make art."

And yet, thought Famke, Albert was remarkably impatient. Just now he was wearing that gray heel of bread down to his fingers, and crumbs were flying everywhere. The page before him was a smear of pale blue. It was time for her to do or say something, lest he succumb to self-criticism and despair.

She covered the chamberpot and put it back in its place. Still naked, thinking how best to distract without annoying him, she climbed into bed and buried herself up to her eyelids in blankets, then looked to the window. The sunlight was already waning, but it showed the roofs had grown dirty, the day's warmth turning the castle ruins from a palace of snow back into mere rubble.

"Do you think Christiansborg burns to a purpose?" she asked. "Do you think it is destroyed because it is not perfect?"

Albert glanced out the window, too, and what he saw there seemed to calm him. "No." He picked up his brush again. "The Danes do not behave that way. Not since the Vikings, at any rate." He turned to a blank page and said, ruminatively, "Perfect . . ."

The sheets now felt as warm and soft as bathwater; Famke slid down them like a happy eel and tried to imagine a world she might create if invited to do so. She had only the dreamiest sense of what it might be: warm, yes, but with jigsaw-puzzle blocks of ice and flowers and pickled herring and definitely Albert. The thick smell of linseed oil and the bite of turpentine, rainbows of paint under nails and across unexpected stretches of skin. There would be no farmwork, no housework, no church services; only art. She would never cough. Instead, she would stand in the middle of this world, or lie in it, perpetually still, with her clothes off and her eyes lost in Albert's.

It would be this life.

"New pots for old!" sang a tinker passing down the street below.

Famke looked up and suddenly the light was gone; even the keenest eye couldn't stretch it any further. Albert sighed and put brush and palette down on the rough board table, where Famke would clean them later. Wiping his hands on what he must have thought was a rag—a camisole she'd left to dry over the back of a chair—he looked from the easel to the bed, from pencil drawing to paint sketch to the real, living girl watching him and trying not to cough.

"I think it is going to be . . ." He paused, searching for the right word: "beautiful."

It was an ordinary word after all, but nonetheless exotic to her, for he said it in English. Famke felt a rush of hot feeling—not the ordinary fever of her disease but a new kind that Albert had passed on to her, a kind that felt hotter and stronger each time it came over her. She threw the covers off and held out her arms to him, unconsciously splaying her hands in much the same way as Nimue did.

He came toward her, repeating, "Beautiful . . ."

When he was undressed and in the narrow bed himself, he hoisted Famke up and—her arms braced against the sloped ceiling for balance— slid her down onto him. She wobbled, unsure just what to do now; and he kept his hands on her hips. He held her still while he began to move.

Famke looked down into Albert's face; and then he looked up into hers, the planes of it in twilight shadows. Famke removed one hand from the ceiling and pulled her hair to the side so that, behind her, he might look on the face and form of his Nimue, his masterwork, his violated virgin.

"Ah . . ." Very quickly, he gasped and began to shudder.

As she rode that wave, Famke knew that he was seeing her as his heroic nymph, and she did not mind one bit. She had a lovely warm, shimmering feeling, a feeling that—like the new fever, but different—made her *want* something . . . As Albert quieted beneath her, she felt the shimmering rise and then fall away, leaving in its wake a vague sense of longing and that familiar tickle in her lungs.

Famke coughed. The contractions pushed Albert out of her, and he slid back, to where the bed met the wall.

"Really, darling," he said as she got up and, for want of a handkerchief, coughed further into the paint-stained camisole, "you should take something for that dreadful hack." He swabbed at himself with the bedsheet. "I'll get you an elixir the next time I'm out."

Famke shook her head, yes, no, feeling herself cold and wet and somehow bereft, but still with that sensation of wanting inside. She lowered the camisole and smiled at Albert, and he said again, "Beautiful."

Kapitel 2

. . . . .

English is spoken at all the principal hotels and shops. A brief notice of a few of the peculiarities of the Danish language may, however, prove useful. The pronunciation is more like German than English: a is pronounced like ah, e like eh, ø or ö like the German ö or French eu. The plural of substantives is sometimes formed by adding e or er, and sometimes the singular remains unaltered.

K. BAEDEKER,
NORTHERN GERMANY (WITH EXCURSIONS TO
COPENHAGEN, VIENNA, AND SWITZERLAND)

Famke was not virtuous when she met Albert Castle. According to the Catholic precepts by which she'd been raised, she was no longer truly virginal, as she confessed to him in a bedtime conversation. Few orphan girls, even those raised by the good sisters of the Convent of the Immaculate Heart of Mary, could lay claim to that desirable state once they entered the wider world—and why should they bother to hold on to something that would be taken from them once they'd passed communion and were placed in service with some family inevitably headed by a prurient husband, a curious son, or a querulous grandfather who *would* have his way?

"Darling, you're so fierce," Albert said as he squeezed her.

"It is a fierce world," she said. "*Overhovedet*, especially, for a girl."

Besides, immured in her orphanage, Famke had found the idea of sin exciting. It offered the possibility of something other than what she had, something that must be at least pleasant, if not delicious, since the straight-backed nuns who had married Christ were so vehemently against it.

So Famke had taken sin into her own hands. The boys on the other side of the orphanage were just as curious as she, and intrigued by her interest. She courted them first through a crack in the wall separating the boys' and girls' dormitories. This was during the exercise period, when the children were encouraged to enjoy fresh air and wholesome movement, trotting up and down two barren courtyards, occasionally playing desultory games of tag or statue around the lone elder tree in each one. Famke would lean into her wall and see an eye, almost always blue, peering back at her through the rubble and leaves. They would talk, whispering arrangements for *rendezvous* that, under the nuns' watchful glare, never came to pass. Once, Famke wormed her thin hand along the crack, and the boy on the other side (a Mogens, she believed, or maybe a Viggo—there were so many of both, arriving with those un-Catholic names pinned to their diapers so the good nuns felt bound to retain them) managed to reach just far enough in to touch the tip of one finger. The contact gave her a thrill she'd never known before, and for a good many months it was what she thought sin was, this furtive touch within a wall.

She actually saw boys only during the daily chapel services; the sexes even ate separately, so as to avoid the inevitable temptation. While the priest droned on about the blessings of humility, meekness, and poverty, she flirted through fanned fingers. Breathing deeply, she smelled the strong cheap soap the older girls made in the orphanage yard from ash and fat. For the rest of her life, it would be that smell—even more than the smell from the place that the nuns would refer to only as Down There, when they admitted it existed at all—that made her heart pound with excitement.

To the priest's soporific cadences, in that edifice of gray-painted brick, Famke's azure eyes winked and fluttered. The boys were helpless: She glowed like the rosy windows that Catholics could afford only in non-Lutheran countries. At the age of twelve, her breasts already brushed against the plain gray uniform, and the figure growing inside that rough sacking seemed to color it rainbow bright.

The nuns did not fail to notice her blossoming. Soon, Famke had to sit through services sandwiched between two severe gray bodies.

"She has always been wild," the Mother Superior said in one of her frequent conferences with the wisest of the nuns. "We saw that from the first."

"And the visitors saw it as well," said Sister Saint Bernard, Mother Superior's second in command. "The basest peasant can recognize such a spirit, be the little girl ever so pretty. It's no wonder they always took a different child."

Mother Superior said absently, "We do not speak of our patrons that way. Or our young charges." She was thinking, as was the rest of her council, of the high hopes they'd entertained when the baby turned up on their doorstep one late October day, still wearing the black hair of the womb, wrapped in a soft wool blanket and bearing a note that said simply, "*Familjeflicka.*" This, they had thought, was a child destined for one of their rare adoptions.

Young Sister Birgit, who had been born in southern Sweden, had said the word came from her country and meant either "a girl who stays at home" or "a girl of good family." Given the quality of the blanket and the notorious fact that gravid Swedes often took the short boat ride over to Copenhagen, where mothers' names were not required for a legal delivery, the note seemed to promise great things. But the sisters found no family portraits, no silver spoons, no precious jewels hidden about the infant's person; only what one might expect to find in a very ordinary baby's diaper, and that they gave to one of the novices to deal with. The baby screamed at their inspection, and screamed when she was washed, and nearly took her own head off when she was put to bed with a bottle. The sisters decided to let her cry till she slept, and in the morning they found her whimpering more quietly, but with a mouth stained from blood, not milk. Her tough young gums had broken off the glass nipple.

Sister Birgit was delegated to pick the splinters from the baby's lips, using tweezers and the light of a good lantern. She had to dose the squalling patient with brandy to make her lie still.

She's nothing but breath and bones, Birgit thought. *Only breath and bones.* Though it wasn't true—the baby's limbs were nicely rounded, her cries lusty—the phrase made Birgit feel tender. It gave her patience.

In the meticulous work, which took all day, Birgit came to love the little girl. She murmured endearments over the drunken body and torn mouth, and it was then that she shortened the Swedish word to "Famke," the name that would follow the girl even after her official christening as Ursula Marie. When Famke woke up enough to be hungry again, Birgit would have fed the baby at her own breast, if she could have mustered anything more than prayers. Instead she dipped one corner of Famke's blanket in a cup of warm milk, freshly bought at the market on Amagertorv, and coaxed the sore lips and tongue to suckle.

In later years, as the growing girl's cough turned bloody, Sister Birgit would accuse herself of having missed a shard of glass somewhere. She fancied that Famke's lungs were lacerating themselves as they tried to get rid of that last fragment. Though Birgit and many of the other nuns were also afflicted with persistent coughing, she felt, against all reason, that the unusual event of Famke's infancy was the source of the girl's affliction—never mind that she bore no other scars. Birgit prayed for forgiveness, and for Famke's cure, and she nursed Famke all the way to solid food at the age of five months. Thus she made the best possible use of the "good family's" sole patrimony; the baby sucked the blanket down to meager threads.

"Sister Birgit," the Mother Superior reprimanded her gently in private, "you have become too attached to this one child. You must divide your care among the children equally, as our Lord divides his love among us."

Birgit tried to do as she was told. Though she could never give the chaotic horde of orphans the impartial and impersonal affection required by her order, she could offer them the semblance of equal treatment. In everyday life, the life the other sisters shared, she nursed the orphans' colds and coughs and combed their hair with the impartiality of a Solomon; when a child died, Birgit washed the body and lifted it into its pine box.

But when she was alone with Famke, Birgit hugged the little girl as tight as she dared, so tight that their bones ground together. Birgit would not have chosen convent life for herself; that had been her parents' wish, as they'd grown too old and tired by the time their seventh daughter reached adolescence to do anything more for her. Her eighteen-year-old body was starved for physical contact, and Famke's round little arms gave her the greatest comfort she would ever know.

In these moments of privacy, Famke took shameless advantage of Birgit's unstated preference. She played by sliding the gold band from the nun's finger and sticking it on her own thumb, then popped it in her mouth and impaled it with her tongue to make herself laugh. On the unusual occasions when there was candy at the orphanage, Famke knew that even after all the other children had received their justly measured shares, there would be an extra piece or two in Birgit's pocket. She knew also that if Birgit, and Birgit alone, caught her in some wrongdoing, she had only to place her hands on each side of the nun's face and kiss her nose to be forgiven and pass unpunished. No one else would learn of her crime, and her bond with her fellow-Swede would grow.

．　．　．

In Famke's twelfth year, Birgit's affections led nearly to disaster. As one of the physically stronger nuns, Birgit was asked to supervise the annual boiling of soap. She had been doing it for some years and had the routine chore mastered: rendering the waste fat saved from stringy Sunday joints, adding lye made from stove ashes, stirring endlessly. The older girls were excused from lessons in order to perform this stirring, for production of a good soap, the nuns argued, was of as valuable practical use as hemming the countless towels and blankets they made to sell—all skills the girls would take with them into service—and perhaps even more necessary than lessons in the use of Danish flowers and herbs, or reading the Bible and other useful books.

That year, Famke was big enough to help. Sister Birgit smiled as her darling took the wooden stirring-stick from the orphan ahead of her and began to draw it through the liquid viscous with long boiling. Famke closed her eyes and breathed in the odor that, to her, meant the belly-fluttering thrill of flirtation and the promise of something she didn't understand but knew, absolutely *knew*, would be wonderful. And so when one of the older Viggos, a large-eyed youth now nearing the age of confirmation, approached with wood for the fire, Famke smiled and shimmered at him. And he was lost.

Just then Birgit's attention was momentarily diverted—and for this the other sisters blamed her—by a cloud of bees threatening to swarm either the soap pot, the heavy-blossomed elder tree near which it rested, or the fair stirrer of soap herself. Birgit took off her apron and flapped it vigorously at them. So she did not see Famke slow down in her stirring, gazing at this Viggo, lost in her own hazy ideas of sin. And then Famke lost the wooden plank, or most of it, in the soap pot. With a cry of dismay, she lunged after it; the boy dropped his wood and lunged, too, to save her hand from scalding—and as a result it was his hands that scalded.

Viggo howled with pain and ran toward the well. Famke ran after him. She nursed his burned hands as she'd been trained to do, with cold water and bandages swiftly torn from her petticoat. And finally, as a much-stung Sister Birgit abandoned the bees and came to the rescue, Famke dropped a tiny illicit kiss on one clumsy knot she'd tied over the boy's wrist.

In that moment, with no interchange of plank and air to cool it, the un-stirred fat reached a crucial temperature. The whole soapy potful burst into flames. The conflagration blew toward the elder tree and, as Mother Superior said in yet another council meeting, "We were an angel's breath from burn-ing up ourselves."

Indeed, a spark landed in Famke's hair and started to melt. With a hurt hand, Viggo smothered it, and Famke collapsed in his arms in gratitude. She never mentioned the singeing of her braids to anyone else, but she was to suffer a fear of fire the rest of her life.

Sitting and tallying up the damage, Mother Superior said, "I believe some punishment is in order. For endangering not just herself and young Viggo but the entire orphanage as well, for being . . . Nå, for . . ." Everyone on the nuns' council knew what she meant. Famke had been born with a character that had no place inside convent walls, and Sister Birgit had only strengthened it. They were all thinking one word: *wild.* "This time her transgression itself was slight, but it might have had serious consequences for all of us."

Sister Saint Bernard said cryptically, "When Lucifer and his angels fell from heaven, their wings burst into flames."

"Så," said the Mother Superior, "it is time to take Ursula in charge."

Birgit prayed for humility and for strength. She knew she was to be dis-ciplined by having to join in the disciplining of her favorite, and she could say nothing aloud just yet.

"She should be isolated from the other children," suggested Sister Casilde.

"She should have bread and water for a week," countered Sister Balbina.

"Bread and water *and* isolation," said Sister Saint Bernard, sending up a quiet prayer of thanks that the year's vintage of elderberry jam and wine had not been threatened.

The nuns discussed this punishment eagerly, piling on mortifications that they themselves might have embraced in a more idealistic, ascetic or-der. One sister, who had been in the convent so long that she'd gone deaf with the silence, even shouted that Famke should wear a hair shirt.

"Sisters!" Birgit bit her lower lip, shocked at her own forcefulness. What could she, so largely responsible for the disaster, say to them? "Famke is just a child—"

"Her first communion is not far away." Sister Casilde offered the sacrament as a threat.

"Punishment will do no good," Birgit said with the authority of the one who knew Famke best. "She is wild, yes, but we must tame her gently. Violent restrictions will only make her rebel—and she only dropped a spoon, after all."

The other nuns gaped.

"Our order does not advocate violence," Mother Superior told Birgit on a note of reproof. "No one suggests we cane her, for example."

"It would not be a bad idea," Sister Saint Bernard said under her breath.

Birgit pressed her palms against the table. "I am to blame," she declared loudly. "I should have been watching her. So I will do penance, say extra prayers . . . I will wear a hair shirt, if that is required."

The nuns stared. They had never seen such passion in Birgit before. Nearly all felt a little ashamed; each asked herself, *Would I wear a hair shirt for someone else's sin?*

Mother Superior relented. "And Ursula will pray with you. No hair shirt will be necessary."

While Birgit prayed, the good sisters plotted a course of action. One after another, they lectured Famke about minding the clock and always, always keeping her eye on a burning fire. Sister Fina instructed her to sleep on a wooden board, Sister Agnes to cross her ankles, never her knees, when seated. Mother Superior had her read stories of the saints' lives to the younger children—endless tales of patience and suffering, including the story of Famke's own namesake, Saint Ursula, who had fled pagan England with an army of eleven thousand virgins only to be mown down in Germany.

Sister Saint Bernard swore her to secrecy and gave her five good whacks across the bottom with a cane.

Knowing this was mercy, and feeling very bad over what had happened to Viggo, Famke obeyed them all. She adapted easily to the manners of a good girl—but they suspected she would as naturally have taken on those of a strumpet. So she was forced to bide her time, peeking through the prayerful fan of her fingers with a nun on each side.

"Why do you twitch so?" she whispered, sitting next to Birgit; but the nun said nothing, having resolved, despite Mother Superior's injunction, to wear the hair shirt in silent mortification for three full months.

At the end of that time, Viggo's hand had scabbed over nicely and the women hoped he would one day be able to use it again to lift a pitchfork or curry a horse. A bumper crop of elderberries allowed Sister Saint Bernard to forgive both Birgit and Famke, and Famke forgave herself. She began begging to help with tasks that would bring her to the other side of the orphanage.

But, bolstered by her own penance, Birgit held firm. She kept the girl with her during exercise periods, and she herself plastered every chink she could find in the dividing wall.

"You will understand one day," she said as she brushed Famke's mass of red curls before bed, "and you will be grateful."

"But in the outside world," Famke pointed out, "there will be nothing to save me. Shouldn't I learn the worst of it now, while I still have you with me?"

Birgit gave a few vigorous strokes to a particularly stubborn tangle. "Perhaps you won't need to join the outside world. Perhaps you'll stay here . . ."

"What, with you?" Famke turned and gave her a big hug, slightly frightening to Birgit in its intensity. "I would love to stay with *you*. But I'll never be a sister. Instead, maybe I'll take you with me when I go into service."

Birgit picked up the brush again, disciplining herself to make firm, even strokes, and then to braid the girl's hair tight. "What would I do in the outside?" she asked.

◆　◆　◆

Since it was impossible to reach the boys' side of the building, Famke turned her attention to the part she herself occupied. At night in the dormitory, she lay awake listening to the other girls breathe, feeling the heat radiate from their bodies. She wondered why she had never noticed that Anna had a loud, tickling laugh or that Mathilde's hair was long and bright. Mathilde also had large and capable hands that nonetheless managed to look graceful as they scrubbed out a pot or picked up a stitch dropped in

Famke's knitting. Mathilde smelled good, like bread and soap. She began to interest Famke very much.

She was thirteen, a year older than Famke and a suitable model for the younger girl's reformation. The nuns looked on their friendship with relief and, as Famke took on some of Mathilde's habits, with complacency. They saw that she washed herself frequently, volunteered to help deworm the littlest orphans, and even rose early, with Mathilde, to make breakfast.

Famke's hair curled in the steam as she stirred the enormous kettle of *havremels grød*, the oatmeal gruel they ate each morning. Through the dully fragrant cloud of it, her eyes kept seeking Mathilde. She knew no love poetry, except what was found in the Bible, but she thought there must be some nice way to describe the curve of Mathilde's back as she bent over the bread board, or the graceful undulations of her hands as she kneaded the dough.

"You look like a fish," Famke blurted out, and Mathilde's eyes got wide. Then, out of embarrassment, Famke laughed; and Mathilde, with an affronted air, turned wordlessly back to her work.

In the end, won over or perhaps worn down by that persistent blue stare, it was Mathilde who approached Famke over the bubbling pots, who kissed her and set her heart pounding, who held Famke close and hard and gave her a taste of that delicious, elusive shimmering feeling.

"You are *my* little fish," Mathilde whispered into the red curls. Famke felt glad all over.

That night she was awakened with a tickle in one tightly curled ear. "Let me in," Mathilde whispered, tugging at the blankets that the nuns always snugged like winding-sheets around the children's bodies.

Famke wiggled herself free, emerging from her cocoon warm and white and fragrant. Mathilde slid in beside her and, with little ado, put her supple lips up to Famke's, her hand on the region Down There.

Famke jumped. "*Fanden*," she swore, daring to speak the name of the devil for the first time ever.

"It's all right," Mathilde whispered, touching Famke through her nightgown. "You see, there is a little cottage Down There, with a little roof of thatch. A little fire burns on the hearth."

If there was indeed a fire, it was drawing water to it; but the water did not quench, only made the fire hotter. Famke remembered the day of soap and flames: the smell of ashes and fat, the heat of Viggo's hand under her lips.

Mathilde's finger moved. "The cottager comes home to warm himself." But the cottage door was closed, and Famke yelped in pain.

"I see." Mathilde propped herself up on an elbow and retreated to the roof of thatch. "The cottage-wife has built herself a wall. Shall I look for a window?"

Mathilde's hair shone white in the light of her eyes, and all around them the darkness crepitated. Famke realized that cottagers were coming home in the ward's other beds too. That thought made her bold, and curious; her fingertips itched.

With the swift motion of sudden decision, Famke pushed aside the other girl's nightgown. "There is a net. There is a fish and—a pond? Yes, a deep, deep pond . . ."

"Be careful," Mathilde whispered breathlessly; "there must be nothing larger than a fish. Someday I shall be married."

It was the first and for a long time the only secret Famke had from Birgit.

"A schoolful of Sapphos," Albert said when she told him, laughing out a puff of smoke. "What a picture that would make. A cottage . . . a pond . . ." He hugged her close to his chest and deposited a kiss of his own on the crown of her head. She felt him stirring against her hip, and that was all she needed to know about anyone called Sappho.

Famke told him, with an air of great revelation, that romantic attachments were not uncommon among the older girls, or even among the novices who were expected to take holy orders. Some of the girls swore these orphan embraces would prove the best of love, for they came without responsibility, without danger, without babies. But somehow they weren't enough for Famke. She longed for the open space beyond the orphanage wall, for the freedom she associated with the wind that occasionally rattled the leaves of the elder trees; for the forbidden boys.

Famke was sad when Mathilde left, placed out in the village of Humlebæk. But then there was Karin, and then Marie. Famke became a fish herself, swimming through the ranks of girls, toppling them onto their backs with a flip of her tail. But she was careful to stay on the shore of every pond, the doorstep of every cottage; each Immaculate Heart girl who managed to marry bore all the signs of innocence to her husband.

And soon enough it was time for Famke to go. At fourteen, she'd finally been confirmed; she was capable of earning a woman's wages, and there was no reason to burden the city's few Catholics any longer. Sister Saint Bernard was in charge of placing the grown orphans, and she found a position for Famke as a goose girl and maid-of-all-work in a village called Dragør. Famke mucked out the goose pen, made cheese, and fended off the attentions of the gristled farmer who'd consented to take her. She talked to the girls on the neighboring farms—none of them smelling of soap or bread or ponds, only sweat and dung—and concluded that it would be no better anywhere else; so she hid her unhappiness even in her monthly letters to Sister Birgit. For her second Christmas, Famke's employer allowed a traveling neighbor to carry her to the orphanage with a couple of geese he'd had her kill and pluck. She attended Mass, turned the geese on a spit, and hardly had time to exchange two words with Sister Birgit; but she set off for the farm in new Swedish leather shoes.

There was no cart now, and no one on the road. Famke had walked halfway to Dragør when a fit of coughing doubled her over. Her mouth was suddenly full and tasted horrible—so she spat into the snow and saw a drop of blood. It froze quickly, to glow like a ruby in a bed of spun silk. She kicked the snow over it and walked on, refusing to think of what that droplet meant.

Summer came, and Dragør steamed. Famke told herself she was resigned to her lot. She let the farmer kiss her cheek and even, once, put his hand on her bodice. She attended services at the village Lutheran church and talked to the other farm girls. She met young men, too—hired boys in no position to marry; they gazed at her with the same covetous eyes she saw in the farmer. None of them managed to interest her.

But then, wonder of wonders, a foreigner appeared, dressed in blue and driving a carriage. He stood a long while at the fence rail, watching her shovel out the goose pen; he held a leather-bound book before him and a pencil in his hand. From time to time she wiped the sweat from her face onto her sleeve and cast him a glance from the corner of her eye. When at last he approached, she saw his book contained a collection of drawings. He turned the pages back to reveal a moth, a chicken, and one of *her*.

There she was—she who had rarely seen her own face in a mirror—with all her busy motion stilled, looking slyly up from a white page. The real Famke, living and flushed, straightened her apron and pushed her hair under her cap, trying to look like the good Christian maiden she'd been raised to be. She knew she reeked of goose.

"*Beautiful*," the stranger said in his own tongue, perhaps guessing this word was universal; but she looked at him with the round eyes of confusion. Then a slow smile crept across Famke's face, to be mirrored in his. She put one damp finger to the page and accidentally smudged the drawing.

In gestures, the stranger asked her to fetch him a glass of water; he pantomimed that his labors had exhausted him. She brought a dipperful from the farmyard well, lukewarm and tasting of the geese and horses and pigs that trotted across the packed earth. As he drank, she took the opportunity to engrave his face and figure onto her mind. He was tall and sticklike, with thin blond hair combed into a semblance of romantic curls; his green eyes immediately reminded her of a frog's. But he gave her a nice smile with slightly crooked teeth, and he bowed as if to suggest that he considered her every bit as good as he was.

He returned the next day in a carriage decked with flowers, and again she served him a dipperful of water. The flowers drew butterflies; in a cloud of pale yellow and white, their wings dipped from eglantine to *glem-mig-ikk'*, and she thought she'd never seen anything so pretty. She would find out later that the carriage had been decorated for a wedding; when the young man hired it he had asked to keep the flowers, and the proprietor even threw in a bouquet of lilies left from a more somber occasion. Famke's suitor handed them over with a flourish, and she blushed. She looked from the carriage to him— "Albert," he said, with a thump on his chest—and felt her eyes shining.

Albert drank. As he swallowed, his throat made a little croaking noise, and he and Famke laughed together, like old friends. Before she knew it, his hands were making signs to offer her a ride into the city and an engagement as his model and muse. That she would be mistress as well, Famke had no doubt; her fellow-servants in Dragør had told her what young men who fancied themselves artists were like. She watched this one thoughtfully as he argued his case. From time to time clasping her hand, he repeated two words so often they seemed like a name, *Lizzie Siddal*, though it had no meaning for her. Finally he kissed her grubby sixteen-year-old palm. When she pulled it away and put it to her face, she smelled his soap. Genteel, perfumed, but made of the same basic ingredients as orphanage soap. Ashes and fat. Prayers and hope.

So Albert and Famke rode away in a cloud of heavy dust, with the geese honking and the pigs squealing a charivari of farewell. The butterflies accompanied them, draining a few last drops from the wildflower garlands.

Famke had no notion where he'd take her and was delighted to find herself returning to Copenhagen, to the harbor district of Nyhavn. This time her experience of the town was different, lighter and lovelier, though almost as sequestered as in the orphanage. She stopped wearing the servant-girl caps and utterly abandoned the crossing of her ankles while seated. She found the life of a model so restful that she put on weight, and for the first time her breasts fit the cups of her hands rather than the flats of her palms. From Albert she learned English; she learned to call the shape of her mouth a Cupid's bow—perfectly formed even after the mishap with her infant bottle—and to appreciate the line where the red of her lips met the white of her flesh. He taught her to read English as well, in the guidebooks he had brought. From them she learned that Denmark was flat and that the Danes were thrifty people who enjoyed flowers, sunshine, and making butter and beer. She much preferred Albert's version of her country's history, with the thrilling princesses and long-ago warriors.

Inevitably, she compared being with Albert to being with the orphan girls, and she quickly decided she liked him better. He pleased her in different ways, without hands or mouth, and he took pleasure from the way she sucked on his flat nipples:"No woman has ever done *that* before," he gasped. And when they were working, he looked at her the way no girl had ever done—no man, either, for no one before Albert had thought to preserve her and her beauty for the generations.

Albert once explained to Famke that he'd come to Denmark in hopes that, in a land without a significant artistic or cultural tradition, he might find some last remnant of the medieval life depicted by the Pre-Raphaelite Brotherhood to which he aspired. At home in his father's overstuffed, overheated rooms, he had thought of Famke's land as historically backward—or

primal, he amended when she'd learned enough to protest the first term—
populated by simple peasants in wooden clogs, flower crowns, and brightly
colored folk costumes, still living out the stark paradigms of Nordic mythology. He'd found more of the curlicued Renaissance and overstuffed nine-
teenth century than he'd anticipated, but nonetheless he'd fallen in love.

When Albert said that, Famke felt a thrill in her stomach, as if she were
going to be sick, but in a good way. It left her belly tingling. But even though
Albert repeated the word "love" quite slowly, she wasn't sure exactly what it
was he'd fallen in love with. Before she could muster the courage to ask, he
had moved on to another subject.

"If I hadn't come here, I would have gone to America. To the west."

Famke stared up at the ceiling, which was water stained but marvelous,
Albert said, for reflecting light onto color. "America . . . But that is so far
away, so . . ." At Immaculate Heart, there had been a jigsaw puzzle from
America, a picture of a vast snowy mountain ringed with purple wildflow-
ers. The children had called it Mæka.

"That American west is a new land, and it holds a host of wonders for
the artist—and yet it has seen no truly great painter. Yes, had I had the
funds, that is where I would have gone . . . to the forests primeval, the
mountains and plains, the mines, the canyons . . ."

Albert had reason to respect Mæka's ancient woods, for it was from
good American cedar that his family's fortune had been made. His father
would buy nothing else to make the innovative graphite pencils he manu-
factured, from a money-saving design that allowed six, rather than five,
hexagonal cylinders to be cut from one block of wood. And just after Castle,
Senior, decided to affirm his new social status by purchasing work from the
era's fashionable artists, Albert's determination to become one of them had
been born. The poet and painter Dante Gabriel Rossetti came to the house
to hang the Castles' first acquisition, a portrait that reminded Albert's father of the dear wife who had died shortly after presenting him with the
boy for whom he had finally found room in his budget. Thin and hollow-
eyed, but with a smile and a chin-chuck for little Albert, Rossetti had spent
an hour or so in the gloomy cedar-paneled parlor. That brief moment of
kindness had been a ray of moonshiney hope for the anxious little boy, who
hid behind a tasseled settee and observed the careful measuring of the wall,
the straightening of the frame, the earnest discussion between the sober

factory man and the painter in prime of life, both widowered. That afternoon, nine-year-old Albert decided to learn this magic trick for pleasing people. He would use every technique in Rossetti's arsenal: the goddesses, the eye for details, the colors.

To Famke, however, the most beautiful thing he had ever made was that first plain sketch from Dragør. When he wanted to toss it in the fire, claiming it was far from perfect—even far from a likeness—she whisked it out of his hands and wept so stormily that at last he allowed her to tack it to the wall above the washtub. It was the one work that he held inviolate, and as Famke scrubbed at the paint stains on his clothing or soaped her own legs and arms, she liked to look at it.

Her face, looking back at her, forever exactly the same.

Kapitel 3

· · · · ·

The Danes had a splendid record for fighting in the middle ages and up to the last century, but have become an agricultural people, and their activity is devoted to making butter and beer, and raising poultry and hay. Copenhagen is the only city of any size.

WILLIAM ELEROY CURTIS,
DENMARK, NORWAY, AND SWEDEN

In a rare moment of introspection, it occurred to Famke that other people might consider she was making a fool of herself. She'd thought the same in Dragør about a milkmaid who trailed around after the local doctor, begging for rides in his buggy and dreaming up reasons he should examine her. And at the orphanage, when one of the girls developed a crush on Sister Birgit—the last person, Famke had thought with scorn, who'd look at an orphan *that* way—Famke had kissed the girl herself and deflected destiny. But now it might seem that she, too, Famke of the Immaculate Heart, had developed hopes above her station.

She was in love, with all the passion and force and urgency and trepidation of her years. She did not precisely look on Albert as a savior, but her life was vastly more enjoyable with him than without, and so he was a sort of hero. She had fallen in love by that first night, with pain and blood marking the sharp dart of love settling into her flesh. He smelled good, including the cheroots. She even loved his odd, froggy eyes, so placid in sleep that she kissed them tenderly as she watched over him. He was the first man she had known well, and because there had been nothing like him in her life before, she occasionally suspected it was foolish to hope he would always be there. And just as quickly, she dismissed those notions—after all, Albert himself told her all those nice fairy tales and myths, and hadn't he mentioned that the Pre-Raphaelites were prone to marrying their models?

One night, Famke felt Albert prop himself up among the pillows and gaze down at her. "'He who loveliness hath found,'" she heard him say, "'he *color* loves, and . . .'"

Her eyes flew open at that. She rolled over and poked Albert to make him speak more. "John Donne," he said, laughing. "Color is beauty, and you, darling . . . it would take a whole dye shop to describe you." Then he sobered and took on that tedious tone of the bedtime lecturer, sinking back against the pillows, telling her about something called Old Masters and the National Gallery, the dulling effects of old varnish and the traditional artists' mistaken assumption that to paint like the masters they must limit their palettes to gray and brown . . . Albert intended, like his idol Rossetti, to reintroduce color to loveliness.

To Famke, all this meant was that he loved color; and that itself might mean . . .

Love gave her the stamina she needed to pose the long hours Albert demanded of her; and those hours were growing longer and longer, as he had determined that *Nimue* would be the first picture he finished: She would be perfect, complete, in all senses of the word. Accordingly, he studied the pose from every viewpoint and considered every nuance within the story. He moved the angle of Famke's arms a degree up or down, adjusted the backward thrust of one leg, tried combinations of hair braided and unbraided while Famke basked like a cat in the feel of his fingers. Again and again her lips, nails, and nipples turned blue, but Albert said that was appropriate— "because even a nymph would feel the chill."

At last they had the pose just right, and Albert spent some days drawing intently, sometimes in charcoal, sometimes in graphite. He tacked the studies of Famke's face and body to the walls of their garret. And only when he had the picture fully realized—Famke in her magician's stance, the dance of her hands shaping turrets of ice—did he begin to prepare his canvas.

Albert had decided that this picture would be big, of a size that only a museum gallery could accommodate properly. He bought four straight pieces of Norwegian fir five and seven feet long. He nailed them together in the loft, borrowing a hammer from the landlady. When the frame wobbled, he acquired four more stakes and nailed them into an airy latticework behind.

From an importer on Bredgade, he bought the finest canvas in Copenhagen. There was no cloth bolt wide enough to cover the entire space, so the

lengths had to be sewn together. Even with Famke's help, the stretching itself took days. They laced all four sides over the frame with a series of
cords—not unlike the strings that closed a corset, thought Famke, who
longed to wear such a garment herself and feel like a lady.

No easel could support a canvas so tall and heavy, so Albert went back to
the lumber dealer and fashioned six little props of wood; three he nailed to
the ceiling, and three to the floor. He nailed the fir frame to these blocks,
and Famke at last stopped tripping over them. The room's peaked ceiling
was scarcely more than seven feet at its highest point, so the canvas stood
there, neatly cleaving the space in two. Albert bought a ladder from a bank-
rupt apothecary, a vast tarpaulin from a French painter who had married a
Dane, and then his workspace was complete: windows, paints, and platform
on one side of the canvas; bed, door, and clothes cupboard on the other.

"Subdividing, are ye?" asked the landlady, Fru Strand, when she came to
retrieve her hammer. Never having caught on to the niceties of Albert's profession, she thought he was tiring of Famke and had erected a partition so
he wouldn't have to look at her all day.

When Famke dutifully translated, Albert laughed and offered to buy Fru
Strand a pint of frothy Danish beer, which she loved as much as her seafar-
ing tenants did. The two of them stomped downstairs merrily, leaving
Famke behind to sweep up the sawdust and bits of canvas thread.

"Subdividing," she muttered, having taken on Albert's habit of repetition. She put away the broom and sat down in a chair by the window, to
watch the sailors staggering up and down the street like drunken elves in
their double-pointed winter hoods. Albert and Fru Strand were nowhere in
sight.

That night, and for several nights thereafter, before he would so much as
touch Famke, Albert wetted the canvas; every morning he tightened it, until it was so taut it sang like a bell when she tapped it.

Meanwhile, Albert sketched more Nimues. "She must be *perfect*," he insisted, shading in a sketch he had allowed to progress rather further than
the others.

"Perfect," Famke echoed. Then she giggled, noticing what Albert habitu-
ally omitted. "But no hair," she said. To her, perfection meant an exact likeness. When Albert blinked at her, she touched the picture and explained,

"Down There, she has no hair . . . She hasn't even a sex. It be as if a cloud passes over."

"Sexual hair is not a subject for art," Albert said on a note of reproof. "It is not for ladies to see, even if they know it must be there."

Famke subsided with, "*That* is not like nature." She thought of Albert's *Pik*, so surprisingly rosy in its dark-gold nest. She wondered if she should be shyer about looking at it—if perhaps he didn't like her to look . . . It was the artist's job to look, and to have opinions, never the model's.

. . .

When she wasn't posing, there was little for Famke to do. She'd washed all the bedding and every garment the two of them owned, and she'd had a long wash herself. There was nothing left to clean, and no stove on which to cook (for which she, with her dislike of fire, had always been grateful). She had even grown tired of looking at sketches of herself. So when Albert took out his tubes of paint at last, Famke breathed a sigh of relief. But he explained that before he would need her again, he had to lay down a white ground. Layer by infinitesimal layer he built it up, and the seams in the canvas disappeared.

"Let me help you," Famke begged, eager to hurry the process along. She churned the brush through the thick gesso, and Albert lifted her hand away.

"It must be absolutely even," he said. "It's really best that I do this myself." He explained that only against a smooth, hard whiteness would his colors glow—"and I want you to glow, darling," he finished. She almost didn't need him to look at her then; these words were enough to keep her warm for the rest of the day.

The time it took for the white coat to set, they spent in bed. The sun's hours were getting ever shorter, and despite her boredom during daylight, Famke was quite happy in the dark, keeping Albert gladly distracted.

On the morning that they woke to find the canvas's final white ground was perfectly smooth, dry, and hard, Albert gulped. He lingered in bed much longer than was his wont, and Famke practically pushed him out of it. "You said today you should start," she said. "So start!" When still he dallied, looking at the vast blankness with something akin to despair, she got up and led him to the chamberpot; she saw him finish, then put a morsel of dark bread between his lips and bade him chew. She fed him cheese and sausage in this way as well, and then she—still naked herself—helped him don his layers of clothing.

Only once Albert was fed and dressed did Famke pull Nimue's bloodied chemise over her head. She tugged Albert toward the canvas and put a stick of charcoal in his hand, climbed onto her pillowed platform, and struck the pose. "Now draw me," she ordered him.

After a moment, Albert began. Hesitant at first, then more sure, he marked the canvas with the line of her nose, then a bit of her shoulders, and her breasts, belly, and legs, through the cobwebby cloth. He consulted his sketches and made a few refinements to the piles of pillows. Last he did her arms and the cascade of hair. Then, having outlined his magnum opus, he threw away his pencil and with a cry raced out into the street.

Famke, shivering, quietly picked up the pencil and put it with his other painting things. She wrapped herself in a blanket and stood before the canvas, trying to see, in the rough lines of black against stark white, the image of herself that would eventually live there.

To her, the space looked nearly empty.

◆　◆　◆

Once the real work got under way, Albert could scarcely tear himself away from his *Nimue*. He swore that she would hang in the English Royal Academy's annual exhibition, win him respect and commissions, *and* convince his father to continue the financial support—if Albert even needed it after his success-to-be. He congratulated himself on having chosen such a quintessentially English subject as Merlin, believing that the familiarity of the myth would help his cause.

He divided the canvas into small spaces a few inches square and took one as each day's assignment; sometimes he exhausted daylight trying to cover his allotment. Famke thought he was slow because his brushes were so fine that some used only a single hair, but these were part of his way of working and she said nothing about them.

Painting, Albert started at Famke's fingertips and worked his way slowly downward, spending as much time on the background portion of each square as he did on Famke's body. No matter what he was rendering, she stood there locked in her dramatic pose, her stillness and exposure reassuring him that he was indeed at work. If he wanted to talk, she listened.

He liked to tell her stories: of the Pre-Raphaelite Brotherhood and their ladies, of the Nordic myths she'd never heard, and of unusual events all over the world. Famke's interest in Nimue's lack of hair Down There suggested the tale of John Ruskin, the Brotherhood's father-figure, who had been divorced because of unexpected difficulty with that unaesthetic region. "He had never seen a real woman without clothes—he had only seen painted ones—and he was ill prepared for it! On his wedding night, he ran from the room in a fit, and they lived together chastely until she sought annulment." Famke laughed until she fell off her platform.

That story reminded Albert of the Norse myth in which the trickster Loki had stolen Thor's hammer and cut off the hair of his wife, leaving the thunder god powerless and his wife both lightheaded and angry with her husband. And then he remembered that, just a few years ago, a French matron had received a life sentence for murdering her husband, based largely on the fact that, like any good housewife, she had entered the prices of her murder weapons (shovel, hammer, boar trap) into her account book. Around the same time, an American circus master had marched twenty-one elephants across a New York bridge to test the strength of the steel. Albert dreamed aloud of pictures he might paint from these tales, collected from newspapers and pot shops in his native land. Famke listened hard, though she couldn't visualize the pictures he described and sometimes the blood puddled so in her limbs that she could barely think, much less translate the stories in her head. She concluded that she would never know much of the world; and so she let her mind go blank and simply posed.

Albert's conscience was pricked one day when she fainted clear off the platform, disturbing the careful arrangement of pillows and giving herself a large red welt on one leg. After that, he told her to listen for the church bells and to make sure she had a pause every hour. Then, while she stretched, he could clean his brushes, mix more paint, or occasionally make one of the crazed runs through the street that restored balance to the hand that held the brush, discipline to the eye that plotted composition and detail.

Famke's fall also made him realize how deeply dissatisfied he was with the pillows. They were solid, yellowish-white, soft—not at all the crystal daggers that a scorned nymph would erect around her ravisher. So when he came back from one of his wanderings, he was lugging a chunk of ice. He heaved it onto Famke's platform and stood admiring it.

"I fished it out of the old harbor," he said, pushing it a little to the left. "I'll paint this for today—so you may continue to rest, my dear." He was as excited as a boy with a new puppy, or a youth with a first love. When he pulled off his gloves, his fingers were purple. It took a long time to warm them enough for work.

"*Fanden*," Famke said in a pleasant enough voice. She felt rejected, dejected, but the word relieved her feelings somewhat. Without bothering to hunt for her clothes, she climbed into bed. The cold had tired her out, and she told herself to be glad to have a cozy afternoon. It was nice to have pillows on the bed again.

"*Fan'n*," Albert repeated absently as she sank her head in the downy softness. Curled on her side, she watched him gaze deeply into the ice, as into a crystal ball. He mixed several shades of blue-white and began dabbing at the canvas with them, lost in his new idea. Eventually, lulled by the soft brush-brush of his work and the little wet sounds on the palette, Famke fell asleep.

In sleep, her mind flew back to the orphanage. Now she was boiling soap again, as she'd been allowed to do that one time; all was just as before, except that it was Viggo, not the cauldron, that burst into flames. She felt the heat from his body, and she turned around to see the orphanage building was made of ice. Sister Birgit's eyes filled with water and she was about to say something to Famke, but—

Famke woke when she heard a crash in the street, followed by a curse from the same general area. Albert had thrown the ice block out the window.

"It melted too fast," he said with a shake of the head. "I couldn't get the *essence* down—look, this bit will have to be painted out. I need you now." Unceremoniously he dragged Famke from the bed and barely let her rub the sleep from her eyes before standing her up on the platform again.

Famke didn't attempt conversation; she tried not even to think about Albert and his mood. As she stood still for the remaining hour of daylight, she wondered instead what it was that Sister Birgit had wanted to say.

Famke was no more superstitious than she was religious, but she felt there was a message in the dream, if only her mind could see it. And she suddenly realized that she missed Birgit; since leaving the farm on Dragør, she had been in no position to turn up at the convent orphanage.

"Left leg bent," Albert said crisply, and Famke came to attention. She had straightened her leg without knowing it; she'd have to focus on the pose or risk Albert's wrath. So Famke made her mind a blank.

Kapitel 4

· · · · ·

There were electric lights. They are one of the most beautiful things I have ever seen. Compared to an electric light a gas flame looks like a dismal tallow candle.

JULIUS PETERSEN,
LETTER, 1887

Over the next week, Albert spent an hour or so each day down by the water, observing ice and trying to sketch it. The harsh December weather made his work difficult because he couldn't get his fingers to move as they needed to; he complained bitterly and refused to paint at all until Famke persuaded him to concentrate awhile on her and leave the ice for later.

"There will always be ice," she said, feeling her English so improved she was able to make a little joke. "This is Denmark."

So Albert painted Famke, day after day, hour after churchly hour in the loft at the top of Fru Strand's house. Occasionally he brought in a lump of ice for her to pose with, and then they had to close off the fireplace and open the windows to keep it from melting. But Famke did not complain: She felt they were as happy as they could be.

· ◆ ·

One night near suppertime, when the streetlamps had long been lit, Albert returned sweating and full of ideas. "I ran all the way from Carlsberg brewery," he panted, unfastening her hair. "I've solved the problem of the ice!" He seemed inordinately pleased as he turned to her bodice buttons.

"Why were you to the brewery?" she asked, shrugging docilely out of the sleeves. She did not allow herself to glance at the fried fish congealing on its plate; art would always take precedence.

"I watched the workers as they left for the day," Albert said, tugging on her skirt. "All those faces, so tired, so cold, under that harsh light"—the brewery had gone to electric power that spring— "and I realized Nimue must have *faces* in her ice blocks. Her early victims. Isn't it brilliant?" As the skirt came down, he looked up at her with the bright eyes of a schoolboy.

Famke hesitated, holding the string of her bloomers. The hair on her body was already standing stiff in the cold. "Did you not say your Nimue must be virgin?" she asked.

"Yes . . ."

"So if Merlin is her first lover, should—shouldn't—he be her first . . . victim . . . as well?"

She saw immediately that she'd said the wrong thing. Albert's face fell, and he himself dropped to the floor, where he sat bent-legged and plainly miserable. Famke cursed herself and then, to distract Albert, ripped away the cord of her bloomers and stepped out of them.

He noticed nothing.

"I think Nimue is beginning to bore me," he mumbled into his lap. "I've nearly finished painting you, and the thought of rendering all that ice . . . Some faces inside would make it more interesting."

"But then the painting would be . . ." Famke hesitated; she was not used to speaking in conditional tenses, any more than she was used to voicing opinions on matters of art—". . . less good. For those who see it, I mean to say. In your first plan, as you have said, they will see the moment of Nimue's transforming into a villain, as well as the transforming she makes for Merlin. If you put in other men, she is not a virgin, and she is not changing."

In his glum silence, she wrapped her arms around herself for warmth. During several long minutes, Albert continued to stare down at himself, until finally he drew himself up and said, "I am going out again."

. . .

When Famke opened her eyes the next morning, the sun was already shining with a bright yellow light. One golden ray picked out a small silver box, slightly battered but gleaming, lying forgotten on the mantel.

"Christiansborg," she said without thinking.

Her voice woke Albert up. He smelled sour as he yawned and stretched, reaching for her as if he'd forgotten their last conversations; perhaps he had drowned his frustrations more deeply than she had thought when he came home. He spoke as if he had a headache. "What was that, darling?"

"I want to go to Christiansborg," she blurted.

"In the daytime? With all the guards about?"

"I am going," she said, knowing she sounded childish. "And you may come. I have an idea."

To her surprise, Albert yielded. Perhaps he knew she couldn't be pushed too far this day, or perhaps aquavit (that was what she decided it had been, rather than the more prosaic beer) had set carpenters pounding in his head too hard for him to work. The two of them dressed and went out, breakfasting on fresh bakery bread.

It was a short walk, accomplished in silence. In an unexpected thaw, much of the recent snow had melted, and most of the slush was gone from the roads. Famke held her skirts up but sank to her ankles in mud. Albert's boots were already dirty, and he didn't seem to notice they were getting dirtier. He was too glum to catch Famke's smoldering excitement.

Without the shroud of snow, Christiansborg's ruins made a black scar in the golden stone of the quarter, and the last harbor ice reflected their shadow. As yet there'd been no talk of rebuilding; the royal architects would have to outdo themselves, and perhaps they needed summer's sun for inspiration. Troops of blue-coated guards still marched a circle round the ashes, but without real fervor; the valuables had already been recovered, either by royal servants or by looting commoners such as Famke and Albert. A good deal of the debris had been carted away as well, and men were working among the rest with shovels and a wagon. Overcoming her dislike of things related to fire, Famke headed immediately for them.

"*Hold op!*" One of the workers whistled. "*Hvad laver De?*"

Famke had a story ready. She explained that she only wished to look, that her mother had worked in this palace and died in the conflagration. She and her brother—she motioned to Albert, who had the grace to nod—had come to mourn. She let the light yellow shawl slide off her hair and gave the men the most demure expression the nuns had taught her. She even worked up a tear, more easily than she would have thought, to emphasize her point.

"*Kom så venligst.*" One after another, the workmen invited the two of them closer, won over more by the beauty of Famke's face than her flimsy story. Even the guard who had dutifully appeared waved them on.

"What is it you want here?" Albert asked.

"Shh," she whispered. "No English. We are pretending you be a Dane." To the admiration of the men watching, she began to step delicately through the ash heap, like a figure in a painting about sainthood or loneliness. The effect was good; no one seemed to notice the rough cloth of her skirt or the mud on her one pair of shoes, and even Albert appeared impressed as he followed her.

"What are you looking for?" he whispered meekly.

"I have an idea," she said. "It is about ice."

He did not question her after that.

.   .   .

Guards, workingmen, Famke and Albert: The only person whose presence among the ruins could not be explained was a tall gray-complected man in a dark suit and hat. He carried a long cane with a metal tip and he was poking it here and there into the ashes. Albert watched him moodily as Famke, on her knees, dug through the rubble. The workers and guards politely pretended not to notice what she was doing, thinking perhaps that she was looking for some last remnant of her fictional mother. The man did not look at her either, as her head was covered with the yellow shawl and they were too far apart for any but the most startling features to stand out. Still, Albert felt vaguely as if the other man had insulted Famke in some way, and he wondered what right such a fellow in genteel but shabby costume had among this royal ruin.

The explanation came clear as the gray man drew closer, poking that long cane into the debris. The wind blew past him and up to Albert, who nearly gagged at the strong stench of camphor and formaldehyde. Obviously the man was a kind of mortician, or a mortician's assistant; an apprentice to death, Albert thought, and savored the phrase. An apprentice to death, himself impregnated with needlefuls of scientific fluids that saved the body from the corrupting rot of blood. He must be out to drum up some business, though any reasonable professional would expect all the bodies to have been removed from this place by now. He passed on without looking at Albert or Famke.

Famke rocked back in the mud. "*Værsgo*. Here. Albert!"

He looked down into her face, so delightfully full of life and color. The undertaker hadn't registered with her, beyond a brief cough at the smell he carried.

"Albert, see," she insisted, blinking up against the sun.

He avoided the beseechment he expected to find in her eyes. "What do you have there?" he asked, as one might ask a child.

She was holding something about as big as her fist. Albert watched her spit on it, then rub it on her sleeve, and at last hold it up to him. "Glass," she said simply.

He examined the thing. It was oddly shaped and heavy, a pale shade of green under the grime. He turned it over in both hands. "Yes, I see," he said, though clearly he wasn't seeing what she wanted him to.

Anxiously, Famke got to her feet. "*Glass*," she said again. She turned the lump so he was looking into the spot she'd cleaned. "Some melted. In the fire. Some is from windows, some from glass boxes and other things." Excitement was chopping up her English. "Does it not resemble ice?"

There was a brief pause as Albert took this in.

"Darling—Famke—you're brilliant!" It was his turn to fall to his knees; not to embrace her, as his words might have led her to hope, but to scrabble through the ashes in turn. "You clever, clever girl—there's bushels of it here!"

"I know this," Famke said modestly. "I saw such glass when some boys burned down the Dragør church. Now you may use it for ice in the painting. And," she added on a practical note, "we may keep the windows closed."

◆   ◆   ◆

As the guards continued to look the other way, Famke and Albert collected as many molten shards as they could carry. They took the largest ones they could find and filled Famke's small pocket, then the multiple flaps of Albert's coat. Famke unbuttoned her bodice to tuck a cold lump inside. When they left the plain of rubble and made their way home with the booty, their movements were slow, freighted, and they sank deeper into the mud. But the new prospect made Albert very happy, and Famke's heart caught some of that infectious warmth. She imagined it lighting up her chest like an electric globe.

She was feeling hopeful, in fact, and as she and Albert left, she noticed the gray mortician; he seemed to be lifting a scrap of embroidery from a heap of ash, and she wondered if perhaps he had really lost someone in the flames. When he stood, she turned a dazzling smile upon him. He was clearly surprised, but he touched his hat to her in a gentlemanly fashion, releasing a new wave of pungent scent that made both Famke and Albert cough and the glass in their pockets rattle.

The mortician reached into his pocket, simultaneously depositing the embroidered wisp and withdrawing a stiff cardboard square. "In case of need," he said mournfully, and passed by them like the god of death, poking his cane into mound after mound. They watched him pass through the iron gates and disappear into the fog.

Famke translated the card for Albert:

EMBALMING PERFORMED

•*reasonable rates*

•*lifelike appearance*

•*excellent value*

GAMLE KONGEVEJ 16

"It would appear he's in need of his own services," Albert joked, and Famke was so glad to feel she had pleased him that she laughed right along.

Kapitel 5

· · · · ·

If I say that the houses did not disgust me, I tell you all I remember of them;
for I cannot recollect any pleasurable sensations they excited; or that any ob-
ject, produced by nature or art, took me out of myself.

MARY WOLLSTONECRAFT,
LETTER FROM DENMARK

Thus it began, their best time together. Now Albert had models for
both Nimue and her ice; around Famke's feet he painted the Christiansborg glass many times larger than it was, filling in his little
squares with vivid and detailed renderings of all he saw there. Famke, for
her part, was glad not to be quite so chilled while posing, and even to have
a day of rest here and there while Albert worked on the ice. She had caught
a cold, or one had caught her, and it wouldn't let go.

She coughed and blew her nose until Albert was quite exasperated.
"Darling, *really,*" he said; but then he fell ill, too, and resorted to the comforts of long dark hours of bed rest and Famke's loving ministrations. They
spent candlelit time together poring over Pre-Raphaelite prints; but in the
morning, all was work again.

On one blue afternoon, as he refined the lines of Famke's streaming hair,
Albert even mentioned his plans for the future. He rubbed out a red strand
with a handful of bread, then bit the bread absentmindedly and said, chewing, "I quite like your country. I am finding it every bit as rich in inspiration
as I'd hoped. Perhaps I will come back."

Famke felt suddenly more naked than before, and completely tongue-
tied. Here it was, what she was longing to hear: almost a promise for the future.

"Of course," Albert ruminated, "that can be only after I am accepted as a
member of the Royal Academy. After I am able to live from the proceeds of

my work. I might even do some portraits then—let the ladies' commissions pay for the models' fees."

This was an interesting notion. Aside from her room and board, Albert had not yet given Famke an Øre for her work; but then she did not wish him to. He had once explained that ladies posed only for portraits, for which they paid, while the hired models who lent themselves to narrative paintings belonged to a category just slightly removed from the *Ludere* strolling up and down the frozen canals. "Not you, of course," he had said hastily, seeing her crestfallen. Somehow, not being paid removed her from the unpleasant models' class; and Famke generally preferred pictures that told stories anyway.

She summoned all her courage to ask now, "Will you paint me again?"

"Of course." He sneezed and blew his nose, carefully turning away from the canvas.

"Will you be glad?" She waited a moment, and when he didn't answer— he was still emptying his nose—she added softly, "*Vil du elske mig?*" Will you love me?

He didn't seem to hear, and he would not have understood the Danish words; but Famke took his silence for all the affirmation she needed.

"Darling, please stop smiling," he said, looking up. "Remember, Nimue is angry."

But in the warmth of her smile, he was inspired to pull out a pair of dried butterflies—saved, perhaps, from that bridal carriage ride—that might alight on the ice blocks and freeze there, to represent springtime and the love that once existed between Nimue and Merlin. He bought some silk flowers, frayed and faded them, then painted them withered and bewormed in the ice. Famke did not need him to explain that symbolism.

In this happy time, Albert and Famke often forgot to eat and usually smelled like each other. When he had been out late in the streets, she washed his feet for him with strong, delicious soap and brought life back to his frozen toes. It was while they were doing this that he told her their *Revenge of Nimue* was not the first painting on the subject.

"There is another, called *The Beguiling of Merlin*," he said. "I don't have a print to show you, but I recollect it clear as a summer's day. The colors are gold and blue. Nimue is reading spells from a book, and the ancient Merlin swoons. Her body is big but it moves like a snake's, coiling toward him."

"Shall there be a book in our picture?" Famke asked.

"Darling, that is hardly the point. No, my *Nimue* will be an entirely new composition; I cannot imagine Merlin in a hawthorn bower. Perhaps that is why Burne-Jones's painting failed."

"Who was his model?" Famke asked, rubbing his arches with her thumbs. She hoped it had been Fanny Cornforth, the tavern-girl with hair down to the floor; she had posed for several Brothers and became Dante Rossetti's mistress.

"Maria Zambaco, a wild, dark gypsy-woman."

"Was she his . . . Did he *fokk* her?" she asked, reaching for a word the sailors used.

"Famke!" Albert pretended to be shocked, but he shot her an amused look. "Well, yes. She wanted him to leave his wife for her."

"But he didn't," Famke guessed. She pushed the basin aside and began rubbing Albert's feet with a rough towel.

"No, even though Mrs. Burne-Jones was being courted by William Morris . . . Ouch, darling, not so rough. *His* wife, Jane, is said to have been entangled with Rossetti after Lizzie Siddal died."

"*Fanden*," Famke said, "are all of your Brotherhood loving one another's wives?"

"Not everyone in the circle is like that," he said, in a tone she would have thought priggish from a Danish man. He held out his feet, dry now, so she could slide them into heavy wool socks. "There are men of great honor and women of great virtue."

Famke's cheeks reddened at the thought of virtue. "There are women in the Brotherhood?" she asked innocently.

"Yes, there are women. Some of them even fancy themselves artists," he added, again in that priggish tone. "Rossetti tried to teach Lizzie to paint. Even Maria Zambaco, the earlier Nimue, takes up the brush from time to time, and she has a friend who makes photographs. But most of the true ladies are content to give quiet support. Euphemia Millais, for example, has been her husband's mainstay—since she divorced Ruskin . . ."

Famke could not repress a snort. A divorce caused by private hairs.

"Well," Albert concluded, gazing at his warm feet in satisfaction, "that divorce was quite a *cause célèbre*, but Millais says he'd be nothing without her. And there are other virtuous women. Georgiana Burne-Jones has remained loyal to her husband, and their daughter, Margaret, is quite lovely."

As Famke carried the basin to the window, she noticed that although Albert referred to the male painters by their last names, he felt on first-name terms with the women. She glimpsed, fleetingly, a time when the two of them, Albert and herself, would be known as Castle and his Famke. She thought she could be content as the quiet support in the background of his life, if she could be the chief figure in his paintings. And if he would leave the Brothers' wives alone.

. . .

On Christmas Day, Albert announced it almost shyly: "Darling, come down from your platform. I believe you are complete."

He had finished the figural work.

Famke stepped slowly from the pedestal, struggling with a dual sense of loss and happiness. She had dreaded the day when Albert would not need her to pose—but what a marvel he had made of her! When she looked at the canvas, she saw herself, every bit as beautiful as she wanted to be: eyes like two sapphires, lips like two rubies, skin luminous as a pearl. The fiery hair crackling down her back, the strength of her arms and legs showing through the icy net of nightdress—Famke almost pitied the poor wizard who must, she thought, stand a few feet beyond the farthest reaches of the canvas, where she and Albert were standing now.

Albert breathed: "It is . . . yes, perfect."

He looked about to dash out for one of his mad runs; so to hold him where he was, Famke said that the picture did not *quite* capture her: If he were truly to paint life's every detail, he would break with convention and show the hair Down There.

Albert took this with good humor. "Hush, hush, Miss Famke," he chided, ruffling up the hair in question and sending her into a fit of giggles. "You know we must retain our icy cloud. But here's a thought! Perhaps you will understand better if you become a painter yourself. I shall make you my apprentice"—he smiled—"as Merlin did with Nimue."

It was the finest gift he knew of, and it would more than compensate for the little wood-framed mirror she had given him the night before. He put a brush in her hand and wrapped her fingers around the handle in a way she considered awkward.

"But I have never painted," she said, staring down at it. "*Ellers*, I've painted only fences and the goose pen, all in white—er, white—"

"Whitewash," he said, pushing her up the ladder. "So then you can paint ice . . . Mind your skirt, darling, we don't want you to trip; perhaps you should take off the nightdress . . . Here, you may start with this corner. Only try—remember, many English ladies paint."

"I am not a lady," she said, but she let herself be pushed.

"Ladies paint in watercolor anyway," he said, and his argument was so nearly logical that she capitulated and put a tiny, all but invisible dot of pale blue in the farthest reach of the left-hand corner.

Behind her on the ladder, he praised the dot extravagantly. "That's splendid, that's really wonderful! Such sensitivity, such finesse—you are a born artist. In that little spot you have captured an eternal truth about the nature of ice, about its essence and symbolic weight in human and natural history . . ."

"Stop!" She laughed as his hands reached up, caressing first her bottom, then her waist, then dipping into that controversial thatch of hair. "I must concentrate on my art!"

That day she made two dots more before Albert pulled her off the ladder he'd so insistently pushed her up. He took her to bed, where both were very happy.

Over the next days, Famke discovered that she liked painting. Albert seemed genuinely grateful for her help with the dreary ice, especially as she was willing to lay the base of blue-white and mottle it over while he walked the streets in search of breakfast or inspiration. She was careful to keep her brushstrokes as smooth and flat as the white gesso, and enjoyed squeezing the clean-smelling paint from its metal tubes—rather like milking a cow, she thought at first; then, when more practiced, like holding a girl's breast so long that a drop emerged. The very thought made Famke retire for a moment to bed. *This is a cottager coming home to warm himself . . . This is a fish . . . This is a paintbrush grinding a pearl.*

When Albert came home, he did the finer work, adding nuance to the ice, a bubble or a flower here, a crack or a worm there, more of the reddish glow that signified not only Nimue's magic but her virginal anger as well. Soon the canvas was finished.

Albert bought wide strips of gilded walnut for a frame, then proceeded to bury the gilding under a thick layer of more painted flowers and butter-flies. He could hardly wait till the paint was dry before he fit the frame around the canvas—up into the very peak of the roof—and laid a thick coat of varnish over the whole.

"While *Nimue* dries," he proposed, "I should do some smaller pictures. Maybe the Amazon Queen Calafia. Or perhaps Flora, goddess of spring-time, as we still have those silk flowers; or Salome, if we can borrow Mrs. Strand's brass platter. What do you think, darling—are you prepared to surrender the brush and pose for me again?"

Famke dared a sly suggestion: "Perhaps," she said, "you could paint John Ruskin on his wedding night, seeing the whole truth of a woman."

Albert smiled at that but said, "We have no one to pose for the male fig-ure. No, I think we shall try Salome."

So she stood before Albert again, draped in filmy veils torn from Nimue's nightdress, with the brass platter reflecting back her own face in-stead of John the Baptist's. She smiled and smiled, gazing at that honeyed image.

Kapitel 6

. . . . .

If you want a golden rule that will fit everybody, this is it: Have nothing in
your houses that you do not know to be useful, or believe to be beautiful.

WILLIAM MORRIS,
THE BEAUTY OF LIFE

Finally, the great day came: Nimue was ready to descend to earth. It was the middle of March, the ice in the harbors had all but vanished, and Albert's father expected him in England. The paint and the sealing layer of varnish had dried to his satisfaction, so there was no reason to delay. Thus, despite what he'd come to think of as an artistic idyll with Famke, he had bought a ticket that would bring him home on time.

"I did not know it would be so soon," Famke repeated, day after day, until Albert asked her to stop.

Her lover had larger concerns. Exactly how was it possible to remove a six-by-eight-foot assemblage from an attic with a winding stair? He refused to break down the frame and roll up the canvas; that might crack *Nimue*'s paint and would surely ruin the harmonious whole. He finally decided to remove the glass from two windows, cut away the wood between them, and lower the painting in the manner of a piano. He engaged the finest box-maker in Copenhagen to prepare a crate and deliver it below on the day of departure. Meanwhile, Famke, bereft and occasionally indulging in a sob, sewed a wrapping of fine linen over the whole piece.

On the day itself, Albert hired a team of the soberest sailors he could find to handle both the demolition and the lowering. He stood down in the street with an umbrella to ward off the splinters of glass and wood, and he shouted instructions, which Famke translated into Danish as an amused crowd started to assemble. Several of the neighbors were already drunk and ready to laugh at ten in the morning. The landlady, Fru Strand, was drunk, too, and in a stupor; so it wasn't until all the windows were broken and the wood supports gaping like a toothless mouth that she came boiling into the street to give Albert a what-for. As she raged, he nodded politely, most of his mind on the work above: The sailors had roped up his linened *Nimue* and were pushing her over the jagged edge. Albert still didn't speak a word of Danish.

"Lay some blankets on the sills!" he screeched, and Famke had to translate. For good measure, she also offered Albert's apologies to Fru Strand, but the woman's protests didn't halt until Albert shoved enough *Kroner* at her to buy new glass for every window in the building, and for a good long soak in her favorite beer-hall. At that, she stood back and watched with the rest of the crowd as the well-cushioned canvas slid stiffly toward them, then lurched over the edge and caught with a jolt on the ropes. The linen covering billowed like a sail. Famke's stitches were loose, and they had torn on the broken glass; so as the picture descended the linen peeled away, until around the building's second floor it blew off entirely and Famke was exposed in her near-naked, seven-foot-tall glory.

The sailors whistled and threw their elfin hoods in the air. The prostitutes stamped. A passing housewife looked scandalized, despite Famke's cobweb of ice Down There.

Famke knew she should blush, but she was much too pleased with the effect—she'd never seen the picture from far enough away to appreciate it fully, and she realized again in this moment that it was splendid, very like her and yet far more beautiful than she could ever be. She whirled and flung her arms around Albert, her lips on his lips.

It was the last kiss they would exchange. Albert put her firmly from him and shouted more instructions to the sailors, and Famke had to translate again. "To the right!" he called; and *"Til højre!"* she echoed.

"Careful!"

"Pas på!"

"She's not some clunking sea chest!"

Famke thought for a moment and told the sailors, *"Elsk hende som en Kvinde . . ."* Love her like a woman.

Albert's ship was sailing from the old harbor in less than an hour. He pulled out his watch and glared at it with bulging eyes, a gesture that worked in any language. Famke shivered as the wind grew colder.

"I'll have to have the linen resewn on board," he muttered, tossing the loops and strips up over the frame as it slid into its slender crate.

Up until the last moment, Famke hoped Albert would ask her to come with him. But even in their happiest time together, he had said nothing about doing so; and why should he? She was just a model, and he had important things to accomplish in London; things that required not a model but a sharp, clear head for business. She would only be a burden.

Famke had reasoned all of this out in the last days, but even as she accepted a generous purse as a parting gift, and even as she watched the nails driven into the picture's box, watched Albert climb with his bag onto the hearse that was the only carriage big enough to transport *Nimue*, and watched him drive off with a casual wave of his hat—well, she kept hoping.

"Tell me how it goes with the Academy exhibition!" she called after him, and she thought she heard him shout back in assent.

It took a long time for Albert to disappear. The traffic was thick, and everyone wanted to get a look at the foreigner escorting the long, flat coffin. A couple of serving-girls even gave him a flirtatious titter, and he flicked his hat again in grudging pleasure. Famke pulled her shawl over her mouth. And at last the crowds and other carriages swallowed him up.

When he was well and truly gone, Famke trudged up the stairs she'd so often flown up with a fragrant dinner or some other little token for her lover. Fru Strand's wrath had renewed as Albert disappeared, and she dogged Famke's steps.

"Good window glass, to say nothing of the wall, and now I'm left to find workers to replace it all in dead of winter!

"Coming and going all hours of the day and night, and banging the doors each time . . .

"You told me he was gentry, but I never saw it . . ."

At last they reached the studio, now open to elements that included the stiff breeze that would soon bear Albert away. They found the cheap clothes closet in fragments, Famke's few garments scattered over the floor.

Fru Strand crossed her arms over her beer-stained bosom. "I'll never rent to artists again," she said.

. . .

Albert had meant to leave Famke enough money to get through the spring, but he hadn't bargained on Fru Strand. She was not used to lodging single females, and though she didn't mind the sailors' occasional cohabitation, she very much minded the suspicion of housing a prostitute. Famke protested that she was no such thing, and that she and Albert were married; indeed, as Fru Strand grudgingly admitted, Famke never received a single visitor, man or woman. Nonetheless, guessing that Famke had some means and wasn't going anywhere while they lasted, Fru Strand began to chip away at the girl's modest hoard.

"Your . . . husband," she said one day, hesitating over the word just long enough to make her point, "*nå*, he didn't leave enough for the windows."

It was useless for Famke to argue; there was no one to back her up, and Fru Strand could, with little trouble to herself, have had her thrown into the street. So Famke handed over the sum demanded. Of course the glass did not materialize; Famke dwelt in the darkness of boards nailed over the huge hole Albert had left, and she paid through the nose for candles.

Another time, Fru Strand announced that Famke had fallen behind in the rent.

"I'm certain Albert paid up till summer," Famke protested.

But Fru Strand shook her head. "I've seen this sort of thing before," she said with crafty kindness—the girl was young, she thought, and a little sympathy goes a long way with those who have recently left their parents. "Do not think you are the first girl to have been used and left in the lurch. Just be grateful it's only a few *Kroner* you lack—thank God he didn't leave you missing your monthlies."

Silently, Famke laid the money in the beer-stained palm.

"I am right, am I not?" Fru Strand asked, hovering on the threshold. "He didn't leave a bit behind, did he?"

"No," Famke snapped, her hand on the doorknob. "He did not!"

It was a pleasure to slam the rickety thing in Strand's disappointed face. And to know she now had every right to stay until mid-May, if she wanted to.

. . .

No, Albert had left precious little of himself behind. She had done his packing and knew very well that, except for the tinderbox he'd given her and the sketch he'd used to woo her, she'd been scrupulous about returning everything he'd ever touched or used. She had even returned the bits of costume he'd assembled for her to wear in some of his tableaux: Nimue's filmy shift, Calafia's tin sword and the shield she'd used to hide her missing breast, the shiny tears shed by the love goddess Freya when her husband lost himself among the nine Norse worlds. Freya had wept liquid gold; all Famke had had were a handful of spangles she'd stuck on with Albert's pomade, and even those were now rattling in one of his trouser pockets.

For the most part she avoided intercourse with the outside world. While she wasn't with Albert, she would be alone; she would wait. But one day, drawn by curiosity as much as by the idea of making some money, Famke roused herself to visit the Royal Academy of Art. Her pulse fluttering with nervous excitement, she presented herself as a professional model, and as it happened one of the life-drawing classes needed a girl that very day. Famke disrobed and sat as the instructor told her to do, with her knees pulled to her chest and head bowed, her neck and spine exposed. It was a relatively easy pose. When the students filed in she peeked around a kneecap and searched their faces eagerly: Perhaps, she thought, there would be another Albert among them—not a replacement, for no one could replace him, but someone with the same sort of vision. Maybe several such someones.

But it was not to be. The boys, a few of them younger than herself, darted quick, dispassionate glances at her, saving their true focus for their sketchpads. Of course, she thought as she shifted her pose after the first fifteen minutes, Albert had parceled out their time together in much the same way. But even when one of his artistic fevers took him, he had reflected her back at herself in that form she found so appealing.

She had expected that Albert must have been that way as a student as well. But he was nothing like these pimply-faced boys with their noses to the drawing boards, their bodies slouching almost as if the task at hand bored them. Albert must always have been different.

When she strolled among these students at break time, Famke realized the difference was that he *wanted* more than these boys—more detail, more beauty, more of the world. She felt less exposed now than she ever had been with him, and she was the one getting bored. All she saw on the students' sheets was a collection of body parts, arms and legs and ribs and, occasionally, a cloudy rendering of her area Down There. In these sketches she was just a woman.

The *Kroner* she was given for posing were as negligible as the artworks; she spent them on the way home, buying an orphan's treasure of licorice and chocolate, most of which went stale before she had a chance to taste it.

So Famke stayed in Albert's studio—now reverted to a garret, and a murky one at that—and spent her days in silent meditation. She ate little but didn't seem to feel hungry. She rubbed the tinderbox, thinking sometimes of her days at the orphanage, sometimes of the farm in Dragør, but most constantly of Albert and those few happy months. She even took out the matches, always slightly frightening to her with their potential for harm, and lined them up like soldiers. There were twenty-three of them: a number in which she could invest no significance.

There were, of course, times she'd walk out to the market and occasionally to the King's Garden, to look at the still-intact Rosenborg castle and turn her face briefly to the sun. Feeling reckless and extravagant, she paid the two *Kroner* which gave her the right to enter the gates during certain hours, brush away the frost, and sit on the dark benches there, surrounded by maidservants, nurses, and a few strolling prostitutes of exceptionally high class. With warmer weather, the wealthy ladies came out, too, twirling their parasols above bonnets and curled fringes, letting their bustles bounce beneath their short jackets in a way that Famke found very fine. She imagined that someday these ladies would stroll past Albert's paintings—perhaps his *Nimue*—in a big museum; they would wonder about the artist and the model. She felt a thrill of anticipatory pride, and again of hope. It was as if these elegant ladies had promised her that when he achieved his success, he would come back. After all, he found Denmark inspiring, and Pre-Raphaelite painters sometimes married their models.

While Famke waited, she did a few small things to improve herself. She visited one of the new department stores and bought herself the much-coveted corset. Though it did indeed make her waist even smaller, she didn't like it. No one had told her it would be so very tight, that it would cut off her breath and make her feel as if she were being smothered with a pillow. Albert didn't like corsets anyway; he thought they distorted the body, made the spine unnaturally straight and the waist unsupple. She put it at the bottom of the little pile of her clothing.

On her next excursion she bought a book from a stall by Gråbrødretorv: a Danish-English dictionary. The cover was tattered and some pages missing, but Famke thought the little book would be very useful when Albert came back—or sent for her to join him. Perhaps if she had bought such a book long ago, they'd be together now. In any event, Famke set herself to learn twenty words a day. Her progress was swift; she knew a bit of the pronunciation already, she had a good memory, and there was little else to do. She recited the words on her walks, barely noticing the tulips that bloomed in the tenement yards or the strings of smelly flounder stretched to dry among masts in the canals and harbors: *Pellucid . . . effulgent . . . gorgeous . . .*

She thought of writing Albert a letter using these words, but she didn't know his address. If she'd had the money she might have traveled to London to look for him; but what a girl might accomplish in person would be impossible for a mere slip of paper. A letter would never find him, whereas he knew exactly where to find her.

So Famke merely sat and waited for life to begin again.

Kapitel 7
· · · · ·

[. . .] a pleasant park, originally laid out in the French style but afterwards altered in accordance with English taste. It contains two cafés, a pavilion for the sale of mineral waters, etc., and is a great resort of nurses and children.

K. Baedeker,
Northern Germany (With excursions, etc.)

Finally, there came the day Famke had food only to last out the week, and no money after that. She would have to find work. But who would engage a seventeen-year-old orphan who'd run out on her last position? She had no references, no friends, no way of earning next week's beans and bread without selling herself.

Nå, she had one friend. With her last Øre she bought a sheet of writing paper and a pencil, and she wrote to Sister Birgit.

They met outside the King's Garden. Birgit had stolen a few minutes by announcing a trip to the market; she carried an old basket heavy with withered apples and potatoes. Trying to please, Famke took the basket as she and Birgit walked slowly before the big fence, just in sight of the bronze statue of Hans Andersen.

They started with tentative greetings, restrained but affectionate on both sides. Birgit gave news of the orphanage. Since last she'd seen Famke, Jesus had lost a number of brides: Several sisters, including Saint Bernard, had coughed their way to the next world. It seemed poverty and hard work were taking their toll on the convent's notoriously weak lungs; the doctors were saying it was the curse of urban living and its attendant excitement, but what were they to do? They had nowhere else to go.

Famke gave a shiver of combined sorrow and fear for her own life. If even Sister Saint Bernard had died of the chest, what would become of her?

But she expressed only an unselfish sorrow, and Birgit received it with an approving smile.

Then Famke told her story. She told it simply and plainly, describing what she had done and how she had lived, and the great passion that had driven her to it all. "I let this man see me naked," she said. "I let him paint me. I let him . . . touch me . . ."

Birgit listened with the silence of a confessor, learned over many years. While Famke spoke, she had time to prepare her response. She folded her hands carefully, and the thin gold band glinted dully on her ring finger. When Famke stopped speaking, Birgit stopped walking.

"My dear," she said, "did we not teach you that your body is a house for the Lord?"

Famke imagined a transparent house with a ghostly God peering through the roof. She saw herself now cowering naked in a corner.

Birgit added, as she had so many times in her conversations with Famke, "A poor girl has nothing but her virtue."

"My virtue." Forgetting her vision of the house, Famke raised her free hand and dropped it helplessly at her side. "What use is that? There's always some man who wants to steal it. So I gave mine to a man of my choice."

"Did he promise to marry you?" Birgit asked.

"He promised me nothing," said Famke, "but you see, I kept hoping . . . We were so happy together. And then he left."

"Do you regret what you did?" Birgit asked, fearfully now.

Famke thought. It had never occurred to her. "My regret is that he left," she said.

Birgit took a deep breath. "Then, if you are not repentant, I cannot help you."

Famke stared. Her loving guardian, the woman who had tweezed glass out of her infant lips, who had given her a name—this woman was repudiating her, dismissing her as roundly as Albert had done. The sapphire eyes filled with tears.

"You are my only hope," she whispered. She put her hands—a woman's hands now, lean and bony—on Birgit's two cheeks. Wetly she kissed Birgit's nose, just as the child Famke had done a decade before.

So Birgit found herself beginning to weep, too.

It was the tears as much as the kiss that did it. And perhaps something more—Birgit, who had not planned on being a nun before her parents delivered her to the Immaculate Heart, who admired the lush paintings in her illustrated Old Testament, could have harbored some secret admiration for what Famke had done. Her tears were tears of passion, too. When they were finished, she prayed. She forgave. And by the end of the week she had found Famke a new position.

One of the orphanage's chief patrons, an elderly importer named Jørgen Skatkammer, happened to be in need of a housemaid. Birgit worked secretly, behind the other nuns' backs, to secure the job for Famke.

"Be good this time," she begged as, once more under Hans Andersen's blank eye, she gave Famke a letter of introduction and ten *Kroner* for a nest egg. "Don't stray. Someday you may meet a nice man and marry him"— Birgit knew it wasn't entirely moral to hold out this possibility after what Famke had done, but she had to give the girl some hope— "and you may put all this behind you."

"But I want Albert!" Famke said, with the same stubborn head toss she'd used to demand the last bit of sugar in Birgit's pocket.

Birgit fingered the rosary occupying that pocket now. It was a cool day for late spring, and the beads felt like ice. "And yet this Albert does not . . . no, he doesn't sound a *pleasant* man."

Famke, clutching the letter that was her salvation, allowed herself to laugh. "He is the most pleasant person I've known!"

"He left you behind, ruined, in order to pursue his own career." Birgit did not add, *As well he might, after you showed how carelessly you value your virtue.*

Famke had no good answer even to what Birgit said aloud; she could only say, lamely, "But you did not see the way he used to look at me."

Birgit sighed, thinking how little she knew of the world and how ill prepared she was to speak now. "Only do well for Herr Skatkammer," she said. "And remember to pray."

"I will pray," Famke said, and added in her mind—*I'll pray that Albert will return.*

Kapitel 8

. . . . .

*The Environs of Copenhagen, as well as the whole of the N.E. part of
Zealand, are very attractive. The rich corn-fields, green pastures, and fine
beech-forests, contrasting with the blue-green water of the Sound, are en-
livened with numerous châteaux, country-houses, and villages.*

K. BAEDEKER,
NORTHERN GERMANY (WITH EXCURSIONS, ETC.)

Famke realized she was lucky to have this position. Herr Jørgen Skatkammer's house, in the pleasant suburb of Hellerup, was large and
well run; she worked only twelve hours a day, shared a room with only
one other girl, and was promised twice the wages she'd earned on the farm.
The fireplaces had been converted to a coal furnace, so there were no
hearths to clean. And certainly no goose pens or pigs, no livestock at all except some stuffed birds of paradise and an overweight white cat that spent
most of its time sleeping.

There was also no Fru Skatkammer, so Famke took orders from the
raw-boned, downy-lipped housekeeper, Frøken Grubbe, who was firm but
not cruel and reminded her of Sister Saint Bernard on a good day. She instructed Famke to brush and rebraid her hair every morning, and to purchase a new blouse. Famke got one nearly new from a stall at the local
market, parting with five of Sister Birgit's precious *Kroner.*

Once she'd tidied her person, Famke's principal duties were washing
dishes, folding the newspapers that arrived from all over the world, and
dusting Herr Skatkammer's collections. By far the greatest claim on her
time was this dusting. Each natural curiosity and *objet d'art* that Herr Skatkammer had bought for his shops was represented in his home as well;
thus, if on one of his excursions he had acquired trilobites from the coast of
Scotland, a large chunk of fossil-rich rock settled on his parlor shelves; if
he'd brought glasswork from Venice, he hung a glass dagger on his dining

room wall. A trip to Egypt yielded a mummified crocodile, displayed along with its coffin and a stone tablet with gold hieroglyphics; at an auction in Boston, North America, Skatkammer furnished the already bulging chiffonier with a new set of silver and what Famke thought was a very ugly black-and-brown urn from a territory called Arizona. That urn alone did not show the coal dust that powdered every surface in the house—and yet it must be dusted. Each object was accompanied with a neatly lettered card identifying its origin and, on the back, its value at the time of purchase. These cards also had to be cleaned regularly, and woe betide the maid who left a careless fingerprint behind.

Famke did not notice the lack of paintings and other fine arts that traditionally furnished the well-appointed bourgeois home. Her months with Albert had not trained her to expect such things; to her mind, they belonged to a world apart from the world of work. And after the first few days, Herr Skatkammer's collections failed to register as exotic or even silly; she grew used to the fact and circumstance of wealth, just as she'd been used to the orphanage, the farm, and the studio. The collections were merely objects of dull labor, to be cared for in much the same way she'd looked after the tools on the farm. Even the carnivorous plants in the small conservatory became, after an initial fascination, just another chore; she spent a maddening hour each day catching flies to feed them.

The one collection of any lasting interest was the set of travel guides in Herr Skatkammer's study. As she dusted, Famke opened one from England and read a page or two here and there, to see what Albert might be seeing: *The walls of the National Gallery are surely unrivalled for sheer brilliance of the images hung . . . Each Saturday afternoon in summer, the fashionable and those who aspire to fashion pour into Hyde Park to take the air, to see others and to themselves be seen . . . The verdant nooks and valleys of Highgate offer pleasant and useful instruction, reminding us that even in the midst of life, we are in death . . .*

In her lassitude, Famke made some mistakes. An elaborately painted Russian vase cracked when she scrubbed it along with the breakfast dishes, and a Chinese rug shredded when she put it through the mangle. The holes were bad enough; but then, with her crude needlecraft, Famke took it upon herself to patch them. The result was a clotted web of strings and colors, barely suitable for the cat to lie on. In the housekeeper's opinion, this last offense was grave enough to warrant a reproof from Herr Skatkammer himself.

In the two weeks she'd been there, Famke had not met her employer, though she had seen him as she passed silently by an open door or two. He was always absorbed in his collections and never gave a glance to the ghostly presence who cared for them. Following orders, Famke washed her face and hands, put on a clean cap, and presented herself in Skatkammer's study.

He sat behind a large mahogany desk, surrounded by papers and fountain pens, with the white cat asleep in his lap. Asian masks leered over his plump form in its ill-fitting suit, and when Famke walked in, his mouth dropped open in unconscious imitation of the mask directly behind him.

"I am very sorry," Famke said. Never having worked in such a fine house, she thought perhaps she was supposed to speak first in such a situation. She heard the faint tone of a bell. "Did I startle you?"

The mouth snapped shut. "No," he said. "Not quite." He put on a pair of spectacles and peered at her through them. A vein throbbed in his bald pate, but he said nothing.

She thought Herr Skatkammer must be very angry indeed. She curtsied as the nuns had taught her. "I apologize for spoiling the carpet. I understand my wages will be reduced." Wages hardly seemed to matter; there was nothing she wanted to buy.

"It was a valuable rug," he said, not responding to the matter of the wages. "But come closer."

Obediently, Famke stepped forward, wondering if he planned to slap her. But he merely gazed, as in another land he might have gazed upon a silk tapestry or marble carving, until she realized that this house posed some of the same dangers that the farm had.

"You are very beautiful," Herr Skatkammer said at last, exhaling. His breath carried the bitterness of one who could not sleep without a stiff dose of laudanum. Though he had hardly moved, the white cat woke with a sudden start and jumped to the floor.

Virtue, Famke thought. She said nothing.

"You are from the Immaculate Heart orphanage?"

"Yes."

"How old are you?"

Before she could answer—she would have had to answer, and her answer would have led to further and perhaps perilous conversation—there
came a discreet knock on the door.

Herr Skatkammer removed his glasses. "Yes," he called in some irritation.

"Herr Skatkammer, the Saints are here for you." Frøken Grubbe cracked
open the door. "Shall I send them to the parlor?"

"No, no, bring them in here," he said with a last lingering look at the new
maid. "And tea. And some pastries."

Mystified, Famke followed the housekeeper downstairs. "What are
these saints?" she asked, but Frøken Grubbe gestured for silence.

Two somber, heavily bearded men were standing in the entryway.

◆   ◆   ◆

Not those plates," Frøken Grubbe snapped, more harshly than was necessary. "Herr Skatkammer uses the Flora Danica for these guests—
though why he honors them, I don't know." With an air of long-tried patience, she unlocked a dark cabinet that held the hundred-year-old china
depicting flowers native to Denmark. It reminded Famke of the carriage
Albert hired the day he whisked her away from Dragør, and she was glad to
touch it.

"Why did you call the men saints?" Famke asked as she set out the
plates. Frøken Grubbe was slicing buttery almond *Wienerbrød*, and Famke's
mouth watered. But she knew it was pointless even to imagine what such a
treat might taste like, so she put her mind to other questions.

"That's what they call themselves," said Grubbe, still irritable. "They are
from America"—as if that settled the matter.

"Are they importers, too?"

The kettle boiled; Frøken Grubbe lifted it off the stove and poured it
over the tea leaves in the Flora Danica pot. "In a manner of speaking. They
import people. They convert good Scandinavians to their religion and then
take them to a desert that they say is God's chosen land."

"Slavers?" Famke asked in fascinated horror.

"No one knows," Frøken Grubbe admitted, warming to her subject as
the tea steeped. Her upper lip looked darker as it dampened with steam.

"But they are said to marry many women and to make them participate in secret rituals."

Famke thought of those bushy, moustacheless beards and shivered. "What do they want with Herr Skatkammer?"

"They want," came the ominous answer, "to convert him. They believe that as a Catholic among Lutherans, he is vulnerable. If they succeed, they will convince him to finance passage for their converts, to let them sail on his ships and to *give them money*—more than a decade's wages for you and me, most likely. They think nothing of asking, and he might think nothing of giving it."

Famke felt a twinge of resentment that brought her into communion with Frøken Grubbe; it was almost as if the Saints were stealing from the two of them.

"They're a strange bunch," Frøken Grubbe continued, fishing out the tea strainer. "They pray to God's wife, though everyone with a right mind knows He is a bachelor." She sighed, as if suddenly weary. Then she picked up the tray of steaming tea and sweetly fragrant pastries. "I will bring this upstairs," she said with a sharp look at Famke. "I think it's best if you stay out of Herr Skatkammer's sight."

• • •

Famke was grateful to have found a protector in the spare and unlikely form of Frøken Grubbe. She avoided Skatkammer as best she could; and even when he asked for her by name, the housekeeper would send another maid in her place or do the errand herself.

Eventually Famke realized that Frøken Grubbe's cooperation could point in only one direction. *She loves him,* Famke thought, and was astonished. She felt as if she'd received a revelation: At the advanced age of nearly forty, and suffering a lack of personal charms, a woman could fall in love. That this particular woman was besotted with an even less attractive and more aged employer, and hoped he would come to love her as well—Famke thought it very sad indeed.

What was more, the housekeeper's unhappy story made Famke realize her days in the mansion could well be numbered as the hairs on her head. Even the kindest of women—and Frøken Grubbe certainly was not that—

would not harbor the object of a beloved's lust for long. Indeed, her re-proofs of Famke's mistakes were becoming sharper and sharper, and once or twice Famke found that after the other servants had eaten there was no meat for her own dinner. She made herself adopt the meek manners of the convent and tried to please Frøken Grubbe whenever possible. This was not a job a girl should throw away, especially not a girl who'd lost her virtue.

Famke's virtue remained unmourned, nearly unremembered except for the two mementos of the man who had taken the last shreds of that ephemeral purity from her: the silver tinderbox and the sketch he had made of her in Dragør nearly a year before. She would not tack it to this wall, but when she had a moment and a candle and her bedmate was sleeping, Famke liked to unroll the delicate cylinder of it and spread it on her own bed. She still thought it was Albert's finest work. There was always some new detail to be noticed: a wrinkle in the ribbons of the cap so carelessly shoved back from her head, a bend in the curls that escaped from her braids, a spark of sunlight in her eyes. And finally, as a special treat, Famke might turn the paper over and read the words written there—words she had not discovered until she unpinned the sketch from Fru Strand's wall and rolled it up to come to Skatkammer's. Albert must have written them just before he left:

> To my sweet, lovely Famke, who rescued her face and my fate from the fire—
> Had we but world enough and time, this parting, darling, would be no crime.
> Best regards from a rushing heart,
> A. C.

They were beautiful words, words that—she thought—made it plain he did not wish to leave her. It was only the uncertainty of his own future that kept him from begging her to be his permanently. Had she but means, she might have gone to him and said that none of the rest mattered . . .

These thoughts never failed to make her weep, until, romantically, she doused the candle with her tears.

Kapitel 9

. . . . .

Behold, my house is a house of order, saith the Lord God, and not a house of confusion.

PEARL OF GREAT PRICE 132:8

Alone, depressed, and bored, Famke's mind needed some occupation, and the strangest of the strange attractions in Herr Skatkammer's household were the men who called themselves Saints. They were not Skatkammer's only visitors, but they were the most fascinating; they came to the house regularly, and when a visit was expected, Famke found herself choosing to perform certain duties that lay in their path. She brushed the animal heads in the hallway or polished the sabers on the front stairs, allowing Frøken Grubbe to chase her away only after she got a good look. Men who married more than one woman at a time . . .

"*Polygamy,*" she said, trying out her dictionary English in the privacy of the servants' outhouse. "*Fidelity. Darling.*"

What if Albert had been able to marry both Famke and another girl? Would a half share in Albert have been enough?

He had been gone for more than two months. At night, when her bed-mate, Vida, fell asleep, Famke recalled his amphibious eyes and touched herself Down There. *The cottager holds a paintbrush . . .* She rolled a pebble of her own flesh and felt something pleasant, but not the shimmering feeling, the wanting feeling, she got with Albert. In time even that pleasure disappeared; but she was interested in no other kind. Vida was chubby and smelled like Herr Skatkammer's cat, and she was not Albert. Famke had to take some other action.

. . .

With April and the British Royal Academy show well in the past, Famke took advantage of her first Thursday halfday and trudged into Copenhagen. Albert had promised to tell her how Nimue fared, and her faith in that promise had only grown in the absence of other hopes.

Fru Strand's rooming house looked more dilapidated than ever, now that Famke had Herr Skatkammer's villa to compare it to. The landlady still had not replaced the windows Albert had removed, and she probably never would, Famke thought as she rapped at Fru Strand's door. There must be plenty of sailors who were willing to take that room; when in port, they lived in the darkness and slept in the daytime, so the boards would be no hardship for them.

When the door opened, Famke was surprised to see not Strand but a hunched-over man of early middle age. He was in his shirtsleeves, a napkin glistening with fish scales around his neck; when he saw her, he whisked it off, revealing an equally discolored shirtfront, then wiped his mouth and tossed the napkin into the shadows beyond the door. With lips still shiny, he smiled and tried to straighten, but he was unable to do so fully.

Famke hesitated, but she remembered the boarded-up windows above; she was in the right place. "Nå . . . I came to see Fru Strand."

"She is gone," he said, and made a courtly little bow. "I am Ole Rasmussen, her nephew and the new proprietor. You are a friend?"

"I lived here once," Famke said. "Just a month ago. With my husband." She felt it was only polite to ask, "Where has Fru Strand gone?"

"To the other side," he said delicately; then, when Famke still looked blank, "She is dead."

Famke received this news with a shock that surprised even herself.

"She fell into the canal," Rasmussen said helpfully. "She was—er—"

"She was drunk," Famke said.

"Nej, sadly, she was set upon by thieves. They were never found, but they took even her gold tooth."

There was no predicting what might happen—accidents, footpads—oh, Albert!

Famke swallowed. "I have come to ask about a letter," she said, willing her voice to steady itself. "My husband was to have written me here. His name is Albert Castle, and mine is Famke—or Ursula." She didn't know which name Albert might use in writing her, or whether he'd try giving her a last name.

Ole Rasmussen opened his door wider, and for the first time Famke saw into the landlord's lair. It was the dirtiest place she had ever seen— broken-down furniture and newspapers, indeed papers of every sort, everywhere, and a thick pall of dust choking the air itself. Fru Strand had left a filthy mess for her nephew; but then, judging by his shirt, filth appeared to be a family trait.

Rasmussen gestured at the moldering papers that had burst from a pigeonholed desk like stuffing from a sofa. "There may be something," he said. "*Fanden*, I think there is. I remember your name, and your husband's, from one of my aunt's record books—she kept several, in various places—and perhaps your name was on a letter as well. But I must sort through all of that again before I can say for certain."

Famke's heart leapt. "I could help you," she said.

"*Puhha*." Rasmussen blew out, and she smelled the herring on his breath. "I don't have time to look for a letter today. There's a window to fix upstairs first, and I have the glass waiting."

It seemed terribly cruel that Famke should be kept from Albert's letter—if there was such a letter—by a violence that Albert himself had done to the building. She wondered if Rasmussen might have been more inclined to help if she hadn't introduced herself as a married woman.

"I could look for myself," she offered. "And I could sort the papers for you. I am employed as a housekeeper . . . just until my husband returns."

But her employment was no guarantee to Herr Rasmussen, who looked distressed at the thought of a strange woman excavating the desk before he had his chance. There could be money in those heaps . . . He blinked at her with palpable suspicion.

"Or I can come back," she said, mustering her dignity. "Perhaps in two weeks?" It would be at least that long before she had another half day.

"Maybe." He coughed into his already grimy sleeve, then sighed and extricated a handkerchief that had worked its way up to his elbow. He blew his nose. "Or you can leave me your address and the money for postage, and if there is something for you I will send it on." He tucked the crumpled handkerchief back into his cuff, clearly aware of having offered her a great favor.

Famke realized that whether she accepted this offer or not, she would have to tip the man a *Krone* for his goodwill. She might as well add the few *Øre* needed for a local-delivery stamp; though she disliked giving money away, that would be the fastest means of getting Albert's letter, when it was found. She wrote out her new address and handed it to Ole Rasmussen with the coins. Still, she resolved that she would keep visiting until Rasmussen told her for certain whether a letter for her might lie somewhere in Fru Strand's pigeonholes.

"Thank you so much," she said as she turned away, preparing herself for the long walk back with neither more nor less hope than had accompanied her into town.

◆　◆　◆

Famke tried not to think about a letter. She tried not to run for Skatkammer's post when, at the strokes of ten and three, it arrived each day. She set herself other tasks—memorizing lists of English words as she dusted the collections, practicing the gestures of the Three Graces as she made Herr Skatkammer's bed. She learned the solemn Saints' names, Erastus Mortensen and Heber Goodhouse, and found out as much as she could about them. Though they still had brown hairs among the gray, they both looked old to Famke, perhaps even older than Frøken Grubbe, though not so old as Herr Skatkammer. They earned her gratitude for using none of the pomade she had to wash out of the antimacassars when other visitors left; they smelled only of the plain soap she was used to and liked. They wore round spectacles and always had a book in hand—*En Sandheds Röst, En Røst fra Landet Zion, Mormons Bog.*

Ah, Mormons. Famke had heard of Mormons before; in Dragør there was a man who'd come to proselytize—maybe one of these very two—and she had heard that right by the town well he had preached crazy miracles and said the Garden of Eden was in a place called Missouri. The good Lutherans of the village had chased him away with pitchforks, and for weeks afterward they warned their women that when a Mormon came to town, it was to steal Danish girls and lock them inside a hidden temple. They also reported that the patriarchs married their own daughters. Everyone knew that the Mormon symbol was the beehive, which they claimed signified hard work and sweet rewards, but which others knew meant a tower of pain and poison to outsiders. These two looked harmless enough, but now Famke saw them through the misty veil of legend. They were both wicked and alluring.

She began to listen behind the office door when they were there, and even hung out the windows to get a last look as they left. She learned that Mortensen's father had been Danish, a good friend of Herr Skatkammer in the days when both were Lutheran. This long-dead friendship explained why Herr Skatkammer indulged the frequent visits—this, and perhaps the same kind of fascinated curiosity that drew Famke to them. Otherwise she could not explain his hospitality, for Herr Skatkammer had to listen to endless pleas for money.

"We have engaged a ship to transport us from England," Mortensen said one day in his near-perfect Danish. "The *Olivia* will leave Liverpool in a fortnight. We have over three hundred converts eager to reach Zion, and nearly half of them lack the funds for the journey."

Goodhouse, whose mother had been a Dane from Jutland, added, "We also need a ship to bring them to England. And once they have arrived in Zion, we would like to establish them in the silk-growing industry—we shall need mulberry trees and worm eggs, spindles and wheels . . ."

Herr Skatkammer merely grunted. He must have pulled the bell that rang for servants, because Frøken Grubbe turned up immediately. She glared at Famke as she opened the office door.

"More cakes," said Herr Skatkammer.

The three men peered past Frøken Grubbe and saw Famke. "Have Ursula bring them," Herr Skatkammer added.

So Mortensen and Goodhouse learned Famke's name, too. From that day on, the slightly younger one, Goodhouse, took to greeting her as they passed. "*Goddag*, Ursula."

"*Goddag*," she replied, stealing a last look as the housekeeper whisked her away. Americans spoke through their noses.

On another visit, Goodhouse managed to get her into a corner. She thought with momentary dread of her virtue but was relieved when he merely whispered, "Can you read, Ursula?"

"Yes," she whispered back, eagerly and in English, "and I read your tongue, too. Do you wish to give me a book?"

So, when Frøken Grubbe wasn't looking, Famke accepted the same tracts the Saints had brought for Herr Skatkammer: *A Voice of Truth, A Voice from the Land of Zion, The Book of Mormon.*

She was glad to get them. Now she could read of these fantastic people who married many women; in a household that refused to gossip, these books would tell her about the world. Even better, she would learn how to make English sentences. The dictionary was thick going, and she still considered it of utmost importance to become fluent.

You never can know the future, she reminded herself. *Any day there might be a letter.* She must remember that great work, *The Revenge of Nimue,* whose success would surely make Albert think of her . . .

Famke's roommate noticed the tracts (disappointingly dry, Famke had discovered, but useful for the English) and reported them to Frøken Grubbe.

"You'd better take care," the housekeeper warned as she broke the pamphlets in her hands and consigned them to the kitchen stove. "Do not be foolish. I told you what happens to their women."

Famke replied with confidence, "I am not that kind of woman," even as she reminded herself: *This parting, darling, would be no crime.*

.2.

PEARL OF GREAT PRICE

Again, the kingdom of heaven is like unto a merchant man, seeking goodly pearls: Who, when he had found one pearl of great price, went and sold all that he had, and bought it.

MATTHEW 13:45, 46

And in that day, seven women shall take hold of one man, saying: We will eat our own bread, and wear our own apparel; only let us be called by thy name to take away our reproach.

BOOK OF MORMON, 2 NEPHI 14:1

Chapter 10

Ye Saints who dwell on Europe's shore,
Prepare yourselves with many more
To leave behind your native land,
For sure God's judgments are at hand.
"THE HANDCART SONG"

New worlds for old," Famke whispered. It was a phrase she had read in one of Herr Skatkammer's English newspapers, and she'd remembered it because it reminded her of Albert: building, upon the ruins, a new and perfect world. "*Nye Verdener for gamle.*"

A dark wind swallowed her words; but they did not sound so good in Danish anyway. She had never known such a wind: It seemed to come from some deep part of the sky, well away from any known world; for it was an effortless wind that carried none of the heat that propelled the ship forward. Rather, it buffeted the steam engines, forcing them to chug and labor for every inch they won from the constantly shifting waves.

Beneath that blast and under an arc of star-pricked, moon-tinted blue, the earth had become a flat plane of deep black; when she stood at the rear of the steerage deck and looked backward, she was the only figure in the landscape. Out of its braids, her hair made a tunnel over the water; and overhead, against the dark canvas of the sky, that wind hurled the white engine smoke straight back, like an arm reaching toward its home port. Nonetheless, Famke, with plain pink hands clenched around a ship's iron railing, was being carried forward, to America.

America: where Albert had gone in search of new mythologies, colorful new mysteries for his art. Mountains, goldmines, deserts. Savages. It was a printed fact.

Back in Hellerup, Famke had been on the rear stairwell with an armful of Herr Skatkammer's foreign newspapers, which were needed in the kitchen, when a small paragraph in English caught her eye:

> . . . The passenger list of the S.S. Lucrece will include one lately a student at the Royal Academy, so nonplussed by the Academy's return of what he had hoped would hang in its annual Exhibition that he has determined to try his fortunes in the farthest reaches of the land to the West. Claiming that the flames of inspiration have suffocated in our cold climes, he has, we are told, exchanged the rejected work for his passage to the desert. It is to be hoped that, on shores less known for artistic achievement, the miners and ranchers of his eventual destination will be more receptive to Albert Castle's style and subject matter . . .

The name leapt from the page as if inscribed in red letters; as if it were itself a picture of Albert's green eyes, his thin hair, his cheeks flushed with excitement.

Famke sat weakly down on the stairs, newspapers sliding away from her in a great fan. So Albert had gone to America, left England and his father and the hope of joining the Brotherhood. She barely noticed that *Nimue* (she, Famke) had been sold to some ship's owner or captain.

She dropped to her knees and scrabbled through the newspaper's scattered leaves until she found the *Lucrece*'s date of embarkation: June 29.

Today was June 30.

Famke refused to feel dismay. If she could not sail on the same ship as her love, she would take one soon afterward. This was the sign she had been waiting for, the kind of message that prompted people to do great deeds.

She ran up to her room to put on the despised stays, which she thought gave her an air of respectability, tied up her few possessions in her yellow shawl, and began the walk into Copenhagen, to the address printed inside the Mormon tracts.

Heber Goodhouse was palpably surprised to see her. "Ursula! Do you have a message from Herr Skatkammer?" he asked hopefully. He spoke English, and Famke realized she might not hear her native tongue again for a long, long time.

"No." She stared into his peculiar beard, which was full of the crumbs from his dinner. At the last moment she was having some qualms. But she reminded herself of Albert's dear amphibian eyes, drew a deep breath, and announced, "I want to come with you! I am Mormon!"

. . .

Goodhouse ushered Famke into the mission office and seated her at the table that served as his desk. He even brought her a cup of rice tea, clanking against its saucer.

But what was this trembling in his hands? He folded and clenched them, and the tremors retreated deep into his bones. Of course the housemaid's conversion was a boon to the mission. Women were still somewhat scarce in the American West, and many young Saints found wives difficult to come by; the un-Saintly men who paid for women often paid very dear—or so Heber had heard. Yes, any female convert was welcome, especially one used to a life of labor. As Brother Jedediah M. Grant had written in one of the tracts now in Heber's luggage, new arrivals had to expect "to leap into the mire and help to fill up a mudhole, to make adobes with their sleeves rolled up, and be spattered with clay from head to foot."

Heber imagined Famke working in this way: dress tight over her bent back, hands slapping adobe into the wooden molds, muddy from crown to toe. Despite the girl's pallor and slenderness—to him, she looked as breakable as glass—he had seen her hard at work on many occasions, and this imaginary picture was a pretty one. He reflected that in Utah, along with the mud, she might also stain her white hands green, chopping mulberry leaves to feed a hatching of silkworms, or wrap herself in a gossamer web as she carefully, slowly unwound the cocoons that would make the Saints' fortunes. Yes, as a model of industry, she would be an asset both to the Church and to his hometown, Prophet City, which he had instantly decided would be the best placement for her.

"It is a fairly recent settlement," he told her as he stirred the gummy fluid in his own cup, "just ten years old, and much of the land has yet to be worked. There have been troubles with certain crops, but Brother Young's writings suggest an answer: silk. The climate in our corner of Zion is ideal for the mulberry trees on which the worms feed. I had just started to plow the orchard when I was called to this mission, and while abroad I ordered one hundred seedlings for my sons to plant. The leaves are now profuse enough to feed a hatching of good Chinese silkworms—white mulberry, you see, produces the finest fiber—"

"Is your farm near a train?" Famke asked when she could stand no more.

He looked slightly hurt but answered nonetheless: "My property is five miles from Prophet itself, and approximately twenty miles beyond that lies Salt Lake City. The railroad passes through there. You will not have to walk, if that is your concern . . ."

"Så." Famke looked down at her hands, chapped and callused from cleaning for Herr Skatkammer. Once she knew where Albert was, she'd be just half a day from the means of travel to him. She allowed herself a slender, happy smile, a smile she thought was hers alone.

". . . the future of the Saints, then, is in threads!" Clearly thinking the smile was meant for him and his clever phrase, Heber Goodhouse topped up her cup; but as she became aware of him once more, the smile faded: She had been rude to him, and she needed his help. With a pang of guilt just slightly outweighed by cunning, she pretended interest: "How many children have you?"

He answered with pride. "Three sons. Ephraim, Brigham, and Heber the younger. And there are four daughters. They all earn wages under the United Order . . ."

He didn't name the girls, and Famke didn't ask. She didn't ask what he meant by the Order, either; she was much more interested in a question she had long wanted to pose him: "How many mothers?"

"One," he answered calmly, as if he'd been asked this many times before. "Sariah, my wife of seventeen years. We have been very blessed."

Seven children out of one woman, Famke thought, looking down at her own squeezed-in waist. What must the poor thing look like?

"In any event"—Heber was returning to the matter more immediately at hand—"we will have to arrange for your passage." He gave a delicate cough, and Famke took advantage of it to vent a rougher one herself. "Ursula, I know you have worked for Mr. Skatkammer only a short time. Do you have the means to pay for your tickets? I am afraid that they can be quite expensive, and though we try to help as many as we can, our funds are—"

"I have almost four *Kroner*," she said bluntly. "How much do I need?"

Heber sighed. He looked at his own hands, soft and pink as a pair of marzipan pigs. "I am afraid," he said again, "it is one hundred and twenty crowns just to cross the ocean in steerage—with food and clean water extra—and you will need a hundred and forty-five crowns more for the rails. The train," he added, in case she hadn't understood.

Famke echoed his sigh. "That is a lot."

"Yes."

There seemed to be nothing more for either of them to say. They retreated to their own thoughts.

Heber took off his glasses and polished them, mentally running through the mission budget. In their eagerness to return home, he and Erastus Mortensen had already promised aid to half the Danes they'd won over, and the missionary in Sweden (a most unpleasant country) had offered even more. The Scandinavian share of the Perpetual Emigrating Fund was exhausted. And yet—he looked at the girl again, sitting with heavy eyelids downcast and hands on her bundle—slight as their acquaintance was, he felt certain that *this* particular convert was worth extra trouble. Perhaps there was one already on his list who was less devoted, less worthy?

The clock on the mantel ticked. It was time to make a decision.

Famke decided first. She drew herself up, untied her bundle, and took something out. She clutched the object hard in her fist before laying it on the table. "So—I have this."

Something small and shiny sat between them, blinding in a ray of light. After a moment of surprise, Heber picked it up. It was of good weight, probably real silver, and from the design he guessed it was antique. It bore a hallmark on the bottom—not one he recognized, but a clear sign of quality. He barely glanced at the design on the top, which was not fit to be examined in mixed company. He had the impression of three women, all naked, two of them standing with their rumps to the viewer. The third one, in the middle—no, no, he wouldn't look now. The women's arms were twined about each other . . . He set the thing down and off to the side.

"What is it?" he stalled. "A—an unusual object, to be sure—"

The girl burst into tears. "It is a tinderbox."

Heber passed her his handkerchief. His eyes grew large and round as teacups: *A silver tinderbox.* In his mind he was already wording a tactful let-ter to Herr Skatkammer, a plea for leniency—though of course he couldn't expect the man to take the girl back. What was Heber to do now?

"Ursula—," he began.

"Famke," she interrupted through her tears. "People call me Famke. Ursula is only for religion—for Catholics."

"Famke," he repeated, finding pleasure in the odd sound of the word. "Famke, you must tell me what you have done. Whatever you say, I shall not condemn you. I will try to help."

Famke raised her head, startled. Could he have guessed about Albert and her fall from virtue? Would he really make her say the words—and would Mormons, these people who called themselves Saints, really accept a girl who had done the things she'd done, after she'd done them so gladly? Of course, she reminded herself, she had never done them for money—and with that thought came a sudden revelation.

"You think I have stolen this," she accused him.

He looked at her gently, so gently that the wires of his beard released their crumbs, which fell like snow upon the table. "My dear," he said, "haven't you? Come, you must confess so that I can help you. Perhaps we can return it before anyone notices."

Famke blew her nose violently. She spoke in Danish. "Herr Skatkammer doesn't collect *tinderboxes.* He likes *big* things—this isn't his."

"Then how did it come to your hand?" he asked, also in her language.

She knew it would be a mistake to say that a man, any man, had given it to her. She thought quickly and started with the truth. "I am an orphan," she said. "I was found on the steps of the convent wrapped in a fine wool blan-ket." The mere act of speaking gave her confidence, so she elaborated: "They also found this little box inside my diaper, and inside the box a slip of paper with a word, *Familjeflicka*—'girl of good family.' The nuns told me my mother must have been the daughter of some good home who was forced to aban-don me but did the best she could to give me a future. Mæka—America— is my future. This is enough to get me there, isn't it?"

As she told her story, Famke almost came to believe it herself. And the passion with which she put the amazing events together almost convinced Heber Goodhouse.

"Even half of this box is worth far more than a single ticket in steerage—," he began.

"Then lend me the money," she said quickly, "and keep this as security, and let me buy it back from you when I have a position again. I will take the cheapest ticket." She knew of this kind of bargaining from listening at Herr Skatkammer's door, and she didn't want Heber to ask her to pay for another Mormon's passage with the surplus. "Please. It is all I have from my mother."

Heber picked up the box again and hefted it in his hand. He asked, "Which orphanage did you come from?"

Chapter 11

·····

I go out on the poop-deck for air and surveying the [Mormon] emigrants on the deck below . . . Nobody is in ill-temper, nobody is the worse for drink, nobody swears an oath or uses a coarse word, nobody appears depressed, nobody is weeping . . .

CHARLES DICKENS,
THE UNCOMMERCIAL TRAVELLER

Famke spent that night in the attic at Mormon headquarters with some other new Saints waiting for passage. She didn't want to talk to anyone else, so she lay down on a hard pallet and used her bundle for a pillow. But sleep was impossible. The women lay elbow to elbow—girls, most of them, from villages and farms all over Denmark and Sweden—and they were too excited to be still. Their clothes rustled ceaselessly and their whispers blew around the room.

"It's a fairy tale," she heard one of them say.

"An adventure, more like. A chance. I've been stuck away in Gilleleje, where everything smells like fish . . ."

"*Nej*, it *is* a fairy tale. We are not wealthy, but we're traveling. We will find husbands. We will have houses of our very own!"

A third voice, older, joined the conversation. "And for this we must thank the Lord, who revealed himself to a Mormon on a farm—just like the kind we are all leaving. Thank the Lord."

The girls were silent a moment, then: "*Fanden*, I'm not going to be stuck on a farm again. I'm going to live in a city . . ."

The voices whispered far into the night, until at last Famke drifted away—willing herself to dream of savages, mountains, canvas, paint.

· ✦ ·

Meanwhile, Heber Goodhouse had written two notes: one to the sisters of the Immaculate Heart, one to Herr Skatkammer. He sent his notes by the last post, asking for a speedy reply.

He, too, found sleep elusive that night. If he were another sort of man, he might have sat down with a bottle of wine or brandy and a good cigar; but he was Mormon. Another Saint might have taken up the pen again and written to a wife; but Goodhouse had in mind that he was sailing in a few days, and he'd reach Utah before his letter would. So instead, in his room just under the attic, he paced up and down and listened to the angelic voices overhead. He could not discern Ursula's—Famke's—among them, but knowing it was a note amid the chorus renewed his sense of purpose. There would be some solution.

The morning brought good news for him and his new charge. Herr Skatkammer did not own any tinderboxes, not of silver or any other metal. He did not consider them modern, attractive, or practical; he preferred safety matches and the spring-lid boxes made for them in France. However, he was surprised by the new maidservant's defection and noted that, as she had served him less than a year, she could hardly expect any wages. He added in a postscript that he didn't think Erastus Mortensen's father would have approved of a son who ran around converting other people's servants under the masters' very noses. On the outside of the envelope he scribbled a last question: "How many wives do you have, Mr. Goodhouse?" But since this wasn't part of the letter proper, Heber didn't feel called upon to reply.

The note from the Mother Superior of the Sisters of the Immaculate Heart was somewhat cooler in tone. She reassured Herr Goodhouse, who was kind enough to inquire about one of the orphans her convent had raised, that Ursula Marie, called Famke, had indeed been discovered in a blanket of unusually fine quality. As to the diaper, she could not recall what it had been made of; likewise, she could not swear there had been a tinderbox inside it. Heber's heart sank a bit at this last, but then it lifted when he read that *as far as the convent was aware* (the words were underlined) Famke's only previous place of employment had been a goose and pig farm in Dragør, where her employer would certainly not have been wealthy enough to possess a silver tinderbox. Famke was a girl of good intentions, and though it was disappointing to find she was leaving the Catholic Church, Mother Superior was glad to know she was still following the Lord in some fashion. The convent sent greetings and best wishes to Famke on her departure for America, where it was to be hoped the clear air would do her some good.

The letter was signed, "Mother Birgit of the Immaculate Heart."

*   ✦   *

So when the 317 newest *Sidste Dages Hellige* (who had learned just enough English by now to call themselves Latter-Day Saints) swarmed aboard that first ship with their meager belongings and high hopes, Famke was among them. This vessel, the *Agnete*, was Danish but did not belong to Herr Skatkammer, a fact for which Famke was deeply grateful.

Nonetheless, she scanned the mob of sailors anxiously. Were there any aboard from the days in Nyhavn? If one of them were to identify her now, she would be lost. The men who had grabbed at her skirts as she passed in the stairway, who had listened to her nighttime tumbles with Albert—who had seen her naked on the day of his departure, even if it was only on canvas—these men could ruin her irrevocably.

"Where are the sleeping quarters?" she asked Heber, and, pretending seasickness, she went immediately belowdeck. Thus she missed the chance to bid her native land good-bye, to watch the spires of Copenhagen dwindle into the sky as the steamship chugged northward.

It took three days for the sleek-prowed *Agnete* to round Denmark's islands and graze the tip of Jutland, that finger cropping up from the European continent, then cross the open sea and snake down the English coast to Liverpool. On the first day, Famke cut off the end of her yellow shawl and made a pocket for her most precious possessions, so she might keep them tied under her skirt every perilous moment of the voyage. The rest of the time, she lay on a hard wooden bunk and listened to the women above and below and around her vomiting into the sand that covered the floor. She wasn't sick herself—at least, not from the sea—and yet she wasn't about to go up on deck into the clean air, among the seagulls and the sailors who might spoil her plans.

During those three days she didn't give a single thought to Heber Goodhouse or his precious Profit City. She thought only of Albert and of *Nimue*. When Birgit's face pushed into her mind—for Goodhouse had shown her the letter, thinking it would make her happy to receive this farewell from the women who had raised her—she pushed it out again just as firmly. She would not think of what she was leaving behind; she was exchanging an old world for a new one. Of course, she might write when she found Albert . . .

There was a night's pause in Liverpool, where the Saints filed off the *Agnete* and onto the *Olivia*. As she started down the jumpy gangway, Famke found Goodhouse at her elbow, asking how she felt now.

There were quite a few sailors on the dock. Famke pulled the uncornered shawl farther over her head; she'd wrapped her few other possessions in her spare blouse, and she held it in front of her body and staggered dramatically. "The sun . . ." She wrinkled her forehead, aping pain.

"Ah yes, it's a bit much after so many days belowdeck." Goodhouse took her arm—ignoring the other Sainted women traveling alone, women who had also spent the trip in their bunks and who were weak from vomiting besides—and guided her solicitously through English customs and into women's steerage.

"Thank you," she said politely, as he lingered on the uncrossable threshold. She pulled the intact end of the shawl across her nose; it would seem that no steerage cabin ever smelled good. "Thank you very much," she said again, as he seemed disinclined to leave her. "I am sure you have much to do."

With visible reluctance, he bowed, and he made his exit just as a stout peasant woman tottered in and retched heartily over the floor.

◆   ◆   ◆

To one who did not go on deck, the steamship journey was an endless parade of stenches: seasickness, overcooked stews, underwashed bodies. Perhaps worst were the unemptied privies, for even with the sparkling ocean all around, they made an inexplicable pocket of dirty water and palpable odor. Nonetheless, Famke spent much of her time there: It was the one place she could be alone and unobserved. In steerage, if the sleeping women woke, they tended to use the chamberpot rather than dress and stumble out to what was only a board full of holes propped over a tub anyway. Famke slept in most of her clothes and trained herself to wake shortly before dawn, secure her yellow pocket, and sneak away to privacy. There at least she could wait, alone, until a finger of gray light filtered through the filthy porthole and illuminated her lap.

For in her lap lay her own face, the face Albert had sketched that first day in Dragør. It was crumpled now from its travels, and the pencil marks—graphite, not charcoal, she thought gratefully, now that she knew more about an artist's materials—had smeared, but it was still there: the work of his hand, the outline of her face. As the light grew, she pulled it closer to her eyes and imagined she was gazing into a mirror, such as the one she'd given him for Christmas. It was some comfort to think that perhaps that glass was reflecting his face at this very moment.

Every night, she mourned the loss of the tinderbox; but she told herself to be content with this sketch, which was surely more precious to her than antique silver, no matter how many queens and princesses might have touched that little box. She waited, dreaming, until she heard the first footsteps on the deck—usually a matter of minutes—and then quickly folded the sketch and returned it to her pocket.

As to her other possessions, they were safe enough on the bunk she shared with another girl; Mormon ladies did not steal from each other, and in their new-convert virtue they even withheld curiosity about each other's bundles. All bundles were assumed to hold roughly the same contents: a few spare garments, contracts of emigration and repayment, pictures of loved ones never to be seen again in the flesh.

All day, all night, the *Olivia* glided over the blue-green, sparkling sea, steaming toward the new life. The polluted air on board made Famke cough; but then, she was not the only one it affected this way. She soothed herself with thoughts of the great clean new country, and occasionally beguiled some hours in the bunk by telling herself stories: *This is a mountain in Mæka . . . This is a miner entering the mountain . . .* Below her, the other women spun more fairy tales, imagining perfumes and silks they would wear in Utah, pearls they might reach down and pry from the oyster beds now, if only they had nets long enough.

◆ ◆ ◆

A few of the women managed not to succumb to sickness at sea. They spent their time in singing what Heber called "glees and catches" and in stitching new sets of underwear: union suits so cleverly constructed that the person wearing one need never be completely naked, even while washing, and tediously embroidered over nipples and Down There with a set of symbols that Famke could not understand but was told were a sort of map, directions that the body could follow to paradise upon its resurrection. She herself was no needlewoman (the yellow pocket twice needed repairs on the journey), and she certainly felt no call for such a garment, which in any event she would not be allowed to wear until after her baptism as a Saint. She was much more interested in the English lessons that Heber Goodhouse gave in another emigrant's first-class cabin. She attended those whenever the ship's passageways were free of sailors.

Under Goodhouse's tutelage, Famke learned that English was the language presently spoken by God. The Saints knew this because God—or his angel, which was somehow the same thing to them—had spoken English to their young prophet, Joseph Smith, as the seventeen-year-old-boy dug his father's field a half-century before. Some years later, God had asked Smith to translate the signs on some golden tablets into the Mormons' new book of holy history and had given him special eyeglasses, or scryglasses, with which to do it. She imagined joking to Albert that he'd taught her to speak divine language.

Meanwhile she plied Goodhouse with questions. What did Joseph Smith's tablets say? What did he mean by "The Miracle of the Seagulls"? How long would the train portion of the journey to Utah take? She made Mormon lore her particular study: Perhaps this could be the mythology that Albert was seeking, the set of stories that would unlock his inspiration and let his artistic gifts flourish. The more she knew about it, the better; it would be her gift to him, as the glass ice had been so many months ago.

"Is it true," she asked Heber Goodhouse, "that you believe your God is married?"

"He is everyone's God," the Saint said in a tone of gentle instruction. "He created us in His image and bade us marry; our world reflects His. Even the savages practice a form of marriage."

"So it *is* true, then."

"Yes." He sighed, as if giving up a battle. "God is a husband. He descended to earth and married the woman you were raised to call the Virgin Mary, who is a treasured part of the Holy Family. We recognize her with our prayers in temple."

Famke spent a moment imagining the Virgin's blue veil replaced with the sunbonnet recommended for Saintly immigrants, then dismissed the image as unappealing. "And why," she asked daringly, "do your people have so many wives?"

Goodhouse's eyes remained steady, though they did not quite meet hers; this was the stickiest of all the doctrines and covenants, and the hardest to explain to young women. "It is ordained by God," he said, conscious of some bravery on his own part: "'If any man espouse a virgin, and desire to espouse another, and the first give her consent, and if he espouse the second, and they are virgins, and have vowed to no other man, then is he justified.' Joseph Smith translated this from ancient papyri—er, scrolls of text—"

"What is 'espouse'?" she interrupted.

"To marry, Sister Ursula." Heber was somewhat relieved to escape explaining the rest: that Smith had bought the papyri along with four Egyptian mummies, all of which had traveled to Illinois in time to vanish in the Great Chicago Fire. The nuances of his people's history were always difficult for the unbaptised, who could not accept that they themselves lived in an age of miracles. "Literally, to take a spouse."

Chapter 12

I saw the Mormon women. Then . . . my heart was wiser than my head. It
warmed toward these poor, ungainly and pathetically "homely" creatures,
and . . . I said, "No—the man that marries one of them has done an act of
Christian charity . . . and the man that marries sixty of them has done a deed
of open-handed generosity so sublime that the nations should stand uncovered
in his presence and worship in silence.

MARK TWAIN,
ROUGHING IT

The boy's hands had healed over nicely, to a network of scar tissue as
pink and white as a well-kept baby's skin. Those scars stood out
dramatically against his slightly darker wrists, but he claimed
cheerfully that they did not hurt. Still, even as she explained her dilemma,
Birgit had trouble looking away. She had scarcely realized, when she summoned him from his village on Amager, that this was indeed the boy from
that dreadful day under the elder tree—the tree so thickly green beyond
her window. A Viggo, not a Mogens; a boy apprenticed to a mortician without the usual fee, because no good family wanted a son who had touched
death. He reeked of the camphor with which he whitened the faces of the
dead; but, she noticed, his hands were very clean, even beneath the nails. At
the orphanage, she herself had shown him how to wash his first corpse, and
he had learned her lessons well.

She opened the simple wooden box in which she kept her important papers, including the slip that had given Famke her name, and took out a fat
packet.

"It is really *two* letters," she said, holding them up so he could see the ad-
dresses and postmarks framed on the backs of each page ("To Famke, who
lived at the top with Albert Castle"; "To the Mother Superior of Immaculate Heart"), but not the texts inside. "You see, the first one arrived at their

old boardinghouse. The landlord sent it onward with a note to the house where Famke—Ursula—was in service, though I can't say how he had that address. Finally the housekeeper of that place had the ragman deliver it here on his way through town. She would not waste a stamp on it. There is some bitterness from the way Famke left, to join the Mormons." She said the last word bravely and with such obvious resolution that Viggo knew she considered this to be her own chief failure, to have raised and loved a girl who would renounce the one true faith.

"What do the letters say?" Viggo asked, sitting up straight as he'd been taught, eyes wide and interested below his carefully oiled hair. He had always enjoyed a good story, whether of saints or of sinners, and this one was turning out fine. He remembered Famke, of course: the red-haired witch who'd beguiled him at her boiling cauldron. That she had forsaken farm life and married a dissolute artist (for such was the impression that Birgit, with painful regard for the boundaries of truth, had labored to convey) did not surprise him in the least. What surprised him was that the man would return to his homeland without Famke; even in memory, Viggo felt a tug toward her, just as a nail might retain its attraction to the magnet that first gave it a charge, or as a body in a coffin might turn toward the fields from which it had dug his living.

"It is wrong to read another person's mail—but," Birgit confessed in a rush most unbecoming to a Mother Superior, even one who was barely thirty-five years old, "I did read both letters, this time, to see . . . The boardinghouse keeper says that in sorting through his aunt's record books he discovered some money was owed to Famke. He did not want to send it through the mails, but it is there for her to collect."

"And what does Famke's husband say?"

Struggling to regain her composure, Mother Birgit traced that letter's original creases, making sure nothing showed but the address in Nyhavn and, on the back, a green blot of sealing wax bearing the imprint "AC" and a date of some two months previous. She was almost certain that she was doing right.

"He . . . wants her to join him."

Viggo was perplexed. "But that is wonderful, is it not? She will have the care of a husband again."

Birgit studied her own folded hands. In fact the letter contained no promise of marriage, but she was trusting to God that such a promise would come if she helped reunite the lovers.

"Yes," she said miserably, fearing that Viggo would never agree to her modest scheme. "But you see, he is in England with his father, and she has gone to America. Someone must give her the letter, someone must bring her back. Or, that is, deliver her to the address in this letter. Hampstead." Surely Albert Castle would do the honorable thing if Famke turned up on his doorstep with his letter in her hand, ready to hold him to his half-promise— and with a strapping Danish protector standing behind her. "I thought that if you, perhaps, could collect the money from the boardinghouse, you could use it to go to America . . ."

"Mæka," Viggo said excitedly, using the childhood name. Birgit remembered that, for all Viggo's knowledge of death, he was only eighteen years old. She remembered, too, that he spoke no English; but she had selected him in part because of his ability to learn, if not quickly, then well.

"Famke will not stay a Mormon if she knows this man is waiting for her. If there is not enough money at the boardinghouse, I could perhaps advance something from our coffers . . ."

"That will not be necessary—I will work for my passage. The landlord's money will give me a start in looking for her once I land. And then I will bring her to this husband."

Birgit noticed that in his excitement, Viggo's scarred hands had turned pink. "Yes," she said, "Famke must be with her husband."

◆ ◆ ◆

When Heber Goodhouse made his proposal, halfway across the Atlantic, it was just as much a surprise to him as it was to Famke. "Marry me, Sister Ursula"—it wasn't at all what he had meant to say, there in the cabin-cum-office in which she'd presented herself for the study of scripture. He could not even remember how he had fallen to his knees, but there he was.

What had he done? To have resisted fleshly temptation during these two years abroad, only to yield at the last hour, on his voyage home . . . If his fellow-missionaries could see him now—let alone Sariah, who as his first wife had the right to approve or reject all wives to come— And yet—yet he couldn't quite retract it.

The girl had him fixed with her blue eyes, fixed like a moth on two pins. Was she angry? To his horror, Heber realized he was babbling, telling her after all about those papyri, the Lord's revelation that they were holy records, and the vision he gave Joseph Smith to translate them on the spot (this time without scryglasses) such that the principles of celestial marriage were revealed and recorded in the sacred Doctrine and Covenants—"for the Lord teaches us to increase ourselves—to swell our flock of Saints, the true souls, the sons of Nephi, lest we be destroyed and step into the celestial fire alone . . ."

"I am afraid of fire," Famke said, her eyes wide with what he now knew must be confusion as well as modesty.

"The Lord himself has married, as you know. Marriage is the holy sealing of souls—"

"I told you in Copenhagen." She seemed to think he was chastising her in some way. "I am a Mormon. I promise. I have done nothing—"

"Of course you haven't," he hastened to assure her. "In our Church, it is not wrong for one woman to draw the eye of another's husband. It is lawful and right for a man to have two wives—or more, unto his means—for as it was in the days of Abraham, so it should be in these last days, and when a man is meant to take a wife, God sends a revelation—"

"Lawful," the girl repeated. Her face was luminous white.

Heber clutched his beard. "Yes, yes, I know it is against some earthly laws," he said; "the laws of Europe and of the United States. For now, we will have to keep the marriage a secret, at least among Gentiles. You will live in the home of my first wife, Sariah. You will call her Aunt. You will share—"

"I don't understand," Famke said, switching to Danish. "Are you really asking me to be your wife?"

The flood of words came to a sudden halt. "*Ja,*" Heber said through dry lips.

"With a wedding? A secret wedding?" *Et hemmeligt Bryllup.*

"Yes. One of the other missionaries can do it while we're still at sea."

There was a long silence. Prosaically, Heber felt his hips aching, locked too long in one position. In the corridor, a sailor took the Lord's name in vain.

"Why?" she asked at last.

"Why? Because I—because God— It is meant to be," he said. "I have had the revelation."

She thought that over, too, neither contesting nor confirming his assumption. Heber began to feel a glimmer of hope, and with it, an admiration for her capacity for stillness. She hadn't moved a hair since they'd begun speaking. She had a marvelous control over her body, a most beautiful propriety. Of course it was right for her to hesitate—she hadn't even been baptised yet . . . He should tell her to pray on the question, but an unnamable fear stopped him from suggesting it. Instead he made her a promise.

"You *are* a Saint," he said. "You are blessed of God. And if you accept me, I will bring you to the celestial kingdom."

"What about now?" she asked, in a tone he felt was both unromantic and unspiritual. "What about this life, this summer—this voyage to America?"

He was glad to answer that one, at least part of it. "My scheme of raising silkworms will ensure prosperity to Prophet City. You will be my wife and helpmate—"

"Will you pay for my passage?" she asked. "May I have my tinderbox back?"

Again she'd dammed his words. But he did not hesitate: "Yes," he said.

"Then, yes," she said. "I will marry you."

♦   ♦   ♦

As soon as Famke had freed herself of Heber's joyful embrace, she asked for the tinderbox. He appeared glad to give it back; perhaps he thought she was being properly modest in detaching from him, protecting herself from the dangers of exuberant flesh. He took the box, wrapped in a handkerchief, from his desk and handed it to her with a little homily about the beauty of maternal love and how she would find a new mother in Sariah . . .

Famke unwrapped the handkerchief and saw with relief that the box was intact; even the twenty-three matches were still rattling inside. She held out Heber's handkerchief, but—

"Wrap it up again," he said, averting his eyes from the naked Graces.

And, thinking the cloth would protect the ladies from scratches, Famke obeyed. She went back to steerage with a merry, light step and crawled into her bunk, still holding the box. That she would soon be a wife and take a man's hand in marriage, Famke hardly contemplated. This wouldn't be a *real* wedding, as it was illegal in most of the world; and from what she understood of Heber's confused promises, there would be no consummation until she'd been accepted by the first wife and "bonded" to Heber in the Mormon sanctum in Salt Lake City. Anything could happen before then.

The first wedding ceremony was celebrated that evening, in Erastus Mortensen's cabin. Mortensen himself presided, and the missionary to Sweden served as witness. Famke had no experience of weddings, so she could not tell if this one were special in any way; to her it felt like just another church service. She had always found priests difficult to listen to . . . She kept her mind on Albert and how this scene might unfurl under his paintbrush: Goodhouse's long tangle of a beard, the yellow shawl over her own head like a veil; Albert might transform them into God and wife, and it would be no more or less remarkable than the pantheon of goddesses under whose names he had already painted Famke. Yes, it was best to see this ceremony as a painting . . .

Even on deck that night, staring up at the stars and watching her hair make a red tunnel in the wind, Famke had a hard time realizing what she had done. Heber, now her husband, was apparently too shy to embrace her; so he was just a disembodied voice behind her back, going on about his plans for the silkworm farm and the great Saintly family they would raise on it. She heard almost nothing he said. *"Nye Verdener,"* she whispered over and over.

Chapter 13

. . . . .

I should say, then, that Brigham Young, prophet and leader of his people, made a huge blunder when he brought them so far for so little. Moses led his people through the wilderness, but he landed them in Canaan, flowing with milk and honey. Brigham was a very poor sort of Moses.

CHARLES NORDHOFF, "SIGHTS BY THE WAY," IN
CALIFORNIA: FOR HEALTH, PLEASURE, AND RESIDENCE

The air is good and pure, sweetened by the healthy breezes.

W. CLAYTON,
THE LATTER-DAY SAINTS' EMIGRANTS' GUIDE

The *Olivia* steamed into the Narrows near New York Harbor on July 18, 1885, having taken twelve days to cross the ocean. The emigrants aboard—new Saints and some others less in evidence during the voyage—were already crowded onto the decks, making the ship top-heavy as they craned for their first view of American shores. Because of her exalted status as the chief missionary's protégée, Famke had a spot on the top deck, near the railing, and so she was one of the first to watch the land come into focus: ugly gray docks and squat warehouses much like those she'd seen in Denmark; a very few trees, and all around a swarm of boats. The *Olivia* chugged up between sprawling docklands, engines groaning for the long-needed rest, and at last settled into her space at the pier.

"Act healthy," she heard someone mutter. Perhaps it was Heber, at her back, but the deck was too crowded to tell.

With the ship anchored at the dock, an immigration official came on board and gave each of the new Americans a card with a number. Famke was glad to see that hers was lower than the other steerage passengers'; she got to descend the gangway before they did, and Heber ushered her through a medical inspection. She held her breath and managed not to cough, but other aspirants were not so lucky. Heber told her that the ill and infectious were bound for a special hospital, and Elder Mortensen would wait with them there. Famke marveled that in America, even a sick immigrant from steerage might be cared for, if he wasn't sent home posthaste.

Yes, she was on American soil. It was unsteady soil, seeming to pitch and roll in much the way the ship had done at first. She realized she had acquired what Heber called sea legs; she was glad to have his arm to guide her onto the barge that would bring her and the other new Saints to a place he called Castle Garden.

Famke's heart flopped in her chest. She imagined a long stretch of lawn hemmed in by flowers, just as in Kongens Have, with a palace like Rosenborg in the background; but here there would also be a gravel avenue that led her directly to Albert. She shivered with each lurch of the barge engines.

Castle Garden turned out to be a huge round structure, formerly a theater, surrounded by ugly gray-brown buildings. Famke crowded inside with the other new Americans, to where the noise was disorienting and the fug of breath fairly choked her. Heber, however, seemed equally comfortable in every element, and he steered her swiftly through customs and up to a clerk who glanced at her through greasy spectacles and made her feel utterly insignificant.

"Have you any prospects in America?" he asked in a drone.

"Please?" she asked. "Prospects?"

Heber spoke for her: "She is free of debt and employed. She will be my servant."

Before Famke had time to sort out the confusion that statement created in her mind, the clerk asked for her name.

Famke had always liked the name Goodhouse and what it meant; she thought perhaps it was a name Heber's ancestors had given themselves when they first came to America. As an orphan, she'd never had a last name, and she wanted one that meant something nice. So, with a quick thought, she said, "Famke Sommerfugl."

Famke Butterfly—she was pleased to think this would be her official designation. Butterflies came in many beautiful colors and varieties, and they flitted lightly from place to place. Albert had often painted her with butterflies, when they suited his subject.

"Summer fool?" The clerk's brow furrowed.

She said it again, even more pleased than before. *Famke Sommerfugl*—it sounded like a song.

"Aha." The clerk wrote down what seemed plausible in the bustle and din of hundreds of foreigners answering the same question: *Famka Summerfield*. He entered it first in his ledger, then on a card he gave to Famke; and by the time she deciphered his spidery handwriting he was already processing the next person, and she and Heber were walking into the sunshine.

"You'll have to wait awhile," Heber said, depositing her on a bench in a broad open area. He was obviously reluctant to let her out of his sight. "I must help the others to register. Some of them have heavy bags that will need to be inspected . . . Soon the other ladies should come through, and they will be company for you."

"I will wait," Famke said, her eyes sparkling with the newness of it all.

"Stay in one place," he said sternly, for she looked very young to him in that moment.

She laughed giddily at his concern. But when he stepped away and she saw his spectacled eyes blinking over his dark-suited shoulder at her, she felt a little pang. She was alone in a strange country. The New York sunshine was sweltering, and she could see steam rising up from the river; no one had told her America would smell so bad . . .

Nonetheless, Famke had no wish to sit patiently with the other lady immigrants. Her idea of one place was bigger than Heber's, and somewhere in the mass of land stretching to the west was Albert—how could she then hold still? She was struck with an impulse to leave the Saints here and pursue Albert on her own. She could get a train today, rather than spending the night in town, and be in Utah (which to her meant the whole western territory) that much sooner.

Shouldering the bundle with all her clothes and possessions, and feeling the pocket with the tinderbox slap against her thigh, she strolled along the waterfront, trying to get her land legs back and guess where the train station might be. A brownish cloud lay over the sun and sky, and below that stretched a complex web of wires—for telegraph and electricity, Famke thought, and perhaps even the fancy new telephones that some Danes thought occupied every American household. She looked around for the wonderful bridge Albert had told her about, the one that had supported twenty-one circus elephants, but in the tangle of steel and stone she could see no such thing. She turned her attention to the people.

Real Americans were milling on the far side of a barricade, in brilliant clothing and elaborate hats. Famke sauntered as close as she dared. The women wore dresses in the most splendid shades of pink and blue and yellow, their skirts draped across the front and puffed out behind over bustles larger than anything she'd seen on a Danish woman. The arrangement made their waists look tiny. These weird, bright creatures were laughing so loudly the sound carried to Famke, and they gestured with silk parasols and ebony canes. They were facing toward the old theater and seemed to have gathered for some sort of entertainment, even as thousands of others went through the business of becoming Americans.

Famke realized with a shock that it was this that drew them, the spectacle of strangers arriving on their shores. Of herself and her countrypeople.

She turned and looked, too, at the flood of new citizens coming out of the round building, all clutching their crisp identity cards. From this distance, they appeared drab, moth-eaten, with the hollow eyes of people who hadn't slept properly in weeks and had vomited up all they'd eaten. She tried to imagine Albert emerging that way a few weeks earlier—but it was hard enough to picture herself, just moments ago, doing the same thing. She felt nothing of Albert here, saw nothing of either one of them in the gray masses. She looked longingly toward the elegant few on the barricade's other side, despising and envying them at the same time. Unknowingly, she slowed her steps till she was barely moving.

"Famka Summerfield," she repeated to herself. She decided the name was pretty, almost as pretty as Famke Sommerfugl would have been. It was an American name.

Soon she might have no right to her own last name anyway; she would be "sealed" to Heber and would be called Famke (or Famka) Goodhouse. Unless, of course, she found Albert before then . . . Hastily she said, "Albert Castle. Famke Cas—" But she couldn't complete that last.

She reached into her pocket and stroked the tinderbox. "Famke Sommerfugl," she said stubbornly.

"I beg your pardon?"

Famke turned around. The voice had come from a man somewhat shorter than herself, wearing a light green suit and long side whiskers. The top of his head was bald and pinkly gleaming in the sunlight, exposed because he had his hat in one hand. He was as pale-complected as a Dane, but his bearing and manner somehow marked him out as American. Such being the case, she assumed he could not be speaking to her, and she turned away again.

The little man stepped swiftly and presented himself in her path. She saw that the hand without the hat held a paper tablet and a pencil; he replaced the hat, licked the end of the pencil, and held it over the tablet, smiling up into her face ingratiatingly. "You spoke," he said. "What did you say?"

"I was not speaking to you," Famke said, then realized she shouldn't have answered him at all. He might not be dressed like one of the Nyhavn sailors, but his intentions were probably quite similar to theirs, and any words exchanged could be viewed as encouragement. She began striding back toward the splendid Americans, trying to land her boots square on the boards of the pier.

It was useless. She stumbled, and the man in green caught her. He also retrieved her bundle, which she'd pitched nearly over the railing and into the river, and he almost lost his hat in the process.

"Thank you," she said grudgingly, as she took the bundle from him.

"It is a great thing," he said, redistributing pad, pencil, and hat about his person (with the hat in its proper position, he looked years younger, perhaps still in his twenties), "to be of some small service to a recent arrival on these fair shores—or, no," he amended, with an expression that looked as if it were meant to be a frown but resembled a smile much more, "a fair arrival on these recently blessed shores."

Famke stared at him. No one had spoken to her this way before. "Thank you for collecting my things." She started off again, stepping even more carefully this time.

"Please." He stopped her, waving the tablet so the pages riffled in the wind. "Do not let my attentions offend you, for they are not meant that way. I am no ordinary gadabout of the pier—"

Famke finally made sense of the objects he carried. She felt a spark of excitement. "You are an artist?"

He stroked his side whiskers. "In a manner of speaking."

The spark burst into a shimmering storm. She forgot all caution and asked, "You draw pictures?"

"You might say I do," he said modestly, "but with words rather than curving lines. I am what is called a correspondent, an inkslinger, a writer for the principal newspapers of this great land. I would like to do a word-portrait of you; I am preparing an article for the *New York Times.*"

He paused for her acknowledgment; she nodded, remembering a few issues lying on Herr Skatkammer's desk.

"I have been sent to report on a shipful of freshly minted Latter-Day Saints," the man explained; "particularly the ladies, you pearls of great price. I—the people of America—would be interested in your views on a number of topics. Tell me, are you grateful for the religious freedom afforded by our great nation?"

Famke barely heard him, aside from noticing that he repeated the word "great" rather often. "You are familiar with people newly come to America?" In her excitement, she pronounced it *Mæka.* "The famous people? Artists?"

"But this piece is to be about commoners—not that there is anything at all common about yourself," he added gallantly. "Their views on religion, their expectations of the new Zion, their family lives prior to arriving on these shores . . ."

"Do you know Albert Castle? Do you know where he is now?"

He wrote a couple words—Albert's name—on the pad. "And who is this? Some Mormon potentate?"

"He is a painter," she said reprovingly. "A great artist, in your country since perhaps two weeks. He is going to the West, but I am not certain where. Will you tell me?"

"Does he paint Mormon subjects?" asked the correspondent. "Perhaps the Miracle of the Seagulls, who flew to Utah to gobble up a plague of crickets, or the Miracle of the Prairie Chickens, who appeared on the hilltop to provide meat when Zion was starving—"

"Albert Castle is no Mormon." Famke thrust her hand down her skirt and into her pocket and came up with the sketch. "He is a *painter,*" she said, waving the sketch under the little man's nose. "Can you help me find him?"

The man's eyes flicked toward the penciled image, then back to the living face before him. "Are all young Saints so interested in art?"

Famke made an angry exclamation and set off walking again. The river breeze nearly ripped the page from her hand, and she folded it up again—

awkwardly, with the bundle slipped over her wrist—and put it back in its pocket.

A crowd of Scandinavian immigrants was waiting outside Castle Garden now, unaware that nearby the splendid Americans were pointing and laughing at them. She recognized several cabinmates, still somewhat green around the lips; she thought Heber would surely be finished soon, and then they would all go to the hotel. If she were going to strike out on her own, now was the time.

She stopped, let the little man catch up to her. She had to be certain of one thing: "Do you know Albert Castle?"

At last he gave her an answer. "I have never heard of him. But let me tell you how to find *me*, should you be so inclined—"

"*Fanden!*" Famke saw Heber, his face grave in its ring of hair as he helped elderly Sister Carstensen to sit on the very bench where he had left Famke. He saw Famke, too, and his face lit up in a smile as he lifted his hand to wave. Then his expression darkened, and she realized he'd seen the man at her side.

The correspondent kept on, blissfully oblivious. "My name—"

"Oh, leave me!" Famke bent over in a sudden fit of coughing.

"The devil, you say!" He stepped back, hesitated, then politely offered her his handkerchief. Famke took it blindly, stoppered her mouth, and fled toward her husband.

No, she decided, it was far better to stay with Heber; alone in this new world, she might lose herself, just when she so badly needed to find Albert. This cough—she bent over again—surely this cough would improve in the clean air of the West, in the arms of her love.

❖   ❖   ❖

Viggo bade farewell to his homeland in the way Famke had wanted to, standing on deck and watching first the fairytale copper church spires and then the prosaic wharves, masts, and warehouses recede. He took with him four hundred *Kroner* in a bag tied around his neck; the prospect of menial work on a steamship bound from Liverpool to Boston; three pounds of arsenic, in case there should be an odd job of embalming to be had; and a fat packet of letters that included a lengthy epistle from Mother Birgit to Famke, wrapped around the note from the boardinghouse landlord, and at the heart of the bundle, the letter from Famke's Albert. Viggo had never seen so much money before, or so many words written to one person. Neither had he a sense of what the work would be like, but at the moment he was feeling a mixture of excitement and trepidation. No one he knew— except Famke—had ever crossed the ocean.

A knot of sailors worked behind him now, their forked caps swaying as they coiled ropes, trimmed sails, and told each other tales of fancy in a mix of tongues:

"As tall as a house she was, with eyes the size of dinner plates and nipples like—"

Here the sailor must have stopped to illustrate his tale manually, for Viggo heard a chorus of whistles and hoots.

". . . nothing but a nightdress to save her from the cold, and that itself made of ice," another voice finished.

Here Viggo stopped even half-listening; he had seen enough women in their shifts, farm wives withered and frail, dead in their sleep.

As he watched, Copenhagen became a smoky scribble against the sky, then vanished entirely. Viggo was overwhelmed with a sense of loss. The *Gunnlod* chugged up the Belt between Denmark and Sweden, keeping in sight of land; but Viggo felt with a rising panic that he was never to see his homeland again, had nothing left of it . . . except the letters written to Famke.

It was no more right for him to read Famke's mail than it had been for Mother Birgit to do so; if anything, it was a graver sin on his part, as he could in no way be considered Famke's confessor. Still, he pulled the fat packet from his rucksack and tore it open. The letter in English he could not read, and the one from the landlord was brief and dull; but he unfolded the outermost letter, the one from Birgit, and began.

"My dear child," he read, "A great deal of sad news has arrived at Immaculate Heart in recent weeks, not the least of which has been word of your departure for Amerika. That you did not write or call upon us to deliver these tidings personally has caused some pain; and yet I do not mean to reproach you here, but rather to pass on this letter from one who now seeks to correct the wrongs he has done you . . ."

Chapter 14

. . . . .

The railways are so poorly constructed that the cars shake tremendously, and
the trains don't go any faster than back home. One English mile costs five
cents, which certainly is not cheap.

LETTER FROM DANISH IMMIGRANT,
IN *BORNHOLMS TIDENDE*

In her new world, Famke was far from alone. There was Heber and the
flock of new immigrants; there was also an American girl called Myrtice
Black, who would be in charge of the women for the rail journey and
whose speech was hard for Famke to understand because she came from a
place called Georgia, where people spoke differently. She wore a hoopskirt
and a small bustle. At Heber's suggestion, she and Famke shared a room
and a bed at the hotel, but Myrtice was clearly in no mood for chatting; she
unbraided her straw-colored hair, brushed it as if disciplining an unruly animal, and braided it up tight again. She slid her somewhat thick body all the
way to the far end of the bed.

Famke gathered that Myrtice was some widowed relative of Heber's first
wife, Sariah, and therefore might be resentful on that woman's account. In
any event, she was glad that, after the tumult of finding the hotel and dining with her former cabinmates, she and Myrtice had a room to themselves—
and, just down the hallway, access to a real flush toilet, in a clean-smelling
water closet where Famke was able once again to lay Albert's sketch upon
her knees and remind herself why she was here, in America, the new world,
a marvelous land where even an ordinary woman was entitled to modern
plumbing.

The next morning, after a flurry of eating, food shopping, and prayer,
Heber and his flock crammed into a series of horse-drawn omnibuses and
let themselves be borne through the packed streets to New York's South

Station. This, no less than the streets outside, was a vast, bustling, echoing place, full of the deafening shriek of engines and wheels, with more cinders than breathable air making their way to the immigrants' lungs. Famke found herself shrinking closer to Heber and Myrtice, even as the latter eyed her with obvious disapproval. Famke had not expected this chaos. How could she ever find Albert, if just one American city had so many people in it?

Famke still wasn't prepared, either, for the interest that a flock of Mormons would excite in the American citizens. Like the yard of Castle Garden, the station was crowded with fashionably attired men, and even some women, all gaping and pointing at the Saints. Despite the heat, Famke pulled her shawl over her head—and then pulled it down again, as she'd already realized that it marked her clearly an immigrant. She followed her husband down the platform.

"This way!" Heber called in the voice he usually used for preaching. A long line of Mormons trailed after him, lugging their bundles and boxes.

Their train was obviously an old one—not at all the sort that Famke had imagined in her visions of America—and its cargo was largely human, groups of assorted immigrants bound for points west. They spoke a variety of tongues whose harsh sounds grated on Famke's ears.

"Come along!" boomed Heber, at the same time as another man, right by their side, yelled it.

Confused, Famke turned to see a large number of grubby children, mostly boys, being herded into a nearby boxcar. The man in charge of them wore the sort of sober clothes that Heber did.

"Are all those children Mormon too?" she asked.

Myrtice answered, in her peculiar voice, "No, those there are orphans being sent west for adoption by Gentile families. The papers call it a mercy train. Charities don't send children to *us*. Now try not to get lost. It is my duty to lead the women to car forty-seven." She hefted her own two satchels and poised to stride away.

"Yes, dear, please keep up with Myrtice," Heber said. "I must see to the men now."

Famke stuck to the Mormon girl's heels as Myrtice wove through the crowds and guided the other women into the car reserved for them; she even pushed her way to the wooden bench that Myrtice claimed inside. To ingratiate herself, she helped Myrtice unpack boxes of silk eggs—Heber's new livestock—from the special trunk that the egg broker claimed to have imported from China.

"They need to breathe," the Mormon girl said, and although Famke was finding it hard to fill her own lungs in here, she saw no advantage in disagreeing. Myrtice had been in charge of those eggs for several days already; her purpose for coming to New York was as much to collect them from the broker as to help Heber with the converts. That morning, Famke had heard her explaining to some of the other women that she was recently widowed, having gone to Georgia for normal school two years earlier and met and married her husband there. Now that he was dead, she was rejoining her aunt and family in Prophet City, to help with the new silk venture and to teach the local children; indeed, her very manner of speaking identified her as a schoolmarm. When she took off her glove to dab her eyes with a black-bordered handkerchief, her gold wedding ring gleamed.

As she and Famke settled onto the hard seat, surrounded by the slim wooden boxes, Myrtice scowled and handed over the handkerchief. Famke realized she'd been coughing. She used the cambric square—she was amassing quite a collection—to expel a lungful of dust and smoke and the stench of half a million people crowded into a city in August.

"There are remedies you can take for that, you know." Myrtice looked pointedly at the wadded cloth. "And a heap of cures without alcohol that are true to our faith. Nobody has to cough anymore."

Before Famke had thought of anything to say—and what could she say? she *did* need to cough, and rather often—Myrtice propped her feet on the silkworms' trunk and pulled out a leatherbound book embossed with a golden beehive and elaborate lettering: THE BOOK OF MORMON. She held it up as if offering it to Famke, who declined as politely as she could. She had found no real stories in her old copy of the Mormons' sacred text, only a series of sermons and some men moving tablets around with considerably less efficiency than Heber and Myrtice were moving the immigrants. She would leave that sort of thing to Myrtice.

Instead, Famke opened Heber's copy of the *New York Times* and scanned the headlines. There was no news of Albert, but then she hadn't really expected any; Albert was in the West, and that was where she would pick up his trail. She was pleased, however, to find a description of the scene she'd participated in yesterday. According to the correspondent, who went by the peculiar name of Hermes, the newly arrived Mormon women were "not without a share of youth and beauty, although the beauty was high in the cheekbones and rather more rugged than that of our New-York belles."

Famke laughed out loud. Though the correspondent did not describe her specifically, Famke had little doubt that he was the one who had followed her by the water. The article had to be about her. She read it several times, glad that in this one small way she might feel at home in the new land.

· · ·

After pulling out of the tangled city, the train's iron wheels ate up miles of green countryside over that long afternoon. Famke saw her first mountains—hills, really, Myrtice said, but to a Dane they looked titanic. She imagined a glittering ice cave deep inside every one.

"Mæka," she murmured. It was as if she'd stepped into the picture on that old puzzle, a season or two after it had been painted. And Albert was just around the next curve, or perhaps the next after that. It was still hard to believe that America was much, much bigger than that puzzle mountain.

The train made stops in towns of varying size and prosperity, and many people got off; just as many climbed on. The boys Famke had seen in the station were unloaded at a place called Buffalo, where the last drops of sunshine vanished in the black shadows of the rail barn. The boys ran after the man in the suit, who looked remarkably placid as his young charges shouted above the engines and stole each other's caps. Seeing Famke at the window, one of them blew her a kiss. Another grabbed at his pants in a gesture she'd seen before.

There was a loud *snap*. Myrtice had pulled down the tattered shade and settled back into her place, glaring at Famke as if she were to blame. After a moment Myrtice dug around in the satchel at her feet.

"Here," she said, "read this." And she tossed a small paperbound book into Famke's lap—not the Book of Mormon, Famke was glad to see, but something much more intriguing: *The Thrilling Narrative of an Indian Captivity*.

"My teachers gave it to me," Myrtice said. "It might could learn you something about life out West and what happens to ladies who don't tend to their persons."

Famke opened the book politely and began, though the car was now rather dark and the print very fine and fuzzy. Myrtice watched her for a few minutes, then pulled the spectacles off her face and handed them to Famke. "You're obviously far-sighted," she said, using a term Famke had never heard before. "See if these help. I have two pair." She closed her eyes and leaned against the seatback, feigning sleep.

Famke slipped the gold-wire curves over her ears and let the small weight settle on her nose. She wondered if they made her ugly. But any such question fled her mind when she looked down at the page: The print was much clearer now, and she quickly discovered that the book was about a woman who'd been known to walk provocatively through the streets of her small town. This woman was captured by savages during a massacre and had to live with them for some years.

Thrilling indeed—fearful and fascinating. She hardly noticed when the train pulled out of the station.

Chapter 15

Nothing can give such a vivid impression of the greatness of our country, and
the adventurous character of our people, as the sight of these boundless prairies
and the habitations of the hardy pioneers who are rapidly turning the buffalo
sod and exposing the rich black soil to the fertilizing action of the sun and air,
and substituting for nature's scant forage, abundant harvests of corn and wheat.

STANLEY WOOD,
OVER THE RANGE TO THE GOLDEN GATE

R ail life rolled on with a clackety-clack. The farther they traveled,
the longer were the stretches passed without seeing another train,
and Famke's boredom was relieved only by the book and a few isolated incidents. Once, in Michigan, they stopped because of an accident on
the rails: Another engine had hit a cow and derailed. Most passengers bewailed the delay, but Famke peered with interest through the window, trying to get a glimpse of the carnage. She saw nothing.

Other events posed more serious threats. The Mormon Saints, and especially their women, were the object of insatiable interest to Gentiles; and
in pursuing that interest, Gentile men occasionally grew violent. After the
Saints switched trains in Chicago, a posse of reporters stormed the women's
car, and the station guards had to help the Brothers beat them away.
Thereafter, Myrtice kept the doors locked. In Des Moines, Iowa, a man actually broke one of the narrow windows in the front of the car; Myrtice
jabbed him calmly with her umbrella until he fell.

Even in the face of violence and chaos, Myrtice was never less than calm.
Despite the wilderness through which they were passing, she insisted on
conducting English lessons for the immigrants, though she excused Famke
with a grudging admission of her proficiency. She was even calm when Heber
stopped in to say a few encouraging words, though Famke noticed they
didn't actually speak to each other. She wondered if that were some particular Mormon custom: a man was not allowed to speak to his wife's niece.

"Is this the West?" she asked in Omaha, and Heber said it was. At her request, he bought a newspaper in the next station, and she opened it with a pleasant surge of excitement. There was nothing about Albert—but perhaps she simply had not come far enough yet.

Thereafter she surrendered herself to the journey, and hills and mountains, forests and prairies swept by the grimy window in a blur. The wooden seats made for sleepless nights, and Famke soon felt as if all life were passing in a daze. Sudden shifts in altitude made her dizzy, and everything smelled like coal dust. Other immigrants were still ill enough to vomit, and many of them coughed all day (though without reproof from Myrtice). Decomposing cows and their shaggy buffalo cousins became commonplace sights; naked bones gleamed whitely in the moonlight. She read *The Thrilling Narrative* several times, until it, too, became dull. She put her ear to the boxes of sleeping silkworms, but the crates were silent as coffins; when she opened them, on the sly, the eggs were so tiny and round and blue-white that she nearly didn't see them and might have squashed them by mistake. She almost wished for lessons, so as to have something to do.

And then at last, just as she was beginning to forget any other life, they were in Utah, in Salt Lake City. Down on the ground, the yardmaster swung his red lantern side to side, and the train braked, blowing sparks and steam from the wheels. The hot brick station into which they pulled looked just like all the other buildings in the West; the lone difference was that here the new Saints were herded out—in rapid time, as a Gentile conductor studied his watch and threatened all manner of consequences if they delayed.

An excited Heber left Famke and Myrtice with their baggage in order to bring the other new Saints to headquarters downtown, and to hire a wagon for his family's trip out to Profit. They wouldn't waste any time in the capital; Heber said they would return anyway in a few days, and Famke knew he was thinking of their official sealing and her baptism in the Endowment House.

She put those events out of her mind and asked for a newspaper. Myrtice bought one at the depot office, then handed it over with the sort of severe look usually reserved for an importunate child. She also passed Famke a bottle of brown liquid proclaiming itself "Deseret's Elixir for Common Coughing, completely free of alcohol and other stimulants."

"You see," said Myrtice, "no one really needs to cough anymore." She sat down on the trunk of silk eggs.

Famke obediently uncorked the bottle and swallowed. What followed was the worst taste she'd ever known—something like the smell of burnt hair, in liquid form. She coughed, and then there was the faint tang of blood.

Myrtice pressed her lips together and glared as though Famke were trying to spite her. Now Famke felt unable to open the precious newspaper. She used it to fan herself, for Utah was hot, and the sheltering bricks didn't stop the station from feeling like an oven. Even the stationmaster gleamed with perspiration, and Famke could have sworn she smelled roasting meat coming from his window.

She thought she might be ill. "Where is the privy?" she asked, too loudly, and Myrtice hushed her with a gesture that managed to communicate that even out West, ladies did not ask for such things.

"We call it the *convenience*," she said. "But follow me." They crossed the depot and Myrtice briskly opened a double set of doors, shutting the last one on Famke so hard that the china knob rattled halfway out of its groove.

For the first time in days, Famke was alone. She locked the door, gathered up her skirts, and squatted down carefully, pondering. All trace of illness left her as she realized that once again she had a choice: She was in the West at last, and she could simply walk out of this station and set off to find Albert. Why waste her time riding all the way to Profit City? Somewhere in this newspaper, or in some other she might buy soon, there would be a clue that would lead her to him.

But there was all the trouble: buying. She would have to pay for newspapers and trains and countless sundry other items, unimaginable now but adding up and surely expensive in the end. Her only earthly asset was the tinderbox, and she did not want to part with it again. No, for once in her life, she would be prudent. She would bide her time, wait for the right moment, the proper clue.

Just as she reached this conclusion, the door was flung open again, and Myrtice filled the doorway. "You listen to me, Ursula"—she looked at Famke the only way she seemed to know how, with a glower—"because this might could be our one chance to talk. I want to say that you may not be married all the way to Mr. Goodhouse, but you're married partway, and you had best be righteous and stand by him or I'll know the reason why! If you can't do that, you might just as well leave us right now."

I'll know the reason why: It was only an American expression, but it struck cold fear into Famke. She was overcome with the unpleasant feeling that Myrtice, like a saint of the early days, possessed the power to read people's thoughts. Once again Famke felt ill.

"Of course I will be right," she said. "Righteous. I am going to Profit City. But how did you open the door?"

"Hairpin." Myrtice held up a metal object, its prongs tangled from having worked through the lock. "Well, any road, I thought you should know where I stand."

"Thank you," Famke said, for she could think of nothing that would get Myrtice out of the doorway faster.

Alone again, Famke took her time in the convenience, making herself as comfortable as she could for the wagon ride to what she must now think of as her home. She washed her face and spit vigorously into the basin, ridding her throat of that awful taste of Deseret's Elixir, then wiped her lips on a handful of the old newspaper squares provided by the depot.

She had to hold her own paper over her head on the jolting ride overland. She had never encountered a sun like this one, not even on the ocean; within minutes she'd soaked through her new underclothes. And yet the sun was no worse than the powdery dust, which caked in her throat and dried it till she knew coughing would be useless. Even the few stray cows they passed on the range looked parched and as if the very blood had left them to blow in the relentless breeze. In fact some patches of dust were not an ordinary brown or black but a sickly red.

Eventually the dust gave way to a huddle of brown buildings that seemed themselves to be made of the dust. The road cut right between them, leaving about a dozen shabby structures on each side. There were no wires overhead, thus no telegraph or electricity; the place was like Dragør, only smaller and much uglier. Heber stopped at a watering trough and let the horses drink. Famke would have liked to join them, but there was no refreshment for people here, and Myrtice's steely gray eye kept her in her place.

"Prophet City," said Myrtice, and somehow Famke knew she had misunderstood the name all along.

"Where are the people?" asked Famke, but she already knew the answer: working, like bees in a hive, chasing an elusive profit promised by an invisible prophet. She stared at the windows around, all curtained against the sun, until she thought she saw a twitch. It was some small comfort to think that there might be someone with the idle time to watch a new arrival.

"You will meet them on Sunday," Heber promised cheerfully. His collar was dark with moisture, and his hat had turned black with it—but he was becoming almost unbearably jolly in his native land, Famke thought. She didn't see why he should feel this way; America was not at all what *she* had imagined.

But when she felt him watching her, she smiled bravely. At that, his eyes grew wide and affectionate, and she saw with some dread where his mind was directed.

Famke looked down at her lap, and Heber pulled at the horses' heads and got the wagon creaking again. "Once our business is established," he dreamed aloud, "we'll have a branch of the railway put through here. It will reduce the price of transport by at least a half, and bring even grander prosperity to the city . . ."

Famke tried to imagine the word *prosperity* applying to this clump of crumbling houses, much less to the disproportionately vast cemetery with its beehive headstones. She did not look back as the wagon left the town behind.

The sun beat down. The dust clouded upward. The Goodhouses entered a field of red dirt and yellow vegetation and traveled down it about a mile before Heber said to Famke, with a touch of pride, "This begins our farm."

She did not know what to say. This patch of earth didn't look like any farm she'd ever seen; there were no crops, only that yellow straw and a stand of yellowish-green trees in a little valley. She couldn't see a stream anywhere.

But Heber was slapping his knee in delight. "Now that I'm back," he vowed, "we will put *every one of these acres under cultivation.*"

Myrtice murmured, "It will be a fine farm," and looked sideways at Famke, who was coughing again.

They pulled up at a dirt-colored farmhouse next to a dirt-colored barn, and there Famke met her new aunt, Sariah. She was as big-boned as Myrtice, though thin and swarthy where Myrtice was stout and fair; and while her brood of small children—the older ones were presumably in the fields—hung shyly on her skirts, she stared at Famke with the same obvious disapproval. One look had shown her everything that had led to Famke's arrival on this doorstep, and she kept her raisin eyes on the new girl even as she hugged Myrtice and delivered a dry auntly kiss.

Heber greeted his first wife with an embrace, too, but his was slightly stiff. He seemed to expect trouble. "Ursula has come to join us," he said, straightening his dark jacket. Famke noticed moons of perspiration under his arms. "Ursula Sommerfugl." He pronounced it perfectly, and the name Famke vanished into the desert air.

"I see that," said Sariah, in Myrtice's same voice.

"She is from Denmark."

"So her name would figure it."

A small Mormon child dared enough to hug his father's leg. Heber leaned down and rumpled the boy's hair as if to find the right words there. "Sariah, my dear, I have married her."

With a word, Sariah sent the children inside. "I reckoned as much," she said when they were gone. "Though what a man like you needs with three wives, I can't rightly say."

Famke snapped to attention. *Three* wives! She looked around and saw no other women. Then that must mean— She looked at Myrtice and saw the girl's face was turned toward the ground. So there was no Georgia husband: Myrtice, and Famke's new husband for that matter, were liars. Famke regarded them both with new interest.

"I have the wherewithal to support all three," said Heber, studiously avoiding Famke's blue stare. "And it will help you to have another pair of hands in the house, what with the new silkworm venture . . ."

"I didn't ask for another wife."

"But, my dear," Heber said gently, "when you asked me to marry your niece, I did as you requested."

Sariah turned suddenly to Famke. "Well, young lady, you want some time to yourself. Myrtice, you, too."

It was clear Famke would have this time whether she did want it or not. After exchanging a long look of wordless communication with her aunt, Myrtice showed her inside, to a bedroom for children; it contained several straw mattresses, a wooden cupboard, and nothing else.

"Could I have some water?" Famke asked. She was rewarded with a reddish glassful and the loud sound of Myrtice's heels clicking away over the floorboards.

Though she knew she wasn't welcome, Famke felt quite at home here. Salt Lake and Prophet and indeed the whole West might be nothing like Copenhagen or even New York, but this barren room was not so far from the studio in Nyhavn. She drank deeply, loosened her clothing, and, while Heber and Sariah quarreled about her below the open window, counterpaned a bed with the *Salt Lake City Daily News*. Using Myrtice's spectacles, she read it thoroughly.

An interview with senior apostle John Taylor, now in hiding to avoid arrest by federal anti-polygamists. An Indian on trial for scalping a Saintly family. A new turquoise mine in New Mexico, silver in Colorado. Advertisements, delicately worded, for corsets. Advertisements for cough syrups. Advertisements for livery stables, buggy whips, railways: Rio Grande Western, Atchison Topeka & Santa Fe, Union Pacific—all the West on the move or dreaming about it. Some train derailments and hotel fires. A new wing built onto a hospital in the far reaches of California. Auction lists. Endless local church reports, and one marriage record after another.

There was nothing about Albert.

Famke sat back, crumpling the newspaper and chewing her lip. She was aware of an impulse to cry, probably because she was so tired—but she wouldn't give in. She wouldn't. It seemed impossible that in all this ugly, empty, violent land her Albert had not made an impression. Famke told herself she should have asked for more than one paper, for every paper in Salt Lake City. Now she had to find a way to get back and collect more news. Somewhere, somebody must be writing about his activities, just as that English reporter had written about his departure. Someone must be watching him create a tranquil, perfect, clean world out of this dreadful one.

She shoved the paper aside and lay down full length, listening to the argument outside. Heber was describing Famke's skills with dustcloth and needle—inventing talents for her, Famke realized with a bleak sort of amusement. Sariah remained strictly unimpressed.

Apparently, then, plural marriage wasn't as joyful to all participants as Heber had made it seem. But the discovery that she was only a third wife made no difference to Famke—truth to tell, she considered it an advantage, for now she knew Heber would have two women to console him when she left.

How curious that Sariah had asked Heber to marry her niece. Perhaps that was the custom among these strange people, but Famke was fairly sure the good sisters of the Immaculate Heart would disapprove ... Sister Birgit would scold! Sister Saint Bernard would take Heber out beneath the elder tree and give him a good caning. Someone such as Albert, however, would be intrigued. He would want to know about the domestic arrangements—Heber flitting from bed to bed like a moth, or hopping loosely like a frog ... He would paint a picture and call it *The Latter-Day Bluebeard*.

Famke rolled onto her side, drawing her knees up toward her chest. For the first time in days she had the privacy and inclination, and she tucked her hands below her skirts. *There is a frog, and in his mouth he holds a paintbrush* ... She had little doubt as to how the conversation outside would end; the fact remained that Heber had married her by most of the laws of his and Sariah's church, and so she had a right to remain here as long as she wanted, to stand by and be Heber's wife. *A lily pad supports a bud, and he will paint the white bud red.* Soon, of course, she would find news of Albert and be gone.

Albert. It seemed forever since she'd seen him, though it hadn't been more than four months. When she tried to think of him now, painting the lily, it was Heber's face she saw, or features of the two somehow combined: Albert's big eyes with Heber's small glasses, Albert's thin mouth with Heber's thick beard ...

The bud withered, the frog vanished, and she fell asleep.

Chapter 16

Behind a high wall, is the Tabernacle, and near by it, on the east, enclosed within the same high wall, are the foundation walls of the new Temple. Within the same walls may be found the Endowment house, of which so much has been written. In this building the quasi-masonic rites of the church are performed.

FREDERICK E. SHEARER, ED.,
THE PACIFIC TOURIST

The ceremonies of baptism, sealing, and marriage were held that week among the bishops of Salt Lake City. Sariah placed Famke's hand in Heber's, and the dourness of her expression was eclipsed only by the radiance in Heber's as he laid his hand on Famke's topknot and pressed her gently into the baptismal tank. Though all present wore special white robes over their clothes and Gentiles were strictly forbidden, Famke thought none of what took place was more arcane than her first communion. She would certainly forget it much sooner. Other pictures already took precedence in her memory: Albert appearing with the carriage that day in Dragør, *Nimue* emerging from her linen veil. The blinding light of Brother Voegtli's flash pan as he captured "The Goodhouses and their housemaid" on glass. Herself in the black horsehair wig that Sariah insisted was proper for a Mormon wife. Heber in bed that first night, for their wedding's consummation.

Sariah's sons had moved out of their room to make way for Famke; they would sleep in the parlor until another room, or suite of rooms, could be added for her and her brood-to-come. Ephraim, Brigham, and Heber the younger would begin mixing the adobe tomorrow; like the rest of the house—Heber promised, as if Famke cared how his house would look—the walls there would be plastered inside and out, and scored to imitate stone masonry. The floors would be pine, finished to imitate oak. They would be fine rooms . . .

The house was ominously silent.

"I have kept my word," whispered Heber, alone with Famke in her night-gown and her special union suit embroidered with the map to heaven. He wore the undergarment, too. "I have honored my wives in turn, first Sariah, then Myrtice, each thrice. I have done my best to give each one a child . . . And I will do my best for you," he said tenderly, reaching through the dark-ness with both arms.

Feeling his movement, Famke backed away, aspirating a cough he thought beautiful in its reserve.

"I—I don't—Heber!" she cried when she could breathe. He'd trapped her against a wall. "I don't wish to hurt anyone . . ."

"You are the wife of my heart," Heber said, still in that tender whisper, then added hastily, "Of course, one tries to love all one's wives in equal mea-sure, and to show no preference among them . . ."

Was this really possible? Famke wondered. If she were married to Heber and Albert at the same time, it would be very clear which one had a greater share of her heart. But even with that thought, Heber's arms, enfolding her insistently, reminded her that she was married only to him.

"Famke—may I?"

Her mouth was still averted, so he kissed her cheek. His beard, so wiry aboard ship, seemed softened now with Utah's dust. His lips were moist and they felt . . . kind.

Heber was surprised to discover his new wife was weeping. Her body barely shook, but the cheek he'd kissed was slick with tears.

The old rush of words poured from him. "My dearest—it does not hurt, I promise you. I will do it gently. I will do . . . my best . . . I . . . love you . . ." He punctuated the last few sounds with kisses, on cheek and brow and hair. A daring kiss fell on her neck.

And then Famke buried her face in her hands. She seemed to say, in Danish, "It does not matter. You may hurt me." But he couldn't be sure, be-cause she was sobbing more strongly now.

He lifted the slender length of her in his arms. She was still just a girl. He carried her to the bed and slipped her between the sheets the way he'd done with his daughters when they were small. Then he slid himself in next to her.

So I have come to this, thought Famke. A detached part of her mind was coolly observing even as another part of her, the feeling part, continued to weep. To be a bride and a Mormon: This was her destiny, for now. She had to play the part.

Famke bit the inside of her cheek until she felt quite calm. Then she hesitated. She fumbled. She half-invited and half-allowed. The tears still flowed, but more slowly, as her body and her mind gradually became intrigued. For Heber's touch was unhurried, and even through the cumbersome underwear's embroidery it lingered on her tender parts in a way that Albert's beloved hands had rarely done.

Famke relaxed. Heber pushed her nightgown up over the union suit and undid buttons where they needed undoing, but he left her mostly clothed; complete nudity, it seemed, was un-Saintly even at a time like this. He kissed her long and gently, and she barely remembered to clench herself hard, very hard, at the moment when his map met hers.

"My dearest," he whispered into one ear, in which the tears had puddled like stars, "it will be soon. It is decreed . . . I must . . ."

He kept chanting those words, but it wasn't over soon. He dipped in and out of Famke like a pen filling at an inkwell, ready to add shades and subtleties to those maps. Famke began to shiver, but not unhappily, and Heber stopped speaking to kiss her again and again: little stippling kisses on her eyes and lips. His hands opened her map further and explored the earth and forest beneath.

"My *darling*," he breathed, and at the word a sudden wave of feeling swallowed Famke. Her breath caught and she heard her throat make a little noise, while all over her map the earth began to shake. She barely noticed that he, too, was gasping, or that he'd flooded her, or that Myrtice and Sariah were now pacing in the hallway outside.

In a moment, Heber slid away. Suddenly his hands were clumsy, and they fumbled with the buttons on his own underwear, closing his map again. Famke felt her mountains and plains turned to one vast briny lake, and she tried unobtrusively to mop it up with a wad of nightdress. She was not sure how a chaste Saint would respond, but she herself had always disliked that ticklish leaking sensation.

Heber touched Famke lightly on her shoulder and felt how hot she was. He was certain that her whole body was blushing at the first assault to its virginal perfection; neither of his previous wives had reacted as violently as Famke did, and he could not help being pleased with her refinement. So he inched considerably to the very edge of the bed—where, much as he would have liked to remain a comforting wakeful presence, he fell fast asleep.

When Heber began to snore, the pacing in the hallway stopped. Lying in the messy sheets, Famke heard other noises as well, but after a few sharp exclamations and stamped feet, the house settled in for the night. The hour was already quite late; there was work in the morning, and nothing to do about what had already happened.

Famke was tired, too, and strangely relaxed and dozy, but she pinched the skin of her thigh hard and made herself keep awake. Heber's breathing evened out and deepened, until Famke thought she felt him dreaming beside her. Dreaming, perhaps, *about* her, which was an uncomfortable thought.

She had to begin.

Famke drew in her breath and coughed. She coughed as hard as she could without shaking Heber awake. There was just the smallest taste of blood, but it would be a start; and the rest was not so unlike what he had left behind. As he snored beside her, she wiped her hand between her legs and then on the sheet beneath. She coughed again.

In a little while she felt the tickle growing stronger in her chest. There would be an abundance of coughing that night, many chances to weave this illusion.

And so, as in the days of Abraham, it was.

.   .   .

On the long voyage, as his hands blistered and burst and blistered again, Viggo came to depend on Birgit's letter. The pages on which it was written became worn and velvety along their creases, faded where he'd held them in the sun.

The letter was his one contact with his vanished homeland and mother tongue, for his fellow sailors were of varying nations and spoke an abbreviated English together. It was also his connection to familiar people, Birgit and Famke and, by implication, the orphanage and all Danes. Finally, from that letter he was able to piece together a most fascinating story: a story in which he, in some significant way, was participating.

Birgit was somewhat more candid in writing to Famke than she had been with Viggo in her office—but only somewhat. He read of Famke's "mistake" and, more gravely, her "fall." He could not believe that these terms applied to her conversion to Mormonism; however painful that was to Mother Birgit, in the outside world he had found religion to be of little importance. After several rereadings, it occurred to him that Famke's "fall" might refer to something else entirely. Perhaps, he thought with slow-dawning awareness, she had never married her painter.

An unwed orphan living with her artist-lover, still under the protection of a Catholic nun: that was an intriguing situation. What was it in the girl that made the Mother Superior stand by her, despite what Birgit clearly saw as a betrayal? Viggo conjured up that picture of young Famke bent over her soap pot, stirring and smiling, peering through the steam at him with those brilliant eyes—surely the last image that would appeal to a nun . . .

Finally, just a few days from Boston Harbor, a thought crept into Viggo's mind: If Famke's painter had not married her, she was still free. She could fall in love with somebody else.

Chapter 17

. . . . .

The district was a barren and unpromising desert, but the industrious Mormons set to work at once to plough and plant and began that system of irrigation which has drawn out the latent capabilities of the soil and made the Utah valleys among the most productive regions in the country. [. . .] in spite of numerous collisions with the U. S. Government on the question of polygamy, the history of the city and territory has been one of steady progress and development.

BAEDEKER'S UNITED STATES
(STATEMENT DRAWN UP IN THE OFFICE OF THE PRESIDENT
OF THE CHURCH OF LATTER-DAY SAINTS)

The morning after Famke's second wedding, the silkworms hatched. In the adobe hut that Heber's sons had built for the textile business, they came crawling out of their tiny blue egg sacs and launched themselves at the mulberry leaves that the three wives hastily chopped and mashed for their infant jaws. With the older children, Famke was allowed inside the hut to marvel at this miracle of transformation and the future of Prophet City, the larvae and their mash laid over wide tables that smelled of the linseed oil (remnant of a previous venture in flax) stored beneath.

"But hold your breath," Sariah cautioned Ephraim, Brigham, Anna, and Nephiah. "You can blow a thousand of them away at once, they're that small. And"—she looked hard at Famke, who was gritty-eyed from lack of sleep—"no coughing."

Famke wondered if Sariah might have listened through the night and guessed the secret of the bedsheets; but she put the suspicion out of her mind, deciding that Sariah would never say anything to Heber about such an indelicate matter. She attended, instead, to the worms, which seemed a remarkably frail vehicle for the hopes of a township. They were invisible until she adjusted her expectations and found the yellow-gray wisps, smaller than her own fingernail parings, that lay like a web over the pulped leaves.

They seemed to have nothing in common with the sturdy pigs and geese of her Dragør days.

Heber, however, was enraptured with this increase in his livestock, an advancement in his grand scheme. "This will be something to show the naysayers in town," he said in a rare moment of boastfulness. "All those who doubted the plan!"

Sariah laid her hand on her husband's arm. Her eyes actually appeared to be moist. "'They that fight against Zion and the covenant people of the Lord shall lick up the dust of their feet; and the people of the Lord shall not be ashamed.' Nephi 6:13."

"Very true, my dear." Heber patted that bony hand, still gazing at his new pride and joy, his voice containing only the slightest hint of reproof. "And of course if we arouse shame in our neighbors, we hope it may turn them toward respect and industry."

Famke suppressed a sound. By her own observations, this was not an industry in which the townspeople wished to share.

It was, however, an undertaking of significant interest to those who followed Mormon affairs. In the next days, both the *Salt Lake City Daily News* and the *Daily Tribune*—one Mormon, one Gentile—sent correspondents to inspect the nursery tables (now prudently covered in thin layers of cheesecloth, to keep the growing worms where they belonged) and to question Heber about his plans. "The future of the Saints is in threads," Famke heard him say again, and the correspondents nodded and took notes: one focusing on Heber's early failures with wool, cotton, and linen, the other on his almost certain future success.

Famke managed to take each man aside for some questions of her own. Neither one had heard of Albert Castle or indeed of any British painter in the region, and under the other women's steely, speaking eyes, the reporters' initial gallantry turned to priggish rebuke, as if there were something wrong in Famke's artistic interests, something that did not fit their notion of a good Mormon maiden.

Such was not the case with another correspondent, one whom Famke was most surprised to see under Utah's unforgiving turquoise sky.

"Harry Noble," he introduced himself, with one stubby paw shoved toward Heber's midsection, "also called Hermes. You may have read me in the *New York Times* or *Frank Leslie's Illustrated Journal*. I am presently scribing a series of articles about the Latter-Day Saints for the papers back east, and I'm interested in this silk-spinning venture of yours."

With his usual goodwill, Heber took the man's hand and shook it. "I am afraid I do not recollect your work, but I'm pleased to help you if I can. Ursula!" he called over to the clothesline, where she was hiding behind bedsheets and union suits. "Our housemaid, Ursula. She will ask Sister Goodhouse for the key to the silk house."

Ducking her head in obedience, Famke rushed off to find Sariah. She felt vaguely uneasy at seeing the man in green here; it was as if he had followed her. But of course she was being silly—she could scarcely expect him to remember her at all.

And yet it turned out that, once he saw her full in the face, he did. "We meet again," he said, grinning and sweeping the hat from his balding head. He held out his hand once more, as if he expected her to shake it as well.

This was provocative news to Sariah, coming along with her ring of clattering keys and her forearms steaming from the washtub. "Where'n have you two met before?" she asked.

"In New York, at Castle Garden." Noble fingered his side whiskers. "Just as the ship—what was she called? The *Olive Branch?*—arrived with her cargo of new Americans. A most charming scene that was, lending itself to picturesque description. And how are you finding life in Utah, Miss . . . Mrs. . . ."

"She's Miss Summerfield," Myrtice supplied. She, too, appeared most interested in the proceedings, and had left the children at their lessons under the lone oak tree in order to investigate. Arms crossed, she stood beside her aunt and watched.

"Miss Summerfield?" continued Noble. "Utah and the work of a housemaid, supported by your new faith and a new head of hair—is it the life of which you dreamed?"

Famke would have liked to slap this Harry Noble. All the Goodhouses were looking at her now—even the children—and there was practically no chance that she could take him aside and ask if he had news of Albert. Indeed, she had to prevent him from mentioning Albert now, for if he did there would surely be questions to follow: Why was she, the virgin whom Heber had espoused on board ship, so interested in an unknown painter traveling the West? Who *was* Albert Castle to her? How would she feel about being tossed into the streets of Prophet without a penny to her name?

"Did you not," said Harry Noble, clearly enjoying himself, "come here with more artistic views in mind?"

Before Famke could panic entirely, and even before she could answer Noble's question, Sariah rattled her keys. "I'm afraid we can spare just a few moments for the viewing," she said. "There have been many journalists of late, and we've the work of the farm to do. Ursula, you may return to the laundry. Mr. Noble, if you will follow me . . ."

"That unpleasant man," Sariah called him later, in her confidential hours with Heber. "Did you smell the tobacco on him? And he lifted the gauze and took up a handful of leaves with worms. They'll die sure as I'm born," she said, and her brow wrinkled; for even without the correspondent's interference, the little things were shriveling up at an alarming rate.

"Sariah, my dear," Heber said, yawning, "you fret entirely too much."

Chapter 18

. . . . .

*Unless I am deceived, the younger generation—the children of Utah—show
in their forms the bad fruit of this hard life. They seemed to me, as I studied
them in the car coming down, and on the streets the next day, under-sized,
loosely built, flabby. Certainly the young girls were pale, and had unwhole-
some, waxy complexions.*

CHARLES NORDHOFF, "SIGHTS BY THE WAY," IN
CALIFORNIA: FOR HEALTH, PLEASURE, AND RESIDENCE

M y dear," Heber said on Famke's next night with him, "I could not
but overhear some part of what that correspondent said to you."
Famke's fingers went suddenly cold, and she felt the perspiration freezing over her body. She sat up and coughed.

Heber waited patiently. He was still sticky and hot, but he reached
across the space between them and patted her on the back. The Utah dust
often affected immigrants this way, and his newest wife would soon learn to
live with the tickle in her lungs.

Famke gathered her wits. "Men who write for papers are prone to lies,"
she said, though she did not quite believe it herself. Did not the papers say,
just beneath the titles, *All the truth that's fit to print?*

"I can't think why he might lie about this," Heber said, patting her again
although there was no need. His hand lingered on her shoulder blade and
melted the ice there. "Is it true you have an interest in art?"

How delightful, he was thinking; Famke had that refined European sensibility by which even a housemaid could appreciate the best of culture. He
imagined the two of them strolling arm in arm down a long gallery of glass
and steel, discussing the sculptures on either side. Tall white figures from
mythology, suitably draped; potted palms and, somewhere in the background, a fountain's song, perhaps a violin. But galleries like that existed
only in Europe.

Famke said cautiously, "I do like to see paintings. Some paintings."

Paintings, then—panelled walls with green-brown oils: Romantic land-scapes, pastured animals, peasant girls with clean white feet. Heber felt a warm wave pass over him, and his hand moved to the other shoulder blade.

"There is a small museum in Salt Lake City," he said, "run by a Professor Barfoot directly across from the Tabernacle. Perhaps the next time I go into the city, you could accompany me."

Famke's skin flushed, the chill fully past. It was perfectly natural to ask, "Could we go soon? I would like it very much."

Heber pulled her into his arms, his brown beard tangling with her flame-colored curls. "As soon as I can manage it, my dear. Perhaps after the silkworms pupate; you will not be so needed here then. They are delicate, you see, at this stage in their lives. We must do all we can to provide them with the proper climate . . ."

While Heber dreamed aloud of his people's future, Famke sank back onto her pillow among the damp bedclothes, worn out by both the promise of a treat and its deferral. She might learn something about Albert in this museum . . . She went to sleep and began to dream instantly. In that dream, worms were gnawing their way into her lungs.

The next night, the worms emerged from her mouth and nose, spinning their artful cocoons to smother her, and she woke up clawing at her face. After that, on the nights Heber spent in her bed, she occasionally woke to find her arms shoving him away, as if he were to blame—though, curiously enough, the times she was able to breathe often came at the end of his map-making, when they lay in each other's arms and sweat glued their under-clothes to their skins. At those moments she felt cleansed, and she imagined the dirt of Utah had left her body; then her lungs moved quietly, and she was able to think about how much better still she would feel once it was Albert who took her in his arms, Albert who entered her body and watched the changes in her face and gave her that gorgeous, hungry feel of *wanting* something . . . the feeling that Heber also gave her, true, but in a much less exquisite way than she knew Albert could. Albert always left her wanting, and the tremblings that Heber effected put an end to want.

"Could we visit the museum soon?" she asked each time, and each time Heber promised it would indeed be soon—but not immediately.

Soon, Famke thought, she might give up. She was exhausted: As the weeks ground on, the work grew even more strenuous and unrelenting, and at seventeen she was not getting any younger. She was trapped under Sariah's virtuously callused thumb with no real news, despite Heber's thoughtful provision of as many papers as he could come across. She thought longingly of the time on ship and train, when she had felt she was accomplishing something, even if it was only motion for motion's sake; when she'd seen the West as a patchwork stitched with clues that would lead directly to Albert.

"*En Pige der bliver hjemme*, a girl who stays at home," she said out loud in her bedroom, smoothing the old sketch over her wickedly naked knees. It was good to hear someone speaking Danish again, even if that person were only herself. "A girl of good family . . ." She promised the peasant girl in the sketch, whose face was now shadowed with smudges, that soon she would have a good home, a little family of two with Albert; and he would paint beautiful pictures and join the Pre-Raphaelite Brotherhood and the Royal Academy, and she would at last be able to breathe easily in this dusty, hot, tiresome, frightening new land.

Had we but world enough and time . . .

In Utah, Famke never had enough: enough air, Albert, paintings. She missed the nourishing Danish food, pickled herring and dark rye bread and the salmon that Skatkammer's servants had muttered over four nights a week; here, on a diet of oatmeal, salt pork, and squash, she was growing thin. Even the sliver of ice that a neighbor brought as an unofficial wedding gift—even that disappeared before she could enjoy it fully, nourishing as it was to a Nordic soul trapped in the land of dust and heat. Sariah seemed to consider ice as sinful as good food; she took the slab away from Famke and plunked the whole thing into a vat of the nasty Brigham tea she brewed from mountain rushes, then served it to the family before sending Famke out to the mulberry grove again.

Having stood up to his first wife in the one great matter of taking a third, Heber seemed to be letting Sariah have her way with everything else. She determined Heber's nightly schedule among the women; she decided when Myrtice would hold classes for the children and when Famke would take a nasty draught of Deseret's Elixir for Common Coughing. She burned *The Thrilling Narrative* in the cookstove, for anything thrilling must surely be sinful. She questioned Myrtice delicately about the state of her health, evidently hoping that the girl would be feeling faint or suffering from indigestion. She told Famke when to feed the straggly chickens and lone pig, when to give public witness to her faith, when to haul water for washing dishes, laundry, and bodies. She, herself, dusted the line of little black coffins marching across the parlor mantelpiece, each box sealed with a pane of glass, and explained tersely that the white manikins inside represented the four babies she had borne and buried, children Heber never mentioned.

The Mormons were a fiercely clean people, and amid all the scouring Famke began to detest the smell of soap that she had once liked so well. But she rather enjoyed standing in the middle of all those well-washed worshippers and making up stories to prove she knew Sainthood was the only true path.

"My faith was first revealed in my native land, in the home of my master, Jørgen Skatkammer . . ." When she grew bored with the simple version, she added little embellishments: "I was dusting his glass sword, an artifact of Venice . . ." The Saints' ears pricked up; they'd never heard of such a thing, and several of the ladies asked her about it afterward. Famke added next time, "The sword hung above a collection of eastern mummies . . ."

Sariah stopped Famke's recitations when it was clear the third wife was drawing too much attention to herself. "Don't create such a fuss," she said. "Now of all times, my word."

Sariah would never admit it outright, but Famke had realized that this was a difficult time around the Goodhouse place and in Prophet City generally. When the Goodhouses drove into town, they felt suspicious eyes upon them—not because of the clandestine plural marriage, for many of their fellow citizens had similar arrangements, but because it had been Heber's idea to follow the United Order of Enoch and its principles of complete sharing. He had been gone so long that the most prosperous citizens had forgotten why they'd thought this idea was a good one. There were mutterings, of which Heber remained blissfully unaware, that it would soon be time to dissolve the Order and appoint a new man who would lead the Prophetians to true greatness.

Famke paid no more attention to those rumors than she did to reports of drought, dropping beef prices, crickets in the crops, or a string of explosions in hotels and opera houses that were leading sheriffs and Pinkertons to suspect that a band of outlaws was at work throughout the West. Gossip was just the grinding of so many jaws, or so many priests giving lectures;

she closed her ears, fanned herself, and thought of more pleasant topics. Snow and winter. And Albert.

Alone, as she bent over to slap mud and straw into the molds that would make the adobe bricks for her very own room—that wing of the house in which she was determined never to live—she used one finger to trace his features in the yielding muck: his artfully rumpled curls, his prominent eyes, his dear little soft chin. How refined he looked, how elegant, even sketched with an untrained hand in base clay—imagination created the likeness, and Famke quite melted at the thought of him.

"My dear, are you unwell?" All at once, Heber was at her side. He helped her to sit back, plucking the wig from her head and using it to fan her face. He seemed eager to find her ill, as eager as Sariah was with Myrtice. "Shall I bring you a draught?"

"No"—Famke shuddered— "please, no draughts. Some water."

While Heber went to fetch it, Famke pressed the heel of her hand into Albert's face, erasing the image that had brought her momentary joy.

*   *   *

The experiment with the wet brick inspired Famke with an idea: All around her lay the materials for making art. She might be starved for the sight of pictures, but she herself possessed the means of making them. What was earth but powdered stone? And Albert had told her that ground stone was the base for those paints he bought in tubes. The powder was mixed with linseed oil, exactly what was stored in the textile house.

That evening, after her chores, a wigless Famke filled a drinking glass with blood-red dust and sneaked into the worm hut, where the sound of vermian chewing was faint but quite pronounced. She set a kerosene lantern beneath the table and poked a knife through the cheap tin of an oil can, and then, kneeling down beneath the worms, she let the oil drip in thin golden drops into her glass. She stirred it with her finger till it was of approximately the right consistency. Then, with nothing else to paint upon, she sat back against a table leg, pulled up her skirt, and stretched the petticoat taut over her knees.

For a moment she actually wished for her black wig; the coarse hairs would have made a good stiff brush. Instead, she unpinned her own hair and let it tumble. It was certainly long enough that if she separated out a strand and held herself carefully, she might dip the ends in this rough red paint and trace an oval on the petticoat.

But the paint was clotty, the makeshift brush too soft. Famke tried and tried, but she managed nothing that even faintly resembled a face before the door flew open and Myrtice cried, "Ursula! I saw a light in here and— For shame! What on earth can you be about?"

Famke pulled her skirts down hastily, and in their breeze her lantern blew out. Myrtice had her own light, however, and she made Famke display her petticoat.

"I declare I've never seen the like." Myrtice studied the crude scarlet curves. "Whatever are you doing to yourself?"

"I am painting," Famke said with all the dignity she could conjure. "In oil."

"I learned how to watercolor at the normal school," said Myrtice. "Your posture is all wrong, and you should put on your eyeglasses."

For a moment Famke was quiet, and the sound of worms growing fat filled the little hut while she thought of all there was still to remember and learn. "But this is oil paint," she said at last.

"Then it shall be all the more difficult to wash out," Myrtice said, and tugged at Famke's arm to raise her.

Famke scrubbed for hours, but the red marks never washed away completely, and for this she was stubbornly glad. She was glad, too, that when Sariah started asking after the missing lantern, Myrtice seemed to have forgotten it, and it remained under the table in the textile hut. Famke was pleased to think she was depriving the Goodhouses of light.

Chapter 19

. . . . .

*The intelligent observer who comes to the United States and takes the oppor-
tunity to study American art as it is to-day cannot but be impressed with the
value of its present achievement. The high place it is destined to occupy in the
future is plainly indicated in the startling rapidity of its progress and the
earnestness of purpose of the artists who are each day adding to its renown.*

BAEDEKER'S UNITED STATES

ariah scolded everyone about the lantern, from the smallest child to
Famke and Myrtice; only Heber was exempt. And she had ample
chance to scold, for the next day was Sunday and the family rode the
wagon to Prophet's ward house.

"How a lantern can go plain missing, and our best lantern at that, I cannot understand," she said yet again, her words contorted as she swayed and
bumped with the road.

"Might could be the savages," fat little Miriam suggested.

"What would savages want with a lantern? They see in the dark."

"Sariah, my dear," said Heber, "I do not quite think . . ."

He began an excursus on the habits and abilities of the Indians, and
Famke spun herself into her own thoughts.

Draped now over her lap, dry but limp, was her first painting. It had utterly failed: Not just for lack of technique and materials, but for want of a
proper subject as well. Those ovals and squiggles taught her that memory
was a poor model and dirt a bad medium. She would not attempt to paint
again, or at least not until she had a mirror and some real paint.

Her thoughts jolted away when the wagon came to a halt at the ward
house. Myrtice half-stood among the children in the back: "Is that not one
of those journalists? Harry Noble, I believe?"

Sariah shuddered. "That dreadful man." She looked around nonetheless.
"I swan, what is that he's sitting in?"

It was indeed Harry Noble. And he was sitting by the ward house, locked in a small square cage made of strap iron.

This was such an unusual sight that a crowd all but hid the cell, and it was clear that the meeting would begin late today. The Goodhouses were no less intrigued than their neighbors. Like seven hungry fleas, Heber and Sariah's children hopped down from the wagon and ran up to get a look. From her vantage point on the now empty backboard, Famke could see that Noble was still in his green suit, though somewhat the worse for wear. He looked to her like one of the exotic stuffed birds in Herr Skatkammer's collection: just as colorful, just as forlorn.

Heber made inquiries of the menfolk as his wives watered the horse. "He insulted one of our sisters," was the final word; Heber delivered it as Brother Ezekiah Donnelly, the week's spiritual leader, appeared outside to call the loiterers in. "He was preparing one of his features on Mormon life, and he simply would not desist from a most unpleasant line of questions." For some reason, this made Heber look at Famke, but she was looking neither at him nor at Noble; instead, her eyes were focused on a cricket that she was crushing into the dust.

"I warn't aware we had a hoosegow in town," said Sariah, nodding to Brother Donnelly. She retied her straw bonnet and started toward the ward house. "And a right odd jail it is, too."

"The brothers tell me they brought that cell in pieces from Salt Lake last year," Heber said with a tug at his beard, "but there's been no need for it. And I do wish they felt no need now."

"Once there is a jail," Myrtice said with her most schoolmarmy air, "there will be people looking to fill it."

"Such is the unfortunate nature of humankind," Heber sighed, "even Saints."

Myrtice flushed with the pleasure of being right. "Any road," she said with elaborate humility, "the man did insult a sister." Famke wanted to kick her.

The crowd around the cell had largely dispersed by now, so the Goodhouses were able to get a solid look at the offender inside. With his green-trousered bottom perched on a crate stamped *Needles and Pins*, he was waving the hat before his face to create a breeze; the balding top of his head was clearly sunburned and about to crack and peel. Perspiration glittered like diamonds in his hair and side whiskers.

"Ah, the Goodhouse family," Noble called out, mustering a smile as if to prove he was perfectly comfortable and ready to receive a social visit. "It is a lucky thing indeed to see you. As it happens, I was on my way to pay you a call when this"—he gestured around at the six walls containing him—"occurred. I wanted to bring you my feature on your silk enterprise."

If he intended to prompt them toward some kind of action, he failed. Collecting the children one by one, Heber and Sariah strode by without acknowledging him; Myrtice would have done so, too, if Famke had not seen an opportunity to step on her shoelace and force her to kneel and retie it.

Seeing the family stop at various lengths from his cell, Noble pulled a wilted scrap of paper from his coat pocket. He managed to keep his stream of chat fluid. "Thought you'd want to read it—it makes for a most ripping yarn, with some fine description of the gowns and slippers for which your caterpillars are destined, if I do say so myself."

When the Goodhouses merely looked away from him, he cocked his head at Famke and held the scrap of paper toward her. "Miss Summerfield, how do you fare this fine Indian summer day?"

Famke, who had been savoring the scent of tobacco smoke that steamed from his clothes in the sunshine, dared to step up and reach for the clipping. He, however, pulled it away before she could touch it.

Noble put his mouth close to the iron slats. "There is a lovely little paragraph about you," he said in a whisper that made Myrtice's eyes narrow and the leather shoestring snap in her hands. "If I do say it myself, a lovely paragraph. Yours is a face, adrift in the desert, that inspires men to heights of artistic—"

"Ursula," Myrtice said loudly, "will you *please* help me knot this lace?"

Famke hung breathlessly on Noble's next word.

"—achievement. Indeed," he continued, as if he could not see her flush, "I recollect you have a passion for the arts, do you not?"

Famke suddenly remembered caution. She dropped to her knees, heedless of her ugly homespun skirt, and tried to help Myrtice, thereby entangling the process further. Myrtice made a sharp exclamation and hobbled toward her aunt, leaving Famke to topple into the dust.

"Yes," Noble ruminated, "I recall that you were most interested in art and artists."

Famke got to her feet.

"Or, no," he corrected himself, "I believe there was a particular artist—was he a sculptor?"

"A painter," she mumbled, with her heart hammering at her ribs. "Albert Castle. Have you heard something of him?"

Noble ran his hand over his flaming head and dropped the hat on it with a wince. He seemed to be searching the far recesses of his memory. "Alas," he said at last, with every appearance of regret. "I can tell you nothing. Nothing, that is, while I am in—"

"So you do know something?" she asked eagerly, forgetting to soften her voice. She recognized that he was about to shift conversation to his own predicament, and she had no wish to discuss what she felt she could not change. "You have seen him? You have found his work?"

"Ah, Miss Summerfield, but ponder this: how little a particular man, even an artist, matters in the face of art itself. A hundred years from now, when we are dead and our small struggles and plans forgotten, citizens of the world will marvel at a charming watercolor, savor an exquisite poem, polish up a marble—"

"Hurry," Famke hissed, as Sariah started toward her.

"Have you sought your answer in prayer, as your new faith counsels you to do? Perhaps your present God's earthly wife would be sympathetic to—"

"*Have you seen Albert?*"

"Regrettably," Noble said, with no appearance of regret at all, "any information I might have is at my hotel." Just as Sariah was upon them, he slid the article between the bars with two fingers.

Famke took it and, for want of a better solution, stuffed it hastily down the neck of her blouse. Continuing the same movement, she also pulled a thin steel hairpin from her wig and poked it through the bars, hushing Harry Noble's thanks with an icy stare.

Then her co-wife took her by the elbow and dragged her back to the bosom of the Goodhouses, who were—all of them, even the children, even Heber—now regarding her with suspicion.

"Brush off your skirt," Sariah said. "It's filthy."

But Myrtice was the one to ask what was in everyone's mind: "That man—did he follow you from New York?"

"Of course not," said Famke; yet, that afternoon, when she unfolded the clipping at last, she was startled to find a rectangle of stiff paper tucked among the creases. It had been professionally printed in thick black ink, with a border of twining vines:

Harry Noble, also Hermes
~traveling~
Temporarily to be found at the Continental Hotel,
West Temple Street, Salt Lake City

Now, why did he do that? she wondered. He couldn't really expect her to go to him there; how would such a thing be possible? She tore the card into bits and burned them in Sariah's cookstove.

Then she began to plot.

Chapter 20

·····

*In considering the modern "Movement" in New York it is fair to say that we
cover the whole country, and the condition of the fine arts in the United States
may be measured by applying the gauge to what is to be seen in New York.*

<small>BAEDEKER'S UNITED STATES</small>

It was Viggo's first day in America, and already he was doing his work.
He still thought of it this way: his work, as assigned by Mother Birgit;
and yet it was what he wanted to do, an undertaking that sat very close
to his heart.

As soon as he stepped out of Castle Garden, he asked about trains
to Utah and learned that there would be one in the morning. Then, having
done as much as he could to find Famke for now, he decided to detect what
he might about her husband, the painter. With his knapsack on his back,
he wandered into the street and used his shipboard English to ask a pair
of gentlemen with fine whiskers and tall hats where artists tended to con-
gregate. He did not mind the gentlemen's sneers and stares, for they answered him, and he went to all those places. The Italian restaurants on
Sullivan and MacDougal Streets, the French restaurants on Greene Street
and University Place—in their dark, smoky dining rooms, he stared at
the shabby men and women tucking in to messy plates and declaiming
passionately in a vocabulary he could not understand: *gesso, craquelure,
chiaroscuro.*

Viggo asked the monkeyish man at the cash register where he might go
to see some paintings.

"At seven of the evening?" the little man said with what Viggo supposed
was a Roman snort. "The galleries, they are shut." But he directed Viggo to
another restaurant, one where the owner was in sympathy with Bohemian

ideals. He allowed some of his favorite artists to buy their meals with paint and canvas which he hung on the walls.

This establishment was French and, perhaps because of the exceptionally heavy cloud of wine and smoke in the air, most of the paintings looked blurry to Viggo. He had difficulty deciding what some of them were meant to depict. Was this one a haystack or a fat frog? Was that a gentleman in a frock coat or a widow in weeds—or perhaps a cart horse wearing a hat?

He felt more comfortable with a few small canvases tucked into a corner near the kitchen. These were simple compositions and very realistic in their details: one of a glistening spill of dead fish, mouths gaping in a way he recognized and understood; one of a rose and a fly, with every vein in petal and wing finely traced; and one of a ship on the sea.

Having recently been on a ship himself, Viggo devoted most of his attention to this last. It was, he thought, very nicely done, with many masts and a wild hard wind blowing holes in the sails. The waves on which the ship rode rose high and luminous green, crashing into soap-white foam. It was small wonder, then, that the lone human element in the picture—the ship's figurehead—looked terrified: her face and bosom blunted, her long red wooden hair licking down the hull like a flame.

It was a fine picture indeed, and every detail suited it but one. Bending very close, Viggo saw that the wave in the far right corner was, yes, about to enfold a castle such as he would expect to find only on dry land. He made out the sharp peak of a turret and a crenellated square to the right, with an open space where the far wall would be. He did not quite understand why it was there until he blinked and saw that the castle was actually a blending of two decorated letters: a towering A and a fortresslike C.

Painted around the frame's four sides, he read:

· *Remember me when I* ·
· *am gone away Gone far away* ·
· *into the silent land.* ·
· *Christina Georgina Rossetti* ·

The words were simple, and he understood most of them. A.C., the man who wrote to Famke, was in Mæka looking for her. Viggo's eyelids fluttered in a way that, to the restaurant's other patrons, made him look most artistic.

. ♦ .

Even on a Sunday, farm life centered on the silkworms, which were grow-ing fat, sluggish, and ready to spin: pregnant with their own next selves. Soon the yellow-gray bodies would make white-gray cocoons, and the Goodhouses would be one step closer to securing prosperity for the Prophetians. That afternoon, as she lifted the veil over the largest table, Famke imagined a worm writhing through the eye of a needle, being stitched into a delicate map of paradise. And as she spread the chopped mulberry leaves, she envisioned worms wiggling their slow way through her own petti-coat, right where she had painted the bloody ovals that never became a face.

Six weeks, she thought. *If they are going to spin, I have been here six weeks.*

Famke heard her name. Heber and Sariah's oldest daughter, Alma, was standing in the farmyard, calling her into the house. Famke scattered the last leaves haphazardly, and as she replaced the linen, her toe collided with something hard that gave a liquid slosh: the lantern. Famke poked it farther beneath the table and its gauzy skirt.

"Gadding about the farmyard again," Sariah commented, when Famke joined the family where they had gathered in the dun-colored parlor. All the Goodhouses looked somber, but then it was hard to look otherwise when seated below so many white manikins in black boxes. Sariah held a heavy book that she placed in Famke's hands: *The Silk Farmer's Guide and Almanac.* "It is time we learn how to take the next step." Apparently there was no more sin in reading on a Sunday than in feeding the livestock.

Sariah pointed out the passage Famke must read, the chapter that de-scribed baking the cocoons and spinning their threads. Sariah herself would read privately about reserving a few pupae for breeding, and the manner in which to encourage mothly mating. While the children played Emigration with peg dolls and iron handcarts, and Sariah cut the sacred symbols from a worn-out union suit that was ready for the rag box, the two younger wives took turns reading aloud. Together they memorized instructions for wind-ing a cocoon's outer hundred feet or so onto one set of wooden reels, the finer and more valuable inner thread onto another, and twining four of those strands together on the spinning wheels that Heber had bought at auction.

Heber, sitting with a favorite Mormon tract, spoke up when Famke paused for a sip of water. "Four," he said, "is an ideal number. Where four are bound together, there is great strength."

Sariah and Myrtice pursed their identical mouths, and Famke excused herself to visit the convenience.

She sat on the hot wooden seat and opened Harry Noble's clipping again. This she read avidly, savoring the descriptions of "frangible threads into which the caterpillars' lives will spin, to be cut by a fair flame-haired Atropos; eventually to adorn the ladies Eastward in ruffles and flounces of softest, buttery silk, to line their slippers that they may walk on air, while the lovely Mormon Fates labor in their simple homespun . . ." Naturally she overlooked the last part. She would not wear homespun forever.

Nor would she stay in Prophet forever. That her departure was imminent, Famke was certain: Harry Noble had information about Albert—he had been coy, but a promise had been obvious beneath his words. If he turned her hairpin to good purpose, he would be back in Salt Lake City soon; and he would probably leave just as quickly, fleeing whatever sense of justice had put him in the hoosegow. He would take all news of Albert with him.

Shifting for a more comfortable position, Famke weighed her possibilities, devised a dozen plans and discarded them all. She must get to Salt Lake, which was now her Zion as well as the Mormons'; she must convince Heber to bring her—but how? She had wasted so many days here already . . .

The moths will hatch and die and have their babies before I escape. And I will have to raise the babies.

Then it came to her. She stuffed the clipping back into her bosom and fairly ran into the house, arriving flushed and unsteady on her feet.

"I am ill!" she declared. "I am in a condition! I must see a doctor immediately."

Chapter 21

. . . . .

With an energy and push that had scarcely been expected from the disciples of Mormonism, this work was crowded with all possible speed.

FREDERICK E. SHEARER, ED.,
THE PACIFIC TOURIST

G ood-bye, Sariah and Myrtice; good-bye, Prophet City; good-bye, ward house, where the empty hoosegow still stood in dire commemoration of Harry Noble's visit. Famke beamed alike on all of them, and she waved to her former neighbors as the wagon rolled briskly by. Heber caught some of her gaiety, saluting with the whip and his hat, forgetting to worry. He had not felt so happy, so carefree since leaving Denmark—though of course he would not wish to return to the days abroad, he reminded himself soberly; for Copenhagen was far from his home and children and business, and he'd hardly known Ursula—his Famke—before loading her onto the *Olivia*.

He thought how like a bride Famke looked now; the bride of a rich man setting out on her wedding trip. "My dear, you are radiant," he blurted as they left the little town behind. If he could have trusted himself to say it right, he would have told her this: He'd fallen in love yet again. How could Sariah say that Famke was no more in a condition than she herself or Myrtice? It was clear that the most delightful change of a woman's life was upon her. One picture had filled his mind's eye all night: Famke lying in a bed, her beautiful face strained and exhausted, but a new little life tucked into the circle of her arm. Heber felt dizzy with pride and pleasure.

"You are wise to ask for a doctor," he commented, his throat choking with emotion. "That cough of yours might prove troublesome as your . . .

condition progresses. But Doctor Finstuen used to tend several of Brigham Young's wives; there is no one better."

Famke's mind was working too fast to reply. Inside its hoopskirt cage (borrowed from Myrtice, never to be returned), the yellow pocket slapped against her thigh. It was laden now with her tinderbox, the sketch, three newspaper clippings, Myrtice's old spectacles, and thirty dollars Famke had taken from the cashbox at the back of Sariah's wardrobe. Yes, she had money now, the means of travel; she had only to elude Heber, and she would be stepping into her destiny.

Heber said gently, as if breaking unpleasant news, "I am afraid we must make the most of our time in the city. You may rest in the doctor's office as long as you like, but I will have to visit the warehouses to see about buying some spindles. Sariah says our supply is much smaller than I had thought, and we must have them when the worms do their spinning."

Famke suppressed a smile and imitated Myrtice's manner of speaking when she murmured, "Of course I understand. I am sure I will be quite comfortable while you are gone." That had been a stroke of inspiration— burning half the spindles in Sariah's stove last night, dropping them one by one through the lids and stirring with a vigorous iron poker.

"But we may enjoy this drive together, any road," Heber said, and he let his arm brush hers in a daringly open manner. He drove slowly, protecting his most precious cargo.

Famke could say nothing against it, but with each turn of the wagon wheels, her impatience grew. Every time Heber paused to let another traveler by, her stomach clenched until the butterflies inside it threatened to choke her. She had to ask Heber to stop the wagon so she could relieve herself, and she spent precious minutes checking the contents of her pocket behind a bush.

She imagined Albert's face among the stunted branches. *Albert, I am coming.*

They reached Salt Lake City in late morning, navigating through countless buggies and wagons, men on horseback, ladies strolling under parasols, housekeepers toting baskets. Traffic was especially thick in a section of town lined with fruit trees, where the smells of peaches and plums—fruits Famke had scarcely ever seen, let alone tasted—weighted the air, and narrow ditches of running water sparkled in the yellow light. Train whistles were the sound of sweet music, every bit as lovely as the lyrics the farm girls had sung around the well in Dragør. Already she felt closer to Albert.

In Doctor Finstuen's book-lined, leather-upholstered waiting lounge, Heber took a lingering leave of his youngest wife. His gestures were tender and solicitous, treasuring her, as if he expected yet another profound change to overtake her with the examination.

Famke looked past Heber's dusty spectacles and into his kind brown eyes and felt a now-familiar twinge of guilt. He had been good to her, and she discovered she actually liked him. Life on the farm was not so dreadful after all; there were those nights with him, and she liked his young daughter Miriam. But she wouldn't miss Sariah or Myrtice or Heber either; why should she think so? So she did not kiss him (which would have been unseemly in a doctor's office), but merely thanked him for bringing her this far and wished him luck with the day's transactions.

"Do not rush," she said, knowing nonetheless that he would buy the spindles as fast as he could. "Aunt Sariah says the price is always high to one who shows haste."

Heber allowed himself to squeeze her slender hand, its bones like a bird's wing in their white cotton covering. What an excellent helpmeet she was proving to be.

◆ ◆ ◆

There were 132 rooms in the Continental Hotel, and the desk clerk refused to tell Famke which one contained Harry Noble. "I will send a boy with a message," said the spotty man who had first declared himself her servant and then looked askance when told of her wishes. "Please be so kind as to wait."

Famke flung herself into a blue plush sofa and waited with very little grace. She was vexed with the clerk and with Doctor Finstuen, who had poked and prodded and asked her repeatedly if she was absolutely *sure* of her condition. A plea for a glass of water had been all it took to run out and escape while he was at the taps. And then it had been an easy matter to dash from Finstuen's office on South Temple Street to the hotel on West Temple;

but now she was caught up in a web of rules, and she had to play the fly rather than the spider. Her head was throbbing, and she would have been glad for that glass of water.

After nearly an hour, the spotty clerk approached again. "So sorry, madam, but Mr. Noble is not in. If you would like to leave a formal message—"

"Tell him that Ursula Summerfield wishes to see him, after saving his life," she said, and flounced out to the street again. She had no clear idea where she might go—she knew there was little hope of finding Noble in the city—until it occurred to her that she might walk directly to the newspaper offices and speak to local correspondents. Perhaps she could even place a notice: "Nimue, Calafia, Gunnlod awaiting Albert Castle at Continental Hotel." Naturally she would not use her actual name; she was determined never to return to Prophet City, never to be traced by the Goodhouses.

But the newspapers, large and small, were scattered throughout the city, whose grids looked so deceptively tidy from the hillside and were so entangled when one was in them. Walking in the hoopskirt whose caginess now reminded her of Noble's hoosegow, Famke was afraid to ask directions. She didn't want to call attention to herself—or, worse, to run across Heber in the streets—and once she reached the office of *The Utah Daily Miner*, she realized that placing an advertisement would engrave her in the inkslingers' minds forever, such that it would be all too easy for the Goodhouses to find her before Albert could. She made a vague and fruitless inquiry about him, then left.

Much better to return to the Continental and wait for Harry Noble.

After confirming with the clerk that Noble had not returned, she settled on the plush sofa again. She was vexed, hot, and agitated, but she was also worn out. She sank into soft blue cushions that reminded her of something, something from the orphanage, perhaps a statue or a picture . . .

She slept.

◆ ◆ ◆

A woman approached from the far side of the lounge, gazing at Famke with Sister Birgit's sad eyes. Those eyes were exactly the color of the thick blue veil draped over her hair, though she appeared to be wearing nothing but a nightdress, and it was made of ice. The nightdress crackled as the woman bent over Famke and slid a thick needle made of glass through her left nipple. In the needle's eye there writhed a worm.

The woman vanished somewhere to the left. Famke lost interest in her, however, because she discovered that her own body had become transparent, and by bending her head she could see deep inside. She was not surprised to see the worm gnawing away at her lungs, growing with each thrust of the jaws, for she had seen it many nights in the past. But this time there was one difference: Its top was the normal blue-gray color, yet its back end was swollen and red—like the head of a lucifer match, she thought. And indeed the worm's red part began to glow, and it made her hot, and hotter, till she rocked with the heat . . .

Famke woke. A new clerk was shaking her, an older man with a mustache that made Famke think he probably was not a Saint. Famke opened her eyes pushing against him as if he were Heber.

"Miss," he said, withdrawing in alarm, "you can't sleep here. If your husband or father would like to engage you a room—"

"I am waiting for a guest," she said with all the dignity she could muster. Her hair and wig were soaked with perspiration; the dream had brought on a fever, and Famke recognized, in the corner of her mind that was all she could spare for such thoughts, that the illness was waxing within her again. More than ever, she needed to find Albert, to take away that sickly morbid feeling and replace it with the lovely longing live one he had given her all through the winter. She pulled off her gloves and fanned the flush on her face.

The clerk remained at her elbow. Famke emphasized, "I am waiting for Harry Noble," and picked up a magazine from the array on the side table, for all the world as if she had an actual right to be here in this hotel lounge. Nonplussed, the clerk faded away, murmuring something about the mail.

There was quite a choice of publications: *Harper's, Godey's, Frank Leslie's, The Wave.* In *Harper's,* Famke thumbed past a vaguely worded report of new electrical vibration devices that brought on "hysterical crises" in various patients; she read a feature on the Bohemian girls of New York City, who worked as writers and illustrators for newspapers and who were known to drink, smoke, and "softly!" swear. In the engraving that accompanied the text, they were all dark and tousle-haired, with round shadowed eyes that spoke mutely of their dissolution. What would Albert have to say about such behavior?

Famke felt a surge of impatience, as if she were living in the marvelous glass-domed house of another picture; as if someone had thrown a brick through the wall and filled her skin with prickling slivers. She was no Bohemian girl, but she was no longer a Mormon wife, either. It was time to be doing something, taking action.

She tossed *Harper's* aside and took up *Frank Leslie's Illustrated Magazine* because it was, as its title promised, full of pictures, and pictures suited her restless mood. There she came upon something that interested her very much: a feature about the propriety of unclad female forms in artwork. There were a few engravings on the first page, naked women bathing or dreaming, all with that artistically misted cleft. This she had to read about. It seemed that, in the words of one gallery superintendent, "when a painting of the nude by its spirit and surroundings directs the mind away from the element of artistic beauty it becomes vulgar." Famke gathered that this meant Americans did not want naked women to remind them of sex, nor in fact of real women, only of beauty. Indeed, the reporter—a female herself, perhaps one of those same Bohemians—drew much the same conclusion, and she dropped some dark hints about America's Puritan heritage. The next page promised several tasteful representations of paintings recently sold in New York.

When Famke turned the page, her eye fell on what it knew instinctively was an enormous canvas. An enormous canvas with a fierce nymph. A nymph creating a prison for the wizard who had betrayed her.

Nimue, in her filmy nightdress, surrounded by bloody ice.

The engraving was no bigger than Famke's palm and, to her eye, crude, but even under the title *Vivien* it was clearly Albert's masterwork—which she learned the captain of the *Lucrece* had sold at a recent auction for "a mere two hundred dollars" and which constituted "no great accomplishment for this promising artist, but nonetheless a work dedicated to beauty and not in the least bit vulgar."

Nimue. Albert.

And here at last, the clue she'd been seeking: "It is to be hoped that the artist, reportedly bound for the mines near Denver, Colorado, will bring the same sensibility to painting the women of that wilderness."

Famke's eyes danced feverishly around the lounge. The page swam before her, until she could not make out the least detail, and the magazine dampened in her hands. She grabbed another journal from the table and coughed into it.

.3.

SLIM PRINCESS

One face looks out from all his canvasses [. . .]
A queen in opal or in ruby dress,
 A nameless girl in freshest summer-greens,
 A saint, an angel;—every canvass means
The same one meaning, neither more nor less.
He feeds upon her face by day and night,
 And she with true kind eyes looks back on him
Fair as the moon and joyful as the light:
 Not wan with waiting, not with sorrow dim;
Not as she is, but was when hope shone bright;
 Not as she is, but as she fills his dream.

CHRISTINA ROSSETTI,
"IN AN ARTIST'S STUDIO"

Chapter 22

Among us, when an unhappy woman succumbs to these distractions her fate
is determined by poverty, betrayal, or some other motive springing from the
mysterious depths of the heart. From the little I gathered concerning these
poor girls, I judge that here this is not so. Rather they dispose of their attrac-
tions as a piece of merchandise. The traffic is in cold blood, as if it were a
question of liquors or cloth. [...] And jewelry shops, restaurants, hotels and
dance halls stimulate business by the presence of a pretty woman, much as
they might employ a music-box or a bowl of goldfish.

GUILLERMO PRIETO,
A JOURNEY TO THE UNITED STATES

The city is full of thrift, of life, and trade is always splendid.

FREDERICK E. SHEARER, ED.,
THE PACIFIC TOURIST

Heber returned home the next morning with a heavy heart and no
Famke. As the Goodhouse family poured out of the house and stable and worm hut into the weak yellow sunshine—somehow the
season had turned to autumn—he saw his other two wives casting their eyes
about, looking for her. One light, one dark, they exchanged a speaking look.

But the children claimed Heber's first attention. They jumped about,
putting their hands into his coat pockets and tugging at his shirt. "Candy!
Candy!" the little ones shouted. Ephraim, Alma, and Brigham stood apart
with their arms coolly folded as if the three of them, at sixteen, fourteen,
and thirteen, were above it all. They wanted the candy as much as the others, but they would not let their father know.

Heber had forgotten to buy sweets, and in fact he had returned home
only on the slender chance that Famke would have found her way there before him. For these various reasons, he and his children were disappointed.

"Where have you been?" Sariah hissed, as Heber directed the boys to unpack the crates of wooden spindles and reels he had bought while Famke put her belly up to the doctor's inspection. Sariah's voice sounded sharp, but she laid a gentle hand on his arm. "I didn't sleep a wink, I was that worried about you."

"And where is Ursula?" Myrtice asked. In this light she looked pasty to Heber, and her usual robustness was subdued. He couldn't tell if she were hopeful or solicitous when she asked, "Is she rightly ill?"

Heber leaned against the wagon to keep from collapsing. He hadn't slept either, spending the night combing the streets for his young wife instead. "Ursula has disappeared."

"What?" the other two exclaimed together.

Heber closed his eyes, lest he see un-Saintly glee in theirs. "I left her at the doctor's surgery," he explained. "Finstuen says she ran out before he could examine her properly—perhaps it was her first visit to a doctor, and she did not know what he had to do. He said she seemed agitated and jittered when he—" Heber looked at the children, round eyes blinking up at him. "I spent all night searching," he finished, "but she seems to have vanished completely. I fear she has fallen into a bad element."

Sariah and Myrtice were silent, and he imagined the two of them exchanging those glances that excluded everyone else, even the children, even himself, from their wordless communication. But then he did not want to see anything; he kept his eyes closed, feeling light-headed enough to swoon. If Famke was not here, either, she was well and truly gone. Vanished into the dust of the Salt Lake City streets.

"She'll turn up again," Sariah said at last, and she pulled her niece forward.

Myrtice put her arm beneath Heber's elbow and kissed his brow, for all the world as if she were his mother rather than his wife. "I have some wonderful news," she said.

◆   ◆   ◆

It must be good to be a man in Denver, Famke thought, especially a man with money in his pocket. Perhaps he had just sold a horse or a cartful of silver ore; perhaps he'd been cowboying upon a ranch in the flatlands. He might be light or dark, speak English or what she thought must be some savage tongue; perhaps Mexican. Whoever he was, here he could buy himself not only a woman's company but also an evening's entertainment, a meal with fresh meat, a new suit of clothes. But Famke was a woman, and young, and not terribly prosperous.

She tried to convince herself that the huge, rough, rushing city of brick buildings and carriages resembled Copenhagen. It emanated the stench that accompanied all flourishing enterprises: coal smoke, sewers, carthorse dung; and in that respect it was like home. Within fifteen minutes of leaving the station, she had seen three mutilated Indians, five gun-holstered ranchers, and whole flocks of what must have been *Ludere*. Seeing how many of them had curled and fluffed their hair to wildness, she wished she had not been so quick to toss her plain black wig into the darkness when at last her train crossed over the Utah border. She who had always enjoyed being looked at now felt painfully conspicuous, walking the boards of Holladay Street in her yellow shawl, casting about for a hotel or restaurant that might shelter a lone female and give her a moment in which to think. She was thirsty and wished she had a change of clothes, something nicer than her Mormon homespun; she also wished she had a companion who might know where to start seeking one British painter in a warren of brash, confident, spitting westerners. She had not counted on Denver being so big.

Famke stopped and let the foot traffic flow around and occasionally bump into her. She wetted the shawl end in her saliva and dabbed at her eyes, but even when she was finished, they felt gritty, in testimony to her lack of sleep—she had watched the sun rise somewhere around Delta, Colorado, where a stockyard filled the air with the reek of blood and the mountains of white and brown bones inspired a lonesome feeling that very nearly made her cry.

Seeing those jumbled ossuaries, suddenly she'd been homesick for Prophet, for Heber's kind arms and the intimate bustle of family life. She had to remind herself, firmly, that she was sicker with longing for Albert, that she had fit much better into his life than into the Goodhouses', that he had almost certainly sent her a letter at Fru Strand's house (of course he had!) and must be waiting and wishing for her now. How happy he would be to see her . . . If only she could sit and catch her breath and wits, she would devise a course of action. It was not as if she could go into the next building—the bright blue tiles on the doorstep spelled out M. SILKS—and ask for advice. Indeed, she saw only men passing through that elaborately carved door, and with a quick suspicion of what the place was, she walked briskly on until she could turn a corner.

Even there, however, she was unsafe. A man stepped up as soon as she appeared, and she saw a long chain of suits and hats and cigars scattered down the boardwalk.

"Do you have your own room, sister?" This one's hair was barbered and he wore tidy if inexpensive clothes; he even held his hat in his hands as he addressed her. "How much for an hour?"

Famke understood immediately: The finer prostitutes had their houses on the big boulevard, but the itinerant lower class took to the side streets, among the Chinese laundries and the bright posters advertising Bones and Tambo minstrel shows, patent medicines, and lawbreakers with a price on their heads. Wherever she went, she was bound to be taken for a *Luder*, for she must have about her the air of a woman without a man's protection—a woman looking for a man.

Her hesitation gave this man confidence. "Eight bits should be enough," he said; "I won't take the whole hour." He seized her elbow in a gesture far too eager for gallantry.

"*Fanden!*" Famke shook him off, frustrated and enraged. She summoned her best English to shout, "You bloody, miserable devil!"

But that was not what rid her of him. In her access of emotion, she bent over in a paroxysm of coughing, and he fled in disgust.

Yes, in Denver it was best to be a man.

＊ ＊ ＊

These are for my brother," Famke told the hairy little clerk in the cloth-ier's. She held up two white shirts, nearly identical; she couldn't see why one should cost seventy-five cents and the other a dollar, so she chose the cheaper one. Another $1.25 bought a pair of gray cotton-blended trousers that the clerk assured her could not be distinguished from pure wool "except on very close inspection, ma'am." He smirked, as if to imply something about the inspection she might be giving them.

Famke leveled him an icy blue stare and ordered a cotton coat to go with the trousers, even though the clerk hinted with the same disdainful delicacy that wintry weather was coming soon. She rounded out the costume with a string tie for seven cents, suspenders for a quarter, and a soft felt hat for fifty cents, and she left the shop having surrendered $6.07 and a good deal of her dignity, which she hoped to regain as soon as she could change into her new apparel.

It was miserable to be a woman in Denver, she had decided, even a Bohemian one. And it seemed so easy to become a man.

In the simple hotel room she'd engaged, the Mormon union suit came in handy; she had forgotten to buy masculine underwear, and the clothes would not hang right without it. Yet despite that Saintly intervention, she found the pants chafed her inner thighs, and when she belted them the inseam rubbed uncomfortably Down There, where the embroidered map grew scratchy. Well, she could not imagine dressing this way long; she would ignore this little discomfort as she had ignored so many worse ones while posing. Her own boots were fine for now, and when she coiled her hair up into the hat she thought the hotel mirror reflected a passable young man. On the thin side, perhaps, but so were many who came to town after weeks of eating hardtack and working a mine.

She had hired the room for herself and a husband, so she expected no difficulty in coming or going as either man or woman; and indeed the proprietress (furtively enjoying a bottle of bitters beneath her counter) paid little attention as Famke strode through the lobby imitating Albert's firm, fast gait.

So here she was, on a Colorado evening, looking for one man in a territory pockmarked with small towns and deep shafts that could hide anyone, even an artist featured in Frank Leslie's magazine, for weeks. It was a daunting task. But walking like Albert had given her an idea; she knew what he liked.

The first saloon she entered was much like the beer hall she'd once visited with him in Copenhagen. It was louder, yes, and it looked dirtier to her; but it was a place to start. Pitching her voice deep, she asked for a glass of the cheapest and some information about strangers in town.

The man behind the bar rolled his eyes. "Brother," he said, "everybody in this town's a stranger."

"I'm looking for an artist," she said stubbornly. "A painter. His name is Albert Castle."

"What's your interest?" He looked dubiously at her slender form, around which the obviously new jacket and trousers bagged. "If you're a Pinkerton, I'm a dancing girl."

Famke had read of those detectives—brutal men. "I am his brother."

"Well, I ain't heard of any Albert Castle," he said, and turned to rinse some glasses in a sinkful of brown water. When he set one of the glasses in front of her, she shuddered, paid him the nickel he seemed to expect, and left.

It was the same story in every saloon she visited: Famke asked after a brother called Albert and was told that no one knew anything about a particular stranger or an artist. There were many saloons, and she grew terribly thirsty. After a while she began to have a few sips of beer in each place and soon felt giddy; then she stopped drinking and her head began to ache. Finally, when the beer halls closed with the sunrise, she walked into a pharmacy and asked for a bromide, anything to relieve the pounding in her skull.

"Want summat for that cough, too?" asked the pharmacist, and she shook her head. In fact, she was hacking so much from fatigue and the city fumes that she couldn't have answered.

While she waited for him to fill a bottle, she managed to calm her lungs enough to ask, without any real hope, if the pharmacist had had any dealings with an artist called Albert Castle.

"He the one that's painting Amy Oggle's girls?" the man asked, and Famke's heart stopped.

"Painting girls?" she croaked, holding back another cough.

"The soiled doves, the fair but frail, the ladies as paints themselves. Amy's got some feller making up a portrait of them all." He pushed the bright green bottle toward Famke and stared at her curiously, flushed as she was beneath the drooping hat. She must have appeared very young or very naive, for he said finally, "Holladay Street at Fourteenth. It's a bagnio, my friend—one of the very places causing the Holladay family to agitate for a name change."

Famke did not know that word, *bagnio*, but she recognized the street name.

"He came in here for white lead and arsenic to help the girls' complexions," the pharmacist concluded, with an early-morning yawn. "That's Amy Oggle's. And yours'll be nine cents."

"Thank you," Famke murmured in a voice not at all like a man's. She was so distracted by this information that she pulled a dime from her pocket and did not wait for the change.

Chapter 23

One feels a sense of exhilaration in the atmosphere of Denver. The bland but bracing breezes cool the fevered pulse and the abundant oxygen of the air thrills one like a draught of effervescing champagne.

STANLEY WOOD,
OVER THE RANGE TO THE GOLDEN GATE

The contagion of soul, says the ancient philosopher, is quicker than that of the body, and I have yet to see the one with soul so dead as to refuse a venture in mines, and wholly resist the fever which spares neither age nor sex, yet is not fatal or even unpleasant.

SUSAN E. WALLACE,
THE LAND OF THE PUEBLOS

LOTS OF BOARDERS—ALL THE COMFORTS OF HOME. WELCOMING GUESTS FROM THREE O'CLOCK ONWARD: That was the legend above the door of Mrs. Amy Oggle's house, which was further identified with her name tricked out in red tiles on the step, glowing lurid in the afternoon sun. And yet, with her thighs rubbed nearly raw and her feet blistered from walking like Albert—and most of all because the prospect of seeing Albert himself made her tremble—Famke hesitated. What if he didn't recognize her as a man? Well, she might take care of that in a hurry— but what if she found him . . . painting another woman? Certainly she, Famke, had the prior claim, and naturally she would forgive him, but still—

"What's keeping you, brother?" asked a man behind her. His battered boots had obscured the *Oggle* on the doorstep, and his dark hand, too, was poised to knock. But he seemed to expect her to do it, and so she did.

The door was opened immediately by a tall, bulge-browed man who somewhat resembled Brother Erastus Mortensen and introduced himself as "The Professor." He looked down at the two ragged and unpromising customers, and he sighed. But nonetheless he held the door open for them and offered to take their hats. Famke kept hers and even clamped a hand on the crown, as the irrepressible curls threatened to send it flying.

So this was a bagnio, a house of sin, *et Bordel*; the kind of place the nuns had hinted about and that Sariah had bewailed but never described. It was not what Famke had expected. It wasn't lush or velvety, was not swagged or gilded; though the madam had made an effort to decorate it luxuriously in pink brocade, every cushion and chair was of a slightly different hue, and all were shabby around the edges. It was barely as nice as the Goodhouses' parlor, and Famke and this skinny brown fellow seemed to be the first customers of the day. The time was a second past three.

But there was a table for drinks, and there was a piano at which the big-browed Professor sat down and began to pound. Music came pouring forth, and with it about a half-dozen girls in gaudy dresses streamed in from a hallway. They toyed with colored ribbons and false curls, and though their giggles began to sound forced within a very few seconds, at least they made an effort at welcome.

All females. No Albert.

The girls sidled over, batting their eyes like wind-up dolls. They brought with them whiffs of stale cologne, alcohol, and smoke, and they gave the two customers their names:

"I'm called Bett."

"Spanish Sadie."

"Big Kitty," declared a tall bundle of curves, "two hundred and five pounds of lovely!" She tossed her light brown mane and set her impressive flesh to billowing.

The other girls ignored her.

"I'm Jo, and this is sweet Giulietta."

"Golden Lallie."

"Duchess Irene."

Famke was overwhelmed, confused, and powerless. Somehow she found herself seated with the other customer on a smoke-yellowed sofa, clutching a watered-down whiskey in one hand. She kept the other hand on her head, still holding the cloth hat down. Lallie, a dirty blonde, perched on the arm at the thin man's side, and Big Kitty nearly unbalanced the couch at Famke's.

All the girls giggled and purred; Jo and Giulietta stroked each other's hair with gestures obviously calculated to please the viewer.

And then the madam swept in, Mrs. Oggle herself. Her hair so white it was nearly blue, she was wearing a dress of emerald green silk dark at the armpits. She looked sharply at Famke.

"What'll it be," she said, "boys?"

Famke felt Amy's black eyes poking at her. "I am seeking—," she began. When the girls looked at her sharply, too, she remembered to pitch her voice lower and said, "That is, I—" She couldn't finish.

Mrs. Oggle pulled out a newfangled brown cigarette and lit it, peering steadily through the smoke. "Not from around here, are you? What did you do, strike a mother lode?"

The other man snorted, claiming his share of the women's attention. "Money ain't in the digging these days."

"You said it, honey." Amy looked around the room at her pathetically bright girls and sighed.

"I have money," Famke blurted out, and she felt the prick of Amy's gaze again.

The piano music got stronger; someone had given the Professor a drink.

"You may have the bones, young fellow, but we'll take care of your friend first," said the madam, not allowing Famke or the other man a moment to protest that they weren't friends. "Which of these lovelies will you have, good sir? Cash up front and in my hand, given the times you've fallen on."

Famke watched the man make the difficult choice. Jo was striking, with her dark hair and good skin, but there was something fascinating about the size of Big Kitty, and Giulietta had a nice pink smile. In the end Lallie's breasts were nearest, and as they pressed in closer to him he took the easiest decision.

"Ten dollars," Amy said.

Famke was surprised; the man in the street had offered her far less, and she'd dressed herself for a fraction of Lallie's fee. Women must be more highly valued here than she thought.

The door banged shut under a legend that read, SATISFACTION CHEER-FULLY GUARANTEED.

Once he was gone, the atmosphere in the room shifted. The other girls pulled out cigarettes, too, and they turned away from Famke. One or two of them wandered off to sit with the now-idle Professor and plink halfheartedly at the keys.

"You may as well go," said Amy. "We don't serve women in here."

Famke wasn't too surprised; in the gaslight, she'd already felt exposed. Anyway, she didn't see how her disguise would help her now. So she dropped all further pretense and said, "I am not here for a girl. I am looking for Albert Castle."

The girls' heads whipped around, and Famke felt the hearts about her beating fast. Clearly this was a name they knew.

"Is he here?" she asked.

Amy exhaled a long gray breath. "Albert Castle," she said. She bent in closer, pulled off Famke's hat, and unpinned her hair familiarly. "And who are you to him, if I might ask?"

"Please, if you know where he is, tell me," Famke said, as the hot waves of hair settled over her shoulders. She felt tears in her eyes, and she brushed stray locks away impatiently. "Is he in Denver? Is he—here now?"

Amy shook her snow-white head. "No, hon. He left a couple days ago."

"He painted all of us," Big Kitty interjected. "It's going to be in the newspaper."

"Has been," said Bett. "Days 'n days ago."

Famke felt her eyes welling up, and one traitorous tear slithered away. She couldn't speak.

"Would you like to see the picture?" Amy asked, offering her a cigarette at the same time.

Famke shook her head at the cigarette, but she managed to squeeze out, "Yes."

Jo grabbed Famke's hands and pulled her upright. "Turn around," she said.

The painting hung above the very sofa on which Famke had been sitting. She'd been too overwhelmed to notice it when she entered, and truth to tell it was not a very remarkable work; but now she studied it hard. The composition featured nine women—all these girls, plus Amy and another—arranged singly and in groups of three around an olive grove and mostly naked, with assorted props placed so as to accentuate their charms and hide the problematic hair Down There while at the same time suggesting it was present in abundance. Famke recognized a scroll, a flute, and a pair of large masks: one frowning, one grinning lewdly. Without these familiar props, she would hardly have recognized the canvas as Albert's. The details were imprecise, the lines hurried—and then, too, it was a *finished* painting.

Amy told her, in a puff of smoke, "The boy said he's traveling around the West, earning his way with these pictures."

"You asked him to paint this?" Famke asked, feeling a telltale tickle in the lungs. "It was a job"—she'd learned that word from the men of Prophet— "not a work he chose for himself?"

"He came calling, and I said yes. Most houses like something to show off their girls, but your average picture's only a photograph. I say a painting's got more tone, especially when it's Greek like this one." She shook her head, obviously delighted. "I think it turned out, wouldn't you say?"

Famke couldn't answer at first, for she had to give in to the tickle. While she coughed, brown-haired Irene touched the canvas and set the whole picture slightly off balance. She seemed to speak of Albert with a special eagerness. "There's his mark. He makes 'AC' look like a castle . . ." She glanced down at her fingertip, now faintly green with paint, then rubbed it with her thumb until both were deeply stained.

Mrs. Oggle reproved her, "I told you not to touch that thing. He said the quality stuff would take a while to dry, so don't chafe it all away." She combed through Famke's hair with her fingers and said, "Jo, get this girl another drink. Get her some of your laudanum."

Jo vanished under the Satisfaction sign.

Fragile Bett, who looked hardly older than Sariah's eldest boy, gave Famke her handkerchief. "He was very nice," she said. "I hope you find him."

Famke was afraid of just how nice Albert had been to all of them, and she could have wept from the unfairness—the paint was still wet but Albert already gone, without even applying a layer of varnish that would preserve the image. Yet she held her breath, swallowed the draught that Jo brought, and kept studying that canvas.

Nine girls in the painting, eight in the house, if you included Amy herself. That left one extra. As Famke looked at that one, a shadowy, nearly faceless figure alone in the background, her stomach fluttered. All of the women at Mrs. Oggle's were blonde or brunette, but that one figure wore a wreath of rosebuds and butterflies atop flaming red hair. And it seemed to

be her lips that voiced the words painted around the frame: *Nine Muses ·
Inspiring Pleasant Thoughts · in a Grove · "Had We But World Enough."*

The laudanum took quick effect. Famke's cough faded and her eyelids
drooped; she smiled. "Do you know where he is now?" she asked.

"You might try the smaller towns. Fair Play, Leadville, Boulder," Amy
told her, still stroking Famke's hair. "But what do you want to rush off for?
A girl with your face and your hair could do well for herself here."

Chapter 24

. . . . .

The Railways of Colorado are famous for their bold engineering, and their wonderful achievements in the passage of lofty mountains and unparalleled gorges. They have been built in advance of population, and the rapid growth of the State is in part due to their agency.

Moses King,
King's Handbook of the United States

The big, loud trains that had borne Famke across the country were no good in these complicated mountains. Carrying a secondhand satchel with her female clothes inside, she bought a fare on what the ticketmasters called a Slim Princess: a narrow-gauge train that could negotiate the cramped tunnels and precarious passes. The Princess was only a third as wide as the big trains, but she was better tended, with bright red and green paint and shiny brasses.

That first morning, Famke felt well rested and full of energy, thanks to Jo's laudanum (a mere nickel added on to the dollar charge for her whiskey), and took heart at the sight of the pretty little locomotive puffing steam through the station. She mounted with a light step and found a bench to herself in second class, mindful that a man would sit with ankles and knees apart, rather than pressed together in the way of lady Catholics and Saints. She was proud of another detail that had occurred to her that morning: She had hung the yellow pocket around her waist with the tinderbox inside, where its bulge added an authentic touch to her male impersonation. She had also slicked her hair down with macassar oil and pinned it tightly, with the willful hat practically sewn down on top. She would keep it on during the ride.

"Morning, ma'am," she greeted a fellow-passenger, and then had to fight to keep the grin from her face. From the woman's scandalized expression,

Famke could tell her disguise was succeeding, and she had been what Sariah used to call "overforward."

But the day did not go as Famke had hoped. After riding as far as Fair Play at a bone-jolting sixteen miles an hour, she came to an impasse: Although she visited all five of the town's inexpensive bagnios, called boardinghouses, and paid an extra premium for a drink at a fancier parlor house, she found no trace of Albert.

After some moments' despair, she decided he must have continued west. So she bought another ticket and breezed toward Garo, found nothing, and went on to Buffalo Springs with the last train. This was home only to a hog ranch, which Famke deduced after some confusion meant a warehouse for decrepit prostitutes who sold themselves cheap. The "ranch" was a flat, unpainted building in the middle stages of falling down; about a dozen aging women lurched around it baring pockmarked breasts and gap-toothed smiles at all comers. They'd never heard of an Albert Castle, and they laughed at the thought of being preserved on canvas.

For economy, Famke spent that night among men in a nickel-a-night flophouse that looked like a cousin to the hog ranch. Bedbugs, nerves, and the men's various means of leaking wind kept her awake, but at least no one recognized her as a woman. Lying there with her hat on and her face pressed to a drafty chink in the wall, she made up her mind to travel as far as Leadville, as she was familiar with that city from her newspaper reading; it was the sort of violent, wild place that would attract a man in search of new myths and inspiration. It was also the city of highest elevation in North America, and Albert must be interested in a place with such a pedigree.

Another Slim Princess pushed her deeper into Colorado, gliding down tunnels and over bridges, through clouds of butterflies dying with the autumn. This was dramatic, terrifying country. While the other second-class passengers kept up lively discussions, played cards, spat tobacco, and ate noonday dinners, Famke gazed transfixed at sheer dropoffs and mountainsides blazing with color. She saw huge hollow bowls in the earth from which silver had been pulled, conical tailings where the waste dirt and rock slag were piled. In prosperous regions there was scarcely a tree to be seen, as they'd all been harvested to build a town or shore up a mineshaft.

In midafternoon the Princess dipped sharply south to round a towering mountain, then turned north again at Buena Vista and labored upward.

Under the engine's soothing rhythm, Famke began to give in to her drowsiness. But then, a few miles above Granite, the Princess began to shriek. Her brakes dragged along the rails, and sparks flew up to strike the windows.

Famke pulled back in alarm, as if the glass were no protection. She came fully awake as the ladies in the car around her exclaimed, and a few of the children began to cry. They all sat in suspense for several long minutes, breathing in the smell of hot iron, speculating wildly on the delay.

Eventually a gangly conductor burst into the passenger car and rushed down the aisle, on the way to something important. A rough-looking man in front of Famke grabbed him by the arm; the conductor's cap fell from his head and nearly knocked Famke's hat off too.

"What's the production?" the man demanded.

"Derailment," the conductor said. The passengers around him gasped. "Not ours," he reassured them hastily. "Word is it's a mercy train jumped the rails. Fortunately we're going uphill, so we stopped in plenty of time."

"A mercy train!" repeated the rough man's refined wife. She wore a high comb in the back of her hair, like a Mexican woman. "All those precious little orphans . . ."

"They're right as rain, ma'am," the conductor assured her as he detached his sleeve from her husband's grasp. "Nobody hurt at all. Nobody *there*— the engine's warm, so we know it happened within the afternoon, but we can't find trace of the merest orphan or minister or any other body. No engineer, either, or coal stoker or conductor. Now, if you'll pardon me—" He retrieved his cap and dashed off again.

The Slim Princess waited long hours while the crew got word to Granite, where the stationmaster telegraphed a warning northward to organize a locomotive with a team of men and mules to right the derailed mercy train. It took many more hours still for them to effect the movement, using the light of the moon and the lanterns they'd borrowed from idle miners. Famke's fellow-passengers cleaned out their picnic baskets; those with first-class money descended upon the dining car, where the Chinese waiters emptied what was left of the larders. The commotion outside meant there was little sleep for anyone that night, but Famke could not have slept anyway. She shook with chills and worried that if Albert were in Leadville, as she had managed to convince herself he must be, he might move on while she was stalled here, a captive of the rails.

As she lay on her hard wooden bench, she imagined Albert in Leadville's famous Opera House, or ensconced in a fine room in the Grand Hotel, drawing or painting. No, he would choose a simpler hotel, one with good light and a low price, just as he'd done in Denmark . . .

"Honestly," the lady with the comb whispered to her husband, "the manners!" That lady was forced to sleep listing on her husband's wakeful shoulder.

It was midmorning before the Slim Princess had a free path, past noon when Famke got out stiff and sore in Leadville. She was glad to find herself on the ground again, using her legs among good solid wood and brick buildings. She made a few inquiries, then headed for the business district on Harrison Avenue.

Within a very few steps, Famke felt her breath begin to fail. Here the air was thin indeed; any exertion seemed to weaken the supply to her lungs. She loosened her masculine collar and leaned against the depot bricks: *Breathe in, breathe out.* It was like being drunk. She felt cold, too, and wished she'd bought the more expensive wool jacket in Denver.

As if in a dream, she found a small boy was tugging on the cotton jacket tail, blinking up at her with practiced winsomeness. "Spare a penny, mister?"

Famke was too weak to deny him. She dug into the pocket of her jacket for her money, which was still knotted in Sariah's handkerchief, and gave the boy exactly what he'd requested. He didn't ask for more but didn't thank her, either; he stood watching expectantly. Famke forced herself to walk on.

The farther she got from the station, the more slowly she had to move, until it felt as if she were crawling. She stopped again to sag, gasping, against a saloon wall vibrating with music. Inside she could make out the words to a song that would have raised Sariah's hackles—

> My sweetheart's a mule in the mine
> I drive her all day without lines
> On the car front I sit
> And tobacco I spit
> All over my sweetheart's behind . . .

Famke felt a surge of nerves and a consequent constriction of air, but she managed to drag her feet toward a general store with a soaring false front.

There, she thought, she might take a seat with the customers around the cracker barrel or checkers table, perhaps drink a refreshing bottle of blood-purifying sarsaparilla and soda and, eventually, ask about a man who'd come to paint the women of the town.

She was in luck. As she sank down into a chair, surrounded by shelves comfortingly laden with foodstuffs, clothing, and hardware, she found a pair of old-timers already discussing art. Nodding to acknowlege the addition to the group, a maimed man continued drawing in the air with one good hand and one wrist that ended where a hand would begin. His friend hung on every word; he seemed to be missing most of a leg, but from the way he was sitting Famke couldn't be certain.

"The dangedest thing you ever saw," said the man with one hand, "and it's all painted on the same canvas you'd use for your wagon."

Famke forgot to breathe. "What do you mean?" she asked.

He looked sideways at her, and she knew she hadn't pitched her voice quite correctly. Yet he trusted her enough to report that a Mrs. Suky Rummell had just decorated her boardinghouse lounge with a portrait of her nine girls, all in their prettiest dresses and posed as if they were virgins from good families whose fathers were arranging a coming-out ball.

"Do you know who painted it?" Famke asked.

"Does it matter?" The one-legged man, hitherto silent, spoke up and crowed. "Suky's got the freshest gals in town. Expensive, too."

"But that picture ain't a patch on what's over to Dixie Holler's place," the one-handed man continued as if he hadn't heard. "Now I'm gonna get all poetical, but that's just what this picture makes you feel. Dixie's got a band of girls all dressed up—"

"Or undressed, more like," said his friend.

"—as an army of lady warriors, all iron girdles and horned hats. Angels with swords—they could slay a man and collect his thanks along with his scalp."

Famke listened breathlessly, trying to silence even the beat of her heart. As the one-handed man described it, the lady warriors clustered worshipfully about the figure of a man whose head was half-turned from the viewer and partially veiled in one woman's flowing hair: "That rapscallion could be any man, you or me or your brother, and that's just how I like it."

"That do sound like a picture," the other man said, "but I patronize Ma

Askling's myself. Her girls is all wool and a yard wide, and they're at bargain prices every day."

"No, Dixie's is worth the extra," promised the first. "Not just for the girls, but because of this thing she's got hanging there—makes even the old hogs look plump and tender. Bill, my friend, you won't believe your eyes, and you'll want to give 'em a dig for yourself." He swished his tobacco wad to the front of his mouth and spat into the brass cuspidor.

Famke couldn't help it. She coughed. She coughed so hard the tears squeezed from her eyes, and she didn't want to look at what was left on her handkerchief. The two men watched her, impassive.

"You new to town, boy?" asked the man with one hand.

Still coughing, she nodded.

"A lunger," he observed to Bill, shaking his head wisely. To Famke he said, "You got no business going down the mines, boy—you'll be laid up inside a week. Look what it did to me." He held up his stump. "And I was pert as a parrot when I stepped in."

Belatedly, Bill thumped Famke on the back and very nearly knocked her over.

"I am not a miner," Famke said, when she could speak. The cough had made her voice appropriately gravelly and deep. "I have no intention to go down."

The portly shopkeeper came toward her with a tray, saying in a stout voice, "That's fine, my friend. The air aboveground'll do you a world of good." He set the tray on the barrel; a collection of bottles, blue and green and clear, tall and thin and short and squat, rattled upon it. "Meanwhile you might want to throw down a taste of these cures."

"No, thank you," Famke said, thinking of the nasty taste of Deseret's Elixir.

"Just a sample, why not," the shopkeeper wheedled. "First swig free of charge."

"Doesn't pay a man to be in any business but cures these days," said Bill, with a sigh and a twitch of his leg stump. "Silver ain't worth the sweat it takes separating from the rock."

It was much the same opinion as Famke had heard in Denver, and his friend agreed. "May as well get into the burying business. For folks like us, no money a-tall's to be got *out* of the ground."

Chapter 25

Leadville is one of the most interesting cities in the world to the tourist. It abounds in scenes of a novel and characteristic nature, and presents views of life entirely foreign to the conventional.

STANLEY WOOD,
OVER THE RANGE TO THE GOLDEN GATE

That evening, having fortified herself with a bottle of sarsaparilla, a dose of Dr. King's New Discovery for Coughing, and a handful of oyster crackers, Famke contemplated the daintily lettered sign hanging over the door to which the ex-miner had directed her: IF AT FIRST YOU DON'T SUCCEED, TRY, TRY AGAIN.

She took this as a portent of encouragement, hoping that Dixie Holler would shout out some news of Albert, perhaps even produce him from some paint-splattered studio. So she knocked on the door with masculine force, and when the door was opened—this time by a tarnished blonde in a yellow-and-black striped dress and heavy face-paint—she gave a lecherous grin and made sure her arm brushed the girl's breasts as she entered.

The girl threaded her arm through Famke's. "My name's Myrtle," she murmured, just a little too loudly, in the neighborhood of Famke's ear. Famke gave a start. Myrtle concluded hopefully, "Some folks call me Sweet Myrt; have you heard of me?"

Famke had to shake her head at that; she'd startled only because of the similarity to her former co-wife's name. Imagine seeing Myrtice here! Of course that was a silly thought. And yet Famke suspected that no one in Prophet City would be entirely surprised to hear that *she* had been to Dixie Holler's, or that she'd come as a man. Even Heber must know by now that she was not what she'd initially seemed to him.

"I'm new to town," she said to Sweet Myrt. "But I've heard there is a beautiful painting of you here."

At that, the practiced smile that had never faded from Myrtle's face grew wider and more genuine. "Yes, hanging over a sofa in the parlor, the most rightful little portrait of the six of us you've ever seen."

She brought Famke straight to it, past the row of handsomely made up boarders and the stout carrot-tressed madam in black silk and lace. "See!" Myrtle said proudly, waving her arm to display the painting and her bosom at the same time. "It's called"—she frowned, recollecting— "*The Hero's Rest in Valley High, Among*—"

"*The Hero's Repose*," corrected the madam, "*in Valley Hall, Among a Passel of Walled Kiries.* That's a kind of bird."

This frame showed no title, but that did not matter; for once Famke knew words that an American did not. "Valhalla," she said. "And Valkyries. They are women who care for the men who have died well." She did not have the vocabulary to correct the word *passel*, though it sounded wrong to her. She pulled Myrtice's spectacles from her pocket and fumbled with putting them on so as not to disturb her slicked hair. Closer inspection showed the plain gold frame did bear the faintest trace of lettering, as if Albert had begun to paint his title there and then grown dissatisfied with it, or perhaps pressed for time.

Dixie decided to indulge her customer. "Whatever it's called, it's sure pretty, isn't it?"

So, clad in the scantiest of costumes, with the customary girdles of mist, the proud warrior women of Norse legend had gone the way of the Muses. The colors were pleasant and the likenesses good, though even less detailed than in Amy Oggle's painting; the carefully arranged Valkyries-for-hire fawned over their faceless hero and wove a web of silken hair about him— golden, ebony, brown, and brilliant red. In the lower right-hand corner, nearly lost against the hero's silver shield, stood the peaked castle made of the letters A and C.

Famke felt tears springing to her eyes.

Dixie sized Famke up. "You need a drink, my friend. What'll you have?"

Famke hesitated. "Whiskey." It was the only drink, other than beer, whose name she knew in English. "How long have you had that picture?" she asked in her deepest voice.

Dixie did not hear her, for at that moment, the doorknocker sounded. The professor at the piano said, "Company, ladies," and played even louder.

A second blonde went to answer the door. Sweet Myrt, still hanging on Famke's arm, spoke up again: "You talk like him."

"Who?" Famke asked.

"The man that painted us." Myrtle combed her bright yellow locks with her fingers and fluffed up the fringe in front. "He had that way of sounding a word. Are you from England, too?"

The remaining girls, now perched on chair arms all around the room, looked at Famke with renewed interest.

"I'll be switched!" Mrs. Holler said. "Could you be his brother?" She took Famke's chin in her hand and turned her head sideways, looking for resemblance, until Famke grew nervous and jerked away.

It appeared she'd given a decisive nod. The girls squealed in delight.

"Albert's brother!" Myrtle was so excited that she tore an artificial tress accidentally free of its pins and had to hide it behind a sofa cushion.

"Do you paint?"

"What's your name?"

The new customer entered then, and he thought the question was aimed at him. "Bill," he said, looking around with the authority of a man who knew just what to expect from a place like this. He was the one-legged man from the general store and had obviously been lured here, as Famke was, by the tale of the marvelous painting. Leaning on a crutch, the empty trouser leg pinned up by his belt, he, too, stood looking at the Valkyries a long moment, comparing their faces with the faces in the room.

The girls paid him scarce attention, fascinated instead with the man they thought was the painter's brother.

"What's your name?" repeated a girl who looked like she might have a bit of savage blood in her.

Famke gave the first that came to mind, a name suggested by what she thought was her special familiarity with Albert's history: "Dante."

"Don Tay?"

She spelled it aloud: "D-a-n-t-e. Dante."

"Dante!" They all repeated it at once, savoring the exotic taste of it.

At the sound of her voice, the new customer looked over and lifted his chin in recognition. While she nodded back, blushing unaccountably, the girls avoided meeting Bill's eyes. A Dante was much more fascinating than a Bill.

"I must find my brother," Famke said desperately to them, her head down. "Do you have any—do you know where he has gone?"

Before anyone could answer, Dixie Holler snapped her fingers. "Ladies," she warned, and that was enough. They lined up in front of Bill, dutifully displaying their figures in the tight colorful frocks, inviting him to choose.

In the commotion, Famke touched the canvas. Dry. She sank down on the couch, feeling her lungs constrict.

Bill took a girl with pale brown hair—bottom left corner in *The Hero's Repose*—and despite her lingering look back at Famke they disappeared down the hallway. An IF AT FIRST YOU DON'T SUCCEED sign hung over the inner door, too.

As soon as Bill was gone, the other girls began to chatter. Apparently they had liked Albert very much, for they were eager to make friends with Dante. They began by telling him their names, none of which Famke could make out in the din, and they plied her—Dante—with questions about the accomplished brother, for all the world as if they'd forgotten the reason Dante gave for coming here.

"I need to find Albert," Famke broke in at last, though she felt a strange reluctance to say the name out loud again. She was aware of being somewhat rude. "You know more about him now than I do. Where is he?"

Mrs. Holler said shrewdly, "Doesn't know you're coming, does he?"

"I believe he never got my letters." This much was true, as she had never written any.

"Well, my boy, your brother ain't in Leadville anymore. Said he was moving on to Denver. Were I you, I'd look for him down Holladay Street."

Famke nodded dispiritedly. It seemed she had stepped backward, not forward, in her search; she looked again at the Valkyries and sighed. "After Denver? Did he say where he would go then?"

The madam shrugged, and all the girls appeared to wait for her answer. Myrtle surreptitiously reattached her lost curl. "You might try the towns north of there," said Dixie. "Maybe Box Elder. Or south—Greenland, Monument, Pueblo."

While Famke digested those names, Myrtle presented herself in Famke's line of vision again, her hair now intact but slightly askew. "Would you like to see my room?" she asked, with a note of wistfulness beneath the brass.

Dixie Holler licked her lips and made ready to name a price.

Famke was spared the possible embarrassment of a reply: The door-knocker sounded again, so hard and rapid that everyone startled. It kept going for nearly a minute while the professor stopped playing and the girls turned white.

"Any of you in trouble with the law?" asked Mrs. Holler.

No one bothered to reply, and the knocking continued. It seemed likely that some very bad news had arrived.

"Lazy Izzy, you go," said Mrs. Holler, but nobody wanted to wait; if one girl was going, all would go, and the professor with them. They all forgot about Dante for a moment and trooped into the foyer, some of them holding hands.

Famke lingered behind. She knew this would be a good opportunity to make her exit, but she wanted a few moments alone with the painting. She stood and examined it again, marveling that Albert had allowed himself to finish and frame what to her was so obviously an inferior example of his work. These Valkyries were pretty enough, it was true, and their colors were vivid and clear, but where were the finer points that had distinguished Nimue? The delicate tracery of her veins, the fine shadows of her garments; the details, the grace.

Grace. She thought of her silver tinderbox and patted herself to make sure it was still there in the yellow pocket inside her pants. Looking up at the picture, she wondered if there had ever really been a time when women wore helmets with horns, particularly with so little on their actual bodies. Somehow it was easier to believe in the absolutely naked world of the three entwined Graces.

Dixie Holler alone had not answered the strange knock; she leaned in the doorway, watching Famke like a stout but agile cat, always with a view to the kill. She scratched with one finger among the carroty curls that—Famke looked again to be sure—were brown and gray in the painting. "Now, sir, if you don't like Sweet Myrtle, we have many beauti—"

She would never complete that sentence. Suddenly, at the back of the building, there was a tremendous explosion. A lamp fell from a table, a shepherdess from a carved shelf, and then the shelf itself. Both Dixie and

Famke were knocked down. *The Hero's Repose* dropped from the wall onto the sofa and bounced face down to the floor.

There was a moment of strange, false silence, not really silent at all. Famke's ears rang. At the front of the house, the girls wailed and wept— Valkyries sorrowful rather than celebratory. Bill's voice came from somewhere farther off, cursing a blue streak. Plaster rained over everything.

When the world seemed settled again, Famke slowly picked herself up. She felt dazed, unsure what had just happened, and her lungs rasped on the dry dust. Dixie Holler half-sat on the floor, hacking, the plaster giving her the lips and cheeks of a corpse. She waved Famke away.

With nothing else really to do here, Famke pushed down the foyer and through the girls who were toppled willy-nilly over the front steps and down into the street. Still confused, she stood looking up at the sky, at the haze of dust collecting beneath the stars, while women and men in various stages of deshabille poured out of the boardinghouses around her and someone, far away, set to a piercing howl. She stood in the way of a swarm of boys, and they skirled around her, bumping and shouting until they'd spun her dizzy and breathless once more.

Now there were running bodies everywhere, and voices, snatches of conversation.

"Dynamite—"

"—mines—"

"—Pittsburgh—"

"—Matchless—"

"—Blaze!"

It seemed that, behind the row of fancy-houses, a fire had started. There was another explosion, or perhaps just a loud crash, and the first flames showed above the roofline. A fire wagon jolted by, the horses' eyes showing the whites. The crowd drew Famke along toward it. When she rounded the corner she found that the house directly behind Dixie's was on fire—that might explain the knock on the door . . . She tried to turn back away from the flames, but the press of bodies made it impossible. And then she saw that the flames were licking not just at Dixie's place but also at Famke's own hotel, at the very wall behind which she'd secreted her female clothes.

With the crowd stopped dead around her, Famke stood in the street, mouth open to smoke and astonishment. She was utterly terrified. For nearly an hour she watched as flames writhed toward the sky like worms that would gobble the stars, and ashes flew from them like moths; the firemen's feeble hoses could do nothing against them.

Ashes of wood, of paper, of cloth. The homespun skirt from Myrtice, the nice blouse she'd bought in Copenhagen, the petticoat on which she'd essayed her first artwork—the yellow shawl . . . All Famke's feminine belongings, everything that made her Ursula Summerfield Goodhouse. She owned nothing in the world now but what she carried in her pockets. Famke wiped her nose on her sleeve and realized that she had become, to all intents and purposes, a man. A man with no reason to stay in Leadville any longer, with every reason to flee it.

She fought her way through the watchers and headed for the train depot. Others would be fleeing here soon; she had to arrive first. Heedless of the pain in her lungs and the dizziness in her head, she consulted the chalked schedule and saw a train was due in under half an hour—"Fare for one," she gasped out at the ticket window.

"Denver or Climax?"

She remembered the list of towns Amy Oggle had mentioned. "Boulder."

"You'll have to round the mountain and pass through Denver." The agent, chafing at having to remain at his post while others investigated the events downtown, pushed a scrap of beige cardboard under the grille. "Two dollars and twenty."

It seemed like little enough. Famke leaned against the counter, searching her jacket pocket for the handkerchief that held what was left of the thirty dollars she'd brought with her. It was not there.

Trembling, her left hand dove into the other pocket and explored it thoroughly before Famke faced the ugly fact: Her money, like her clothing, was gone.

"*Fanden!*" Too late she realized what had happened: The boys who swarmed around her in the street had found out where she kept her money and, when an opportunity arose, took it from her. Probably the one who'd begged a penny of her when she arrived had done the scouting. As she groped further in her jacket, she realized the thief had even taken Myrtice's spectacles.

"If you pay no money, you get no fare," the agent snapped. He pulled back the cardboard stub and retreated from the window.

Chapter 26

. . . . .

An untraveled man's idea of a mountain is of a tremendous, heaven-kissing surge of rock, earth and snow, rolling up at once from the dull plain like a tenth wave of a breaker, and fairly taking your breath away. But a mountain range grows upon you gradually.

BENJ. F. TAYLOR,
BETWEEN THE GATES

Viggo never tired of looking at these American hills, blazing yellow now on this October afternoon. In Denmark, it was said that if a man stood on a beer crate he could see from one end of the country to the other; but here, it seemed, there were more mountains than towns, each one as magnificent as the picture on the jigsaw puzzle he'd played with at Immaculate Heart.

Mæka: After swooping from New York to Chicago, through the Midwest and over the vast stretches of Nebraska and Wyoming, the continent to him now was like a giant puzzle of cities, plains, and forests, cut into pieces by rivers and streams that grew rarer with each mile traveled west. The most splendid pieces were the mountains, whether craggy and brown or still lush with lingering leaves and flowers. Viggo looked toward them now as the farmer's wagon jolted slowly away from the big, quiet metropolis of Salt Lake and toward the little town called Prophet, where the Mormon officials had told him he might find his fellow-orphan. He watched the mountains turn bloody red, reflecting the sunset, as he climbed down in front of Brother Nathan Fitzhenry's house and memorized directions for the Goodhouse place.

"You might stay the night in town," Brother Fitzhenry said, scratching his beard. "They've had some trouble out at Goodhouse's lately."

Viggo's brow furrowed. If such were the case, it was imperative that he go there immediately, tonight: Famke might need him. He had a clear picture of her now, with long wet red hair and a terrified expression, just like the ship's figurehead in that painting in New York. He would reach her before the waves swallowed her up.

"Thank you," he said to Brother Fitzhenry. "I will walk."

En, to, én, to, Viggo recited to himself as he marched, soldierlike. The sun finished sinking and the hills turned black; it was a long hour before the moon rose high enough to light his way, and then the coyotes began to howl. Their howling grew louder as he took the turn for Goodhouse's farm, and louder still as an odd-shaped muddy house came into view, its yellow lamplight illuminating a farmyard containing a half-built hut and a large square barn. Viggo heard horses and cows bellowing inside the barn and chickens squawking in their coop; every animal on the place was disturbed and protesting. It was small wonder, then, that no one answered his first knock. He had to knock twice more before a short, skinny boy opened the door and stared up at him with dark adult eyes.

"What do you want?" the child demanded rudely.

Viggo smiled and extended his hand for the shaking. The boy seemed fascinated with the knotty scars over it, and he poked the back of the hand as if to make sure it was real.

"Heber the Younger!" a woman's sharp voice cried out in irritation. "You close that door now—I can't stand that howling another minute!"

"It's a stranger, Ma!" the boy shouted back, and that brought the woman at a run, shoe heels clicking against the floorboards.

"Who are you?" she asked, almost as rude as her son had been. Viggo noted a distinct family congruence, though the woman's face had settled into hard lines.

"My name is Viggo," he said in his best American. "I have come for Ursula Marie. For Famke."

Sariah Goodhouse folded her arms. "You aren't another correspondent, are you? We've had enough of *them*, coming down from Salt Lake in their green suits and side whiskers, claiming she left them messages in their hotels . . . not that we'd disbelieve that for a minute . . ."

"Our Mother sent me," Viggo said, as clearly as he knew how.

"Ursula's mother!"

"She told us she was an orphan," the little boy said on a note of triumph.

"*Gud, nej, jeg mener*—er, our mother the nun. From the orphan home."

Sariah pulled him inside amid a torrent of language—exclaiming over his resemblance to Famke, introducing herself and her children, seating him at the long family dining table and offering him a lukewarm and distinctly unpleasant brew she called "tea." It was clear she now assumed Viggo must be Famke's relation, but he did not disabuse her of that idea even though he knew the two of them were in no way alike. He did everything as she guided him, meanwhile looking eagerly around at the bare white walls, the old oak sideboard with its stacks of chipped dishes, the lone photograph of too many people crowded into one frame.

The room filled up fast with an abundance of children who looked like clumsy copies of their mother. Where was the fire-haired sorceress? "Is Famke well?" he asked. But no one seemed to hear.

The last arrival was dramatic: A stocky blond woman, bearing the same facial traits as all the others under a blanket of extra flesh, staggered in from somewhere upstairs. She was led by a little girl and held a handkerchief to a green mouth. "So you are Ursula's brother!" She gasped, falling into a chair. "I am Myrtice Goodhouse Black, a widow."

Viggo noticed a newish gold band on the woman's left ring finger. That she was pregnant, though not swollen yet, he could see just as easily; he wondered if she might like some of the camphor in his bag to offset her nausea, but he could think of no way to offer it without broaching what ladies thought to be a delicate topic.

"But where is Famke—Ursula?" he asked, when he felt it was polite to do so.

Myrtice Goodhouse Black mopped at her forehead. "You aren't the only one who wants the answer to that question. Why, right this very minute, Brother G—"

Mrs. Goodhouse silenced her with a look.

Viggo struggled to maintain his good manners. "I think I perhaps misunderstand."

"She is gone," Mrs. Goodhouse told him starkly. "And so is my husband, looking for her—he has some idea she must be among the Catholics to the south of here. She has ruined our family business, burned down our silk house, and robbed us blind. I hope you intend to make some restitution."

* * *

The three silver Graces still entwined each other in their dance, smoother than satin, softer than silk. Alas, however, they now did so in a shop-keeper's window rather than in Famke's pocket.

The little box was all she'd had of value, and reluctant as she'd been to part with it, Famke had done so as soon as she could the morning after the fire. The shopkeeper had said the silver was of little valuation here, but he'd pay her for the artistry; yet ten dollars was all that had been worth to him, and when he put the box in his window it was dwarfed by a large, striated cube of pyrite. Fool's gold.

As the train steamed downhill away from Leadville, Famke did not weep. She merely opened the yellow pocket and rearranged its contents: Albert's blurry sketch of herself in Dragør, the newspaper clippings about him and herself, the twenty-three royal matches (heads now blunt and nearly phosphorusless, thus of no use to anyone but her). Then she coughed away a few cinders and left her seat to find the primitive water closet at the back of the car. It was almost as nasty as the shipboard latrine, but it would serve her purpose: The wall held a tiny rectangle of polished steel, and she could see well enough in it to cut her hair.

With fifty cents of her precious haul, Famke had bought herself a sharp Bowie knife for protection, thinking no boy should pick her pocket again. It lay on the lip of the washbowl now as she doffed her hat and unpinned her hair, letting its gleaming waves fall past her waist for the last time. She re-fused to look long at it but picked up the knife and began to saw away just above shoulder length, where most of the miners and ranchers seemed to keep their hair.

It was quick work. The bright hair filled the washbowl to overflowing and dripped in ringlets on the floor. Famke ran her hands through it; how quickly it had gone cold, away from her body. She selected one of the longest tresses and rolled it around her finger, then tied it with another strand. This memento could sit with the matches and papers in her flat-tened yellow pocket. The rest of the hair she stuffed down the hole of the latrine, to land on the tracks and blow away. When she was finished with that, she put the hat back on her head.

It was far too big for her.

◆   ◆   ◆

The Denver newspapers were already full of the misfortune Famke had witnessed at Dixie Holler's. "Leadville: Dynamite Gang Strikes Again!" boomed the headlines in the *Daily Times*. As she waited for a connection to Boulder, Famke bought the paper, particularly intrigued by that word "again"; it was most interesting, and perhaps somewhat comforting, to think that the fire that had robbed her of so much was one in a chain of events plaguing the region. After a vivid description of the blaze, the correspondent described the culprits:

> This raging inferno was almost certainly the work of those whom the press are now calling the Dynamite Gang, believed to be a band of miners turned away from Golden Junction for questionable morals. Those same individuals are charged with having captured a shipment of Swedish-receipt dynamite destined for blasting the riches from those hills. They appear to be traveling throughout Colorado, and the recent disasters at Gunnison, Central City, and Salida are laid to their account. Their method is unmistakable: a fire set first for distraction, then an explosion that destroys what is loveliest and most valuable in the city's monuments. The Grand Hotel here lies in rubble, along with its collection of marble sculptures in imitation of Canova and its copy of Rubens's Little Fur.
>
> Several places of low repute burned also, including the notorious Dixie Holler's boardinghouse. No decent person can much regret the closing of Mrs. Holler's business, or for that matter of the unsavory hotels, catering to itinerant miners and ne'er-do-wells, directly behind it. What we must regret is the impulse toward violence and destruction that prosperity seems unable to breed out of those who enjoy it, even as we celebrate the enterprising spirit that caused one Leadville shopkeeper to declare, "We will build again, bigger and better!"

When she came to that hopeful conclusion, Famke searched for the author. She thought the article sounded like something Harry Noble would have written, but the writer's name was not one she recognized. She looked, then, for news of the art world in the rest of the paper, but discovered only some directions for making a Dove-in-the-window patchwork quilt.

The best use for this newspaper was as a blanket. She draped it over herself and slept fitfully, compensating for an equally fitful night in Leadville's depot. In those mountains with their switchbacks and branch rails, Boulder was several hours and another change of trains away.

When Famke climbed out, stiff and sore, to begin her rounds of watering holes and boardinghouses, she had a bit of luck. In a saloon where the sign above the piano read, PLEASE DON'T SHOOT THE PIANO PLAYER; HE IS DOING THE BEST THAT HE CAN, she recognized a painting hanging over the bar. This one featured seven Muses, plus a red-haired eighth and ninth holding a pen and paintbrush. All were lined up quite tidily, like soldiers presenting themselves for inspection. The frame was inscribed: *Had We But World Enough and Time . . .*

"You'll be wanting Ma Medlock's girls," said the professor at the piano. He looked hardly older than Famke herself, and his hat sat almost as far down on his ears as hers did. With his fingers still dancing over the yellow keys, he gave her directions to the house in question— "the finest girls, sir, the very finest. You'll see the picture don't do 'em justice. But there ain't any with real red hair, or at least there wasn't at the time the picture was made, which is why those two don't have much in the way of faces. Two of the brown-hairs went red since then."

At Ma Medlock's place, she found seven girls eager to chat with Albert's brother, to stroke his soft hair and kiss his pale cheeks and tease him about ways to put meat on his manly bones. The other customers looked old and tired and were scruffy besides; a tall young fellow in a fairly clean suit was both a treat and a good prospect.

"I—I am so sorry," Famke stammered as one hand found its way dangerously close to the inseam of Dante's trousers. "I haven't money enough. I am looking for my brother."

At that, kindly Ma offered her a job repairing an outhouse damaged in a thunderstorm. "Your brother ain't here," she said, "but leastways we can give you something to go on with."

Famke patched the back wall gratefully though clumsily, developing an enormous blister on her right hand and a black thumbnail on her left, when she hammered it instead of an iron nail.

"Tch," clucked Ma, bandaging both of Famke's hands. "You're far too delicate for the life out West. I hope you find your brother soon—and do something about that cough of yours." She gave Famke a dollar and a swig of Piso's Cure, then found her a ride in a customer's wagon through the hills to Nederland.

There, in the salon of a Mrs. Armstrong, a half-dozen fair but frail Nederlandish Valkyries hung on the wall assisting the repose of a hero who, this time, seemed to stare out of the canvas with a pair of rather prominent green eyes. The Valkyrie with the reddest hair had a clouded face and re-markably pretty calves.

Famke touched those calves. Sticky. "Do you know where the artist went?" she asked, feeling as if her real fleshly legs would hardly hold her.

"Only two places to go from here: Boulder and Tin Cup."

From another brothel customer, Famke begged a wagon ride as far as Tin Cup, where she found nothing but a hog ranch. After a few tired tears and an unpleasant encounter with an old *Luder* who seemed to consider Famke her last hope for a customer, she walked and rode back to Boulder, ignoring the ache in her legs and the cough that refused to abate. With a few hours to fill before the next train, she revisited Ma Medlock's and found a house of mourning.

"Ruby is gone," Ma said. Her eyes were pink with weeping, and she wore her genteel black silk with new conviction. "My oldest, my own girl. Diph-theria."

Famke was not sure she'd ever heard that word; she wondered if it re-ferred in some way to a venereal infection. "I am sorry to hear it," she said politely. She thought she remembered a Ruby: the darkest of the Muses, with thin, sharp features, a gold front tooth, and a somewhat splotched com-plexion. She'd been near the center of Albert's painting, her bare knee over a grinning mask denoting comedy. So she was Ma Medlock's own daughter.

"A beautiful girl," Famke added, again out of politeness, and Ma re-warded her with a luminous smile that had been greatly aided by a draught of laudanum.

"She's been most beautifully laid out," said Ma. "Would you like to see?"

This was Famke's first foray down a boarders' hallway. It was dark and stuffy, but the doors were decorated with gaily painted plaques bearing the girls' names: Laughing Laura, Virginia Candy, Ruby. Ma had locked the door to that room; she now unlocked it and led Famke inside, where the curtains were drawn and a lamp was burning low.

Dead and prepared for the grave, Ruby shone with a loveliness Famke had not remembered as hers in life. Her skin had gone waxy yellow, but her cheeks were painted a dainty rose; her black hair waved gracefully away from her brow, and all the switches and tails seemed to match. Her eyelids were sewn shut so delicately that Famke could not see the stitches. Clearly, this was the work of a loving hand, and it was perhaps that love that had kept the body relatively uncorrupted and only slightly odiferous, despite the absence of an embalmer's fluids.

"A beautiful girl," Famke repeated, holding a handkerchief over her face.

Ma Medlock interpreted her gesture as a paroxysm of grief. "Do not be sad," she said bravely. "My Ruby has gone to a better place." She ran a hand gently over the corpse's brow, her cheek, her arm. It looked to Famke as if she left a blue shadow wherever her hand passed.

Ma wiped her nose and was suddenly all business. "I have a proposition for you, Dante Castle. Your brother is a great artist—tell me, do you share any of his skill?"

"I—" Famke remembered the days painting ice for Nimue. Albert had praised her work then. "I am not sure."

"Let's go to my office." After carefully locking Ruby's door, Ma took Famke's arm and leaned on it, all the way to the end of the hall. Her pigeonholed desk there was as vast and messy as Fru Strand's, and she sat down before it with the air of a lost soul.

"I want another picture painted," said Ma Medlock. She took up some papers and shuffled them, perhaps simply to give herself something to do. "One of just my Ruby. Looking as she does in your brother's painting, but wearing a pretty dress as she is now."

"I cannot paint a likeness," Famke said. "I am sorry."

Ma let the papers drop. They scattered over the floor as if taken up in a gale, and two enormous tears seemed to well up out of the black centers of her eyes. "The burying's on Tuesday," she said tragically. "And not a painter in town who can touch your brother's talent—only *diggers*." She fairly spat the word.

With one hand on her thigh, where the pocketed sketch would have crackled if it were fresh enough, Famke thought hard. Her mind was whirling, but, "I might contrive something," she said at last.

"I will pay gladly," Ma Medlock offered, reckless this once. "I would like something special to remember my girl by. Something decent and artistic."

Famke was struck with the idea that, now the madam had been introduced to art, it was an essential element of her life. Those who had witnessed a magic such as Albert's could not return to their ordinary lives: Just so had his artistry ensnared her in Dragør.

"Yes," she said, "I think I have a scheme."

• • •

To be fair," said Myrtice Goodhouse Black, with a gray eye on Viggo, "the silk house burned two nights *after* Ursula left, when we brought the candles in to watch the worms spinning their cocoons. And she took only thirty dollars."

Viggo now realized that the hut in the farmyard was half-destroyed rather than half-built, and the odd shape of the house itself might be the carving work of an inferno.

Sariah pressed her lips together and pushed another cup of the lukewarm tea toward the other woman. "If she hadn't hid that lantern beneath the table where it had no business, we would still have our silk house—one accidental kick from Alma and your dropped match would not have sent the whole place up in flames. And"—she turned to Viggo—"with that thirty dollars we could have bought Myrtice the medicines to ease—"

"Our faith does not condone the use of stimulants *or* relaxants," Myrtice said stubbornly, looking now at her hands. "Thirty dollars would do me no good."

"Maybe," said Sariah, "but then Heber wouldn't have had to sell that quarter-lot in order to travel . . ."

It was fairly clear to Viggo now that the women were disagreeing solely to be disagreeable, and he thought it was up to him to end their bickering. "I have an idea," he said. "If you wish to find Ursula, should you make people know? In all Mæka, I have seen pictures that say, 'Wanted . . .'"

Sariah and Myrtice stared at him.

"That *is* an idea," Sariah said. She looked at the stranger with approval, something like a smile beginning around her lips. "Do you have any knack for drawing?"

Chapter 27

. . . . .

If a man is fortunate enough to find a steady job he can earn a living more easily here than in Denmark. Back in Denmark one can toil from early in the morning until late in the evening for only fifty Øre a day, and in many places the food is bad, too.

Søren Petersen,
Aarhus Amtstidende

Famke's mind was a stew of dynamited walls, Dove-in-the-window patterns, and memories of wielding Albert's paintbrush. She had a fever, inspiration, and good intentions; what was more, Ma Medlock had promised her twenty dollars—the equivalent of two turns with one of the girls, or a hundred miles on a Slim Princess—if she did well.

Famke fetched *Twilight of the Muses, with Their Various Attributes*, from the saloon and set it up in Ma Medlock's office. She located the Muse who was Ruby and got out her Bowie knife. She said, "*Fanden,*" then sent up a hasty prayer to the immaculate Virgin Mary. She didn't want to think what Ma Medlock might do if Famke failed to produce the desired results.

Squinting in the absence of Myrtice's spectacles and working carefully, Famke ran her knife around the outline of the painted Ruby. Albert had as always stretched his canvas well; the fabric was taut and the cutting was easy, from the black ringlets atop Ruby's head to the grinning mask at her feet. In a very few minutes Famke had a silhouette of Ruby and a portrait of the Muses with a large hole in the center.

For once Famke wished she were a needlewoman, as she threaded Ma's thinnest one with cotton and began to sew Ruby onto a canvas square she'd framed and stretched herself. She quickly learned to punch a series of careful holes where she intended to stitch, so as not to crack the paint; there was a delightfully crisp pricking and sliding sound as the needle passed through the taut fabric.

Once Ruby was in place, she mixed a primer using what she could re-member of Albert's recipe and daubed it first around the seam, then over the rest of the canvas, spreading it as evenly as she could. -

That night, while Famke slept, the base dried quickly, cracked, and flaked away. By noon it lay like a drift of dry snow over Ma's desk.

"Yes, it is going well," Famke said that afternoon, buttering a biscuit for her breakfast with the fair but frail.

Ma began to weep again. "Ruby's starting to turn. She has to go into the ground tomorrow," she said.

The biscuit in Famke's mouth became very dry. She swallowed hard, choking at the crumbly sensation in her throat, then excused herself from the table and went to Ma's office. With another prayer, this time to the Mary who was the Mormon god's wife, she mixed and applied a new primer. The drying went more slowly, which she considered an encouraging sign.

While she waited, she turned her attention to the Muses painting, where she would have to perform the same sort of patchwork operation. It turned out that the Muse farthest on the outside was a phantom-faced red-head; with a sense of pleasure, Famke cut her away and set her aside, to be stitched into the gap left by the excised Ruby. She rebuilt the framework smaller and stretched the cut canvas over it. Feeling very clever, she nailed the canvas in place, prick-sewed the red-haired Muse into the center, then spackled over the seam with her new primer. She considered this arrange-ment even more of a triumph than the original.

Now came the most delicate work of all. The Ruby on the new canvas was naked, and Ma Medlock wanted her wearing a frock. She also needed a setting, "something cheerful."

Famke's experience in this area was very limited, but she thought that as the painting would rarely be exposed to anything stronger than seduction-level gaslight, she just might manage something passable. She mixed several tints of white and blue, as she had helped Albert do in the past. Then, painstakingly, she dabbed a filmy gown over Ruby's naked shoulders and bosom. This was very different from painting with mud on her own petti-coat; for one, the canvas was taut, and for another, there were already lines to follow. She managed a passable gown. She wasn't too confident about her ability to shade it properly, so she kept it thin and cloudy, blurring away from the body—the impression of a dress rather than the detailed rendition of one. She left the mournful mask by Ruby's feet and painted a wispy skirt over the legs behind it. Then, with a sigh of relief, she returned to what she knew. All around Ruby and her laughing mask, she painted a cave of ice.

The bigger canvas was hardly any trouble at all; Famke knew Ma Medlock cared little about it anymore. She splashed an aura around the transplanted Muse and tumbled into her borrowed bed with a feeling of a job done as well as her capabilities would allow.

Coughing a little, waiting for dreams, Famke thought that she had rescued something beautiful from the shambles of Ruby's life. The portrait would show very well at the funeral, and as for the painting of the Muses— no one would look closely enough to find a seam there, surely.

Once again, she was Albert's collaborator.

◆ ◆ ◆

Although Sariah Goodhouse and her niece were clearly angry with Famke, Viggo could not complain of their welcome to him. They thought the Wanted poster a very good plan, and while they worked on it they let him sleep in the mud barn, like a hired man. He helped them by making much-needed repairs to the burned part of their house.

Impervious to flame as the mud walls seemed to him, apparently there was enough straw in their composition to smolder like a big hot coal when the fire traveled from the silk hut to the owners' residence. Thus the east side of the house was nearly gone, and Myrtice had had to hang a couple of quilts over the holes in her walls. Viggo saw the lamplight shining through them at night, when he lay in the hayloft trying to sleep and she sat up, ill, or laboring over the drawing that was going to help him find Famke. They were like the stained-glass windows of wealthy Catholic churches he'd heard described at Immaculate Heart.

By a fortunate circumstance, Myrtice had spent two years in the reluctant study of art; it had been a required course at the normal school she'd attended in Georgia, which was also where she told Viggo she had met her husband, Sterling Black, and lost him.

"He was in cotton," she said, avoiding Viggo's eyes. He got the sense that she would prefer not to answer any more questions about her life before this stint in Utah. Probably questions were distressing to women in what Sariah and Myrtice referred to as a delicate condition.

And Myrtice was very delicate indeed; Viggo could see that. Her hands trembled and she perspired, even in this cool autumn weather, as he watched her labor over her ink sketches of Famke. She had a large photograph of Famke posing with the Goodhouse family—standing next to the patriarch, no less—and she kept it propped in front of her as she worked, carefully expanding the ill-defined pale face, enormous eyes, and strange topknot into a head-and-shoulders rendering that she and Sariah found representative. Myrtice was not very good at drawing; but then she said she did not consider the skill proper to the young Saints she taught, and she had not bothered to keep her hand in since returning to the house where she'd grown up. She tore up or crumpled most every sketch before it was finished.

Looking at the photograph from which Myrtice was working, Viggo felt himself pulled to Famke more intensely than ever. He now had three memories of her: the witch at the cauldron, the figurehead on the prow, and this plain, overexposed housemaid. That the last was so ugly and atypical made him the more eager to rescue her. He imagined her adrift somewhere on the vast prairies of the West, or tucked within the folds of a mountainside, probably suffering a loss of memory or a surfeit of shame. Myrtice Black's drawing would be of great help in finding her. Viggo would comb those prairies and hills, showing the posters around every town and nailing them up in prominent situations; surely somewhere someone would be able to tell him something about her.

He and Sariah and Myrtice agreed on the wording of the notice, to be typeset by the same printer who would copy the image:

WANTED

Information as to whereabouts of Ursula Summerfield,
formerly of Prophet City, Utah Terr.
Hair red or black, eyes blue, build slender.
REWARD
Respond to Heber Goodhouse of that town or to any officer
of the law in Deseret County.

"It reads just right," Myrtice said, looking over Sariah's shoulder at the document on Heber's desk.

"Might could bring that correspondent back, however," Sariah said dubiously. "He turned up from Salt Lake not two hours after Brother Goodhouse left again to look for her," she explained to Viggo, "a man calling himself Hermy Noble. He always did have an interest in your Ursula—risked another trip to the hoosegow, coming back here as he did. Of course we didn't tell him anything about her."

Viggo did not understand much of that speech, beyond the fact that another man was looking for Famke. He felt a stab of jealousy. Perhaps this man was her artist, the man who had painted her . . . But there was some comfort to be derived from the idea that he hadn't found her yet, and Viggo had the cooperation of the family.

Myrtice twitched: A gas bubble had escaped. Politely pretending it was a cough, Viggo passed her his rough cotton handkerchief, and she dabbed her mouth with it. He felt the heat coming off her body as she smiled at him more warmly than the favor required.

Sariah was oblivious to what was happening in her background; she held the pen poised over the word *reward*. "I'm not sure we should include this," she said. "Getting these posters printed will cost a small fortune as it is, and we don't have Brother Goodhouse's approval for a reward."

"'Reward' is a general enough term," said Myrtice, tucking Viggo's handkerchief into her sleeve. "It might be the satisfaction of a job well done, of helping a lost soul come home."

"Exactly right." Satisfied now, Sariah laid down her pen, leaving a large spot on the blotter.

Chapter 28

· · · · ·

The traveler will notice that the names of the stations have assumed a
Spanish form, and should he happen to address any of the swarthy men that
chance to be lounging around the stations, he would very likely to [sic] receive
a reply in the language of Hispania. The Spanish spoken is not Castilian by
any means, but is about as near it as "pidgin English" is to genuine Chinese.

STANLEY WOOD,
OVER THE RANGE TO THE GOLDEN GATE

She looks just like an angel," Ma Medlock sobbed into a scrap of black
lawn no less ethereal than the frock in which Famke had clothed the
painted Ruby. "The angel she is now . . ."

The funeral was a splendid affair, as a good segment of Boulder's population came out to see Ruby off. The fair but frail and the grimy miners
agreed: Ma's pride and joy had never looked better than she did nestled
against the auroral satin of her coffin—unless it were in the glistening Heaven
of her portrait. It was a shame to consign the one to the earth, but there was
the other for consolation. The mourners gazed upon the picture after the
burial, while tucking into the baked meats and fruit pies that Ma had commissioned and listening as the young professor played a hymn about the
passage of time. Everyone allowed as it was a wonderful funeral.

In her grief and gratitude, Ma gave the artist an extra ten dollars, and
Famke felt she had recovered much of what she'd lost in the hills of Colorado:
She had the same financial stake with which she'd set out from Utah, something like the same hopes, and, she felt, a valuable new skill. She resisted the
urge to return to Leadville to redeem the tinderbox, but rode instead to
Denver with renewed purpose, which translated to more manly firmness in
her step.

She did not let herself slide into feminine ways when once again she visited Amy Oggle's house. The paint was now dry upon those Muses, too, and
by pressing the girls—almost all turned redheads—to search their memo-

ries, she settled upon what seemed the most likely itinerary for Albert: through mining country and down to the land of the savages.

"You look different with your hair cut," beautiful Jo said wistfully. She ran her fingers through it, almost as if Famke were a prospective customer.

Amy rubbed at a smudge on Famke's cheek. "Complexion's going the way of your hair, too. You need some Eau de la Jeunesse."

"Glycerine, spermaceti, and almond nut cream," Big Kitty translated.

"At a reasonable price," Amy added, and Famke bought a small jar.

The madam said nothing of her feminine earning potential now, but she did permit Famke to take down Albert's picture and paint a few Muses' hair red, and gave her ten dollars for the afternoon's work.

•   •   •

For the next two months, Famke traveled: in train and wagon and on foot, going from salon to saloon to general store, to a nightly pallet in a flophouse where the men around her snored and gassed while she tossed and coughed. Lugging a carpetbag heavy with painter's supplies and Eau de la Jeunesse, with the keepsakes associated with Albert still swelling her secret pocket Down There, she headed first south and then west through Castle Rock, Greenland, Pueblo, Huerfano Station; circled through Hole in Prairie, Rocky Ford, Apishapa; swept through Alamosa, Tirrietta, Servillela. She sought Albert among miners of gold and silver and turquoise, ranchers of cattle and sheep, the Indians and Chinamen and Negroes who served them, and always, always the fair but frail.

Even if there was no direct news of Albert, there was usually word of some artwork. It seemed art had become the currency of the day, and everywhere a local bar or brothel was boasting about its new masterpiece—an oil over the piano, a watercolor in the washroom, a sculpture (but she wasn't interested in those) adding a note of gentility to the red plush salon where girls were auctioned off at so much the hour.

Wandering through those parlors, she studied each picture in depth. Most of them meant nothing to her, and she left before she could be charged for a drink. But when Albert's work was there, she recognized it immediately. She noticed he was painting many warrior women these days; they seemed to be a generally popular subject among the prostitutes who wanted to think of brighter times, for every whore had a nice word to say about armor and swords. But Famke knew, also, that these subjects had always been dear to Albert's heart and brush, so she hunted until somewhere, in some curl of limb or smoke, she found a little castle formed of two letters.

Most significant of all, she felt, was that many of the women—all of the princesses—had red hair. Among the Amazons, she might find long red tresses flowing over one naked breast and into a brief set of armor, so obviously belonging to the Princess Calafia; and the queen of the Valkyries, the goddess Freya, draped the same coppery curls over a shadowy hero.

Albert remembered her. It was clear that he *could not* forget her. So even as she was shoved out of the salons for not hiring a girl, Famke felt a glow deep in her belly; no, deeper than that, down in her bones.

When there was a chance to make money with her new skill, Famke made it. She cut and repainted pictures to their owners' specifications, reflecting changes in taste and personnel; she did an even brisker trade by persuading madams to let her brush on a layer of varnish to seal the paint—a nicety that Albert had apparently felt too rushed to provide often. She undressed the nymphs and Muses, dyed the drab locks golden or red, painted her own blue eyes into the mysterious blurred faces that Albert had said could house the features of girls yet to come. She painted out freckles and brought certain popular figures to the foreground, relegating others to the shadows, and in the dim light of gas globes and oil lamps the seams were invisible.

These diverse gifts with artwork fascinated the girls: Dante Castle took something his older brother had made and thought perfect, and he made something more useful out of it. He so eclipsed his brother that no one noticed if he patchworked a Valkyrie over Albert's ingenious signature. Anyone would rather look at a pretty girl than a silly building anyway.

Once in a long while, Famke painted an articulate shadow around the sex of a girl near the back of the composition. The whores who giggled at the misted-over genitals, as Famke had once done, crowed when they saw this hint of real hair. In Mirage they banded together and presented her with a wreath woven of their own private locks.

"I shall wear it over my heart," she vowed, and then slid it into her pocket to coil with her own long red tail.

For a time, she was happy. Her hopes were strong; the madams paid her decently; the whores did not bore her by describing their trade. And from each canvas, no matter how she altered it, Famke took the comfort of seeing some new beauty in herself, or at least in the ephemeral Famke that Albert remembered: the roundness of her former breasts, the fluid lines of her arms, the once-brilliant hues of her cheeks and eyes and hair. Those insights, as much as anything else, kept her moving forward, even as in each town she whispered a hope that this time, here, she would find her lover still at work, and in each town she was disappointed.

There were delays and complications: a fierce rainstorm that washed track away one afternoon, a fire set in a sculpture-rich parlorhouse the next. A little boy in Box Elder stole her hat, and evidence of the Dynamite Gang was everywhere. Fortunately she had learned to keep the bulk of her money in her secret pocket, where it rubbed against the goose girl's penciled features and blurred her face into complete unrecognizability.

Holding that now-faceless girl, Famke ran her eyes over the graphite shadows and tried to conjure them back to their original crispness. She did not dare try to touch them, not even with the brush she was learning to wield with more confidence. Just before putting the sketch away, she would turn it over and look at the words, which were blurring, too. Some of the letters had already disappeared—

o   *love Fam e*
  ad   *wor* *no gh an* *me, t is pa tin* *da l ng w* *b*
 n cri e
    B

Eventually, the only word Famke could truly make out was "love"—and by then it was almost too painful to look.

Chapter 29

*The electric air excites the nervous systems of newcomers to a high tension,
producing a sort of intoxication of good health, with keen appetite, perfect di-
gestion and sound sleep.*

MOSES KING,
KING'S HANDBOOK OF THE UNITED STATES

The elder tree in the girls' courtyard was losing hold of its autumnal
gold. Every few minutes it shed a pinch of ore as a leaf fluttered
down to the dark earth below, skittering through the square panes
of the old-fashioned window.

Birgit's hands were shaking so badly that she knew she'd tear the thin
paper, which was much weakened and begrimed by its long journey. She
took the time to hunt out her letter opener—plain, functional steel with a
slightly broken tip—and slice open the clumsy gout of sealing-wax. For a
moment the blade reflected the yellow tree outside, and then the letter fell
limply open in her hands.

Dear Mother,

*I think you must wonder what I am doing and where Famke is and the
answer to both is I don't know but I have a few suspicions. I have been in
Amerika five weeks now you know and it is a good country as imagined.*

*But not cosy for finding somebody being so big. I don't think you should
worry she is dead because everybody says she is very* dygtig, *the word they use
is "scheming" which should make you glad. I met the family in Utah and they
are unhappy she is gone but are helping me to find her with some pictures of
her face drawn by the teacher. The husband is away. They seem to be good
people and not like the Mormons we hear about in Denmark. They say she
was happy here so that should comfort you but not so happy she didn't want*

to run away, and maybe she'll come back if she can't find her artist and marry him again. Though I don't know for certain that is why she left. Maybe she realized he was not for her and is trying to return to Denmark, I believe I will find out if I ask at the rail stations. She will need this money which I have been saving because it is hers. My money is in my left boot and Famke's in my right so you needn't worry I will lose any of it.

I am sending you a handbill because I think you might like to see it, none of us ever had our picture taken and it is a good likeness in my opinion even if her hair looks peculiar, it is not in the fashion of women here either but maybe the fashion has changed.

Writing letters is still hard for me in spite of all the pains Sister Saint Bernard took over it.

Respectful wishes,

Viggo of the Immaculate Heart

Birgit stood at the window, gazing with blind eyes into the courtyard. So Famke had moved on; she was no longer with the missionary, perhaps no longer even a Mormon. That must be to the good—or was it? Even after decades in the black habit, Birgit could not muster the hopefulness and trust that came naturally to the young mortician's apprentice. She would have preferred for him to find Famke immediately; she would most have liked to open her arms and find the girl walking into them, borne forward by a swift steamship and a repentant conscience.

But it was not to be, not yet. She must go to the chapel and pray.

Birgit put the letter carefully away in her desk and would have locked it if a key existed. Then, upon reflection, she took the paper out again and tore it into shreds. There must be nothing for prying eyes to find. But that did not much matter; she had already committed every word to memory.

• • •

Viggo was raised by Catholic regulation, according to which each time of day had its particular duty and prayer, and to that groundwork the master-mortician had added scientific method. Thus Viggo was nothing if not systematic: He could not approach any task but in an orderly fashion.

So, as he marched away from Prophet City, he planned a course for finding Famke.

He started by interviewing Doctor Finstuen, the last person to see her before she vanished. "I've already told her husband all I know," said Finstuen, looking askance at the shabby man who could scarcely string together an English sentence, who reeked of camphor and something suspiciously like alcohol besides. "He tried the hospitals and found nothing; I believe the woman has disappeared."

Viggo thanked the doctor and asked him to post the handbill that Myrtice had designed. It was the first posting, and he thought the yellow page showed very well against Finstuen's dark paneling.

With Famke's picture in place, Viggo headed out to the streets of Salt Lake. To be thorough, he first checked the Deseret hospital and a few genteel restaurants—the same places Heber had made his inquiries—but he knew that widening the field would yield the best results. He had the advantage of knowing names Heber had never heard of, or at least that Heber thought insignificant.

A man who paid not one but three visits to Prophet City, and gave particular attention to Famke upon each of those trips, must be significant. Viggo decided to try tracing Harry Noble, and he made the round of hotels on his second day in the capital city. At the Continental, he learned that Noble had indeed been a guest, and—most interestingly—while staying there he had sent an urgent telegram eastward. There was still a record of it in the desk.

"You a Pinkerton?" asked the spotty clerk.

Viggo did not know what that was. "I believe not," he said politely, wondering if he should enlighten the poor man about the complectual benefits of a light course of arsenic.

The clerk evidently decided that Viggo was harmless, for he turned the telegram book around and let him read. The message had gone to a Miss Mudge at the *New York Times*:

Seeking information Albert Castle, painter. Recently arrived U.S. Anything would help.

Viggo concluded that Harry Noble was not Albert's pseudonym; he was a stranger pursuing at least one of the people in whom Viggo had an interest. So, upon leaving Salt Lake, Viggo went where the clerk told him Noble had gone. Denver first: a dauntingly large city, and dirty beneath its smoke-stained dust of new snow. The people there were not particularly helpful, and an invisible hand cleaned out his pocket the first day—he congratulated himself on consigning his money and Famke's to his boots, where the calluses it formed reassured him as to the stability of their wealth. However, the packet of letters to Famke was gone, and Viggo would have a hard time forgiving himself for that.

In a process he was to repeat often over the weeks, he went to every hotel in town to ask about Famke, then Harry, and beg permission to post a handbill. He found Harry's Denver residence within the first day, but the journalist had already departed and there was no news of Famke anywhere Viggo looked, whether hotel or hospital, restaurant or genteel teahouse. And yet he knew she must have been here; and within two days a Bohemian's offhand remark led him to Amy Oggle's place and its spectacular *Nine Muses Inspiring Pleasant Thoughts.*

Viggo detected Famke's eyes and hair in the background of that painting right away, and he leapt to the logical conclusion. With the definite air of a rescuer, which won him no friends among the girls, he pointed to the shadowy Muse and asked to see her.

"Never worked here," Amy said, blowing a speck of stray tobacco from her tongue. "Just a figure of the artist's imagination."

"But very pretty and very nice," the beautiful girl called Jo said eagerly, and Amy sent her off with the first customer who entered.

Viggo was not equal to deciphering the nuances of American speech yet, so he merely asked where Mr. Castle had gone. He thought they might look for Famke together. Amy gave him the same instructions Famke had received the first time: "Go into the mountains. Fair Play, Leadville, Boulder."

As the door shut behind Viggo, she crumpled the handbill he'd given her and said to Big Kitty, who was eating a box of bonbons left by an admirer, "I declare, the next man who comes in here asking about that girl, I'm sending him to Timbuktu."

"Is that what Mrs. Silks is calling her place these days?" asked Big Kitty.

Chapter 30

· · · · ·

And this [Santa Fé] is the historic city! Older than our government, older than
the Spanish Conquest, it looks older than the hills surrounding it, and worn-
out besides.[. . .] Yet, dirty and unkept, swarming with hungry dogs, it has the
charm of foreign flavor, and retains some portion of the grace which long lingers
about, if indeed it ever forsakes, the spot where Spain has held rule for centuries.

SUSAN E. WALLACE,
THE LAND OF THE PUEBLOS

It was not just the graphite goose girl who was fading: Eventually Famke
had to face the fact that she had developed an array of troublesome
symptoms. Perhaps because of the coughing, her throat was always sore,
and she had difficulty speaking; every bone in her body ached from the rig-
ors of travel, and yet she was unable to sleep. Rising from her bed each
morning required all the energy she had stored between the overnight
fevers and chills. Some days it was all she could do to sit on a plush sofa and
gaze, empty eyed, at clusters of canvas warriors and nymphs and hunt for
the castle made of the letters A and C.

"You look peaked, Mr. Dante," at least one *Luder* was sure to say at each
house she visited. And still she continued her search.

As she grew sicker, the girl whom the whores thought was a boy
brought out the maternal in them. They liked to rub Dante's shoulders and
tell him what they could remember of his brother, without revealing that
Albert had never mentioned another Castle. Dante was so slight, so delicate-
looking, that the girls saw him more as a pet than a potential customer.
They imagined they might take him to their beds and stroke his hair and
talk all night, and in the morning be almost ashamed to take his money. But
he never went with any of them. Maybe he was too young or too sick to
have any interest in that area. Maybe he preferred something else; he was
European, after all.

Dante was such a beautiful, ethereal boy that a fourteen-year-old in Manitou fantasized about painting his face with her rouge; he would look as pretty as she, like a great doll grown up. An older woman in Wild Horse thought she might suckle him and thereby restore vitality to a breast that drooped after maulings by miners and ranch hands. So, even without making the trip down the bagnio hall, Famke found her head pillowed against a series of soft bosoms. She was dosed with soothing laudanum and the alcoholic draughts shunned by Saints: Piso's Cure and Dr. King's New Discovery; Bull's Cough Syrup, Schenck's Pulmonic Syrup, and (furtively) Lydia E. Pinkham's Vegetable Compound, "developed by one woman for the complaints of all women." She wasted a day bathing in hot springs that promised relief "not only for respiratory complaints but also for rheumatism, skin diseases, derangement of the kidneys and bladder, and especially all venereal diseases."

None of it brought any change. Her cough and bone-weariness increased. She had waking dreams about worms and knives and needles, dreams of slapping mud into frames for adobe and of stirring enormous steaming pots that made her arms ache all day. Night after night, she fell into a flophouse bed and wept like a kitten, disguising the sobs as snores until she passed into a kind of sleepless stupor.

Only the thought of taking Albert into her arms, and of being taken into his, roused her from exhaustion. Once they were together—*then* Famke would sleep, then she would fatten, and then her lungs and bowels and blood would settle into normalcy. The sooner she found him, the sooner she would enjoy not just the lovely, shimmering feeling of want but also the bliss of painless, feverless sleep and easeful breath. And so she pushed on.

"If you do not like the way that painting looks now," she forced herself to say to each madam, "I can adjust it for you."

· · ·

By the time November readied itself for serious snows and wind, Famke was at wits' end. She spent a long night in Coal Creek, a rough town with a large Indian population, drinking whiskey and thinking she might give up.

"Looking for my brother," she mumbled drunkenly as the saloonkeeper sloshed gray water over a basinful of glasses. "Went away and never . . . wrote a poem, 'Had we but world enough and . . .'" She broke off to cough. "You don't have any boardinghouses here? Only the streets."

"Plenty of strangers come through asking after girls," said the saloonkeeper, shaking water from a glass he'd decided was clean enough. "The sheriff won't allow it. He's got a daughter and a wife in town. Wouldn't tolerate saloons, either, except he likes his drink."

Famke grunted and ran her fingers through her hair. She was mildly surprised to feel that it was dirty and that several strands came away in her fingers. They drifted lazily to the floor.

Feeling conversational, the saloonkeeper leaned comfortably on his elbows. "There was a fellow here a few days ago. Funny kind of cuss, with round bug eyes and hands colored up like a harlot's face on Saturday night. Said he was looking for whores, too, as he had a business proposition beyond the ordinary. Well, the sheriff thought he was some kind of procurer come to corrupt the town's daughters, and he scarce escaped a lynching. I pointed him toward Santa Fé."

While Famke tried to clear her head, the man slid an extra fifty cents from the pile before her, as recompense for his time. "There *was* a lynching over in Crested Butte last week. Folks thought they caught one of the Dynamite Gang and strung him up. Turned out to be some farmer just down from the Dakotas—but the opera house blew up the next morning anyway. The papers said it was definitely the Gang, as they were using dynamite they'd stole the month before . . ."

Famke could bear no more. "You said Santa Fé?"

"New Mexico Territory," the man said. "You'll need a train and a wagon to get there."

◆   ◆   ◆

The old city rose from the valley floor as if the earth itself had heaved it up—which was in some sense the case, as the larger number of its houses were made of adobe, smooth and untextured and even more unabashedly dirt than the walls of Prophet. They were festooned with red peppers and multicolored maize hung out to dry—food that reminded Famke that one cup of milk in a *cantina* wasn't enough to keep a day's hunger away, especially after a bone-jolting thirty-mile wagon ride. Still, she thought she could not manage a real meal, not after the sun and the dust and the biting odors; her throat was throbbing. She rocked on top of a bale of sheep fleece in the back of a rancher's wagon and clutched the malodorous wool for an anchor. She concentrated on staving off nausea by reminding herself how the vomit would sting her gorge on the way up.

At last the rancher set the wheelbrake. They'd reached a wide plaza of patchy naked cottonwood trees and more mud buildings, some of them augmented by wooden balconies and ornamental log pillars. A raven-haired Indian seemed to stand or sit by each one of those pillars, and most looked as tired as she. To think she had once thought them thrillingly dangerous . . .

Dante Castle jumped down, then held a dollar up for fare.

"The houses is a couple blocks south and west of the Plaza," the rancher said, pocketing the coin and jabbing a stubby finger forward. "Marcy Street and thereabouts. I recommend Ethel Comfort's—she's cheap but the job is good."

Famke thanked him and set off in the direction he'd indicated. When she rounded the corner she saw signs for a dozen businesses—Mrs. Comfort's, Ramona Peter's, Esperanza Espinosa's, and more, stretching into unreadable profusion. Where could she possibly start?

Defeated, despairing, Famke returned to the Plaza and found a shop marked *Tienda* where she bought a fresh bottle of Pinkham's—never mind that the Spanish storekeeper looked at her askance. After a long draught of the liquid said to cure all woes that beset the female body—and which did in fact ease her throat a bit, coating it with a viscous layer—she returned to the store for an evening paper. It seemed the easiest way to start, and she could lean against a gas lamp as she began to read.

More reports of the Dynamite Gang; runaway Chinese cooks, weary socialites, and predictions of snow. Word that Mrs. Opal Cinque was the latest in a series of Marcy Street businesspeople to install electrical wiring.

Electric light—like the Carlsberg brewery that had once enchanted Albert; but even such a marvel as that had lost its allure for Famke now. She was about to turn the page when a single word made her read on.

This correspondent is certain that the new means of illumination will make callers take even greater delight in the parlorhouse's collection of paintings, which is justly famous among artistic types. How lamentable that few of the fairer sex will ever see the collection, "and they fair but frail"! This correspondent himself has already paid a visit and considers the collection worth a viewing even by gentlemen who have no other reason for calling there.

They will find in particular one large canvas of note, completed this very afternoon, that features the ladies of the evening. The piece is praiseworthy for its color, composition, and signature: a small castle in which the artist's identity is ingeniously concealed . . .

Famke did not have to read further. She ran for Marcy Street.

Chapter 31

*But all rich people are not shoddies, and all poor people are not socially out-
cast. [. . .] Our rich men are beginning to learn that there are nobler invest-
ments than stocks and bonds; that life has something grander and sweeter
than the pursuit of sordid gain; that he who would leave an honored name behind him must do something for the future as well as for the past, for the public as well as for self.*

SAMUEL WILLIAMS,
SCRIBNER'S MONTHLY MAGAZINE

By now Famke knew that the girls and drinks a man could buy at a parlorhouse cost twice as much as the boardinghouse varieties; they
catered to a different class of customer. She would have liked to dress
better for this occasion, especially as it was almost certain to unite her with
Albert. But she had only the one—male—suit of clothes, and it would have
to do. She wouldn't be wearing it much longer, anyway.

As she ran, she combed her hair with her fingers and tried to wipe the
dust of the road off her face with her sleeve. Watching her, the loiterers
shook their heads, as if they knew nothing good could come of this excitement but couldn't be bothered to do much about it.

They were much more interested when a short man in a green suit came
along some minutes later, handing out cigars and asking about new arrivals
from foreign lands.

"*No sabe,*" each man said in turn, before asking the stranger for a match.

.   .   .

I'm Margaret." The girl at the door dimpled, looking up at Famke beneath
thickly painted brows. She didn't bat an eye at her customer's dusty di-
shevelment but, as if on impulse, hooked her arm through Famke's and

hoisted herself onto tiptoes to add more intimately, "Or Mag, Cracklin' Mag to some. Welcome to Mrs. Cinque's house."

Mag settled back on her heels, looking as gleeful as all the world. She was dark and plump, if a little flat in the chest, and she used the dimples again to considerable effect. Her ruffly red dress was polka-dotted black as if to draw attention to those pricks in her cheeks.

"I am glad to be here," said Famke. She pitched her voice low, though her arm trembled as she drew Mag closer to herself. She felt she needed the physical support from another human being. "I'm looking for—I believe he's here now—my—"

Mag didn't seem to hear. "You may leave your hat." Fetchingly, she snatched the hat off Famke's head and tossed it onto a green malachite tabletop. She pulled Famke forward by the hand. "What's your name?"

"Fam—Dant—*Fanden!*" As the parlor door opened, Famke clapped a hand over her eyes. Under electricity, the room was lit up exactly like the brewery, so bright that the inevitable pink brocade appeared washed out and the mirror at the far end of the room shone like a beacon. It was blinding, ten times as strong as even the brightest gaslight or the autumn sun, and the effect made Famke sneeze.

Mag sighed and handed her a clean handkerchief. "Mrs. Cinque has ordered new light globes, but there's nothing we can do for now, 'less we go back to kerosene. It takes a mighty lot of getting used to."

Famke dabbed at her eyes and blew her nose, then coughed for good measure. Intending to ask about Albert at last, she raised her head and opened her eyes and mouth—and left them open. For there her eyes had encountered herself: as Nimue.

Nimue towered over the rosy satin sofa on which four blondes sat in an inviting row. Or perhaps "towered" was not the word; the nymph had shrunk. Though still relatively large, she was only half her former height, and just the right size to fit between the sofa's arch and the ceiling's plane. But as if in compensation for the picture's loss in height, the cave had unfurled horizontally, stretching into more ice and clouds of mist. Famke recognized that ice—yes, the same swells and points she and Albert had painted in Copenhagen. She could even tell which lump of molten glass had stood in for a given stalactite; Albert hadn't bothered to design new ice for the extra space but had reproduced the earlier spikes as a series instead.

It was quite a lot to have done in the three or four days since he had left Coal Creek; but then, he'd omitted much of the detail for which he'd hoped to become famous. He was painting now like a Frenchman, in broad, fast strokes, and the likenesses were not good. But there was the little AC of which the correspondent had written, swelling the walls of a stalagmite.

There were other changes. Gone were the flowers inside the ice, gone also the elaborately painted frame. And inside the clouds of Nimue's breath, blowing from one end of the cave to the other, was a host of female faces and forms.

Famke's eyes and throat ached. Dimly she became aware that someone was speaking to her.

"... interested in our painting," Cracklin' Mag was saying. "It has a name—*Evening of the Ladies, Whispering in the Breath of a Nymph Called Time.* And see the wee castle in the ice—"

Famke pulled her arm away from Mag and wrapped it around herself. She needed to concentrate on what she was seeing. Other girls within her own breath ... She compared the *Ludere* on the couch to the ones on the canvas— Yes, each painted face was reproduced in a face of flesh below.

Albert had painted whores into *Nimue.* He had made Nimue herself a madam.

"... I'm at the very top, left-hand side, with that little harp thing," finished Mag, then she seemed to pause expectantly. "My head's the biggest."

Famke could only stare at the canvas. Mag's head was indeed the largest; but more than that, Famke noticed now that Nimue had grown considerably fleshier, and her hair was a loud shade of light orange. Really she looked very little like Famke at all ... Famke struggled to swallow the lump in her throat.

There was a breeze as Mag stood on tiptoe again and peered into her face. Famke smelled the dizzying odor of her armpits. "You all right, lover? Need to sit down?"

The other girls slid down the couch at once. A blonde thumped a cushion invitingly, raising a cloud of dust that shimmered in the bright light.

Famke would not speak, lest she begin to cough. She didn't intend to sit or lie down, either. She swayed on her feet, and as she suppressed her cough she felt her face turning blue.

Mag planted her hand on one hip and studied Famke. "You want dosing, maybe some mercury—why, my sister had that very look when—"

"Enough from you, Mag." A tall woman dressed in peacock blue taffeta came forward through the motto-less inner door, and Mag flung herself down on the sofa, lower lip pouting, bosom heaving. This was obviously Opal Cinque. And she was a stout woman who dyed her hair orange.

Famke did not look at the painting again. Instead she watched Opal Cinque screw a cheroot into an ebony holder with a deliberate motion of wrist and elbow. The cold electrical lights made everything look strange and ugly: They faded the madam's hair to a peculiar pale shade and showed up the wrinkles around her mouth, the dirt on the skirting boards, the worn places on the furniture. They showed the difference between the Nimue found here and the one Famke knew so well.

Mrs. Cinque asked for a lucifer, and for the first time Famke noticed that there were other customers, sturdy men in warm suits looking at the shabby boy she made and laughing at him. She noticed, also, piano music playing smartly. It was a tune Albert had sung her once, about a girl who wandered around crying about cockles and muscles or some such things.

Famke was suddenly tired. She dropped down next to Mag, conjuring her own cloud of dust. Her throat felt terribly sore, and she had to dig her heels into the carpet to keep from sliding down the slippery pinkness. There seemed to be too much to remember.

Standing on the ladder before *Nimue*, Albert just below her, pushing her to paint the ice, pulling her down to their bed . . . Famke was not glad to look up and see, reflected in the enormous glowing mirror, an image of herself crowded together with Mag and the three blondes, beneath *another* image of herself—or someone who had long ago been herself—coughing out a pantheon's worth of whorish Muses. If this was the kind of narrative Albert was painting these days, how far apart the two of them had really drifted.

"Albert Castle," she said hoarsely. "I am looking for him."

"Are you." Opal Cinque took a long drag on her cheroot, the very picture of calm. She offered no information.

"Where is he?"

Mrs. Cinque shrugged her shoulders, exaggerated in their blue taffeta and their wreath of smoke. "Your guess good as mine. What's your interest—are you an inkslinger?"

Famke swallowed hard again. "The paper said he finished this afternoon—"

"Papers lie," said Mrs. Cinque. "You must be a pretty poor correspondent, or you'd know that. Clio, give the boy your handkerchief."

Famke took it without thinking and let it ball in her fist. "I am an artist," she said, blinking rapidly. The electricity had power to addle the brains; it was as if the currents in the walls and floors were making her limbs tremble. She felt all the customers and all the girls were staring at her. "Do you wish any change to that painting?"

"Change the painting?" Mrs. Cinque flicked ash into the cuspidor. A wrinkle formed between her eyes as she looked hard at Famke. "Why?"

"I *love* that painting!" Mag declared passionately. The blondes murmured agreement. "I wouldn't touch a line!"

"What is it you want here, my boy?" asked Mrs. Cinque.

"Yes," Mag said more softly, "what do you want?"

Tingling, with a buzz in her head, Famke turned to Mag. She did not know what to do next. Blue eyes looked into brown; uncertainly, Mag smiled. Famke's ears roared, and there was a lump in her throat so large she could not speak.

She thought of something: She took Mag's face in her hands and kissed her. She made it a deep and hungry kiss, the kind the girls of the Immaculate Heart of Mary had given each other, and she tried to spin one of the old stories in her head: *The cottager comes home and finds his house has been burgled . . .* She pushed her tongue into Mag's mouth, probing it, trying to find what Albert had left there—for she was certain in that moment that Albert had kissed Mag, had perhaps even made love to her. So Famke explored the corners of Mag's mouth, looking for traces of Albert, perhaps even traces of herself. Of this new Nimue.

When the kiss was finished, Mag swayed backward and studied Famke even more dubiously. "You sure do that funny."

At that, Famke opened her mouth again—but not to kiss or speak. She opened her mouth because her throat felt hot and full, and because she

needed to breathe and couldn't. She exhaled, and a flood of heat came pouring over her lips.

"Christ and the devil!" Mag tumbled off the sofa. "That's blood!"

The roar in Famke's head grew deafening. It was much easier to slip into
unconsciousness than to reply. She slid down the pink satin slope and
landed in a heap at Opal Cinque's feet.

Chapter 32

The city [Santa Fé] is free from malaria and excessive heat and cold, and from wind and sand storms. It is supplied with pure water and pure air from the mountains surrounding; it has delightful scenery beneath bright sunshine with glorious sunsets; and besides possessing wonderful health-giving properties, it is one of the most comfortable residence cities in the world. This fact is rapidly becoming known and appreciated.

STANLEY WOOD,
OVER THE RANGE TO THE GOLDEN GATE

For long timeless hours, Famke lay pitching and rolling, throwing sweat-soaked covers off her body one moment and burrowing into them the next, after shadowy hands restored them gently to her. She was aware that she was ill and that her throat ached. Sometimes a basin was held under her mouth or her bottom, and at those moments she was very ill indeed; sometimes a spoon forced her teeth to unclench and dribbled a foul, burning liquid—much worse than Piso's or Deseret's or even Lydia E. Pinkham's cure—down her throat. Almost always, she coughed, and the bed rocked like a ship.

Despite this discomfort, there were moments of beauty. Colors pulsed around her—blue, red, orange, rose, dripping from the ceiling and over the sheets, over her body. She was delighted to discover those colors were there even when she closed her eyes; they were stars that burst and spread across her eyelids, butterflies that flew slowly by, trailing clouds of tiny bright feathers. Waves of luscious-hued feeling washed through her, until she could feel her heart beat in every place she could name.

Opal Cinque visited, and the blonde girls, and Mag. Sometimes they brought curiosities: a dwarf dressed in a tiny replica of Opal's blue gown; or a tall girl who had a beautiful face but no arms, and only one leg to hop about on; or a midnight-dark woman who sponged her gently all over, with special care for her underarms and the furrows between her legs.

Sometimes Mag stayed, and the kisses she gave Famke were deep and re-freshing and delicious. They lingered on her lips and suckled there, as Albert had once done, before moving down to pepper Famke's neck, her bosom, the ticklish line below her ribs, the wing of her hipbone, and then—

Famke groaned and pushed the covers away. The dark hands replaced them. An angel with fiery wings lay against her, rubbing her body on Famke's, her wing between Famke's legs. Famke realized they were both naked. A line of print unfurled before her eyes, at the same time read aloud in what she was surprised to recognize as Myrtice's voice: "*When a painting of the nude by its spirit and surroundings directs the mind away from the element of artistic beauty, it becomes vulgar.*" How funny to find Myrtice here. She would have to tell Heber when she joined him at the doctor's office—if only he would keep his nasty worms from gnawing away at Nimue . . .

"*Fanden,*" she whispered.

"Who are you, really?" the angel whispered back, holding her tighter and tighter, till it seemed Famke's ribs must break and her heart pop through her lips.

◆   ◆   ◆

When he'd written to Birgit, Viggo had felt no need to mention the painting he had seen in New York. He had been even gladder of his decision once he reached Denver and saw the first of what, even then, he suspected would be a long trail of pictures featuring the face that had finally grown so familiar as he gazed into the handbill, now printed on expensive yellow paper. He fancied that if she knew her pet's likeness was found in places the like of which Birgit could scarcely have heard, that news would have the power to strike the nun down, to bring her to bed of chagrin, even to kill her. Women were so delicate. Viggo was grateful to have the means of protecting both of those he knew best; all he had to do was hold his tongue.

Contrary to what he might have expected if he'd thought it all out, Viggo found his love for Famke undiminished by the images he now found up and down Denver's Holladay Street and, as he traveled onward, in the bagnios of the smaller towns. They were all enchanting—the Muses, the Valkyries, the nymphs in their caves. Even the pictures' lesser satellites, those bordello denizens, glowed with the reflected light of Famke's unearthly beauty. Viggo could and did find reason to gaze on the images for hours.

"Are you an artist yourself?" asked Mrs. Maud Dempster, spare-boned proprietress of a house in Frisco, Colorado. Her ochre-tinted *Twilight of the Muses* was the talk of the town.

"No," he replied truthfully, "but I do paint people."

As it happened, Mrs. Dempster's back room held a flower fading fast. The madam was relieved to assure herself of Viggo's services and save the expense of sending to Leadville for a more expensive mortician; and so the contents of the carpetbag came in useful at last. He stayed on a day and a half, waiting for the big girl known as Wobbles to expire of what Maud called fever 'n ague but a more practiced doctor might have named malaria—rare but not unheard of in late autumn. When she was finished, he prepared her for her final party.

"May I place the painting in the room where I work?" he asked, with the scrupulous politeness that was endearing him to the prostitute nation. "I can make Miss Wobbles appear as she was painted."

The result, Mrs. Dempster's girls agreed, was better than life, even better than the painting; and Viggo's future was made. All across the mountains he loved, he might earn room, board, and rail passage by restoring a temporary bloom to the fair but frail women who'd fallen prey to a diphtheria epidemic, laudanum overdose, or the violence of the Dynamite Gang. Bungled abortions did him a brisk trade, thanks to rusty wires and a rumor that a baby would leave a mother quietly if she ate fifty or sixty phosphorous matchheads. Without a mortician's system of tubes and pumps with which to drain the bodies, he could not give a complete embalming; but with the camphor and arsenic he carried, he could do enough to make a corpse look appealing for the duration of a dinner and a wake and the flash of a camera, if there was one in town.

The madams who were willing to pay him for the preservation of these girls—their own favorites, surrogate daughters and sisters—were touched that in his zeal for realism and authenticity he wished to follow these artistic models so closely. Some of them already had photographs they tried to foist on him instead, but he always asked for and eventually received private access to the paintings.

"There is no color in a photograph," he learned to explain. "For life to appear we must have color."

Indeed, in those parts of the West, photographs were most often associated with death, for it was only in extremis that most ordinary people thought to have their loved ones' portraits made. The painted portrait was the living art form, which was why the madams covered those pictures with shawls when the first guests filed in for a funeral. Funerals were surprisingly good for business; gazing on the dead made customers appreciate the living that much more, and they buried their sentimental regrets between the legs of the deceased's sister whores. Viggo never quite realized just how valuable his work there was.

One well-read madam was so mournfully gratified by his efforts that she presented him with a box of calling cards identifying the name and profession she thought were his:

Vigo Hart
- professor of the chthonic arts -
traveling

Viggo saved these cards carefully, in the packet with the diminishing stack of Famke's pictures that he was leaving in the towns and houses he visited. He thought he might never give a single one of the cards out, unless he wrote to Birgit again: In their own way, they were beautiful, too, and must be cherished up and treasured. They wove him into the tapestry of Mæka, the land in which beauty reigned supreme, even after death.

Chapter 33

We can not possibly describe the attractions of these resorts. They are at once terrible, overpowering, lonely, and full of indescribable majesty. Amid them all the tourist travels daily, imbibing the life-giving, beautiful, fresh air full of its oxygen to quicken and stimulate the system; the eye drinks in the wealth of scenery, and loves to note the beauties of the wonderful glowing sunlight, and the occasional cloud-storms, and wild display of power and glory.

FREDERICK E. SHEARER, ED.,
THE PACIFIC TOURIST

On the morning Famke's fever broke, she found that the black hands she'd dreamt of were spooning a gruel down her still-burning throat, and Cracklin' Mag was standing at the room's tiny window, tugging at the curtain so as to see into the litter-strewn courtyard outside. The light was dull and gray, like the once-white walls, and the cloud she thought she'd been sleeping on was a lumpy mattress that seemed to have been set on a boulder. There was a terrible smell of hot flesh that Famke hoped was not her own. She inhaled to find out, then choked. Gruel splattered the bed, the walls, and even Mag, who turned quickly and gave a wide pink grin to see Famke awake.

"I knew there was something different about today!" She bounced onto the bed and, heedless of the sticky gruel, kissed Famke quickly on the brow. The black servant had vanished momentarily. "Here you are, awake at last, and your eyes have a look to 'em they haven't had in a while. You see me now, don't you?" She made as if to drop another kiss.

Weakly, Famke turned her head away and coughed. She was confused—this could be a dream, too, or maybe none of it was. "Can you . . . my . . . Albert . . ."

"Shh." Mag laid a butterfly finger on Famke's lips, then touched it to her own, as if she had an itch there. "You've had an awful septic throat. You shouldn't talk much if you can help it."

The dark servant came back with a wet cloth and swabbed Famke's face clean. "Mrs. Cinque she coming"—the woman's accent was nearly unintelligible to Famke—"and she will know what you be."

"Yes, darlin'," said Mag, "tell us who you are." She laughed quickly, her eyes luminous with excitement—or perhaps with the belladonna that some of the fair but frail used to keep their eyes bright. "All we know is you're not the man we thought you were."

Famke was defeated, and too exhausted to think of a new lie. "My name is Famke Sommerfugl." She whispered because of her throat.

The black and white faces exchanged a look. Both wore the same impenetrable expression.

"Fanny?" the servant tried.

"Summer fool?" Mag echoed the immigration agent from New York, and suddenly Famke felt as if she had made no progress at all, as if she were back at that busy, confusing, hopeful day on the dock. Albert had surely left Santa Fé long ago, and there was no telling how many days she, Famke, had lain here.

"What kind name be that one?"

Famke turned her head into the pillow and wept.

She didn't weep long, however, because Opal Cinque turned up quickly, wearing a red velvet wrapper and an air of haste, as if she'd been disturbed in the middle of a transaction. She was puffing away at another cheroot— much as Albert did, Famke thought; but then again, not like him at all.

"So you must be Bertie's girl."

Bertie. What a dreadful name. "You know him? My brother?" Famke didn't want to tell Opal how the smoke bothered her throat. She tried to lie straight in her sickbed and take shallow breaths. "Did he tell you about me?"

Opal gave one of her characteristic shrugs and filled her lungs. "Your brother, is he."

Cracklin' Mag spoke eagerly into the silence: "Imagine our surprise when we picked you up off the floor and found you weren't a customer at all! You could have knocked the lot of us down with a feather. We thought you were

a newspaperman at first—a good number have come by since we got the
'lectric and that big painting—"

"Mag insisted we keep you here, as a special favor to her," Opal interrupted.

"That's right," Mag interrupted in her turn. "I said, 'We can't just turn a
poor sister out in the cold—'"

"Leastways," Opal continued implacably, "not after giving her a kiss, no
charge. We went through your things to find out who your people were, and
your pockets weren't too fat. So we gave you this little back room here. Our
Chinese cook used to sleep in it before he lit out for the goldmines. It's a
dollar a night."

"I'm sure I'm very grateful," Famke said in her best imitation of Sariah,
though the price seemed high to her.

"I found a nice little picture that looks to be of you," Mag said, plumping
up Famke's pillow, "though the features have smeared. Daisy—that's the
maid—washed that little yellow bag. Don't look so rattled—we put everything back in it, and I mended the seams myself. It's right here on this little
table—"

"Fanny," Opal broke in again, as seemed to be her habit, "are you familiar
with a gentleman who calls himself Hermes?"

Perhaps she should have been surprised, but she wasn't. "I have met
him," she said cautiously. Nothing good had ever come of knowing Harry
Noble.

"He came by the very morning before you did." Mag brushed the dirty
hair away from Famke's brow. "He wanted to find out about the painting—
wrote about it for the *New Mexican*. But he asked about you, too."

Opal inhaled one last time and set the stub of her cheroot down in a
little crystal dish. "Ursula Summerfield, he said, Mag. But I suspect it's you
he's after—there can't be too many red-haired lungers calling themselves
Summer in this territory. He said he'd be in town a few days and to
let him know if you turned up. Maybe you're his mistress as well as
Bertie's?"

"Well," Mag said in the voice of one who knows she is speaking reason,
"a girl must make her way through the world somehow, even if it be as a
mistress—or a—"

"What does he want with me?" Famke wondered aloud. It was becoming increasingly difficult to lie still, but at least she could take somewhat deeper breaths now that the cheroot was extinguished.

"We'll find out soon enough," said Opal, with so much smugness that Famke wondered unhappily if *she* considered herself Albert's mistress. "I sent for him soon as I heard your name."

. . .

Harry Noble breezed in wearing the familiar green suit, or perhaps a fresh one cut to the same pattern, and carrying a carpetbag. He'd been on his way to the station when the maid Daisy had found him, panting up and grabbing his arm as if for dear life.

Famke surprised herself by being glad to see him; his was at least a familiar face. Cramped as it now was, the tiny room actually seemed to expand when he entered.

"I'm off to points north," he said grandly, by way of greeting. He took out a cigar, and Famke resigned herself to another suffocating conversation; but he did not light it, merely ran it under his nose and then used it to scratch an itch among the few hairs that remained behind his left ear. "I'm planning a series of features on the Dynamite Gang—all New York's in a frenzy for them. Ladies are wearing dynamite in their hair and twisting their jewels around it. And I have a theory involving those fellows, one that will make for a most ripping tale if I develop it correctly."

"Why did you come looking for me?" Famke asked, squeaking around the wound in her throat. She remembered now why she disliked him. "How did you know to look in this place?"

His eyes grew big; he was clearly delighted with himself. "My dear Miss Summerfield, you gave me all the information I required. Your interest in a certain artist, one who has made a name—or at least a set of initials—for himself painting the women of the West, your appearance in the works of that artist, your visit to my hotel—"

"So you have been hunting me through Albert's pictures." She didn't know why it hadn't occurred to her that someone might do this, when she had been using the same method herself.

"Yes, and very nice some of them are, too. Quite personable. A few, of course, are less accomplished, and some appear to have been laid waste since first they were committed to canvas. I would say the very pressures of the market that has made your A. C. successful have also rendered him corrupt, a slave to the demands of his customers, as prostituted as they—"

"Have you seen him?" Famke asked. She began to cough, but she spoke through it—without bothering to wonder *why* Harry Noble would have taken the trouble to look for her through three territories: "Do you know where he is now?"

Mag was looking at Harry now with indignation, Opal with contempt.

Noble took a deep pull on his cigar. "Before I answer that question, my dear, I must offer you one small reproach. Why did you not wait for me that afternoon in Salt Lake City? I avow, that very morning I had succeeded in tracking down your friend, and I could have told you to look for him at the home of a Mrs. Dixie Holler of Leadville. Telegraphs confirmed his temporary residence in that locality, and a telegram could have held him there for you. You see, if you had not rushed off—"

Famke cried out, then collapsed in a fit of ragged coughing. Mag, who had been clinging silently to a wall while Noble's tale unfolded, brought a glass of tepid water and held it to Famke's mouth while she drank. She even blotted Famke's lips for her.

Harry Noble shot the two of them a calculating stare, then smoothed it over. "Miss Summerfield," he continued, "haste has been your downfall. But I have a question for you now—"

"Do you know where Albert is?"

"I do not know, but I suspect." He stopped and looked at her gravely; Famke got the sense that he was trying to intimidate her. "And there is more that I suspect, and it is this that I came to ask you . . ."

He paused to enjoy some suspense, and she demanded, "What is it, then?"

Harry Noble drew himself up to his full green height. "Are you, Miss Summerfield, in any way associated with the Dynamite Gang?"

Mag gasped and pulled slightly away from Famke. Even Opal Cinque let a look of surprise flit over her features. Harry laid his unlit cigar down in the little dish and ran his hands up and down his sleeves, like a cat grooming itself after swallowing a bird.

"Why do you ask me that?" It took Famke a moment to realize she should also say, "No. I do not know them. I am not *associated* with them."

Harry Noble would have paced the room like a triumphant general if there had been space enough. "There has been a most intriguing coincidence between your travels—for, yes, I have found news of you in one place or another—along with the work of the infamous Gang. In brief, Miss Summerfield, I have placed you both in the same townships on several occasions. Leadville in particular—did you have anything to do with the explosion that destroyed Mrs. Holler's boardinghouse?"

Opal Cinque and even Mag looked at Famke accusingly.

"No!" she fairly shouted in indignation, or would have shouted if she'd had the breath to do it. "I went there to look for Albert—and some boys stole my money—I had to sell my nicest thing to go onward—"

Harry Noble held up one plump pink hand. "Do not fret, Miss Summerfield. I am merely gathering information. I have not informed the law as to my suspicions, although"—he reached into his vest pocket—"these notices have naturally given me pause for thought."

He drew out a large sheet of yellow paper and unfolded it. Famke read one enormous word, WANTED, and recognized a crude drawing of herself.

"What is that?" she asked, but the answer was perfectly obvious.

"There were several incidents of vandalism in Prophet City around the time of your departure," Noble informed her, not ungently. "Shall I share my theory? I consider this to be the moment. I think . . ." He paused to finger his side-whiskers. ". . . I am almost certain, in fact, that this gang is *not* a band of angry miners, as some correspondents would have us believe. I think—they are orphans." He picked up the cigar again and stuck it between his teeth, grinning widely.

"Orphans?" Famke's voice trailed upward.

"Orphans?" Mag and Mrs. Cinque laughed.

"Unhappy orphans, clearly, left as parentless as yourself. Now I shall explain. There have been several incidents on mercy trains heading west—ministers thrown out of immigrant cars, trains deserted, dynamite stolen on its way to mines. I have put two and two together and come up with a most spectacular sum: The orphans have formed a small army, and they are setting explosions where they will most trouble the wealthy folks who refused to adopt them!"

Harry looked around the room at the three women. Clearly he expected a reaction. "Well?" he prompted them. "Is that not splendid material for my features?"

"It's a story, for certain." Opal scratched her red-wrapped elbow.

"Where do you think Albert is?" asked Famke.

Chapter 34

. . . . .

For strait is the gate, and narrow the way that leadeth unto the exaltation and continuation of the lives, and few there be that find it.
—PEARL OF GREAT PRICE 132: 22

Harry Noble asked the other women to leave the room then, and he leaned in close to Famke and spoke in a half-whisper.

"A most splendid painting was sold at auction in Denver last month," he said. "One of your Albert Castle's finest; an early work, a sister to the canvas that hangs in Mrs. Cinque's parlor now. A much larger sister she is, being at least seven feet tall and sold at a hundred dollars a foot; she is called *Vivien, Betrayer of Merlin.* I interviewed the wily auctioneer, Royal Barnes, who attests he acquired her in New York with the idea of moving her west. In these benighted hills, men are more likely to buy what he calls buckeyes and potboilers; obscure works by unknown artists, Miss Summerfield. This *Vivien* was bought on behalf of a hos—"

"I don't know anything about that painting," Famke interrupted, "and I don't care to know now. Tell me where you think Albert is!"

Before he answered, Harry Noble bit his tongue elaborately, the same gesture a snake might have made; but Famke did not notice. She was listening hard. She heard him say that he could not be certain as to where Albert had gone: Both Albert and Dante Castle had doubled back on their own paths so many times that he'd never been able to sort out exactly when and how frequently, for example, each of them had visited Denver; but there was more than an even chance that, wherever Albert was now, before long he would be joining his painting—which was now in a place called Hygeia Springs, California.

"The buyer is as rich as Croesus"—Famke did not know what that meant, and she didn't ask—"and he owns a mountain that has yielded more gold than most miners dream of. In fact, his wealth comes from the miners and not so much from their gold, as his father, who bought the mountain, rented out the right to mine it and the water with which to sluice the diggings. He made his first fortune before the gold gave out. And now his son is making a second fortune with—"

"Tell me about *Albert*."

"My dear impatient Miss Summerfield, the story goes that this son, once prey to the very same lung fever that plagues yourself—"

"I don't have a lung fever," Famke said. "Cracklin' Mag said it was septic throat."

Harry Noble raised his eyebrows but refrained from comment. He also stopped his story midstream and stood as if waiting for her to prompt him to continue.

Famke did not notice, for her mind was racing. "And this man has sent for Albert?"

"If he has not precisely sent for Mr. Castle, it is almost certain that a painter whose work has fetched such a sum will seek out the man who paid it and see if he is willing to pay more. Your 'brother'—lover, employer, whatever he may be—will surely visit soon and likely stay."

Famke did not respond to the obvious question in Noble's speech; she would not explain her relationship with Albert to him or to anyone. Pressing hard against the Chinese cook's flat pillow, she chewed on her lip and tallied up what might remain in her pockets after Mrs. Cinque had extracted the dollar a day for room and board. How long had she been here? One day? Three? No one wanted *Evening of the Ladies* changed, and anyway, her canvas patchwork would not show well under electric light . . . California would be a long journey at a steep price . . .

"*Hvad behager?*" she croaked, realizing Noble had spoken further. She had virtually no voice left, and her mind and body were exhausted from this conversation. "What did you say?"

"I asked you," he said in a voice so quiet that she actually shook her head and checked to be sure a new man had not entered the room, "if you would accept my protection for the journey there."

◆   ◆   ◆

The first weak snow had come early that year, though as far as Myrtice knew, thus far it had fallen only in Prophet City. Snow lay now over the red-and-brown hills of the Goodhouse place like the talc she'd spilled on her dresser and hadn't seen a need to wipe up yet. Maybe there was no snow anyplace but around this one particular house; she had no means of going elsewhere to find out, and soon it would be improper for her to leave the house even for weekly worship. She would miss the Christmas celebrations in Salt Lake; but perhaps that was best, for the strictest Mormons did not observe the holiday, and Heber and Sariah had always been strict.

So she slouched in the window with her belly pressing against the glass, and she stared moodily out at the snow while she unscrewed the lid of her arsenic jar. She licked an index finger and collected some of the powder, then licked the finger clean again.

This was of course not exactly her arsenic jar but Viggo's, and yet she was so certain he would not return to claim it that she had taken to carrying it around in her apron pocket and having a taste now and again during the day. Some women in the part of Georgia where she was born and where she'd spent those useless years in normal school were said to eat dirt while they were breeding. Myrtice had never seen anyone actually doing that, but she could understand it. There was something deeply satisfying about a bitter taste, aside from the fact that this particular powder would make her complexion clear and creamy. She had had the most embarrassing trouble with spots since becoming pregnant; it was a wonder that nice Mr. Viggo had been able to tolerate looking at her.

"Myrtice, you'll make yourself sick with that junk," her aunt had scolded her that very morning.

Myrtice told herself she simply did not care. Arsenic was neither stimulant nor relaxant, and if she did fall sick she could take to her bed and no one would notice. Heber was gone chasing Ursula and there was no telling when he'd be back; Viggo had gone, too. Any day now the Goodhouse women could expect to hear news that one or the other of them was enfolding Ursula in his arms and carrying her off to enjoy the full pleasure of his attentions. It had been weeks since they'd had a letter from either man, and Viggo's had been incomprehensible, something about the yellow handbills and women dead of diphtheria.

"You don't need to be thinking about your complexion anyhow," Sariah had concluded. She looked at her niece uncertainly, and with more tenderness than her tone had conveyed. True, arsenic wasn't strictly forbidden, but if it was used in Viggo's work Sariah didn't think it could lead to much good.

No, there was hardly any reason for Myrtice to bother with her complexion, except that she had to look at herself in the mirror when she put up her hair. She was still doing that, at least, like a proper Saintly wife with a view to hygiene. She took another tiny dab at the powder.

"Cousin Myrtice?" It was Sariah's youngest daughter, Miriam, the plain and stocky one who resembled Myrtice herself. "Mama says you're to come downstairs directly and help her with the dusting. She broke one of the little coffins this morning and she's in a powerful mood." Miriam looked at the jar. "What's that?"

Myrtice offered her a bitter fingertip. "Taste."

Miriam did, and she made a face. "Heber the younger says some crazy likings take hold of ladies when they're in a condition."

Myrtice's spirits were too depressed even for scandal or umbrage at that remark. She looked out the window again, expecting the satisfaction of seeing her mood reflected in the landscape.

But now there was a new interest to the setting. Coming down the road to the house was a four-wheeled buggy, one as heavy and black as the weeds Myrtice had been wearing this last year. Her heart began to beat fast, her stomach to churn; she sent Miriam to her mother with a sharp word.

Every Mormon knew what a buggy like that would be carrying: men to strike fear into the bosom of every participant in a celestial marriage. That, Myrtice told herself as she lurched for a basin in which to vomit, was the buggy of a U.S. government agent.

• • •

Harry had given Famke money to buy some decent clothing, but she didn't see as it mattered terribly where she got it. She made sure she had her secret pocket tied around her waist—sketch, newspaper clippings, lucifers, a great emptiness where the tinderbox used to sit, a nice heaviness from the coins Harry Noble had left her—and drew the top blanket from her bed around her like a cloak. Barefoot and still quivering from her illness, she took the steps one by one and entered the girls' hallway from the back stairs.

She paused to listen. It was early yet, and from the noise she surmised that all the girls and Opal were in the parlor, listening to the professor's piano and entertaining the evening's first customers; chatting and giving the men an illusion of real friendship and delighted conversation. Famke was safe. She found the room assigned to Mag—the name painted on the door and surrounded in forget-me-nots too reassuringly clumsy to be Albert's work—and stepped cautiously inside. She had no idea what Mag would do if she found Famke there.

Mrs. Cinque's place was so nice that the girls had real oak furniture in their rooms: not for their own enjoyment, Famke realized, but to give their customers the illusion, again, of comfort and refinement. The door of Mag's wardrobe creaked under the weight of its mirror, and when it opened, a strong scent of stale perfume, alcohol, and smoke assailed Famke's nostrils, along with something else that could be described only as the scent of Mag.

The smell awoke the memory of feverish dreams, and Famke sat weakly down on the bed for a moment. She would never know how real those dreams had been or if she'd ever given Mag more than that one desperate kiss the first night in the parlor. Considering how ill she'd been, Famke rather doubted so; and anyway there could have been no harm in it.

Mag aside, Famke had to get to Hygeia Springs, California, as soon as possible; Albert would be arriving any day, and he might leave just as quickly. So she got up and plunged into the soft, bright fabrics, clawing through till she found what she wanted: a relatively plain dress of plum-colored silk, with a ruffled skirt and a high collar to the basque. When she felt its softness, she understood why Heber and Sariah had devoted themselves to cultivating the worms that produced it. Fortunately, Mag was long-waisted, and the pieces fit together even on Famke's taller frame. The Mormon underwear was, of course, gone, but Mag had plenty of under-things too—corsets and corset covers, bloomers, and camisoles lined with starchy ruffles that Famke concluded must be the source of Mag's nick-name. There was a definite crackling noise as she drew the neck string tight and pushed the ruffles into place.

Famke mourned the loss of her own pretty round breasts, but at least there was this way to fill out the frock she'd chosen. Once she was with Albert again, she would eat and regain her curves; for now, the corset made her waist so small she could span it with her own hands, and it gave a wel-come support to her spine as well.

Famke would arrive in San Francisco as a lady, with gloves—she found them in a drawer—and a parasol, a straw bonnet, and an embroidered shawl. She felt some qualms at taking Mag's only overcoat and sturdy outdoor shoes, but she had to keep warm; she could see beyond the window that snowflakes were already spinning around the gas lamps.

Ladies had to coif their hair. The red curls were just long enough now to make a modest knot at the base of her neck, and she used some of Mag's heavy hairpins to do it. She would have liked to fasten a glittering bee or butterfly over her ear, but she wasn't sure a lady would do that. She must hope not to attract notice.

When she felt her ensemble was complete, she studied her reflection in the mirror. She twirled the parasol—black silk trimmed with tassels—and the waft of perfume and smoke blew wisps of her hair about. She added a matching black net purse with a long tassel and turned herself around slowly, thinking of those splendid Americans on the New York dock. Mag's skirts showed a bit too much ankle, and Famke hadn't been sure how to put on the bustle, but she thought she'd done well enough. The wire cage of it slapped first her back, then her thighs, when she bounced up and down. It seemed secure.

She reminded herself that Harry would be waiting for her at the Santa Fé depot next morning. She would have to walk all the way there—tonight, right away. She tried taking a few steps as an American lady, eliminating the masculine saunter and mincing instead. It did not seem too difficult; this was what Sariah had drilled into her, after all. Famke could play the part.

Just as she was about to leave the room, she met her own eyes in the mirror and was startled. She realized she'd been avoiding them, and with that realization she steeled herself to confront what had become of her face. She stepped up to the glass and studied herself. Where was Albert's Nimue?

She found that when she regarded herself as a stranger, she bore more resemblance to the artist now than to the nymph: With the loss of flesh, her eyes bulged in their sockets, her brows were set in a masculine line, and her nose had risen into prominence. Of course, *she* thought Albert was handsome, but did she want to look like him? Did she want him to see her as a reflection of himself?

There were a few things she could do to rectify the situation. Her former hectic flush was gone, a blue-white pallor in its place; but she might pinch her cheeks and bite her lips and be glad to see there was enough blood left in her to redden them. She put some of Mag's lip-rouge in the purse, just in case. Then she dabbed some Eau de la Jeunesse—Mag had a bottle, too; perhaps all the girls did—onto a finger and used it to lift her eyebrows into a nymphly arch. She smiled.

Her face grinned fearfully back at her. The teeth looked far too big.

Famke closed her eyes and thought hard. She remembered cold, ice, the sight of her round breasts bobbing as she clutched the ceiling slope and sailed upon Albert. In her natural state she was beautiful. She told herself that for now, she had done the best she could: She looked as much like the original Nimue as possible. Everything would be set right when she saw Albert again.

Famke gathered herself together to step out the back door and into the frosty night of snowflakes like tiny kisses. Almost as an afterthought, she took out a twenty-dollar gold piece and laid it on Mag's dresser, for all the world as if she were a male customer; she had after all arrived in that guise, though she was leaving as a lady. Then she closed the door and stepped lightly toward the main road, feeling her breath come easier in the cold air. A train would leave for Arizona at 8:12 p.m.

Lying in the Chinese cook's bed that afternoon after Harry had left, Famke had seen no reason to wait for Harry and every reason to avoid him. He'd already listed the trains for her and told her to choose the one she thought best; it was an easy matter to select a different train now and follow the route he'd sketched. She made the depot in good time.

She was so pleased with herself that she failed to notice the ticket agent's critical look—for it was unusual to see a woman who carried nothing larger than a purse when no man, porter or friend, followed her with a valise. She bought a ticket and climbed into the train, happy in her first silk dress and the prospect of resuming a life of art in a big city. She coughed into a handkerchief and threw it recklessly out the window.

.4.

ANGEL IN THE HOUSE

'Twas a cure
He had not ever named
Unto our kin lest they should stint
Their favour, for some foolish hint
Of wizardry or magic in't [. . .]
I bade him come that night. He came;
But little in his speech
Was a cure or sickness spoken of,
Only a passionate fierce love
That clamoured upon God above.

DANTE GABRIEL ROSSETTI,
"THE BRIDE'S PRELUDE"

Chapter 35

· · · · ·

It is a dreadful pity that old cities will burn down and be rebuilt, and that all cities must have such a monotony of repetitions of blocks of houses. By the end of another century there won't be an old city left anywhere in the world.

HELEN HUNT JACKSON, "DENMARK," IN
GLIMPSES OF THREE COASTS

The maid who opened the front door was plump, pale, and spotty of complexion; worse yet, she smelled of cat. Mother Birgit wondered why a fastidious man, such as she presumed Herr Skatkammer to be, and his housekeeper tolerated this indication of personal slatternliness. Perhaps the housekeeper had a damaged olfactory sense; it was only natural, after all the caustic soaps and oils she must have inhaled in her career.

Birgit drew herself to attention. The maid was looking at her suspiciously, as she must look at many black-robed Catholics who came to the door seeking Herr Skatkammer's favor. Perhaps the girl was a Lutheran.

Reminding herself that she was Mother Superior, Birgit held her breath and gripped her basket hard. It required all her courage and sense of purpose to say, "I have heard the master is ill. I would like to bring him these gifts from the children of the Immaculate Heart, to whom he has been so generous."

The maid chewed the inside of her cheek suspiciously, but nonetheless she opened the door and allowed Birgit into the foyer. "Wait here." She vanished, to be heard from soon afterward with heavy steps that could not be muffled no matter how thickly carpeted the stairs.

Standing in the foyer, Birgit had time to study Herr Skatkammer's collections of shadowboxed beetles and butterflies, fossil ferns, and artifacts related to a mummified crocodile. They all bore a layer of dust and ash that put Birgit distressingly in mind of the death that the Catholic network reported was imminent, though she took it as a good sign that much of the anteroom was occupied by several large wooden crates. These presumably contained more collections looking for a home and thus indicated that the owner had not yet given up on life.

It seemed that on restless nights Herr Skatkammer was in the habit of enjoying a cigar and a collection of rare prints in bed. Two weeks ago, the inevitable had at last occurred: The master fell asleep, and by the time his housekeeper had detected the smoke, Herr Skatkammer was nearly a lost cause. His bed was a mass of black feathers and cotton, and he himself was covered with blisters and char. The burns were so painful that Herr Skatkammer begged the doctor several times to kill him, as he seared the wounds shut by burning them further with irons.

One of Birgit's informants had hinted that the ephemeral collection was something scandalous, pictures of men and women from the East doing things no nun should know of; but Birgit hardly believed it. Herr Skatkammer was known to be a most upstanding gentleman.

"I have brought you some elderberry wine," she said to him when at last the plump maid showed her into the sickroom. She peered into the shadows at what must be the bed, presided over by the housekeeper's dark shape. "It is both nourishing and soothing."

Birgit had met Herr Skatkammer only once before, when she came to arrange for Famke's employment; and if she did not know that he alone occupied this brocaded bedroom, she certainly would not have recognized him now, like this. He was lying on his back, wrapped in bandages nearly up to the eyes, and about him there clung an odor of burnt flesh. The pale blue irises glinted as he struggled to look at her.

Birgit closed her eyes a moment and, as was so useful, imagined Skatkammer as one of her orphans. She whispered a prayer for his recovery and finished out loud: "There is wine jelly as well." She set the basket down, fished out a bottle and jar, and held them up where he could see them.

Frøken Grubbe leapt from her seat at the bedside and took the items out of Birgit's hands. "Herr Skatkammer is on a restricted diet," she said reprovingly. She was so thin and her face so lined with shadows that Birgit guessed she must have been spending all her time in the sickroom. A mustache showed up startlingly dark against her white skin.

Birgit addressed herself to the housekeeper. "These foods are made of the purest ingredients, from Immaculate Heart's own trees, and the jelly is of an old recipe recommended for invalids. I boiled it myself." She did not need to point out that there could be nothing wrong with the gifts of a convent; her dark habit and dangling rosary communicated as much for her.

Herr Skatkammer wheezed. "I—am gratified to see you, Mother. A most fortuitous—a welcome surprise." It cost him some effort to speak at all, for the heat of the fire had blistered his lungs; Birgit heard the liquid gurgling like a gutter deep inside. She was surprised when he managed to draw together breath enough to say, "Grubbe, you may—go now. I want to talk to the Mother—alone."

With a disapproving shake of the head, Frøken Grubbe went, taking the convent basket with her. Birgit replaced her in the bedside chair, where the smell was nearly suffocating; she, who was so skilled with corpses and sick children, itched to unwrap Herr Skatkammer's bandages and see what she could make of the wounds beneath. She had to remind herself that he surely had the best of doctors, and it was not her place to interfere in this way.

There could be no harm, however, in smoothing a gray wisp of hair from a patch of brow that had miraculously remained unburnt. When she did so, Skatkammer looked at her with tears of gratitude—so happy, she thought, for the small mercies. "Is there something you need from the Church?" she asked in the voice that she used for soothing agitated novices.

He seemed to feel there was no time for niceties. "That housemaid you sent me," he said. "Ursula. I am told—she was once an artist's model."

Birgit tucked her hands within the folds of her skirts and allowed them to clench each other. "That may be true," she said, her voice and face carefully blank.

Skatkammer would not have noticed if she'd been livid. The pale eyes blinked rapidly. "Do you know where she is?"

Birgit decided there could be no harm in admitting, "I believe she has gone to America." Thinking of Viggo's letter, which had been remarkable in its lack of real information, she stretched the truth slightly and said, "She has gone to join her artist. They are to be married."

"Ah."

With all the bandages, it was impossible to read the wounded man's expression. In the long pause that followed, the housekeeper's voice scolded someone on the floor below, but Birgit could not make out her words.

"I have also heard"—Skatkammer wheezed damply over the aspirated sounds—"that there exists a marvelous painting of her. A barefooted nymph. In a forest of ice."

Birgit chose her words carefully. "I have never seen such a painting," she said, but the image Famke had described to her flashed in her mind: naked but for a nightgown, arms upraised; hair streaming, breath steaming. The thought of it scorched Birgit with shame.

"I read of it in the papers," Skatkammer said, as if winning an important point.

Red-faced but carefully erect, Birgit said, "Naturally Immaculate Heart did not know of Ursula's activities, nor do we approve of—"

"I know that painting has gone to America as well," Skatkammer cut in with an invalid's imperiousness. "But it—has to come back. I want to buy it—I am thinking of starting a collection of art," he added, as if to justify himself to the nun.

Looking around at the already crowded walls, Birgit rather doubted that a new collection would be possible without building another wing onto the house. But she said, "I know considerably less about this painting than you do."

"That doesn't matter now. I can do nothing as I am, and someone—must help me find it." His eyes were leaking into the bandages, where surely the tears would sting the tender skin; Birgit took out her clean, coarse handkerchief and dabbed gently at the lower lids. Skatkammer took advantage of this intimacy to whisper, "Help me." Even his breath smelled burnt, blowing hotly on her face. "I have no faith in the Grubbe woman."

Birgit sat back and tucked the handkerchief into her sleeve, hoping that her face did not show how troubled she felt.

Chapter 36

· · · · ·

At or near the mines you will find the mountain air exhilarating enough to persuade you [. . .] to make a prolonged stay.

CHARLES NORDHOFF,
CALIFORNIA: FOR HEALTH, PLEASURE, AND RESIDENCE

Famke shivered, waiting before a strange door until at last a maid might open it. Beveled glass panes had been set like diamonds in white iron filigree, and the air in front of it glimmered dizzyingly with refracted light. In fact the whole house struck her as peculiar, made entirely of glass and iron and steel, with so many domes and minarets that it looked like something Albert would paint in one of his fantasies rather than the residence that a helpful shopkeeper down the mountain had assured her it was. Even stranger, there was a little white palace, or possibly a church, off to one side of the building, and a strange animal clamor in the forest beyond. Famke put one hand against the jamb and was surprised to feel it was warm, for although there was no snow in these mountains as yet, the day promised a frost. She hoped someone inside would offer her a cup of hot tea.

The knob turned, and the door swung open. Famke jumped back. The girl who stood confronting her now was slender and small, and she had the smoothest skin and narrowest eyes Famke had ever seen. Wearing a strange sort of short gray dress over wide gray trousers, the girl clutched the knob in one doll-sized hand, wobbled on feet no larger than Famke's fist, and asked, "How you come in?"

It took a moment for Famke to make sense of the question, and in that time she coughed deeply and dirtied one of the cheap handkerchiefs she had bought in the Phoenix station. "I came on the stage." She could manage only short sentences. "From Harmsway. I walked from the village and climbed the fence. I am here"—she had to pause and soil another corner of the handkerchief—"for the painting."

"Pain-thing?" The girl's porcelain face wrinkled in puzzlement, though Famke thought she was shamming or perhaps making a joke. The face remained a smooth mask.

Famke leaned forward a bit and peered into the foyer, which was if anything brighter than the sunshine outside. Walking up the graveled drive, she had thought the house was painted green; but now she saw that the impression came from a profusion of plant life inside—palm trees and vines with complicated flowers—especially striking since what grew on the hillside had turned mostly brown and gold for the winter. This did not look like a house that would hold a large painting, and Famke saw no evidence of one in the foyer.

All the way across the west and into California—Albuquerque, Deming, Benson, Fort Yuma; up to San Bernardino, down to San Luis Rey, the slow ride on the eastern spur to Harmsway—the wheels of the train had spun out one name: *Hygeia Springs. Hygeia Springs.* The stagecoach wheels had jolted the name into her bones. Now at last she stood on the doorstep of Ed Versles, the man who essentially owned the town, the man whose father had founded it and built this otherworldly palace in which to live. She would not accept defeat here.

"There is a painting and a painter inside," she said stubbornly. "I am here to see them."

The girl—was she mistress? housekeeper? someone's wife?—pointed back the way Famke had come. "Patient in town. Hospital." She drew out the *s* sound: *hosssssspital.*

"Yes, it was bought for a hospital, but it was delivered here. Several people told me—"

Now a second woman joined the first, dressed just like her in a gray tunic and wide pants but, if anything, even lovelier in the face. "No visitor," she said firmly, and she shut the door.

• • •

Famke had to wait a long, long time for the master to come home. She sat
by the graveled drive on the hillside, out of the maids' sight, and
wrapped herself as warmly as she could in Mag's silk dress and wool coat.
She wouldn't have thought California could be so cold and damp . . . She
wondered where she would sleep tonight, for she was nearly out of Harry
Noble's money, and there were no flophouses for ladies who dressed in silk.
She told herself not to think about it, to trust in Albert instead. She had almost found him—she felt it in her bones, in a pricking there, and in her
chest, where the worms seemed to be chasing the old glass splinters around
and gobbling them hungrily.

After some time, fatigue got the better of Famke, and she entered a
dreamlike state in which she thought she saw impossible things around her.
She watched a family of deer no bigger than dogs as they picked their way
delicately across the yellow grass; when they noticed her, they startled and
showed long gleaming fangs—tusks, rather—then streamed for the naked
trees nearby. From somewhere among those trees came a loud but muffled
roar as of some wild beast. She closed her eyes, and when she opened them
she saw, in the distance downhill, a strange little horse covered in bold black
and white stripes. It tore hungrily at the grass before making copious water
upon it. When she looked again, the horse was gone.

The sun was low and red in the sky before she heard hooves crunching
on the gravel drive and knew the elusive owner had come. She pushed herself off the ground with some difficulty and shook out her skirts, telling
herself that surely a man who loved a painting enough to pay a hundred
dollars a foot for it would be glad to meet its subject and help reunite her
with the artist.

In the fading light, it was hard to make out anything but the vague
dark shape of a rider and horse fused together, like the mythological men-
horses Albert had occasionally sketched. They stopped in front of her without any sound beyond the hoofsteps and a final *chuff* of the horse's breath.

Famke was too tired to be anything but blunt. "I am here about your
painting," she announced without preamble. "The one you bought for your
hospital. I am the model."

The man was silent a long time, until Famke became almost afraid. The horse danced nervously beneath him, but she held her ground.

"You have made a mistake," he said at last.

"This is no mistake." She drew herself up as tall as she could, despite the stiffness in her limbs. "I am the model for Nimue—for Vivien—and I am looking for the painter. He is my brother." She felt the sun's last warmth on her face, and she pulled off Mag's hat and let the red light blaze in her hair. She held her shoulders back and her chin up, just like Nimue's, but nevertheless she heard the man say,

"My picture does not look like you."

The blood drained from Famke's head. Her ears buzzed, and she knew she might faint. In desperation, she admitted, "My—looks may have somewhat changed in the last year."

The black figure glanced up toward his house, the glass panes of which were making it into a giant lamp, magnifying the light inside and casting a net of illumination over the trees and grass that surrounded it. She saw the outline of a long, straight nose and rather full lips.

When he spoke he seemed to voice the words that came first to his mind. "The figure in the painting has yellow hair and a Grecian nose. She is nothing like you. And I don't know where your brother is, either," he added as an afterthought.

Famke coughed a little but didn't need a handkerchief. Unconsciously, her hand groped for the man's stirrup. "May I see it?" she asked. "I have come so far . . ."

"But it is not a remarkable picture," he said.

Famke's hand dropped. This was almost the worst thing he could have told her.

He explained, "An agent bought it for me at auction, and I don't much like it. It shows no sense for nuance."

Famke thought of the hours in the Nyhavn studio, how they had stretched into weeks and months as Albert painted each little square with his hair-thin brush. She said, miserably and by reflex, "If you want the picture changed, I can do it. For a reasonable fee."

"Still," the dark man concluded, as if he had not heard her, "I suppose there is no harm in letting you look." With a sudden gesture of gallantry, he climbed down from the horse and offered his arm to Famke.

As Famke ascended the hill for the second time that day, she was aware that her host was adjusting his gait to hers, that he walked slowly and restrained the impatient horse in order to accommodate her. She was grateful, however, that he did not expect her to make conversation; she didn't have the strength to offer an excuse for her lethargy, to mention the altitude or her long journey and guide his attention away from that troublesome cough that punctuated every third step or so.

For his part, Edouard Versailles was glad that the woman did not require him to speak, either. He was not accustomed to genteel female company, or indeed to company of any sort; it made him nervous, and he hoped that the stranger could not tell that his arm trembled as it supported her, that his feet stumbled even as he guided her steps. He was wretchedly aware that what he'd said to her had sounded rude, and yet he could not think how he might have expressed himself any better.

It had been a long day in "Hygiene"—so called locally because the inhabitants had butchered the name Hygeia Springs much as they had done his own. This trip down the mountain had been a necessary exception to Edouard's usual rules of solitude and silence, and it had exhausted him. In fact, he had begun to wonder if perhaps he had been rash in founding this hospital—but then again, to reserve the secrets of his cure to himself would have been avaricious. Thus he had resolved to keep private only the house and the grounds with their menagerie, and he had made these bounds clear to his servants, who had always been so obedient in the past.

He would, of course, ask them how this red-haired wraith had managed to enter his sanctuary; and yet he could not even find the words to pose her the same question, let alone to send her away. He could scarcely admit to himself that he was eager to let her inside, to see how she looked in the light, to put a visual diagnosis to her pronounced chest-rattle.

This desire to look at another person was unusual; Edouard Versailles rarely even saw his servants, the men he'd saved from slavery on the railroads, the girls he'd rescued from the dreadful cribs of prostitution in San Francisco's Chinatown. He valued them all precisely for their ability to make themselves invisible. So when he tied the horse to its hitching post, he knew a ghostly groom would lead it to the stable; and as he came up the steps with this mysterious woman, the front door swung open silently. He stepped into an empty foyer, just as he wished. The butler, Wong, was standing behind the door, ready to close it and collect his hat and coat from the hall table; but Edouard did not think of Wong any more than he thought of the palm trees and passion vines, the faded sofas and cracked sideboards, or even the maids Precious Flower, Ancient Jade, and Life's Importance, as he followed the trail of gas globes they'd lit in the hallway and entered the one room large enough for the painting he was so reluctantly housing. His office, the most private room of all, where the linen-swathed canvas was propped against two palms so tall that the fronds brushed the filigree iron ceiling.

The strange woman followed him in. She looked even thinner in the light; but that light also emphasized her ethereal quality. Her skin was bone white, her cheeks blood red, her hair a startling dark orange. As she advanced through the potted palms and jasmine vines, she seemed to shimmer, and her image was reflected in the night-darkened walls all around. One or two spectral visitors followed where the fleshly one went.

Tongue-tied, Edouard followed her over to the swathed painting. She put one spidery hand on the drape and plucked feebly; so, feeling he could do nothing else, Edouard pulled the thing free. He remembered, then, the social delicacies of introductions and offers to take a visitor's coat and give her a seat, but it felt too late for them.

Famke was thinking neither of him nor of etiquette, and if he had taken her coat she would have protested, for she was still grave-cold. She stared at the revealed picture and saw that he was right: This painting was not of her.

The composition bore some similarity to *The Revenge of Nimue*; there was a tall woman with her arms splayed, gesturing at a vast cave of reddened ice in which the traces of frozen flowers could be seen. But the face, the form, the character of the model were unfamiliar, and there was no evidence of Famke anywhere. As she searched, she realized this was in fact the picture she'd seen reproduced in *Frank Leslie's*. The whole picture began to swim. She blinked, many times and rapidly, but she could not clear her vision. She put a hand to the glass to steady herself and asked, "Is there a castle made of the letters A and C in the lower right corner?" Edouard Versailles confirmed that there was.

That at least was something.

"The goddess Hygeia," Versailles explained, trying to pretend he could not see her crying. "Thawing the winter of ill health, freeing the afflicted from their suffering. It is to hang in the entry of the hospital I am building in the village." He paused to chide himself mentally: Of course she knew about the hospital already; that was why she'd come here. His hand crept to his woven watch fob and worried away at it. "I have a programme in mind for a general cure of the diseases that afflict the lungs. I cured myself," he ended, weak where he had intended to sound forceful.

Famke burst into paroxysms of coughing and tears at the same time. It seemed that even here, even now, when she most wanted the solace of her own thoughts, she was not to be spared some man's passionate description of his vocation.

"A number of sufferers have already arrived, even before the hospital can be finished, to take the cure in the village. I have great hopes—you see, the cure is based on the principles of water and elec—"

"Where is *Albert?*" Famke wailed, cutting Edouard short.

As if struck by a sudden inspiration, he pulled a black-bordered cloth from his vest and pressed it into her hand. Through the veil of her tears, she saw then that he was dressed entirely in black, as if mourning, though his skin was like the belly of a creature that never saw sunlight. So he, too, had lost someone.

"If I were you," he said, not unkindly but most uncomfortably, "I would go to San Francisco. Every artist in the West ends there eventually. Your brother is probably there now, making more paintings such as this one."

Famke blew her nose, which started her coughing again more violently.

Edouard hesitated, watching her. Now that he'd broken his silence, he could not prevent himself from speaking further: "But you should really think of staying on here, in Hygeia Springs. You clearly suffer from phthisis yourself. The Institute is not open officially yet, but—"

"I have no money," Famke said, stuffing the sodden handkerchief into her tasseled purse without asking him to explain that strange word. "And no time. I must find Albert—everything will be right when I find him."

"You cannot find him if you are dead," Edouard pointed out.

Dead. The word shot through Famke's brain and seemed to explode there. For a minute she couldn't think, could barely keep balanced on legs that suddenly seemed made of water.

Edouard, seeing this, poised to catch her. His arms anticipated that frail weight . . . But what would he do with her once he had her? He began looking around for a sofa he knew was not there.

"You are wrong about me," Famke said when she could speak again. "I am perfectly well." He thought she appeared to derive strength from the words themselves; perhaps that was how she had managed to come so far.

Edouard's arms dropped. "I did not mean—"

"You said what you meant. And I shall go to San Francisco, as you suggest."

Edouard scarcely heard her. His eye had been caught by the reflection in the glass wall: There he saw his own white face and shirt collar, floating above the black suit; and behind him a blur of purple and red and white that was this woman, all gleaming in the wet glow of two blue eyes. He imagined those eyes closed and himself bent over her, administering his cure, watching the healthy color flow back into the waxen skin . . .

Famke thought her answer had struck him speechless: All to the good. While her host's head was turned, she staggered out into the hall and followed the gaslit path to the door and the crisp, clear air outside. By holding her breath, she even managed not to cough until she'd put the walls of glass and iron behind her.

Chapter 37

*Santa Fé [. . .] is one of the most comfortable residence cities in the world,
as witness its growing popularity both as a summer residence for people from
the South, and as a winter residence for people from the North, and as an all-
the-year-round residence and sanitarium for people variously in search of
health, comfort, pleasure and business.*

STANLEY WOOD,
OVER THE RANGE TO THE GOLDEN GATE

Harry Noble cursed himself for a slack-twisted fool. After waiting in
the station until the 8:12 to Phoenix was long gone, followed by
the 9:13 to Denver and the 10:46 to Las Cruces, he finally presented himself at Opal Cinque's salon, only to hear from Cracklin' Mag that
the patient had disappeared early the night before. Then he knew exactly
what Famke had done and where she'd gone, and he knew he should have
thought better than to give her a purseful of money and leave her alone to
spend it. He had no one to blame but himself; it was hardly worthwhile
even to be angry with Famke.

The ingrained habit of the longtime correspondent made him ask, almost without thinking, "What was she wearing when she left?"

Perched on a slippery chair in Opal Cinque's parlor, where Spanish
workers were adjusting the electric lights, Mag dabbed at swollen eyes. "My
new silk dress, the one I was saving to visit my parents in. And my winter
coat, my dark parasol—though what she'll do with that in December, I don't
know—my tortoiseshell combs, a silk purse one of the girls netted me—"

"And you thought she was a sister to you," Mrs. Cinque said in a scold-
ing tone, from her pink plush throne. Already two bulbs had broken, and
the Spanish workers had sworn colorfully, but she was as calm as a queen
overseeing a ball. "More than a sister and less than a friend, I'd say."

Even as sulky Mag spoke, Harry had transcribed her description into
newspaper prose: *The fair but feverish damsel absconded in a frock of lustrous silk,*

a Venetian lace parasol shading her visage from importunous stares . . . "What color was the frock?" he asked now.

The question produced another angry swab at the eyes. "Purple. The loveliest plum color you ever saw—not puce—just what a lady would wear. All Chinese silk. There was ruffles round the hem and the hands, and the sleeves were lined with lace."

Her raiment was the hue of amethyst, and its flounces fluttered in the breeze like so many moths . . . *no, like butterfl—like so many* . . . "It sounds very pretty."

"It was *brilliant!*" Mag wailed, falling prey to another spate of tears.

"What are you going to do, Mr. Noble?" Opal Cinque asked practically.

Noble pulled himself out of his picturesque thoughts and considered the facts. Ursula Summerfield, fugitive and thief. The sturdy little prostitute probably was lying about some of it, but he did not want the bother of an argument. "There is not much for me to do," he said. "I am a mere acquaintance of Miss Summerfield; I had heard she was to be in town and, concerned about the state of health I knew to be hers, I went searching for her. She rejected my offers of help, and the results are as you see." The last thing he wanted was to be held responsible for that dress, which sounded expensive—not to mention the other feminine accoutrements, which he did not pretend to understand.

"She left a twenty-piece on the bureau," Mag reported, with a swelling of rage. "She didn't have that kind of money before you came."

Noble spread his hands as wide as they would go. "My dear young lady, I myself have been robbed. It seems Miss Summerfield was not what I believed and hoped her to be, and now we have both suffered by it. We must move on to the rest of our lives."

"Are you moving on, then, Mr. Noble?" Opal asked impassively, as a stout workman positioned his ladder directly behind her. "To chase the Dynamite Gang?"

Without knowing it, Harry sighed. Pursuing Famke had won him no rewards, and he was suddenly as disgusted with her, for being so elusive and unforthcoming, as he was with himself for chasing her. Damn her for leading him so far and telling him nothing. He felt tired, and the luxury that Famke had enjoyed in a Chinese cook's bed, with the ministrations of a houseful of tender doves, appealed to him mightily. He knew they were not for him, but he saw no harm in having a rest. He made a decision on the spot.

"No, I shall stay in Santa Fé for some weeks," he said, with a tug of the side-whiskers. He felt a tingle in his fingers, as if he were about to start writing. "I have lately been much on the road, and I need some tranquility in which to work. I have a new kind of project in mind," he added with a dawning sense that such a project had sprung full-fledged in his mind, "something that will require a deal of concentration to produce. Your capital city suits me as well as anyplace."

"I hope we shall see something of you, then," said Opal, with the same impersonal hospitality she offered all her guests.

Harry opened his lips to reply, but Mag burst into another storm of weeping, and instead he produced a bit of hard bright candy from his pocket and handed it to her. He gave Opal the cheroot from his vest just as the third light bulb shattered.

"Corruption!" Opal shrieked at last, rounding on the workman. Her chignon glittered with slivers of broken glass. "Are you trying to kill us all?"

Mag popped the candy into her mouth and smiled at Harry, dewy but radiant, as if all were peaceful around them.

Chapter 38

. . . . .

We all discovered that it took a great deal of air to do a little breathing with.

BENJ. F. TAYLOR,
BETWEEN THE GATES

There was an icy fog all around, uniform and black and heavy. It coiled around the body and chilled the bones; it sat on the chest like a panther and sucked out the breath.

But it was not altogether a bad fog, for out of it there emerged a woman of astonishing beauty. She had hair the color of sunrise and eyes like a bright winter afternoon, and her skin seemed made of white cloud—until she touched the dreamer with hands that felt like ice itself. It was then that one knew this was a woman of ice, who had created that black fog. It seeped from her nostrils as she breathed; it plumed from the cauldron she was stirring, stirring, stirring.

And then she thrust her hands into the cauldron and brought them out scalded a leathery pink. Burning hot, she laid those hands about the helpless dreamer's body, on neck and wrists and breasts. She did this for hours, every day. Sometimes she treated the dreamer savagely, breaking bones so they'd fit in a narrow black box. Once the body was inside, she sealed the box with a plate of thin ice, under which one watched oneself slowly freezing white, only to be resurrected with another brush of those scorching hands.

But the strange woman could be gentle as well. She might squeeze a tube of liniment until a fat blue or green snake slithered out onto the dreamer's breasts and began tickling its way down her stomach to the notch of her legs, painting her like a meadow. Or she might bend over until one could smell her soapy breath and feel it, sometimes warm, sometimes cold, upon one's lips. Her icy dark eyes stared until one could see nothing else; and then the eyes did not seem so icy anymore. At those moments the dreamer knew everything was going to turn out well, because she saw herself reflected in those eyes and knew that she looked just like the ice woman; and that woman was lovely. She knew also that her strange nurse was going to kiss her . . . But at that moment, invariably, the woman vanished.

It was on perhaps her tenth visit, perhaps her twelfth, that the ice woman put those hot pink hands into her patient's hair and wormed them in deep, next to the scalp. Once there she began to press and press, as if to crush the skull, to pop the eyes from their sockets, to push blood from the nose and mouth and ears. She bent close and whispered, "Pair of aces. Full house, spades. Royal flush, hearts, with three pretty portraits."

As if those words were magic, another world came rushing in. The ice woman vanished; the patient's eyes fluttered, she looked into a darkness slightly less deep than that she was used to, and her ears heard several voices at once:

"Raise you ten."

". . . bluffing."

"Call!"

She tried to call, she did. But her lips were still frozen. She heard a slap-slap sound, as of wings, and there was a smell of sweet smoke that reminded her of a room brimming over with light; a faraway room in which she had been naked and cold, but not as cold as now.

"Sham!"

"Bastard!"

There was laughter, and the sound of wings again. She wondered if she were in some kind of heaven, or perhaps purgatory, with the angels laughing over her. But how could she have found heaven when she was naked? And who would have thought heaven could be so cold? She tried to sit up and look at the angels, but her limbs were too heavy. Arms, legs, and waist were oppressed with heavy bonds, and all she could move were her eyelids. She wanted water badly, but she could not draw the breath to ask for it; and since she was also sleepy, she let her eyelids droop again.

"Did you hear that?"

"What?"

"Something coughed."

"Some*one*, you mean?"

"It wasn't me."

"Wasn't m—"

"One of *them*, must be . . ."

"Tarnation!"

"Which one?"

This was interesting enough to make one fight to stay awake. And it was the fluttering eyelids that eventually drew the voices, and the hot hands— many of them—about her body.

"She's alive!"

"I knew she—"

"Untie her."

The hands unknotted some bonds, and a pair helped her sit halfway up. Weak yellow light shone all around; she caught glimpses of faces—hairy, plain, masculine faces—and someone held a glass to her lips and let the water run into her mouth and over her chin. Despite the cold, her fingertips burned as if she'd been playing with hot coals. She discovered she was not naked after all but wearing a thin white shift.

She coughed, a good long cough, and someone held a handkerchief before her lips.

"Where am I?" she whispered. It was a strange pleasure to hear her own voice.

"What did she say?"

"Was that English?"

She realized she'd misspoken, that there were words these ugly angels would understand and words they wouldn't. With the effort she might use to push open a heavy door, she thought hard and came up with the right ones: "Where am I?"

Someone said words she thought were "debt hospital," but that voice was quickly hushed. Someone else laughed, nervously. The third voice said, speaking very slowly, "You are in the Anteroom."

"*Hvor?*" She was too sleepy to make sense of it. She was almost sure that her fingers were on fire, but she could not see them.

Another voice said, "The Anteroom of Hygeia Springs Institute for Phthisis."

Words she could not understand; but they were words, and the very sound of language comforted her. She closed her eyes and slept, hearing dimly: "Who are you—miss—what is your . . ."

Chapter 39

. . . . .

Such beauty could not be were it not for the highly reflective qualities of the pure translucent waters which serve as a polished mirror of French plate glass.

"THE GLOWING LANGUAGE OF A MUCH TRAVELED AUTHOR,"
QTD. IN STANLEY WOOD,
OVER THE RANGE TO THE GOLDEN GATE

No one looked beautiful in the middle of dying, Edouard Versailles thought as he stood over the new arrival. She lay sleeping in an effervescent bath, emaciated and whiter than the chalky tiles around her, losing her hair and scarcely breathing. And yet he found traces of loveliness in this patient's face—the cheekbones, the prominent brow, the eyes that must still be bright when her sleep ended and the whisper-thin lids peeled back. About her figure it was impossible to tell; not much to it but bones, with the barest hint of swelling around the nipples and a startling froth of red hair where he had known no woman to have red hair before, between two hipbones that reminded him of plucked chicken wings. It was no wonder that, when she was found waiting in the Springs Hotel for a stage that never came, the nurses had taken her for dead and put her in the Anteroom.

They told him she'd had no pulse then, and that her breath had left no trace on a mirror, but now she showed the signs of life common at the Institute: the rattling in the lungs, the pulse hammering visibly between neck and shoulder. Already one miracle had occurred; if Edouard had time to apply his special cure, she might yet live.

"It is a great thing," he said, as if to himself, "that we included the Anteroom in the architect's plans."

The single nurse on duty here merely nodded. She was working too hard to speak, guiding the heavy rubber hose to fill the patient's bath. Sweat and water coated her and Mr. Versailles in a light spray, and tiny bubbles clung to the sleeping woman's body, for the mountain water was naturally carbonated. Dr. Beachly had prescribed a series of baths, increasing in temperature, to get her blood flowing and to wash away the taint of near-death, and Edouard Versailles would trust no one but himself to supervise. This patient must be cherished, not least because he had suddenly realized she was the means of establishing his hospital's reputation and his own: She could be his first private patient.

The Hygeia Springs Institute for Phthisis was several months from opening its doors to business, but already there was a clear need for certain specialized chambers such as the one in which this woman had wakened. The invalids who had somehow heard of the water's astonishing properties had filled the town to overflowing: all to the good, for there would be many beds in the new Institute's three hexagonal towers, and meanwhile hotels and rooming houses were doing a brisk business. The independent sufferers busied the doctors already on staff. Unfortunately, deprived of the particularly salubrious arrangements of air and water that the Institute would provide—and most of all unable to take advantage of the special electrical cure by which Edouard swore but that even the most sophisticated doctors felt would require at least a gradual introduction—many of those patients were dying. The hillside above town was pockmarked with new black graves, and even before the rooms could be plastered and painted, a few had been pressed into service as operating theaters, intensive nursing wards, a morgue, and, finally, the Anteroom.

Edouard did not know that the nurses privately called the place the Death Hospital. It was there that they sent patients who appeared to have expired but for whom one of the doctors stubbornly clung to hope. The sturdier nurses hoisted these likely corpses onto wheeled gurneys and settled them in one vast room, where a woman was charged with daily pricking their feet with needles and holding matches to their fingers, until the patient either woke screaming in pain or achieved such an advanced state of decay that there was nothing for it but to slide the body quietly into one of the chutes that fed directly into the cellar morgue, thereby releasing such an odor of misused flesh that the chief mortician, Dr. Rideaux, often swore he'd seen the other cadavers flinch in horror. No body had ever wakened before.

Edouard had been most surprised to recognize this miraculous patient as the visitor who had disturbed him some days ago, who had made him even more dissatisfied with his *Hygeia* than before—who had, in fact, almost convinced him to destroy it. After her visit, he had imagined the ranks of the afflicted filing in, wheeled in wooden chairs or carried on comfortable stretchers, beneath the thick nose and limbs of that painted goddess; she was likely to make them abandon hope, and he was tempted to abandon her to the glass house's furnace. That he had not done so was entirely due to the exertions of his butler, Wong, who had become enamored of the painting and had dragged it out to the stable for safekeeping until his master reconsidered.

But now Edouard forgot about the picture as, staring down at Famke, he thought that there could never be another patient such as this one: a woman whose funereal beauty seemed to call into question the capacity of art to represent anything at all.

"Sir?" Dr. Beachly, the Institute's chief physician, entered the room and signaled to Miss Pym to close the tap. "Her warmth is nearly restored. What do you want to be done with her?"

Edouard blushed, remembering he was in the presence of others. Until this moment, he had not been embarrassed to be gazing upon this naked woman, for her eyes were closed. What troubled Edouard Versailles, as always, was the living and conscious.

He had to address two such people now: Lesley Beachly and kind, stout Miss Pym, one of a few female nurses on staff, who had just left to fetch soaps and creams.

"Do we know who she is?" he asked at last, a simple question; one he should have asked the woman herself when he had the chance. He could remember only that she had claimed some relationship to the painter of that ill-begotten canvas.

"We think her name is Fanny," the doctor told him. "She has said it, or something like it, twice in her sleep. She claims to remember nothing, not even her name or where she was born. She had only six dollars in her purse, along with some clippings from the newspaper and a filthy paper that might once have contained writing. All we know is that she is consumptive and . . ." He coughed delicately. "She is not a virgin."

Edouard gazed down at the white figure sunk in the tub. For the moment, her lack of virginity was of no consequence to him. Still, looking at the wounded fingers and feet, and at that surprising red tuft waving in the water, he realized there was one question he did have to ask.

"Has she been violated?"

"Not as far as my investigations have shown," the doctor said.

"She could be married," suggested Miss Pym, coming back in with a tray.

"Perhaps." Beachly reflected that the woman's fingers were so white that they showed no difference where a ring might be, nor was the flesh indented there; but he did not need to point to these facts. "She does not seem to have produced any children."

Miss Pym knelt to wash the stranger's hair with a French soap that Versailles planned to put in all the Institute's cells. She began at the scalp and worked her fingers in, worrying the skull from side to side so that sometimes the stranger's face appeared lovely and vital; at other times, a leering death's head. As she worked, she had to keep taking her hands from the suds to pull away the strands that clung to her fingers; long strands of red clotted the surface of the water and the foam drifting there.

Edouard thought of a print his father had bought long ago, a beautiful red-haired woman floating among flowers in a pond. "I think we should call her Ophelia," he said out loud. "Or Miss Ophelia." It was important to maintain an appropriate formality between doctor and patient.

As if she recognized her name, the woman opened her eyes. They were every bit as blue as he remembered, but she looked at him only a second before she shuddered and they closed. He saw her eyes moving nervously beneath the lids.

Edouard had to remind himself that he was at the door of a great venture, and that this nameless woman—Fanny, Ophelia—might be the key. He cleared his throat. "My—er, Miss," he said, remembering manners that had fallen into disuse. "I have an experiment—an opportunity to propose to you . . . a cure . . ."

"A cure," she repeated in a whisper, still refusing to look. She was too weak to move away from Pym's efficient fingers, which made her head shake on its stalk but nonetheless, for the moment, kept her looking more alive than dead.

"Do you want to be cured?" asked Edouard.

"Yes," she whispered back, as if it were an odd question—as indeed it was.

"Shall you mind an unusual treatment? Free of charge? I assure you it is most effective—I have benefited from it myself . . ."

She made a small mewing sound and fell asleep again. Miss Pym held her head out of the water.

Edouard tried to curb his excitement. "I think we shall move Miss Ophelia up to my house tomorrow," he told his staff, referring modestly to the wonder of iron and glass that the villagers called the Palace. "She shall be my private patient and occupy my mother's old suite."

Dr. Beachly and Miss Pym avoided each other's gaze. Surely, if the Institute's owner wished to take a penniless stray into his own home, where both his parents had succumbed to the disease he had made it his mission to cure in his own most peculiar way, that was his business and no one else's.

◆   ◆   ◆

Ophelia's progress up the mountain the next day would have honored a queen of Egypt or Amazonia. She lay on an oversized stretcher, her body wrapped in wool blankets, her back propped with pillows—hexagonal, she noticed, and rather harder than pillows usually were. With Dr. Beachly leading the way like some high priest, four male nurses carried the stretcher, and as many lady nurses followed with the various bags and bottles they considered necessary to promote a recovery. It was a beautiful, cool, sun-drenched afternoon, and Ophelia felt as if she were in a painting come to life. Within the cocoon of blankets she even pinched herself, just to make sure she wasn't caught in another fever dream.

She had to pinch herself again once the glass house came in view, rising like a glittery moon over her feet. Surely this place was part of her dreams—but, no, Dr. Beachly opened the lacy white front door, and the nurses trooped her over the threshold and through the foyer. The palm fronds and flowered vines closed in around her, and the nurses began a shivery trip up an iron stairway.

She almost forgot she was ill. Everything was white and green and very, very bright. There was even a vine twining up the banister, its tiny star-shaped blooms filling the air with a sweet heavy scent.

"Jasmine," said a nurse, when the patient sniffed. "Mr. Versailles's"—she pronounced it *Versles*, as the villagers did— "father, who built this house, was very fond of it."

Jasmine made Ophelia dizzy. But her room was airy and relatively free of plant life, and so big that the doctor and all the nurses could fit comfortably inside. The ceiling was a gentle dome of glass, and just now it was uncovered; she could stare straight into the sun if she wanted to.

"These are the cords for drawing the shades," said one of the men, demonstrating. "You give a pull here and the drapes will cover the ceiling."

"Or you may ring for a maid to do it," added Miss Pym. "Although Mr. Versailles believes the light will speed your cure."

So she was to have a maid—a fact that fled her mind as she watched the shades cover the sky. They billowed like white sails, stretching by means of a system of wires hidden against the iron framework. This was indeed a marvel, but in turn it was quickly forgotten in the curiosity of wooden furniture, deeply carved and once very elegant, warped and bleached now to the color of old ivory. The bed and a few other pieces were wrought of white iron, but the chest of drawers into which the nurses began stowing her possets and rubs, and the wardrobe in which they hung a few simple white gowns—these furnishings were of necessity made from lightweight materials, and they had absorbed the sun and steam until they cracked. She wondered at a man who not only insisted on living in a house of glass but was also willing to destroy what had obviously been expensive furnishings in order to do so.

The nurses wiped Ophelia's lips and lifted her into bed, where the sheets and blankets were paper-white. Out of nowhere, it seemed, there materialized a lovely quilt composed of little velvet hexagons painstakingly stitched together. Most of them had faded, too, so that what had been crimson and emerald and gold was now shades of dove-gray with gentle underpinnings of color.

"Grandmother's Flower Garden," said Miss Pym, running her hand over the softness as she tucked it around the patient's hard little bones. "That's what this pattern is called. Some woman did fine work here."

One of the younger, sharper women laid another gleaming cord across the pillow. "If you need anything, pull on this—once for us, twice for a maid. As a rule we're to keep out of sight."

"Why is that?"

No one replied; but of course she already knew the reason. The rule that servants should never let themselves be seen till absolutely necessary was doubly important in a glass house. And how well she knew the system, too, although her hand had never before held the silken cord for any purpose but to clean it. She exerted herself to give this one a couple of tugs now and was delighted to see a slender, silent China girl appear in the doorway: hands folded into the sleeves of her cotton tunic, face made perfectly smooth, awaiting instructions.

"*Fanden!*" Ophelia exclaimed admiringly.

Miss Pym nodded dismissively to the maid, then opened a door in the right-hand wall. There was a gleaming flush toilet, its tank and pull-chain suspended from a reinforced ceiling. "This is your water closet. You may use it when you are stronger."

Somewhere downstairs, a parlor clock chimed high and spidery, five times. The nurses exchanged another glance.

"We'll leave you now," Miss Pym said, with a final tuck to the quilt.

"Where are you going?" the patient asked, suddenly afraid of being on her own in this strange place.

Miss Pym appeared to understand, though she did not answer immediately. She held a warm cup to the girl's lips: "Drink this," she said.

Heating had taken the bubbles from the water, and mixed with honey and other flavors came a familiar alcoholic bitterness that reassured Ophelia. She drank, and within minutes she was asleep.

Chapter 40

· · · · ·

There is a saying in South California that if a man buys water he can get his land thrown in.

HELEN HUNT JACKSON, "CALIFORNIA," IN
GLIMPSES OF THREE COASTS

The elder branches were white with an unexpected snowfall, so clean they seemed to glow electrically in the intense blue twilight of mid-afternoon. Mother Birgit entered her office in her winter coat, wearing all three pairs of woolen socks that she owned. She had ordered the sisters not to light the hearth in here this winter; it was, she explained, an easy economy to make, since the office was used primarily by just one person. In her own mind it was also a penance, like the hair shirt she had once worn, for the missteps she had taken in the case of a particular orphan.

Birgit settled herself at the big, plain desk and uncapped the inkwell: It was time to write the letter for which Herr Skatkammer had asked weeks ago. She had promised, and he was an important benefactor—particularly so now that the Queen had opened her *Børnehjem*, diverting the flow of funds and newborns who might have turned Catholic if the nuns had found them first.

Words were slow in coming, and Birgit found herself gazing out at the elder, lost in thought, coughing abstractedly. There came an echoing cough in the hallway; if she listened carefully, there were coughs all over the building—the famous Immaculate chest was afflicting nuns and orphans who had already tired themselves out in the early days of Advent. If only it were possible to keep them in bed rather than in the drafty chapel! But of course no nun should ever think as much. And then there was Famke—out there in America with her splintery cough and no one to care for her, unless Viggo had found her by now . . .

Birgit considered some difficult facts. Above all, she wanted to find Famke, not the alarming painting for which the girl had posed. As far as Birgit knew, the canvas about which Skatkammer had inquired was the only one in existence; if it remained in America and Famke returned to Denmark, she might take up a virtuous life. Even if she stayed in America and married her painter, that country was large enough to absorb the scandal. But in Denmark, a much smaller place, eventually the painting would cause trouble.

A gentle wind blew through the courtyard, and the elder tree shook loose a fine powder of snow. That tree was like a hand, Birgit thought fancifully, with many fingers reaching up to grab—what? The rising moon? She could not see it, could see only a few of the clouds that had dropped that blanket of snow.

She forced tree and sky out of her mind and set herself sternly to the task at hand. First she folded a sheet of paper several times, as if the letter were finished. It made a white pad like a bandage—but she must not think of that either, poor Herr Skatkammer lying so badly burned, poor Viggo the day of the soapmaking, poor suffering Catholics everywhere . . . She wrote the address of Skatkammer's American agent on one of the outside rectangles, blotted it, and opened the sheet again.

Dear Herr Jensen, she wrote at last, with the sense that she was punishing herself, *I am writing at the request of your employer, Jørgen Skatkammer, who has heard of a painting he would like to secure for his collection . . .*

. . .

At the same blue hour, Frøken Grubbe sat down in Herr Skatkammer's parlor to write to Copenhagen's bishop. She wrapped her right forearm in a sleeve guard and brushed a few distracting hairs from her brow: This letter required the full focus of her energies, and it had to look pristine and professional. It must also read compellingly.

Dear Holy Father!

It is with considerable pain that I take pen in hand. But I must inform you that it is time to put stop to an intolerable situation, a disgraceful canker eating away at the body of the Church, destroying your flock as murrain destroys sheep. . . .

If she wrote quickly, she could put it in the afternoon mail.

* * *

In the quiet warmth of his own steam-heated office, Edouard Versailles reminded himself that all good beginnings take into account that they are also endings. This would be the beginning of Ophelia's cure, the end of her illness: poor, memoryless Ophelia, victim of an unknown crisis that had robbed her of that precious storehouse of experience, who couldn't even recall when the phthisis had begun to manifest itself, and who had no idea how such fevers were born. Who had no recollection, even, of the quest that had brought her here—an attempt to locate a brother whose name she never spoke, but who was the author of the painting that now sat in Edouard's stable; a quest that had ended in her collapse and subsequent rebirth into the web of health and hope that Edouard was spinning for some lucky patients.

An unlucky patient's hand sat on his desk now, deformed by disease and stored in a jar of alcohol. Edouard picked it up and set it at eye level on a bookshelf, where it bobbed along to the left. He fancied it was reaching for a fetus miscarried at seven months, now forever cradled in another thin womb of glass. Chemicals and sunlight had combined to bleach both hand and fetus to a pallor even less luminous than the new patient's skin . . . Terrible to think what this disease was doing to Ophelia now.

He turned away from the jars to dig into his desk for an anatomical drawing. He found what he wanted deep in a central pigeonhole: It featured a naked human female, and its contemplation replaced niggling distress with a warm glow of anticipation. His mind supplanted the drawing's expressionless face with Ophelia's visage, and he imagined the effects that his success would work on her: the gradual burgeoning of flesh, the bones and eyes sinking back to their rightful places beneath pillows of breasts and delicate shells of eyelids. Her beauty completed, perfected in the eyes of the world; even more intensely gorgeous to himself, who had helped create it. She would far outshine this bland representation of the healthy specimen, a woman who had probably been born into health and never struggled to recreate herself.

But Edouard also imagined failure: Ophelia's last sour, soughing breath, the subtle fading of her skin from white to waxen yellow, the grave's black dirt clouding her hair. And then there was the damage to himself: Failure would label him as crackpot as his father, the immigrant Frenchman who had perversely refused to mine for gold himself but had made a fortune by buying mountains and rivers, for the use of which he charged those who did the digging and sluicing. The man who did not see his wife or son for twelve years but who built this fantastic house in order to give the woman a view of the outside world when, finally arrived in America, she lay suffering just as Ophelia did now.

Thinking of those awful days, Edouard reflected that it might be time to visit his parents, whose bodies now lay entombed inside a small replica of the Taj Mahal on the edge of the forest. He often went to them at what he thought must be midnight, though the heat and moisture in the house made his clocks unreliable. But then his eye fell on that discarded engraving, and his mind again imposed a picture of that frangible wreck of a girl upstairs, lying in his mother's bed, waiting for rescue.

Edouard felt his muscles stretching in an unaccustomed direction. He realized he must be smiling.

Yes, it was definitely the start.

. . .

Edouard breezed into the bedroom the next morning with an armload of charts and diagrams and tables of facts, lists of substances and behaviors desirable and undesirable. Miss Pym, who had accepted private nursing duty, and the housemaid Precious Flower followed with an assortment of basins, towels, and bottles. Ophelia struggled to sit up, looking expectant and eager.

Miss Pym hoisted the patient and arranged the pillows in a tall mound at her back. As she did so, a single downy feather floated upward in the air, and Edouard caught it in his fist lest Ophelia should inhale it. The patient murmured something that sounded like "Summer fool," and Edouard worried that she already considered him a crackpot. Briskly, as befit a man of medicine, Edouard pulled out a contraption made of two flexible tubes that joined into one and ended at a little metal cup. He anchored the tube ends in his ears.

His Ophelia did not recall seeing its like before. She was taken aback, then, when Edouard placed the metal cup on her chest and she felt the chill through the gauze of her nightdress.

"Don't pull away," he said, giving a little expert frown as he moved the cup slightly. "This instrument lets me listen to your lungs. It's called a stethoscope."

She determined that there was nothing but science in the way he handled the little cup, but what did that matter anyway? She had agreed to stay here, and she would have tolerated almost any strange behavior so long as it produced the feeling of health and release that he promised.

"A stethoscope," she repeated dutifully.

"Yes. It tells me your rattle is not too pronounced; your lungs aren't completely hollow." He sounded almost disappointed, as if he'd wanted her to be sicker than she was. He pulled back the covers and began prodding her legs; she decided to let him.

"Not much swelling here," he said, again with that jarring note of disappointment. "Perhaps no swelling at all. Tell me—how painful are your joints?"

"My joints?" she asked, the repetition this time signifying not passivity but confusion. As far as she could recollect, a joint was a cut of meat.

"Here"—he clasped her knee—"where your bones join together. The disease can settle in them as well."

"Oh. Not bad." She paused as he rustled with the bedclothes, covering her up again.

He twitched at the quilt, trying to make it lie perfectly straight. "And where did you come from? Have you remembered anything? You don't speak with a native accent."

"Nor do you, I think."

"I was born in France."

"I believe I was born somewhere else as well," Ophelia said meditatively. "But I cannot say exactly where."

"I know you have a brother," said Edouard.

Her face did not move; it was as if carved from marble. "I do?"

"And he is a painter. You came here to look for him." Her expression still did not change, and with a guilty sense of relief Edouard nodded to Precious Flower, who placed a chair behind him. He sat and pulled out a diagram. "Perhaps you will remember as your health improves . . . This," he said, changing subject rapidly, "is what a diseased lung looks like."

It was horrible, yellow-pink tissue spotted with grayish holes, looking like spoiled cheese. How disgusting to think that was how she looked inside.

"And this"—he produced another drawing—"is what is making you sick."

"This" looked like a bubble, somewhat elongated and slightly fuzzy around the edges, utterly empty inside. Involuntarily she clutched at her chest.

"Oh, it is very tiny," he hastened to assure her. "So small that you can't see it without a special instrument known as a microscope. Doctors did not discover these little organisms—they are called bacilli—until three years ago. The discovery completely changed the way we think of this disease. Bacilli are *alive*, you know, and we must kill them to make you better."

Edouard pointed from one artist's drawing to another. He was finding it much easier to speak now that he had a clear role to play in the conversation. It occurred to him that the role even required a certain tolerance from those with whom he spoke; doctors were often abrupt, absorbed in their scientific calculations. So: "Each bacillus creates a tubercle in the flesh— these little holes here and here. That is why advanced medical men now call your disease *tuberculosis*."

She appeared never to have heard those words before; to Edouard, it was just as well, for he derived some comfort from saying them aloud. He elaborated at length, pulling out more drawings, diagrams, and cross-sectional illustrations. The girl's eyes glazed over, and she began to cough uncontrollably—or not so uncontrollably, he thought, for wasn't it his clearest mission to cure that cough? He passed her one of the black-bordered handkerchiefs and continued talking.

Precious Flower, standing behind him in her dark gray uniform, thought that the tubercles looked like grains of rice; only of course they were not grains of anything, but hollow spaces where nothing but these bacilli could exist. Tiny spaces, like the crib in Chinatown where she had lived like a bacillus herself, singsonging out to men as they passed: "You want nice China girl? Two bits lookee, four bits feelee, eight bits fuckee..." Until Edouard Versailles had bought her, as he had bought two of her singsong sisters, and commenced the process of bringing them back to apparent good health (Ancient Jade and Life's Importance were still clapped, but they managed to hide the periodic outbreaks) and morals. The process which, she thought as she passed him a pad of paper and a pen, had rendered the girls themselves completely invisible at last.

"I have developed a theory," Edouard said, writing the name *Ophelia* at the top of a page and feeling deliciously like a real doctor as he did so, "a theory that I believe will cure you completely, as it has done for me. It is based on the principle of flushing..."

"Flushing?" The patient looked toward the little room to her right.

"Yes, flushing out these tiny, evil creatures." He motioned to Precious Flower, who poured a glass of fizzing water from the pitcher and handed it to him. He, in turn, gave it to the girl in the bed. "They cannot live in the light, and once we flush them from the body's cavities, they themselves die. This flushing must be accomplished on both physical and mental levels, for a weakened mind weakens the body and allows the bacilli to prey. We accomplish the first by means of copious liquids and purges, the second by creating an environment of calm. And finally, there is a galvanic device I have been developing—"

"Calm?" she said, staring at the hissing glass. She did not care for the bubbles now. "Evil?"

"Yes," he said firmly. "Only someone at peace with himself can truly come free of this disease. A calm mind lulls the bacilli into stasis so they may be the more easily flushed. Now drink, and then I shall have the nurse bring up my machine."

He watched, with mounting excitement, while she drank.

Chapter 41

*Why, Coloradoans are the most disappointed people I ever saw. Two-thirds
of them came here to die, and they can't do it. This wonderful air brings
them back from the verge of the tomb, and they are naturally exceedingly disappointed.*

P. T. BARNUM,
LECTURE

M æka was like a dream, Viggo thought, a dream of a world that
could not possibly exist—but that could not be a dream, really,
because who would ever imagine those vast plains of sand with
their thick, prickly plants; the even stranger salt flats, where nothing grew
and salt lay crusted like ice over swampy earth—the *mountains?* No one who
had not already seen such places could believe they existed, wild places
more fantastic than anything in a fairy tale or martyr's history.

Snow and other weather permitting, he spent the winter on the move,
posting handbills, painting corpses, following the trail of canvas that he was
sure would one day lead him to Famke. He was very aware of the money in
his right boot, which had now callused his foot not quite to the point of in-
sensitivity; with every step he took, that money reminded him of why he
took steps at all. When the trail faded away, he patiently returned to the last
place of certainty and began again, asking about paintings and about "Albert
Castle, the painter," in town after town until he was as well known as the
artist himself.

It wasn't till Mirage, Colorado, that Viggo's method slipped, and he
asked merely for "Mr. Castle, the painter." The *Luder* to whom he'd addressed that question answered it with another: "Do you mean Albert or
Dante?"

Thus Viggo, who had begun to identify himself as the model's brother
for the sake of her reputation, learned that the painter had a brother as well.

When he asked for a description of Mr. Dante Castle, the picture that his interlocutor painted with words excited him so much that he himself nearly became a candidate for the services of a chthonic artist. He spent a febrile, heart-thumping hour drawing rapid conclusions, and he realized what the fancy girls had not: Dante Castle was a fiction; Dante Castle was Famke; Dante was following Albert; and if Viggo followed Dante, he would find Famke. He hoped to do it before Albert did.

So, methodically, Viggo rode back to Denver and retraced his steps. This time through, he discovered that the peculiarities of the paintings he'd seen along the way—the penumbras around certain figures, the elevation of some girls on the plane of the canvas, the occasional visibly clumsy thick layers of paint—were the work of a revisionist, of the "brother" who had followed Albert around, not the original artist's design. This made the paintings all the more precious to Viggo, and he recognized a fierce desire to own one of them, or all—these tableaux that not only represented Famke's face and figure but also showed the actual work of her hands. He felt a kinship with the women in the paintings; they had been cut and reassembled and permanently marked by the object of his quest and dreams.

On his second trip to Leadville, he was able to fulfill his longing in a small way. Whereas his first visit had yielded him nothing, this time some more persistent digging led him to a *Twilight of the Muses*—unaltered—by Albert Castle, in a house inhabited by a very congenial young lady who had once worked for someone called Dixie Holler.

"Dante?" she said meditatively, her breath hot and intimate in Viggo's ear. "Yes, he came by, the night the Dynamite Gang blew Mother Holler's house away. Vanished that very same night . . . So far as I'm aware he never came back, neither, though Bertie did—just a day or two after the explosion. Said he wanted to sketch the . . . the destruction of the imperfect . . . And he wanted to see what Mother Holler would erect in its place . . ."

Viggo twitched. Without his notice, her soft little hand had crept into his trousers. Politely but firmly, he removed it now.

"Well, he painted the girls here, at least." Sweet Myrt sat back and blew at her yellow frizz, the very picture of irritated boredom. "Old Dixie took her business to San Antonio, and I ended up at Mother Askling's, where it's harder than ever to earn a dollar." She stood up but was detained by a last question from Viggo.

"Where is Mr. Albert Castle now?" He thought that this information might be of some use, at least.

Prodded by a reproving stare from her current manager, Myrt stayed long enough to say, "I've no notion," and then flounced over to to perch on the arm of a real customer's chair. "Bill!" She exploded a kiss in his ear.

Viggo paid for his whiskey and left. Out in the cold of early evening, he trudged toward the row of raw-lumbered flophouses that had sprung up in the fire's wake. New snow balled up under his boot heels, so he had to stop periodically to scrape them.

During one of these pauses, as he scrubbed his sole against the base of a gas lamp, a gleam in a shop window caught Viggo's eye. In this town of so much silver, in a region of gold and turquoise and other fine things, there was something in the curve of this object that drew him closer. Pressing his nose against the pane, he saw a delicate silver box with three—three—*Gud*, three beautiful naked ladies entwined.

Accustomed as he was now to spending time with whores, there was something in that particular nakedness that excited him. He thought per-haps it was because of his newly awakened sense of artistry, learned through contemplating the work of Albert Castle and Famke. Yes, with its graceful lines and luminous surface, that box was an object of real art.

But just as suddenly as he'd noticed the box, he forgot all about it. Because in the rank just behind, catching a reflected glow from the many objects of silver, brass, and glazed porcelain, was a scrap that spoke to him even more intimately, even more importantly. It was about the size of his hand, brightly colored—just a flat bit of canvas pinned to a board. It fea-tured a pair of serpentine white arms and a few locks of burnished red hair.

That these elements were mere amputations, ancillary to the scrap's main figure—a curvaceous blonde wearing only a helmet and a cloud about her hips—meant nothing to Viggo. He was familiar enough now with the work of A. C. to recognize one of his hallmarks, the figure of Famke he added whenever a composition required a ninth Muse or a background fig-ure to give the beholder an impression of plenty. He even recognized the composition itself, a *Hero's Repose*; for however Albert's Valkyries might vary in the face, their bodies always assumed the same attitudes.

This was clearly a wisp of what Viggo sought, and it was tattered enough to be within his grasp right now. He knocked on the door till the shopkeeper came to open it.

"Just a bit of the wreckage," the man explained, swiping at a grease-smeared mouth with his sleeve. Viggo had interrupted him at dinner. "Flotsam. Of interest for its connection to the fire, most likely, though the colors were fresh beneath the soot. I can show you something much bigger . . ."

"This one," Viggo said firmly, reaching for his left boot.

Three dollars later, the piece was his. To the shopman's amusement, Viggo untacked it from the board, rolled it carefully, and wrapped it in a clean handkerchief. It might be just a pair of arms and a long lock of hair, but Viggo thought them a very good likeness.

. . .

Stethoscope, microscope, bacilli, tubercles. And now a new word—or rather, a word she had long known but only now was beginning to understand.

Edouard Versailles had made it clear: That lovely, shimmering feeling, the one she had enjoyed occasionally in a faraway past and which left her wanting nothing but more of itself, was the feeling of *hygiene*.

"It is another means of flushing, Miss Ophelia," he explained as he unpacked his complicated machine from its red plush carrying case; "of letting the juices down, as it were, and eliminating the infelicitous bacilli. It is a practice that dates back to Soranus and Galen, who demonstrated in the second century A.D. that it frees the body of evil. But whereas earlier centuries were forced to entrust the process to manual manipulations or to unreliable jets of water, ours has the benefit of electricity—making the cure more precise, more clean, more—"

He broke off, blushing as he looked at the patient in the bed. At this first use of his invention on a woman, Edouard felt an embarrassing hesitation, a shyness most unbecoming in a doctor, despite his carefully written and well-rehearsed explanation of this technique. True, a similar device had worked on himself to perfection, and he had modified it according to his collected anatomical drawings of women; he was as eager to see it at work as the patient was to achieve her cure—and yet for the moment he could hardly bear to look at either it or her, or to be looked at himself.

"Leave us," he said to the three Chinese maids who had lingered to await his bidding. They vanished like water into sand.

Alone, Edouard dared a glance at the patient and saw that, mercifully, she seemed to have fallen asleep. The blue eyes were still, curtained by the paper-thin lids, and her body lay passive. For good measure, Edouard wove a few red locks over her face: a blindfold of Ophelia's own making.

He turned to the thing that waited at her bedside, squat and wide-bottomed, with a rubber handle on one side and, on the other, a bulbous node that suddenly reminded Edouard of a pig's snout. His grand invention, a machine that would root out disease as a pig hunted truffles. He inserted the pronged plug into the wall's current box—rubberized for safety, as his house's metal ribs called for the most delicate precautions—and thought he heard it begin to hum, though he had not yet turned the switch.

In a way, dismissing the maids made Edouard's situation worse, for now he, himself, had to be the person who pulled back the sheets and gently separated Ophelia's legs (nearly weightless, he noticed, though burning hot to the touch). He knew from his own experience that the most effective treatment occurred on bare skin, but he could not bring himself to peel away the thin nightdress. Instead he flipped the switch that engaged the current, and in the sudden deafening roar of it he guided the thing's round black nose to the vee of the patient's legs, where the buzz quieted. Much, he thought, as a baby's crying quiets when presented with the breast.

While the machine hummed, Edouard kept his eyes trained on the ceiling. The glass domes revealed a brilliant blue sky punctuated occasionally by a dry leaf or a bird's leavings, disgusting marks he must have the servants wash away . . . He held the device steady and waited for nature and technology to take their course with Ophelia; tried to ignore the noise and concentrate on theories of disease. He recited the names of Dr. John Butler and Dr. Joseph Mortimer Granville, whose masculine devices, powered by battery cells, had done him some initial good and provided the inspiration for the much more effective machine he tinkered into existence himself. He thought of the long, lonely hours in his office, the specimen jars and anatomical engravings eclipsed by wires and motor parts and electricity manuals, hours filled with happy expectation and occasional tests of the machine on his own anatomy. Could those have been the gladdest hours he would ever know as a medical man? For despite the excitement of this initial use, Edouard was finding the situation painful. Perhaps he should have limited the machine's exercise to his own treatments. But no—again, such reserve would have been selfish.

Edouard was too rapt in his own embarrassment to notice that when he applied the machine the patient's eyes had flown suddenly open beneath their red blindfold. The vibrations in his arm were so strong that he did not sense, either, when her legs jerked and her body recoiled at the touch. In her frailty these movements were slight, and she brought them quickly under control, for despite the strangeness she found the treatment to be not unpleasant. She almost regretted that she had shut her eyes and ears to Edouard's lengthy explanations, for she would have liked to understand what was happening to her now. This strange noise and motion Down There—could they really be part of a cure that would clear her lungs? She closed her eyes again and—subtly, so her doctor would not notice—scooted down a little in the bed, until her anatomy ground more firmly against the machine. She remembered feeling a similar sensation in the past, and she wondered if there would be a correspondingly similar result.

After some minutes the vibrations running through Edouard's arm and across his chest began to weary him, and he wondered when the hygienic crisis would occur. Or could it be he'd made a mistake? Perhaps the device would not prove effective on the female anatomy? Perhaps the woman needed to be awake for the crisis to occur . . .

All at once, his questions were answered and his doubts dispelled. He heard an involuntary cry break from Ophelia's lips, and he looked down to see her whole body in a deep, prolonged shudder. Edouard sighed in relief, so heavily that he blew the red curls away from her eyes. Her face was revealed, and it was smiling, beautiful, looking up at him in happiness. Edouard turned away.

To cover his embarrassment, he made much of removing the plug from its socket—it hiccoughed up a tiny orange spark—and replacing the machine in its case. He had already thought of one or two alterations he would like to make to the device, and he began sketching them out mentally as he coiled the cord.

When he turned back to the bed to replace the sheet, he found Ophelia fully awake and watching him. He tried to assume a professional air. "That was your first hygienic treatment."

"*Fanny*," she whispered, and he wondered if that were the name of some dear sister or friend she had lost. She was unlikely to say her own name at a moment such as this; but then, a crisis of any sort, whether physical or emotional, could spark memory as easily as it could induce amnesia.

"Have you recollected something?" he asked dutifully.

Her light eyes met his dark ones. "No."

Perhaps she was raving. In any event, the blue stare made him distinctly uncomfortable.

"This evening," he said briskly, snapping the locks on the case, "we may repeat the process; you shall have at least two treatments a day at first. But now you must rest."

"I am not tired," she said, as if marveling at the fact of it.

"Then I shall send Miss Pym with a draught." He ran from the room— or would have done so, if it were not for the cumbersome burden of the machine.

Chapter 42

. . . . .

Southern California presents a most gloriously invigorating, tonic, and stimulating climate, very much superior to any thing I know of, the air is so pure and so much drier than at Mentone or elsewhere; and although it has those properties, it has a most soothing influence on the mucous membrane, even more so than the climate of Florida, and without the enervating effect of that.

FRANCIS S. MILES, QTD. IN CHARLES NORDHOFF,
CALIFORNIA: FOR HEALTH, PLEASURE, AND RESIDENCE

Auntie Myrtice looked a right mess. Her hair had come loose from its braids and was soaked with her perspiration, sticking to her face and the pillow and to Mother's and Alma's fingers as they did things to her. They had tied her hands to the bedposts, and it must be her pulling against those ropes that made her perspire so. She'd pulled so hard that the blood was redistributing itself all over her body; her face was puffy and red around the handkerchief they'd stuffed in her mouth to stop her crying. And there was blood all over the bed, too. Probably Auntie Myrtice had vomited it up, the way Aunt Ursula used to do; for as Mother had explained that morning, Auntie Myrtice was very, very ill, and the little children must not come around to listen or watch at her door. That was why Miriam had hidden herself in this camphorous wardrobe, where her view was poor but at least she got some idea about what was happening. Too many people had disappeared from Miriam's life recently; she would not go outside to play with her doll and let another person slip away.

". . . at a time like this," she heard Alma mutter, much as Auntie Myrtice herself might have muttered; and Miriam knew her sister was thinking particularly about their father, who had been gone almost longer than she could remember. Alma sounded quite grown up; she had just turned fifteen.

The last time they'd heard from Heber, he'd written from Nevada Territory, where he'd heard of a lady with red hair who was called Ursula. He'd gone up to the door of her shanty and scared her half to death, but she wasn't their Ursula; she taught school and sewed shirts for extra money. Father wrote the story as if it were a terrible thing, but at the time, Miriam had laughed and laughed.

"The Lord is testing us," said Sariah now, curtly. "Now hold up that sheet."

Alma pulled the sheet off Myrtice's feet, and Miriam couldn't see what was happening down there. She did see her mother ducking under the sheet with a handful of what looked like the threads the little dead caterpillars had made last summer. It looked as if Sariah were going to spin a cocoon around herself or Aunt Myrtice or both, and then they would disappear together.

"No!" Miriam burst from the wardrobe. "Don't go in there!"

•   •   •

Now, at last, Edouard Versailles knew what it was to be happy. Every time he checked Ophelia's pulse and found it stronger, every time he weighed her and another pound registered on the dial, every time he studied her fluids under his microscope, he felt a pulse of feeling he could call by no other name. It was happiness when he treated her with his galvanic invention, when he saw her face flush and her body shudder; happiness when he charted the waning of her symptoms and, inverse to them, the waxing of her health and beauty. He was giving her the great gift of herself—and losing *himself* in the process, as a medical man should.

He abandoned all other projects, including not just his father's menagerie and his own collection of rare plants but also the architects and builders completing the Institute downmountain. How could he care about a new shipment of cot springs or beakers when a miracle was already underway in his own house? Much better to sit at Ophelia's bedside and observe, with an attentiveness that might have seemed religious if Edouard had had any use for religion, the resurrection of her flesh. Just as he had prescribed, she brought all the juices down, and the results supported his theory beyond what even he might have asked. After an initial sluggishness due to dehydration, her body began flushing itself most efficiently, keeping the nurses and maids busy with the bedpans. Every day she had a bath in the foaming waters piped down from Hygeia Spring, and her skin seemed to drink it in and grow each day infinitesimally more supple, more luminous, more full of both life and liquid; with each revolution of the earth, her bones appeared a fraction less prominent, her hair a whisper's breadth thicker. Soon her eyes stopped glittering with fever and shone instead with steady light; best of all, her cough retreated to the tops of her lungs, and the blood faded away until her spit cup often contained nothing more alarming than that of any other resident at the glass house. He taught her to breathe again, deeply and using each muscle in her body; and with practice her breath came more easily.

There was but one element lacking to make her cure complete: her story. But he was convinced that it was a mere matter of time before she recovered her past and, with it, information that would help him understand why her body had become so susceptible to the deadly bacilli. With memory, as with physical hygiene, the cure would flourish, as he would at last be able to put to rest the mysterious demons that plagued her.

"Have you recollected anything, Miss Ophelia?" he asked almost every day. "Perhaps in your sleep?"

Sometimes she answered this question with a laugh; sometimes she shuddered and turned away. Occasionally she began to weep, so stormily that he feared she would do herself an injury; then he prescribed an extra dose of opiate in the broths and waters that the nurses brought.

Fortunately, Edouard's studies had shown opium was an integral and by no means unusual part of most cures for consumption, as it promoted sleep by cleansing and soothing the nerves. Doctors around the world had decided to dose their most wretched patients with the stuff of deep dreams, and this was one method, at least, with which Edouard could find no fault. He himself had occasional recourse to the soothing pleasures of laudanum. Quietly, then, Miss Pym and the other nurses dissolved sticky balls of medicine into Ophelia's food, and Ophelia slept. Under the opium, her dreams appeared to be vivid if not always agreeable; she murmured in them frequently and at length but never described what Edouard suspected must be nightmares. She said she could not put any of her dreams into words but that there were no useful memories in them.

Most nights, Ophelia slept beautifully, reflected in the shiny glass walls; and she woke with ever greater energy. Thus, by the early months of 1886, she had become what Nurse Pym proudly called a handful. Much to her own surprise, Miss Pym had recognized that the electricity was of benefit to Famke. It helped the girl's body to uncurl, to become more elastic, more capable of assuming the postures of good health. Witnessing this, Pym came to have faith in Mr. Versailles's strange theory of hygiene and, even without his knowledge, to promote it subtly in the town below. She was grateful to be part of this wondrous new cure, and from time to time Famke discovered her kneeling on the floor, offering thanks up to God for the gift of modern medicine.

The patient, however, had had enough of her bed; she was complaining of boredom and demanding to be allowed up. Edouard felt strongly about the restful component of his cure, and he would not allow her to rise from the pillows under her own locomotion, even to use the sparkling bathroom nearby; but he knew he was losing control of his patient. Her opiate dosage had reached a level he was reluctant to increase, and he began to cast about for some sort of gentle occupation for her; something not too taxing, for which the occasional drug-induced languor of her fingers would not be a hindrance.

Seated at his great warped desk, Edouard sifted through the drawers where he kept his parents' most treasured personal items. He had long ago boxed up his pious mother's collection of prayer books and crucifixes— Edouard could not follow any creed that celebrated physical suffering—but he had collected more precious memento mori in brass coffers and faded velvet bags: locks of his mother's dull auburn hair woven into bracelets, his father's iron gray strands coiled inside rings and brooches—the jewelry he planned to give a wife if one ever found her way to his lonely mountain. He'd also had hair from both the elder Versailles twined into a wreath that he thought would look very fine atop a bridal veil. The Chinese maids sometimes jested, but always in quiet tones, that there was not a hair left on either head at rest in the miniature Taj Mahal.

He was so used to collecting hairs that now, in another drawer, he had a nest of fiery red locks rescued from Ophelia's bath water, her comb, her pillows. The singsong sisters gathered them without question, drying and untangling each strand, then mounting it all on a hair receiver to await some future grand purpose. The time was early as yet, and of course he would wear no such memento while he was her doctor, but Edouard could imagine weaving Ophelia's hairs into the prettiest object of all. He envisioned an intricate diorama of flowers, bees, and butterflies that could occupy a prominent position in his study. Or perhaps a gleaming watch fob, something he might use to replace the worn maternal one he used for fidgeting. The old woman who had made his parents' tokens had died several summers before, but Ophelia had long, artistic fingers. Perhaps she herself could weave the fob when she recovered enough to be weaned off opium and regain her natural quickness. Or, if she did not recover—

"Life's Importance!" he barked, and the words echoed through the lacy structure of iron.

The maid came as fast as she could, swaying on her crippled little feet. She stopped, face carefully blank to hide the pain, one hand behind her tunic steadying herself against the doorframe.

Edouard assumed the stern countenance of a doctor. "Are you skilled with the needle?" he asked.

The maid nodded. She hemmed and mended his sheets, but he could not be expected to know it, any more than he could know of her childhood spent spinning silk threads, a cricket in a cage at her elbow, to make a trousseau she would never need. She had been kidnapped at age fourteen, just on the eve of her marriage to a man as rich as the one who employed her here.

"Could you make something like this?" He pulled out a bracelet, and she limped forward to look.

Life's Importance had a more than basic understanding of needlecraft, but she could not account for the little quills of hair that spiralled round the thick circlet. She hesitated, then shrugged.

For once, Edouard was irritated at a silence. Life's Importance, who scarcely spoke at all, was normally his favorite of the three maids. "Could the other girls do it?" he asked.

She shrugged again, then bowed her head to show humility.

Edouard sighed and tucked the bracelet back into its box. "Bring me Ophelia's chart," he ordered.

He simply had to refine the treatment. Perhaps an extra session of electricity each day would flush out the bacilli more quickly . . .

Life's Importance disappeared.

Chapter 43

· · · · ·

Nowhere else have so many extensive colonies been successfully planned and started as in California, much of whose prosperity is due to the scientific skill with which its settlements have been established.

Moses King,
King's Handbook of the United States

There came a cold, gray day in February, a day on which the strongest horse would only flounder on the icy path to Edouard's palace. Dr. Beachly put on his thickest boots and headed up the mountain. The latest supply wagon had brought long-awaited light fixtures to the new Institute, and for this Edouard Versailles would be grateful; but somewhere between Chicago and Hygiene the boxes had been opened, and whoever had inspected the contents had repacked them. Luckily, not a single globe or flute was broken; but the new packing materials bore disturbing implications for Mr. Versailles.

"I thought you should see this." Beachly handed his employer a crumpled sheet of yellow paper. "There were several among the crates."

Edouard Versailles took the paper and began the delicate process of unfolding. The page was grimy and soft, as fragile as lace, and it fell apart in places along the creases. Nonetheless he managed to untangle the shreds and lay them out on the desk, atop a diagram of "the inner female parts, with assorted anomalies of size and proportion."

He pieced together a face and a word. Ophelia's face, underneath the legend WANTED. The likeness was crude, the nose too small and the cheekbones too low; but clearly this was his patient.

"There were several of these handbills," Beachly said again, rubbing his hands in embarrassment, "but I believe I have found them all. It is for you to decide what to do." Privately, he hoped Versailles would elect to keep the discovery a secret—as the patient was virtually a secret herself—and continue his mysterious treatment. Downmountain, it was the dawn of a momentous era for Dr. Beachly and his associates, and at this stage Edouard Versailles could only be a nuisance; some months ago he had caused significant delay by insisting the rooms be wired for electricity as well as plumbed for gas. Fortunately, his work with this "wanted" woman, Ursula Summerfield, kept him out of Beachly's way, and the three tall hexagons were nearly ready for real paying patients and their formally trained doctors.

Edouard was silent a long moment, puzzling over the broken text.

WAN ED

Information as to whereabo   of Ursula Summerfield,
formerly of Prophet City, Ut   Terr.
Hair red or black, eye   ue, build slender.

REW RD

Respond to Heber Goodho   of that town or to any officer
of the law in Deseret Cou

"Hair red or black"? "Officer of the law"? And who was Heber Goodho? Edouard stroked his watch fob and thought.

Behind him, Beachly coughed; not as a patient would cough, but as a polite reminder of his presence.

Edouard acted all at once and summarily. He gathered the yellow scraps in one fist and rushed out, leaving Beachly to study the gynecological drawings, and Ancient Jade to sweep up the leaves of jasmine Edouard had torn from the banister in his haste.

Up in her bright, airy room, he found Ophelia moving her hands beneath the bedclothes. When she saw him, she opened her mouth as if to voice some complaint, but at the look on his face she stopped herself.

Silently, upon the faded velvet of Grandmother's Flower Garden, Edouard patched together the handbill.

Once all the facts lay before her, Ophelia chewed her lip and coughed, then fumbled among the sheets for a handkerchief. He felt she was trying to distract him, and he did nothing, though his own linen square remained a damp but clean ball in his hand.

"I . . . that is a strange picture," she said at last, when he made no move toward pocket, basin, or bottle. "I know nothing about it, but that woman is very plain. She does not really resemble me, does she?"

Edouard's voice trembled as much as his hands, but he spoke clearly. "Are you Ursula Summerfield?"

She did not answer but looked as if she were trying hard to come up with words.

Edouard flung his arms wide, losing the handkerchief and disordering his cravat. "You are!" he cried. "And you remember it perfectly well!"

Finally recognizing his absolute conviction, Famke took a deep breath and sighed. She picked at a loose seam in the quilt, feeling sad that she'd never got to use the flush toilet; she had always known this was just a matter of time, but she had hoped to be considerably better before Edouard threw her out into the streets. "Yes," she admitted reluctantly, "my name is Famke Sommerfugl. Or Ursula Summerfield—Ursula is the name the nuns gave me, and Summerfield is what Americans made of my—"

Edouard would not be distracted with etymologies. "But what have you done?" he demanded. "The law is asking for you. Was it murder, robbery . . ." His words trailed away as his thoughts reached toward depravities of which he could not quite conceive.

Famke realized she had not enjoyed her pretense at amnesia; what a relief it was at last to claim her own name and to let herself remember her life. Even to her own ears, her voice sounded different now, more like a real voice. "I have not killed anyone. And I have not stolen anything." Briefly, she thought of the silver tinderbox that Heber had once thought she'd taken from Herr Skatkammer: How long ago that seemed. "I don't know why they would mention the law."

He regarded her through narrowed eyes; for once he was not too embarrassed to meet her gaze. "So now you tell me you can remember? That is convenient."

She would not look up; the quilt top was coming apart nicely. "Yes, I remember. I always have remembered."

Moving like an automaton, Edouard sat down in the chair from which he'd explained the intricacies of tubercle and bacillus, the chair from which he had watched her sleeping and dreamed, himself, ambitious dreams for her cure. *So she remembered.* He was not as surprised as he thought he should be; he thought he must have known this all along. Opiates aside, the woman had always seemed too sharp and too quick of wit, and Edouard knew now that he had been her willing dupe. Even so, he was tempted to believe her protestations of innocence . . .

Irrelevantly, Edouard's mind played a game of word association in his all-but-forgotten native tongue: Famke . . . *femme que* . . . She was *la femme que*—the woman whom—what?

"*Alors*," he asked, in a bit of a daze, "who is this Heber Goodho of Utah?"

"Heber . . ." Famke hesitated. No clever story sprang to mind; all she could think about, inexplicably, was that half-seen flush toilet. "Goodhouse. He is my husband."

Edouard's face went pink. "You have a husband?"

"Yes." She looked away again, feeling rather shy but at the same time suddenly hopeful. She thought Edouard must be thinking of the electrical treatments Down There and what a husband might have to say about them. Certainly Edouard and his nurses had been rather free with her body. Famke wondered what she might make of this; for, just at the moment, she wanted nothing more than to stay right here in Hygiene and continue her treatments, to regain her health completely. Edouard must be made to want it as badly as she did.

"But he doesn't advertise for you under his last name. You are Summerfield and he is Goodho—Goodhouse."

"That is because . . . in Utah . . ." Here her powers of explanation truly failed; she had seen enough of the world to know that Edouard would not be so delicate with a plural wife as he would with the singular companion of a man's heart and soul.

But Versailles read her silence as easily as he read an anatomical chart. "It was a *Mormon* marriage," he guessed, and he put all the proper meaning into the word.

Miserably, Famke nodded.

"And *you* are a Mormon?"

"The proper term is 'Latter-Day Saint,'" Famke said, much as Sariah or Myrtice might have done. She remembered her baptism in the Salt Lake tabernacle, the shock of the cold water and the tangle of undergarments around her body; then those meetings in the ward house, where she had stood up and described the moments at which God had revealed true faith to her. Those had been just stories, but didn't they combine with the baptism to make her something different? Certainly she had done more to prove she was Mormon than she'd ever done to assert her Catholicism.

"I'm not sure if I'm a Saint," she said at last. "I did not want to be one particularly, but I think I was made one when I married—when circumstances forced me to marry Mr. Goodhouse." She felt a twinge of disloyalty, remembering again that Heber had been good to her. It was thanks to him, after all, that she first experienced what she now knew enough to call the healing powers of hygienic crisis. "I was an orphan, you see . . . The sisters raised me in the Immaculate Heart orphanage in Denmark. That is where I got my cough—they called it the Immaculate chest—"

"Catholic?" Edouard interrupted.

"Yes. But when I wanted to come to America, the only way was to borrow money from the Saints . . ." She stopped there, unable to explain her decision to marry the man who had lent her the money.

But Edouard surprised her once more: He seemed exhilarated, running his hands through his hair in delighted agitation and regarding her with the light of a rescuer in his eyes. "You married outside your faith, and you converted under pressure. A Mormon union will be easy to annul. We need merely ask this Goodhouse to sign some—"

"Oh, no!" Famke cried. "He must not learn where I am!" She was sure that Heber would come at once, would assert his right as her husband to sweep her up and bear her off to Utah, where Sariah's vigilant gaze would make it even harder to escape than before. Heber loved her; but Edouard was helping her, though even he did not know how much. Soon she would be cured, and *then* she could leave.

Versailles regarded her hands, which lay weak and white upon the quilt, for a long minute. "Was Goodhouse . . . cruel to you?" he asked.

That could explain a great deal. She thrust loyalty and obligation aside, and scarcely hesitated this time as she said: "Yes."

"And that is why you lied about your memory? So that I wouldn't send you back to him?"

"Yes."

"And when you came here—when you were looking for your brother— it was so he could rescue you?"

"Yes, rescue me."

"Well, then," said Edouard, "we must try to contact him."

We must try to contact him. Famke felt a glow deep inside. At last, she would have help looking for Albert! With the Versailles fortune aiding her quest, it should not take long. She had given up hope that he might find his way here on his own.

Almost perversely, however, her mind recognized a related danger: "Whatever you do, I pray you to . . . You must not use my name at all. Mormons . . . They read the newspapers. They post those signs. They have many ways of communicating—if even one of them found out I am here, they would all know, and then . . ."

"We shall certainly be cautious," Edouard said. "Your brother has a different surname, does he not? Albert Castle?"

Famke thought he was asking for more than confirmation of fact; or perhaps her guilty conscience made her explain more than she needed to. "Orphans in Denmark have only Christian names. We may give ourselves second names if we wish, and Albert lived a long time in England. He thought Castle a good one for a painter."

Edouard accepted this without further question; and indeed much of it was true. "We will use only his name in the advertisements— 'Albert Castle is asked to contact his sister in Hygeia Springs—'"

He continued drafting the announcement aloud, and with each word Famke's heart sank. Albert might see such an advertisement, it was true; but since he had no sister, he would not respond. He might even think it was one of the *Ludere* who had written to the papers. Either way, this would be no help, and it might somehow draw the Goodhouses; but she could not think how to word an announcement that would call Albert and only Albert to her. And anyway, did she really want him to see her like this, with her bones showing and the blood still blue beneath her skin? Perhaps it was best to stay here and wait till she was well, if Edouard would have her.

Meanwhile Edouard's heart was plummeting, too. Already he regretted his offer to help in this way. Of course he was happy to discover that Ophelia—or Ursula Summerfield Goodhouse, as he must now think of her—had family who might come to her aid; but this brother might think she needed rescue not only from the Mormons but from Edouard as well. And then there was the risk that an emotional scene, whether joyful or distressing, would affect the progress of her cure. In point of fact, Edouard thought, it would be best to make no haste with the search.

He let his voice trail away and simply looked at his patient, who was studying her own hands and clearly had not heard him the last ten minutes. *Ursula*, he thought, *named for the saint who led eleven thousand virgins across Europe.* This namesake appeared to be on the point of tears: her lips were very red, and her eyes had swollen. Indeed, as he watched her, one fat opalescent drop rolled out of each eye and trailed its way down her cheek.

"Perhaps we should not risk it," he said in the deep silence of that sunny room. "You need your rest, and travel is dangerous in winter. Your brother might be injured as he tried to come to you. What would you think if we waited till spring?"

He held his breath, studying each nuance of her reaction.

At first she did not react, merely continued her contemplation of her hands and the counterpane. Then she wiped her eyes on the backs of her wrists and looked up at him. "I am grateful," she said, "that you will allow me to stay."

It was clear that she felt emotional, but he was not sure if gratitude were uppermost. Yet her emotions lent her restored face such grace and loveliness that at last his mind completed its *jeu de mots*:

She, who called herself Famke, was *la femme que j'adore*.

Edouard would not let the words' full meaning sink into his mind, not yet. Instead he blurted out the first question that came to his lips: "Are you skilled with a needle?"

Chapter 44

· · · · ·

In any Eastern sense there is no rural life in California, and the thing called
rustic simplicity is unknown. [. . .] The instant you rise to the dignity of a
home, with women and comforts in it, fig-leaves disappear and Eve's flounces
grow artistic.

BENJ. F. TAYLOR,
BETWEEN THE GATES

Among the packing materials for Hygeia Springs' new light fixtures
were not only the Wanted posters but also countless sheets of
newspaper, some of which might have borne nearly as much interest for Edouard as the yellow pages Beachly found. But as the significant
text was small and buried among other notices, Beachly did not see it, and
so it was burned along with the rest of the trash.

Harry Noble, however, had seen the item when it first appeared, in both
the *New York Times* and the *Rocky Mountain News*.

Wanted. Reward.
Information about oil painting. Features red-haired subject, feminine,
posed artistically in a cave. Urgently sought by a serious collector. Painter is
English and canvas is large. Please direct reply to . . .

There followed a New York address, an agent at a shipping company. Harry
had seen no reason why he, whose information was slim but genuine,
should not see what it might yield him. He wrote to tell the prospective
buyer about Royal Barnes's auction of the probable painting; he asked, incidentally, if there were any information to be had about the model. And now
here was the reward: twenty-five green American dollars, as much as he got
for a well-researched story, his simply for writing a few unpublished lines.
The agent thanked Mr. Hermes for providing the name of the painting's

auctioneer and requested that if he came across any other information he should send it on immediately. About the model there was no word.

Harry pocketed the money but made no plan to do further detective work. The funds would buy gaspers and a supper or two in the next month, but then his book would come out and twenty-five dollars would be petty cash indeed.

Or perhaps, he decided on further reflection, he might use this windfall to treat himself to some feminine company. Opal Cinque had recently presented a girl with a cloud of hair as orange as her own, and Harry, like many of Opal's visitors, was curious to see whether the cumulus below matched the cirrus above. The effect must be particularly striking under electric light.

◆　◆　◆

The discovery of Ophelia's true identity sparked a complex reaction in Edouard. With that crude line drawing on the handbill, it was as if a bright light had suddenly shone upon her, revealing details and facets hitherto hidden in shadows. Now, instead of a memoryless waif, she was a wife; and wives commanded respect, even after they had left their husbands. Edouard's own parents had spent more than a decade apart while Edouard, Senior, built his fortune in the mountains up and down California, and their bond had been no less strong as a result.

And yet Ursula Summerfield Goodhouse was a *third* wife; a Mormon. It was a simple matter to rebaptize her, and he had it done immediately; any religion would be preferable to that one and would strengthen her case against Goodhouse, and she knew the Latin catechism well enough. But as long as she stayed married, she was compromised. Who knew what strange rites she might have participated in as a member of that tenebrous faith? What strange beliefs she might now hold? Whether she believed in the infamous Miracle of the Gulls, or that God had a wife to whom men could pray . . . Her mental integrity had been shaken, and though he would never ask her new father confessor to reveal Famke's secrets, Edouard's mind was full of questions. How would it be possible to flush such disturbing notions out of her now? If he could find a way, how rapidly she might improve, how easily she might become fit for a complete life. A complete life such as the one he occasionally allowed himself to envision for himself.

At times, he wandered the grounds, dodging zebra and exotic fanged deer and mulling over other questions. He fed the panthers in the cat house and daydreamed about at last taking a wife and fathering children of his own. He and his hospital would restore life to more than a few; didn't he have a right to happiness as well? But the sight of the small Taj was always enough to pull him up short. Those white walls and moldering sarcophagi marked the fate of those who devoted themselves selfishly to one another, without sufficient view to communal health and hygiene; they indulged in a kind of hygienic flushing, true, through the marriage debt, but it was a limited and necessarily inferior process, dependent as it was upon the passions that so disturbed peace of mind. And yet, Edouard dared to think, with the modern technology there might be a way to introduce the more salubrious galvanic crisis into marriage and still enjoy the other . . .

So the winter waned, and despite occasional setbacks Famke continued to grow stronger. By the time the first daffodils had bloomed, she was able to leave her bed to visit the water closet, and more than once Edouard looked up in his wanderings about the grounds to find her at the windows of her room, gazing down on him. When they met in person, she complained of boredom and asked repeatedly for a pair of spectacles and something to read. He dutifully arranged for an oculist to visit and gave her a book of domestic poetry, and she thanked him unenthusiastically; but he did once catch her reading the more sensationalistic parts of Miss Pym's New Testament—which passages he then carefully excised with his razor, much to Miss Pym's indignation. It was time to find his patient something useful but soothing to do.

Ophelia (Edouard still could think of her by no other name) claimed to be no needlewoman, and the idea of a watch fob made of her own hair struck her as odd; but she informed her benefactor that she had a way with a paintbrush. "Albert taught me," she said. "He told me I had a natural gift for it." Edouard thought of the Hygeia painting and frowned.

"You say you do not like the painting," she acknowledged. "Well then . . . You might let me change it for you—I am sure that will give me useful occupation, and it is quiet work."

Edouard did not confess that he liked *Hygeia* so little that, after Famke's first brief visit to the house, he had almost succeeded in having the thing burnt. Now he told his three Chinese maids to remove the painting from the stable, brush off the cobwebs, and deliver it to Ophelia's suite. It was far too big for the inner staircase, of course, so Ancient Jade had workmen remove a large pane of glass from the wall and slide the enormous picture inside.

Famke nearly swooned with the memory of *Nimue* making the reverse journey out of Fru Strand's rooming house a year before. She could not give in to the impulse, however, for then Edouard would not allow her to leave her bed again; so she bit down hard on her lower lip and said, as she had said then, "Treat it gently, please."

The nurses had been moved out of their bedroom and the space was now dedicated to *Hygeia*, because Famke should not sleep with the odors of paint and turpentine. The inner walls and floor were sealed to prevent the circulation of noxious air in the rest of the house, and Edouard had the carpenters build a special easel and set it against the central wall. The easel could tilt inward, for easy reach. They also constructed a collection of ladders in varying heights, all topped with chairs; no matter what section Famke was working on, she could sit.

But in the brilliant morning sunshine, Famke chose to stand before *Hygeia* in a white wool dressing gown, unsteady on legs that had grown unused to supporting even her slight weight. She put on the new pair of spectacles, made just for her with real gold-plated frames, and studied the canvas gravely. No, certainly not Albert's best work, but his all the same; and because it was his, she found in it a germ of beauty. The ice was very nice, and it contained the familiar dead flowers. Certainly the work held possibility.

She assumed her most professional air, the one she had used to such good effect with the madams and prostitutes of Colorado. "What would you like to see different here, Mr. Versailles?"

Edouard considered the two women before him: the recovering patient and the painted Hygeia. Beauty and a feminine beast, or a princess and one ugly stepsister.

"It is really the central figure," he said at last. "Her colors, her—" His hands made vague shapes in the air, and Famke understood these were criticisms of Hygeia's form.

"I can change those things," she assured Edouard. It would be a pleasure to do so.

While they stood gazing, the light shifted suddenly as the sun popped over the mountainside. When the glass walls magnified the winter rays, the colors of the painting began to glow—all except for those that made up Hygeia herself, for they were curiously dull, as if Albert had mixed them much more hastily and cheaply than he had done with the tints for the background, then laid them on more thinly. In the background, among the familiar jags and lumps of ice, Famke recognized Albert's old attention to detail, and that same painstaking work was found in the castle signature. It was only Hygeia herself—big-nosed, straw-haired, and somehow vague and unformed—who suffered in this composition. And that was easily remedied. Then too, as tribute to Edouard and the living waters that brought health, she might add a series of springs among the ice crystals . . . Surely Albert would not mind . . .

Edouard coughed delicately, to get her attention. "Miss Summerfield, do you think"—he tried to ask as if the idea had just occurred to him, though it was first in his mind— "she might have hair of your color?"

Famke rewarded him with a shimmering sapphire stare. "It will be easy," she said.

*   *   *

I t was as if a figure from a painting had dropped from the wall into his arms. But the girl Viggo held was indisputably alive: warm to the touch, with skin smoother than the most finely finished canvas, and—he sniffed— a most definite odor as well. Tobacco, perspiration, the omnipresent whiskey; a faint scent of something sweet. Perhaps it was lemons. Her likeness hung on a wall in the parlor of her boardinghouse, but this was the real thing. Her hair was pale orange rather than brown, and her lips were thinner, but still she was recognizably the same woman, and in his drunken state Viggo found this simple fact to be fascinating.

She squirmed out of his embrace and struck a pose where he could see her. It was the same pose in which she had been painted as a woman of music; only now her arms held no lyre but curved instead around empty space, and behind her flopped a set of spangled wings. Most of the girls were wearing them tonight, for once a week they played at being fairies. The wings had given the parlor a dreamy atmosphere, and after one glass of whiskey Viggo almost believed the girls could have flown away if they chose.

After holding the position a few seconds, she lifted her hands slowly to her head and untied the ribbon that held her pale red locks in place. The hair was dry and coarse, once curled and now limply straight; but it fell nearly to her waist, and when she shook her head the scent of lemons grew stronger.

She began to undress. Off came the lace-and-spangle wings and the green basque and skirt; she hung them carefully over the back of the room's one chair. Then the ruffly white corset cover, and her breasts were exposed.

Propped up by a dingy white corset, they were small and firm and pink, with a network of blue veins that reminded him of a corpse and the most startling nipples he had ever seen—so puckered and dark they looked almost brown.

"Should I take the corset off, too?" she asked, twisting the ribbon tie around one finger and fluttering her lashes at him coyly.

Unable to speak, he nodded. Any resistance he might have made was lost in a haze of whiskey and curiosity.

"It's two dollars extra, on account of how long it takes to lace up again."

Once more, helpless, he nodded.

So she removed the corset, and her waist expanded as it met the air. Her middle was covered in red wrinkles and welts left by the corset. Then, moving swiftly because the air in the room was chilly, she stepped out of her pantaloons, posed briefly again, and jumped into bed.

Viggo had never seen a live woman naked, and because the madams dressed the expired girls before he painted them, it had been months since he'd seen a dead one. It came as a shock to see the flesh of this one move: the undulations of her breasts, the jiggle under her arms, the dimples that formed in her buttocks and thighs when she lay down. The greatest surprise of all was the tuft of hair that fronted her sexual parts—not just because it was brown rather than orange, like the hair on her head, but because it was there at all. Viggo was so used to looking at the artist's cloudy rendering of that area that to see it now as coarsely covered as his own gave him a lurch in the stomach, as if he were looking at something unnatural.

"What's the matter, lover?" she asked in a low voice, propping herself up on one elbow and holding out the other hand to him. "Aren't you coming?"

Viggo shifted awkwardly, and he felt Famke's money rub against his foot.

In a way, this pregnant pause was Famke's fault, and the Catholic in Viggo blamed her, for his present situation was the direct result of that scrap of canvas that he had bought in Leadville. At first it seemed to have brought him luck; or maybe he had simply scoured Colorado so thoroughly that he was bound to have made some progress by now. Town by town, the various stages of Famke's journey had fallen into place, and he felt he knew exactly where she had been and when. He took the junk dealer's scrap out of his boot every night before going to bed, and in his dreams the hair waved and the arms beckoned him forward.

Now those arms had guided him to the capital of New Mexico Territory, where suddenly he found spring had begun. Very little snow lingered in the muddy streets when he stepped out of the stage coach and inquired, with his beautiful manners and confident new English, where he might find "the district of the whores."

So it was that he found himself in the gleaming salon of a Mrs. Opal Cinque, surrounded by winged girls and gazing at the enormous *Evening of the Ladies*, in which Famke was all but unrecognizable, fatter and paler of hair—in fact resembling Mrs. Cinque more than the Famke he had come to know. In his surprise he found himself accepting a glass of unusually strong drink from a man in a money-green suit, and feeling so awkward and out of place that he actually drank from it. One glass followed another; in short order he was drunk, and was swept dizzily away to a room occupied by a girl whose name he did not know, except that it was painted on her door and had something to do with springtime.

"Well?" She hopped from the bed and took both his hands in hers. Shyly—or with the pretense of shyness—her brown eyes looked up into his blue ones. "This your first visit to a woman, dearie?"

Feeling as if he were in the confessional, Viggo nodded a third time. If he had had control of his feet, he would have run; but he was discovering that whiskey had a number of strange effects. Only one part of him could move now, and it was not a part to aid in general locomotion.

"Well!" she said again, her cheeks dimpling to match her stippled bottom. She put her arms around him and drew him close, so the chill in her body penetrated his clothing, even where his trousers were most warm. "Isn't *that* a treat! Oh, there's nothing to be afraid of. We'll go very slowly . . ."

Before he knew what had happened, he was in this earthly fairy's bed, and his trousers were undone, and her thin red lips were—of all things—down below his stomach, drawing more heat from him than he'd ever imagined.

For the first time in his life, Viggo swore. "*Fanden!*"

Chapter 45

·····

The bee has a full year's work in South California: from March to August inexhaustible forage, and in all the other months plenty to do,—no month without some blossoms to be found.

HELEN HUNT JACKSON, "CALIFORNIA," IN
GLIMPSES OF THREE COASTS

Ophelia—Miss Summerfield, Edouard reminded himself yet again—took an immediate turn for the better when he let her into the studio. With each stroke that she made in her effort to improve upon *Hygeia*, her own health improved as well, and far more rapidly than ever before: Her stride became firmer, her voice more steady; breasts began to push against the warm wool of her gowns. She even seemed to grow taller. It was as if she were painting health into her own body while she made Hygeia more like her.

At least, such were the changes Edouard hoped she was making to the figure in the painting. Famke had forbidden anyone to enter her studio, other than the maids who cleaned her brushes, and Edouard considered it a point of honor not to ask them about her activities. Alone all day, she worked with a dedication verging on dangerous zeal. Very quickly, Edouard realized he would have to limit her hours in the studio or risk seeing her exhausted again. Thenceforth she was allowed only two hours in the morning and, after an enforced nap, one in the afternoon.

"But it is impossible to accomplish anything in such a time!" she protested, angry tears hovering. "I need at least an hour to achieve my inspiration—I mean to feel I am one with the painting. It is," she said with a true burst of inspiration, "as if something inside is telling me what to paint, and I am obeying. You must give me more time."

This argument was virtually the only one that might have swayed

Edouard, and indeed he did waver a moment; it was entirely possible that her newfound health was taking on a palpable life of its own and expressing itself in pictorial form. She might have prevailed if he had had any faith in her teacher. But: "No," he said firmly, "your recovery is more important than a painting. Become fully healthy first, and then you can dedicate yourself entirely to your work." He did not mention that he hoped she would eventually find some worthier occupation. To smother further protest, he ordered her to take an extra galvanic treatment. At least she never refused those, and he was so used to giving them now that he hardly blushed at all. In fact, the treatments were calming to his nerves as well.

Thereafter, Edouard watched the clock carefully during Famke's time in the studio. Each morning, he had a manservant bring a watch up from the village, where the more conventional living conditions made time run more smoothly, and he kept one eye on the slow black hands as he addressed himself to business.

He found much to do around the house. Now that Famke was moving about more, she had complained about the heavy odor of jasmine; so Edouard directed the Chinese gardeners to remove the vines his father had planted and to replace them with frangipani, which Famke liked better. He loved to see her bury her face in the fragrant blooms and come up radiant with scent. He hired another indoor gardener and ordered gardenias, hyacinths, and orange trees; the smells warred with one another and triumphed individually according to the time of day.

In the evenings, Edouard and Famke sat on the mildewed parlor sofa, surrounded by pots of whichever flower she favored that day. Together they read agreeable poetry by the likes of Alfred Tennyson and Coventry Patmore, and he began to postpone his walks and visits to the Taj in favor of the more immediately soothing pleasures of literature.

Famke, however, remained dissatisfied with their reading. She continued to ask for magazines and newspapers, although Edouard had banned them from the house as well as the township.

"They excite the wrong feelings," he explained patiently, "with their sensationalized stories. Such reading is as dangerous to lung sufferers as novels are."

"According to your opinion, even the Bible is sensational. How can it hurt me to read the *New York Times*? It is only facts."

Edouard gave her a tight smile and turned to Patmore again. Thereafter Miss Pym's already mutilated Bible made a swift trip downmountain, never to be seen again, and Edouard was careful to read only from the least religious domestic poets.

During the day, he had time at last to pay old bills and to hear reports of progress on the Institute. The triple hexagons were finished and the exteriors quickly painted honey gold, for his original conceit had been to found a sanatorium on the model of a beehive: The workers, doctors and nurses, would come and go with quiet efficiency, flying in and out of the individual rooms in which ailing kings and queens occupied themselves with nothing other than the effort to get well. At last this dream was taking shape, and the Institute would open its doors to patients in May or June. And yet Edouard found his passion for it had faded, replaced by a burgeoning interest in one particular patient who would never be immured in the Institute herself.

. . .

Famke, meanwhile, had begun to think of herself as trapped; a queen she might be, but among the bees even queens were confined to their cells. She was not allowed outside, her hours in the studio were limited, and now that she had new glasses, she had nothing worth reading. She found she missed newspapers the way she had once missed *The Thrilling Narrative of an Indian Captivity*; she wondered what the Dynamite Gang had done lately and whether Harry Noble had written anything interesting. There might even be news of Albert somewhere. For all she knew, he had sailed back to England.

As she repainted Hygeia's waist, she began to think of leaving; by the time she reached the breasts, her departure became certain. She was still weak, yes, but stronger than she had been when she arrived in Hygiene months before; if she'd been able to travel then, she could do it now. With the painting, fine new muscles had stretched themselves over the bones of her hands. She had breasts and hips again, and although Edouard forbade her mirrors, at night she saw herself reflected in the dark windows and knew she had regained a good measure of her bloom, the gleaming hair and rich complexion she was painting into Hygeia.

"I am beautiful," she whispered to herself. With each stroke of the brush, it seemed to become more true. She fell in love with the woman she was re-making—growing into a far, far better likeness than that horrible yellow handbill—and wondered if Edouard would let her take the canvas with her when she left. She refused to allow him in the studio, planning to surprise him with her achievements once she'd finished.

Mercifully, the three maids who came to fetch her at the end of each day, who helped her uncurl her stiff body, walked her down the hallway, and laid her in bed—these singsong sisters were her accomplices. They kept her confidence and did not tell Edouard how tired and cramped she was after working. In their gray costumes, with their expressionless faces, and on their tiny, pained feet, the girls hobbled along, supporting her and themselves on odd tables and outcroppings of iron. They laid her in bed and cleaned her fingers with turpentine. They said nothing, either, to describe the painting, knowing that he longed to hear about it and would never ask. Had Famke thought about it, she would have seen that they were pleased to keep a small secret from him.

"Missy ready for 'lectricity," they would report merely, and their smooth faces gave no hint of either what Famke was doing or the disapproval they felt for Edouard's device. They did not understand the nature of the crisis that it brought about in Famke, never having felt one induced in themselves, so they thought the procedure was for Edouard's pleasure. If such instruments had been known in the cribs where they used to work as hundred-men's-wives, customers might have paid for the right to use them on the girls; these girls thought it unfair that Famke underwent the treatments without pay. Thus they saw her privacy as her compensation, and if she had asked them to carry letters outside or even sneak her a few dollars, they might have done it—never mind what they thought of the picture itself, which to them was no better than Edouard's anatomical charts and drawings.

If the four of them had been friends, Famke might have told them that with her work, she had begun to relish galvanic electricity even more than before, because she felt it planted the seeds of artistic inspiration in her. When her body started to pulse in the crisis, she saw Nimue, then the brushstrokes she'd have to make to bring Hygeia to look like that long-ago nymph. With those visions, she felt her physical strength grow; and it was a real struggle to bide her time until the next session in the studio. If she could only spend a few uninterrupted days in there, she thought, she might quickly finish and bear the results proudly toward San Francisco.

"I think I feel strong enough to travel soon," she hinted to Edouard one night.

He slammed a heavy book shut, his face as white as her dressing-gown. "By no means, Miss Summerfield!" he said with uncharacteristic force. "You are far below the ideal weight for a woman of your height—you should gain at least twenty more pounds—and you are so easily tired—and you must take care with the air that you breathe, or your lungs might collapse entirely—"

Famke sighed and ignored him, gazing instead at the red-stained edges of his ornate *Collected Patmore*. So he would not let her go; and now she felt she could not breathe. But she had recently learned both patience and prudence, so she forced her lungs to inflate and deflate as normal. She bit down on her tongue for strength and to prevent it from speaking.

There was no telling what Edouard might do if she pressed him; the man who had cut the description of Christ's death out of a Bible would think nothing of locking a door upon a recalcitrant patient or even tying her to her bed. He read aloud for at least an hour while Famke seethed inwardly.

The next morning she felt the old heaviness in her limbs, and it was nearly impossible to drag herself from bed and dress for her hours in the studio. As it was, she arrived late, and stood half-slumbering before the canvas.

He has drugged me, she thought, but she felt too languid to react much. There was no anger, only a mild surprise. She began coughing, too, and lay down on the studio floor—just for a few minutes, she told herself as she sank into velvety darkness. When the maids came to collect her at the end of her allotted time, the filigree floor had imprinted itself on her cheek and arms. All three of them had to carry her to bed.

Edouard appeared to be all concern, particularly when a half hour's electrical treatment failed to produce a crisis. He listened to her lungs with his stethoscope and frowned. "Your system has been strained with overwork and excitement," he said, coiling up his tubes. He hardly dared to look at her as Miss Pym pulled the gown back over her chest. "The bacilli have formed new colonies inside. Or perhaps," he hypothesized, "there are some memories making you ill? An excess of emotion, even when recollected in tranquility, can be very dangerous. It is best to speak them aloud and despatch them."

"I like excitement," Famke interrupted drowsily. It was as if a thick blanket were wrapped around her, cocooning her from the rest of the world and restricting the flow of air to her lungs. Still, she knew she should give away no more secrets, admit to no more illness. "But could you stand a little farther away?"

He did, and he opened a window, which helped her breathe somewhat more easily. His movements were slow, as if he were depressed. "It is a medical fact," he said, "that tuberculosis comes in waves, ebbing and flowing. It is like the pulse of blood through a heart, at times full of strength rushing forward, at times seeping back to rest and renourish itself. You must take rest, too. At least a week, perhaps six, with abundant sleep—"

"No more laudanum," she said, drifting away on a surge of exhaustion.

"You haven't had any in a month," she heard him say from a great distance. His voice sounded so sincere that with the last ounce of her strength she opened her eyes. Mr. Versailles, she thought as she relaxed again, was looking at her almost the way Albert had done.

.   .   .

Viggo woke with a throbbing headache that nearly eclipsed the aches in the rest of his body. When he moved, the pain felt especially strong where the night before the animal part of his body had throbbed even more strongly than his head did now; and not just once, but four times.

How could he write to Sister Birgit now? And how could he look Famke in the face when at last he found her?

The girl in the bed woke briefly as he struggled into his trousers.

"It's forty dollars for the night," she mumbled sleepily. "Plus the two for taking off my corset. You can leave it all on the dresser."

Forty-two dollars, and Viggo's left boot held only thirty-nine. He had to take the rest from the right boot, and when he did it he felt he had sunk to his lowest point. Now not only had he betrayed his love with another woman, he had stolen from Famke as well.

"Come back and visit me again," the girl called with an obvious attempt to be charming, before she leaked a little wind and fell asleep again. On her door he read the name Mag: nothing to do with springtime after all. Clumsy *glem-mig-ik's*—what Americans called forget-me-nots—clustered around the letters, and Viggo felt ashamed. For a moment, he had forgotten what he should most have remembered.

He walked through the muddy streets feeling dirty, sinful, repugnant. It seemed right that a donkey should kick him or a stray dog take a bite from his leg; and yet neither of these things happened. He met only one other creature, a tall man with big funereal eyes, carrying a carpetbag and clearly bound for the depot. He was as lost in his own thoughts as Viggo was, and neither acknowledged the other.

Unmolested, Viggo made his way back to the modest hotel where he had stored his own bag—experience having taught him not to leave expensive chemicals unattended under a flophouse cot—and answered the Spanish proprietor's greeting with a glumly polite "Good morning."

And then came a surprise. "There is someone waiting to see you, Mr. Hart."

Viggo frowned. Looking around the shabby hallway that served as the hotel lounge, he had some difficulty imagining who it could be. There had to have been some mistake.

He said as much to Señor Garcia, who made an elaborate ceremony of checking the register. So the visitor must be a guest at the hotel . . .

"Ah, *aquí.*" Garcia's thick finger underscored a name written in what, even from a distance, Viggo could see was careful textbook script. "Her name is Mrs. Goodhouse. Shall I send my wife to see if she is awake?"

Chapter 46

. . . . .

*Find a place [in California] that seems as isolated as a mid-ocean island,
with neither lightning nor steam, and the dwellers are not prisoners.*

BENJ. F. TAYLOR,
BETWEEN THE GATES

As she regained her strength after the third and certainly final collapse, Famke rediscovered her restlessness and resentment, and
with them a plan. So Edouard wanted to keep her captive, like a
princess in a tower, like a saint in a cell—well then, she would escape. As
she unlocked her studio door for her first day back, she determined that the
very moment she finished *Hygeia*, she would find money somewhere in the
house and buy a ticket to San Francisco—and wherever else it was necessary to go—and then she would catch up to Albert.

Albert. The very thought of him stilled the blood in her veins, and she
nearly dropped to the floor again. She reminded herself yet again that once
they were reunited, he wouldn't need the fair but frail anymore; she herself
would again pose as Calafia, Salome, even Nimue. European painters were
fashionable in America; with the right model, Albert would have a great career here. She reminded herself yet again that once he had established himself, she would be more than a muse. Someday he could paint her portrait.

In a rush of anticipation, Famke slid the drape from *Hygeia*. The joy of
rediscovering her own work—the bright colors, the slim lines, the energy—was surprisingly intense; *Hygeia* was becoming beautiful, and that
transformation made Famke more than usually thoughtful. As she gazed on
what she had done to the body before her, and assessed what remained to
do, she reflected that she was coming to understand Albert and what had
gone amiss with this work—perhaps with all the other pictures he'd

painted on American shores. There was a slapdash rhythm to the brush-strokes in the central figure that reminded her of his mad flights through the streets. He must have painted *Hygeia* under pressure, and quickly; he had perhaps done the background first and taken care with it, but by the time he reached the woman's figure he was feeling a need to escape, and he had dashed her off. No, he had not succumbed to the careless principles of French painting after all; it was merely the duress of the marketplace that had caused him to sacrifice what he held most dear.

Well, Famke would continue to go slowly: The most important goal now was to make *Hygeia* perfect. And then, once she and Albert were reunited—he with his muse, one bringing greater knowledge and understanding to their work together—she thought that she might paint again as well. She might find that she was a real artist; she might paint alongside Albert, matching his strokes with her own, until there was no telling where his work ended and hers began.

It was a heady, giddying thought. She knelt down before *Hygeia* and took deep breaths, just as Edouard had taught her: In, out; in, out; and her head cleared. She rang for Precious Flower and a fresh palette.

When at last Famke stood with brush in hand, the desire to flee ebbed a bit. As she stirred oily spots of color and tapped them gently onto the surface, she knew her painting would be both beautiful and truthful; it would tell the truth about beauty, for, as Albert used to say, in every detail there is a message, and in beauty there is genius. Famke would remain until *Hygeia's* genius was full-fledged.

So in the next days the goddess's lips and cheeks grew even redder, her jaw thinner, her hair thicker and flaming. The mole vanished from her cheek. Her eyes—though Edouard had not asked for this—became a light, luminous green, the most beautiful eyes Famke could imagine, and the lids receded from the orbs. Her smock thinned out where it touched her body, and in those places Famke painted the whole truth of a woman. This, she imagined, must be how the Mormon God's wife felt, helping her husband to create.

At last, one afternoon in April, Famke laid down her brush for the last time. She had done what she could: Hygeia might not quite measure up to the image in her mind's eye, but she'd come as close as Famke could bring her.

"*Færdig.*" She said it first in Danish, to please herself, then translated in honor of Albert: "Finished," although there was no one to hear her.

The word seemed to travel through the walls, however, and in short order Edouard himself was knocking on the studio door.

"Miss Summerfield?" he called, and even Famke could sense his timidity. Though he said no more, she also divined his wishes immediately, and since she was so elated to be through she opened the door to him.

"Yes, I have finished," she said, wiping her hands on her dress and staining it red, green, yellow. She was flattered now that he wanted to see her work, half proud and half nervous. So this was what it felt like to be an artist . . . "Come and see."

Dazzled by the brightness of her smile, Edouard fairly fell into the room. He recovered himself and walked to the easel, where he raised his eyes and took in *Hygeia* all at once.

For a long time Edouard was silent, so silent that Famke heard the blood pounding in her head and suddenly, on its own, her body let down some juices. In an attempt at professionalism, she held her breath, trying not to give in to emotion.

"Well?" she asked at last, her eagerness making her rude. "Do you have an opinion?"

Edouard filled his lungs to the bottom, weighing a speech which he knew was the most important he might ever say to her; there were so many possible words and phrases, and perhaps only one right thing to say. He fidgeted with his old watch fob, which was now worn whisper thin. After the first glance, he could not bring himself to look again at the canvas, which had already burned its image into his brain; he knew his face must be stained with a blush as deep as the one on the painted cheeks.

"It is my opinion," he began heavily, "that, as you know, this painting was not much to begin with . . ." He could not think how to end the sentence, and he stopped to fidget some more and consider.

"There were good parts in the original," Famke said. Her hands were folded, and beneath the streaks of paint he saw her knuckles had gone white. "The ice was very well done." And yet, now that she looked at it again through Edouard's eyes, she thought she might rework it; for Albert had ranged his stalagmites in groups of three, like soldiers marching . . . And how did Edouard feel about her addition of Hygeia's springs? He had not commented . . .

Edouard cut into her thoughts, seeming rather to blurt out his next question. "Would you like to take lessons?"

Famke breathed carefully. "Lessons?"

"I can arrange it, if you want them."

What did that mean? She began with the most hopeful interpretation: "Do you *like* my painting?"

Edouard, too, was breathing with his whole body. "There is a certain . . . vigor to what you have done," he said, obviously struggling to balance tact and truthful opinion. "But I cannot call it quite professional."

Half afraid he had misjudged, Edouard looked back up at the immense canvas, and Hygeia's distasteful green eyes stared glassily back. She stood at slightly more than his own height, as colorful and intricately detailed as a medieval illumination. But those details—the goddess had hair of Famke's shade, yes, but its intricate whorls and scrolls reminded him of hellfire; her round arms and exaggerated bosom were the depiction of *la luxure* as imagined by a terrified peasant. And below the breasts—well . . .

If he were to be truthful, he would say this canvas was even worse than when she began.

"What do you mean by 'professional'?" Famke asked, with perspiration beginning to bead on her brow. "You mean the style of those who paint for hire, to the client's orders, without inspiration?"

Edouard blinked. "I merely referred to a certain . . . polish that is lacking here."

"I can't varnish it yet," she protested. "We have to wait till the paint is dry!"

"It is not the varnish," Edouard said stiffly. "It is the color—garish. It is the lines—exaggerated." When she continued to stare at him expectantly, he burst out, "This Hygeia looks as if she is— That is, she is not entirely the model of—"

"So you *don't* like her," she said, holding herself as still as a stone.

"The picture is not ready to hang." Now Edouard would not look at it or at her. Beachly had been wrong to buy this canvas, and it was his own fault that the thing had only got worse. "The truth, Miss Summerfield, is that there are certain elements of this composition that make it inappropriate for—for ladies and children—"

Suddenly Famke coughed. She turned her head so that she wouldn't spray the canvas; but this was a normal cough, no blood, and for a moment Edouard congratulated himself on what he had accomplished with her cure. She was *his* masterwork.

Even so, the cough was of long duration, and it so weakened her that she dropped to her knees at Hygeia's feet.

"I know—what you—mean to say," she gasped. "Her—hairs—"

"True . . . Such things are generally not painted," Edouard said, fumbling for a handkerchief; for there were tears on Miss Summerfield's cheeks, and he was not sure if they came from the cough or her emotions. "Perhaps you have not been properly exposed to artwork before." He shuddered to think what horrors her brother, painter of the first disastrous *Hygeia*, might have committed to canvas elsewhere.

"But I *have*," she said. She ignored the handkerchief he held out. "I have seen more paintings in one year than you have seen in your entire life of living here. And this is what I think is art." She wiped her nose on the back of her hand and said, "Anyway, you see those hairs every day. You see me."

Edouard felt himself growing warm, and then sickened with a lurch of shame instilled by the religion in which he'd been raised and of which this painting had unfortunately reminded him. He saw those red hairs again in his mind's eye and grew even warmer. "But that is for medical treatment," he said, rather too loudly. Like a proper clinician, he bent knifelike at the waist, then knelt and dabbed her nose with the handkerchief. "What is appropriate to medicine is unacceptable in entertainment. You may have had the best of intentions—" He stopped.

When he bent so clumsily, he'd brushed the peg holding the muslin used to cover the canvas at night. While he spoke, the fabric drifted slowly down, and now the end of it settled on the crown of Famke's head. The rest swirled away to tangle at her feet, and with the two of them on their knees, Edouard felt as if they were at an altar.

His heart pounded. He imagined he were about to place his lips on hers and thereby seal a pact. "You are—ill," he said, taking refuge once more in medicine.

Famke's eyes sank slowly shut, then opened halfway as the blood drained from her face. For once, she appeared to agree with him. "I need to rest," she said, in a feeble voice. But she shrank from his arms, wrapped herself in that muslin drape, and added, "I can walk there myself. You should leave me now."

Edouard felt he could do nothing but obey.

.   .   .

Birgit twisted the ring on her finger, the one that had marked her, at age eighteen, as a bride of Christ. She had lost some weight lately, and the ring was loose; she would have to wrap it in string to make sure it did not slip off her finger.

"Sister," Father Absalom said loudly, on a note of rebuke. The nuns sitting behind him were rigid and still, their faces blank. They would model their behavior, as their attitudes, on his.

"I am sorry, Father." Birgit folded her hands and drew a deep, painful breath; in addition to her other problems, she suspected she had contracted a fever. "What do you wish to ask me?"

She had already confessed to him in private, and her fate was decided, if not yet revealed to her. But it was necessary now to make a second confession to the nuns' council so that she might serve as an example to others tempted to err; and the confession would be extracted in the form of a catechism.

Father Absalom asked, "Were you aware of the girl's immoral past when you sent her to Herr Skatkammer?"

"Yes," she admitted steadily.

"But you secured this employment and vouched for her good character nonetheless?"

"Yes."

"And why did you do this?"

"Because I am fond of her, Father."

There was a silence as this crime sank into the minds of the assembled nuns. No one seemed surprised; truth to tell, it was hard to blame a sister for feeling affection. The lie about Famke's virtue was more serious, but still none of them expected terrible consequences from it.

Father Absalom's tone became somber as he spread a page of writing paper on the table before him. "The letter I have received makes another accusation about your dealings with this girl. Do you know what it is?"

Birgit coughed and then said, "Yes, Father, for you have shown it to me. Herr Skatkammer's housekeeper accuses me of being Famke's mother in body as well as spirit."

Now some of the nuns could not repress a shiver. They were astonished at how frankly, how calmly Birgit repeated the accusation. What could that mean?

"Are you the girl's mother?"

"No," said Birgit, "I am not. When she was abandoned at Immaculate Heart, I had been among the sisters for more than a year. Sister Casilde can testify to my virtue and to the fact that I had not been outside the convent walls in that time."

"There is no record showing precisely when you arrived. And Sister Casilde is ill in bed."

"But when she recovers, she will tell you I speak the truth."

This, however, was unlikely; for as everyone assembled there knew, Sister Casilde was old enough to have slipped back into childhood, and her memory was most unreliable. There were no others left from the bygone days.

"And how do you explain the word pinned to the infant's blanket—a word in Swedish, and you the only sister who could translate it?"

Birgit spread her hands and felt the ring slide again. "Many Swedish women came to Denmark to deliver; it was the one place they did not need to give their names to the midwives. I was not such a woman—it is impossible to think I could be. As I told you, I had not been outside the convent in over a year."

Father Absalom waited.

The nuns pushed their ears from their wimples to listen.

Sister Birgit would say no more.

.5.

LA BELLE DAME
SANS MERCI

I see a lily on thy brow
  With anguish moist and fever dew,
And on thy cheeks a fading rose
  Fast withereth too.

JOHN KEATS,
"LA BELLE DAME SANS MERCI"

Chapter 47

. . . . .

*Among the prospering industries of the Pacific Coast, one of the most inter-
esting and profitable is that of putting up various articles of food and delicacies in cans and other vessels, for preservation and shipment.*

MOSES KING,
KING'S HANDBOOK OF THE UNITED STATES

M ankind's hopes are fragile glass, and life is therefore also short,"
Edouard read out loud. This was the motto, much quoted by his
father, that had been carved over the doorway of the miniature
Taj Mahal; it never failed to arouse deep thoughts in Edouard as he entered
the white marble chamber where his parents lay side by side. The lives of
Berthe and Edouard Versailles, *père*, had indeed been short, their deaths
(one of phthisis, one principally of grief) long; but there was some solace in
the thought of their embalmment, which was guaranteed to preserve the
bodies perfectly for ten years and slow the corruptive process dramatically
even after that. By that reckoning, his father had a year or two of fleshly
splendor left, while his mother's mortal coil must long since have begun to
sink into her coffin's silk lining. Edouard, however, still envisioned her as
she had been when the coffin was nailed shut: her lips red, smiling as if in
relief, the thin auburn hair waving off her brow, white hands clasped comfortably beneath her breasts, which the mortician had kindly restored to
pre-consumptive fullness by means of strategically wadded tissue paper.

Edouard left the iron door open and pulled a chair into the streak of
moonlight that reached into the mausoleum. It was a fine arrangement for
meditation; luminous even at midnight, the tomb had all the sanctity of the
Catholic confessional, and tonight Edouard, for once, treated it as such. He

allowed himself to speak in his native tongue, rusty at first but increasingly swift. It was to him the very language of confession.

"*De verre fragile*," he said to Berthe and Edouard, Senior: And just like fragile glass had his hopes been shattered. His hopes of achieving medical prominence, of doing some real good in the world. All because of that cursed painting—Hygeia, Vivien, whoever she was—and his damnably honest response to it.

Upstairs in the glass house, Famke was sulking over his critique. She had taken to her room and drawn all the drapes, even the ones on the ceiling, and now she refused to emerge for any reason—not to peek at the baby zebra grazing on the lawn, not to read the *Frank Leslie's* he'd reluctantly ordered, not even when he found a former art tutor among the patients in the village and presented the woman through the lacy iron of Famke's door. She even told the maids and nurses she would accept no more electrical treatments, and Edouard was too embarrassed to press his case. Her room was now forbidden ground.

And yet everywhere he went, he was reminded of her, for her cough was shaking the house's foundations. She had hacked elaborately all day and night, and the maids scurried back and forth with covered *crachoirs* that he was not allowed to inspect. Those spit jars told all the story he needed at this stage: His unwitting blunder had brought the illness back in full force.

"*Mais non!*" he cried bravely; if he were not to be honest here, he would be so nowhere. With Berthe and the elder Edouard receptively silent, he said, "I knew. I wanted her to be my *chef d'oeuvre*—I thought that she was that, and that her work threatened mine. But it was my opposition that disordered her fluids, not her activity. *Que je suis pénible . . .*"

He paused, as if waiting for the absolution he still half expected to follow confession. There was nothing: All was silent within the thick stone walls, and Edouard did not even hear the tiny sound his mother's jaw made as it detached and fell upon her collarbone. But within that silence he thought he heard his answers.

He was guilty. He owed Famke a penance, something much greater than a magazine subscription and a lady teacher. And the nature of that penance was obvious: He must find the original author of those artistic horrors, the man who would whisk Famke away. Her brother, Albert Castle.

• • •

Viggo was reassured to find his visitor was not the forbidding Sariah Goodhouse but her niece, whom he had known as Mrs. Black.

"You may call me Myrtice," she whispered when she descended the stairs in her drab dress. "I am not really Mrs. Anyone."

Under the hotel owners' elaborately unwatchful eyes, Myrtice found herself telling Viggo everything. She could not have stanched the flood of words if she'd tried: It was a relief to speak to someone, and Viggo was so kind.

She began with her name. "I am not Mrs. Black," she said with an air of quiet tragedy. "I am not even Mrs. Goodhouse now, but I can't think what else to call myself."

Viggo shook his head as if to clear it, then clutched his temples in obvious pain. Myrtice hesitated; the correct thing to do would be to pack some mint in a handkerchief and hold it to his brow, but when he put his hands back into his lap, her own need to speak overpowered her sense of Saintly charity. She had been traveling so long, and to so many seedy, desperate places, to find him.

"You see," she said, gazing down at her own clenched fists in their faded charcoal gloves, "I am not just my aunt Sariah's niece—but her co-wife as well. Or so I was. I married her husband, Heber; you know that is somewhat the custom among the Latter-Day Saints."

"Yes," Viggo said without moving his head an inch. He had not known, but he was willing to agree to little things. All he wanted was a quiet place in which to lie down, where he might attempt to dream away his memories of the night he had just passed in the arms of the orange-haired whore.

"When my parents died, she alone of all my relations was willing to take me on. And when Heber came through Georgia on his first mission, he didn't seem to mind that Sariah—Sarah as she was called then—was encumbered with a child. You see, he loved her right dearly, and because I was part of her he loved me too. When I grew up, he was even willing to marry me, because she asked."

Viggo remained politely attentive.

"But then Heber married Ursula, too, and everything was ruined!" Myrtice blurted out, and she covered her face in her hands and sobbed. "Of course, some of the blame is my own," she resumed after a minute, whispering even more quietly (Señora Garcia was forced to fetch a dust cloth and hovered nearby, vigorously polishing a battered china shepherdess). "I drew the picture for the Wanted signs, after all. And when those pictures went up in Salt Lake City, the federal agents saw them and formed suspicions immediately. They came to the house, Mr. Viggo, after you left. They said Aunt Sariah is Heber's only true wife, and they told us they would arrest him if he did not have the last two marriages annulled. Well, he was out looking for Ursula in Dakota Territory—and they thought he was already running from *them!* They sent him to prison!"

Viggo tried to hold his head very, very still while digesting this story. There was but one thought in his brain: "Ursula is married?"

"Yes, she is married—to Heber," Myrtice whispered with some of the schoolteacher impatience that had always been her most appreciable flaw. "She is his third wife—or I reckon his second wife now, as *my* marriage has been dissolved. And the federals won't let Heber out of Fort Yuma until her marriage is annulled as well, because they say he must keep his first wife and renounce all others. They have him breaking rocks in a chain gang—because of her!"

Viggo looked confused, even dismayed, but still attentive.

"Do you know how hot it gets in south Arizona in the summertime, Mr. Viggo? One hundred and twenty degrees! And Heber is not strong; he has a cough. So you see we must find your sister at once." She paused now to cough a bit herself, and to wish for a glass of water. It was dry work, spilling all a family's secrets. "I don't suppose you've found her . . ."

Viggo gave a little murmur that she took for assent.

"But have you learned anything at all? I know you've searched all over Colorado—I looked for you there, too, in all manner of dreadful hotels. It was easier to follow you—of *her* I couldn't find hide nor hair."

As to what he had learned, Viggo was reluctant to say anything lest he say too much. He was so stunned by what Myrtice had just told him that he felt he'd have little control over his own tongue, and he must by no means mention that Famke had been masquerading as a man or that she'd been earning her fares in the bagnios. He would not even hint that he himself had been to such places, much less that he had just come from one; Myrtice believed he had returned to the hotel very late and hadn't wished to disturb her until morning. She did not recognize his symptoms, and it would not have occurred to her that a woman's fluids might be drying in his trousers as he sat next to her.

He remembered with a little shock that Myrtice, who had just untangled her web of family for him, still believed that Famke was his sister. And then he remembered that when he last saw her, Myrtice had been expecting yet another addition to the ever-growing Goodhouse clan.

"What is happened of your baby?" he asked, his nerves making him unfortunately plainspoken.

Myrtice flushed brick red, nearly the color, incidentally, of the brothel girl's nipples. "I—er, I was unwell for a time," she said. "The strain of events was too much for my delicate state of health."

Naturally she did not mention the arsenic eating, which had ensured that when the barely formed creature slid out of her womb and its blood was washed away, the complexion beneath was unearthly white. When the almost-baby was laid in its grave, it exactly replicated the new china doll that Sariah enclosed in a black coffin and set out on the mantel along with her own.

"This is what it means to be a woman," Sariah had said, embracing her niece awkwardly after ensuring the coffins were spaced just so.

Myrtice got suddenly to her feet. "You see, Mr. Viggo, we must find Ursula before more tragedy befalls the Goodhouses." She shook out her skirts until she was sure the tears had retreated from her eyes. "Now, if you will pardon me, I am going to find a telegraph office. My aunt will be relieved to hear I have found you at last."

Chapter 48

*This gypsy of a book has few facts and not a word of fiction; not so much as a
dry fagot of statistics or a wingfeather of a fancy.*
BENJ. F. TAYLOR,
"CONFIDENTIAL," IN BETWEEN THE GATES

*It is often said that truth is stranger than fiction; but how much stranger even
than truth is the tale of the gallant Robber Baroness and her brood.*
"TO THE READER,"
IN RUBBLE ON THE RAILS

Edouard's vow of penance had been sincere, but he had difficulty pros-
ecuting it. He sat for hours in his office, attempting to word an appropriate advertisement; but he found his mind occupied instead
with other ways of wooing back Famke's good graces. Perhaps it would not
be necessary to contact Albert Castle after all, or at least not immediately:
Edouard tinkered with the galvanic device, hoping to make it bring down
Famke's juices more efficiently, once she deigned to allow it; he read recent
books on tuberculosis and tested new tonics on himself. Yet long moments
would go by in which he could not have accounted for his time.

On the third day Edouard took a tentative, exploratory cough into his
stethoscope, to stay in practice and regain his confidence; and as he moved
the cold metal disk across his chest, he thought he discovered true cause for
alarm. Ever since the terrible day of *Hygeia*'s exposure, his chest had ached
inside, and when he listened he heard a rumble that could be a sign that disease was returning. He had medical equipment brought down from Famke's
room to his, and he performed a thorough examination of himself, forcing
up bodily liquids and analyzing them under Beachly's high-powered microscope, measuring his hand against the tubercular one in the specimen jar.

He was unable to distinguish his actual symptoms from the ones he'd just read about, and so he decided to seek outside opinion.

It was evening; Beachly would be sleeping far down the hillside, but the household staff could fetch him. From the depths of an armchair grown painful to him, Edouard reached for the tasseled bell cord.

Nothing happened. He pulled again, and still nothing. After his years of insisting that the servants stay out of sight, Edouard wondered if perhaps the staff truly had vanished at last and left him completely alone. He pushed himself out of his chair and up the stairs to their quarters, trailing down the starlit corridor until he found a cell whose light eclipsed that of the sky. Its curtains were drawn, and the room appeared like an immense shaded lantern. He read the name on the door.

"Ancient Jade!" He rapped smartly. When there was no answer, he decided he would simply open the door; and then he found her, to his relief, standing by her washbasin, wearing the bottom half of her simple gray uniform. She had been washing, and her arms and shoulders glistened.

"There you are!" In his relief, he hardly registered her nudity or her slow covering of it with her hands. But now that he saw her, smelled the faint sharp smell of her soap, Edouard's reason for being in this room seemed absurd. Of course he was not alone; he was surrounded by people. And those people not only served him but depended on him to be a model of comportment as well. "There is something wrong with the bells," he said lamely, backing away. "Have them fixed in the morning."

In his confusion, Edouard almost failed to notice that Ancient Jade's washbasin was teetering, for she had shoved something beneath it. But, painfully aware as he was of the traces other people left in his world, he did see it just as he backed over the threshold.

"Be careful," he said, "that basin is about to fall."

The maid twitched; the basin fell and shattered. Edouard saw the object that had destabilized it.

A book in a yellow wrapper.

Even Edouard knew what that particular shade on a wrapper meant: a Dime Novel, the cheapest and most popular type of literature, chronicle of sensational violence and too-yielding despair. Its cover was gaudy, its title dripping purple ink. He picked it up.

"*Rubble on the Rails*," he read out loud, in a tone so forbidding that Ancient Jade nearly toppled over in fear. "*Being the True Story of the 'Dynamite Gang,'* by Hermes, Western correspondent. My word, woman, what you have been reading!"

For all her alarm, and for all her secrecy, a tiny part of Ancient Jade took umbrage that Versailles hadn't noticed what to her was most important: She was reading English—not quickly, but she was reading it. She was no ordinary hundred-men's-wife; she was one who could read.

She watched as Edouard pulled the book closer to his face, though he did not need to do that to confirm his eyes' first evidence. In the year that had brought *The Bostonians*, *Dr. Jekyll and Mr. Hyde*, and *The Evil Genius*, this execrable work—a slim hundred pages long—was illustrated with a picture that gave no doubt as to the story's contents: lively youths in newsboy caps, a giant locomotive, a décolletée heroine whose free-flowing hair bled into the smoke of a billowing explosion. Beneath her likeness was printed a legend, "The gallant Robber Baroness." And her hair was bright flame red.

Surely she could not be . . . but then Edouard was just as sure that she was. Ursula Summerfield Goodhouse had come to him a Wanted woman, after all.

Standing there in the maid's bedroom, Edouard read the first page, and the next. He stalked away to his office with his face still buried in the book.

◆   ◆   ◆

Much to its author's gratification, *Rubble on the Rails* had been circulating through the world for several weeks. When it arrived in Hygeia Springs, it had been an instant sensation, no less than in Saint Louis or San Francisco; the Good Life Mercantile sold all five copies in a day and ordered more, only to find the publisher was out of stock. The precious volumes passed from hand to hand throughout the village, and each set of yellow covers acquired a mosaic of marks and stains—cooking splatters, sprays of blood, fingerprints; from the laboratory of Dr. Rideaux, mortician, a wash of arsenic so dark and final as to make the title unreadable.

Precious Flower had lifted a copy out of Miss Pym's pocket, and she and the singsong sisters practiced their English with it. But this activity they, like Miss Pym, kept secret from their employer; and in this they conspired with the town at large. Everyone knew that with his notions of mental hygiene and tranquility, Edouard Versailles would disapprove. Thus he had remained unaware of the book's existence, even as Miss Pym interrogated the staff about her lost volume and Dr. Beachly himself locked his door and cracked a set of yellow covers.

Famke was equally ignorant. In the past months, she had had far too much to do with her *Hygeia* to think about matters literary.

Now *Rubble on the Rails* utterly transfixed Edouard Versailles. The words of this Hermes had a ring of certain truth, as if the man had written so much and so often of strange happenings as to be almost cold to them now. Edouard read the entire ignoble work that night, and in its pages his hypothesis was tested and proved: The flame-haired baroness with the mysterious accent and the crippling cough, the siren called, with a Keatsian flourish, the Belle Dame sans Merci—this could be none other than his Ophelia. And, oh! the things she had done! The scheming, the deceptions—the men beguiled by butterfly eyes while her team of rebels laid their dynamite, the hotels raided for food and valuables, the brothels paid to provide refuge. In a few chapters, the Belle Dame even dressed as a man, the better to snare her victims.

Edouard knew this was no time to act in haste. He spent some hours considering what he should do and reread John Keats's poem:

> She took me to her elfin grot,
> And there she wept, and sigh'd full sore,
> And there I shut her wild wild eyes
> With kisses four.

How many men had seen those cerulean eyes droop shut? How many had made her sigh—without the medical benefits of galvanic treatment?

He opened Famke's fat file of test results and other documents and reviewed them all thoroughly, including the contents of the pocket that had been found beneath her skirts: some newspaper clippings about artists; a few lucifer matches naked of phosphorous; a scrap of paper that was a great smudge on one side and, on the other, a mysterious scrawl, almost equally blurred. Edouard could make out only four words there: "love," "world," and "no crime." This looked to him like absolute proof, no doubt some communiqué from the Rubblers. He was sure they instructed Famke to feign love, to make love, and in the eyes of the world commit no crime . . . And all those articles about art were probably the research she had done in order to convince him she came from a family of painters—for of course, he realized now, Albert Castle and her relationship to him had been a mere fiction. Her clumsiness with the paintbrush surely demonstrated that.

Amid all these horrors, Edouard felt curiously numb. He picked up the long red curl that had been wound among the pocket papers and sniffed it. It smelled to him of medicine, chemical and bitter, and it shed shorter, coarser locks of brown and gold and black, the provenance of which he did not wish to contemplate—it would seem the Robber Baroness scalped her victims like a savage. He gazed long at the repaired handbill, also yellow, that marked her out as Wanted.

In the small hours of the morning, he took a dropperful of laudanum that calmed his hands, and he wrote a letter that covered both sides of the page; this he tore to shreds. He took another page and wrote a few choice, brief sentences. He blotted the sheet haphazardly, folded it into an envelope marked "Harmsway Telegraph," and put on his coat, for he was strangely frozen inside. Under a fading moon, he saddled his huge black horse and rode down to the Hygiene post office, where he found the postmaster asleep. The man woke easily enough when he realized who was there, and Edouard directed him to take the message and make sure, personally, that the words left Harmsway that morning.

"You may take my horse," he added, and to the postmaster that was almost the most terrifying part of the order. No one but Versailles ever rode the noble black horses. The man left immediately, without even pausing to urinate.

The laudanum surged through Edouard's veins, making his heart weary and slow. He forced himself to trudge back up the hill. He regretted only that he had not been able to deliver the telegram himself; once again, he had too much to do to go abroad. The hospital. The maidservant. Famke herself to deal with—though she, at least, would be staying here some days longer; and now she would be truly his prisoner rather than his patient.

He went upstairs to lock Famke's door, then woke Ancient Jade again and told her to bring warm milk to his office. They had a brief interview in front of the jars of bobbing fetuses and limbs.

"You have aroused my severest displeasure," he said as sternly as he could manage in his weariness.

Astoundingly, she spoke up against him. "Is my book," she said. "My pleasure to read. You give back to me."

Edouard's temper flared. "No one under my roof will waste time on such trash!" he snapped. "If you want a good book of poems—"

"No poem," she said stubbornly. "*My* book."

Suddenly he remembered her standing naked before him, and he did not remember her covering herself; in his mind she stood on display for him as she had done for countless other men, as the red-haired baroness did on the cover of *Rubble on the Rails*. "My house," he said. "And there is no further place for you in it."

Ancient Jade stared at him with glittering button-brown eyes, as if she were putting some Asian curse on him; but she hobbled away without a word.

After she left, Edouard felt exhausted. He drank the last dregs of the milk, which in his distress tasted bitter as opium, and the room swam before him. All at once that faded armchair looked the most comfortable seat in the world, and he sank into it as an eagle might sink into its nest after a long flight.

For some hours, Edouard slept.

Chapter 49

.....

John [Chinaman] is inevitable. He has discovered America, and finds it a good country. But it is ours, and not his, to determine whether he shall be a curse or a blessing to us. If we treat him as Christianity teaches that we ought to treat our fellow-men; if we do unto him as we would that others should do to us; if we see that he is instructed in that which we believe to be right, he may become a useful part of us. Teachable he certainly is; a far more civilized being—or rather, a far less savage creature—than many we get from Christian Great Britain.

CHARLES NORDHOFF,
CALIFORNIA: FOR HEALTH, PLEASURE, AND RESIDENCE

As Ancient Jade packed her few belongings into a shawl, the singsong sisters spoke their mother tongue together for what could well be the last time. Under normal conditions they used only English with each other; their English was good, far better than they let anyone know, and they honed it like a weapon. After having served American businessmen in various ways, they thought someday they might open an American business of their own; but they were so accustomed to invisibility that for now they were keeping their competence, like their aspiration, to themselves. From five years' wages, each had saved nearly fifty dollars toward this enterprise. Tonight, Ancient Jade's banishment confirmed their sense that the safest course was secrecy. They rehearsed the facts to themselves and felt better, because understanding was a kind of mastery.

"For reading a book, he dismisses you," said Precious Flower. "I would like to know how this is just."

"He who is so proud of saving you," said Life's Importance.

Ancient Jade explained, "He thinks Chinese prostitutes make good maids. Chinese readers are criminals."

"He made the red-haired woman read poems," Precious Flower observed—the three of them said Famke's name aloud no more often than they said Edouard's. "She did not want to."

"She wanted to paint," said Life's Importance, "and that was a crime too."

"Especially what she painted," Ancient Jade ended. "Hairy American lady."

"*Eight bits fuckee*," Precious Flower whispered in English.

"But he never got a chance to fuck her," Ancient Jade said, and the three of them indulged in a mirthless giggle that might have sounded, from far away, like the glee of carefree young girls.

◆　◆　◆

When Edouard woke, the house was strangely quiet; even quieter than he liked it. It was delightful. Just as good, the sun stood high in the sky, filtering through the glass and the palm leaves in the way that he loved. He smiled. He stood up and stretched, feeling deeply refreshed despite the crick in his neck and the ache that had spread from his chest now to his spine. He wondered for a moment why he had fallen asleep where he did. Then his eye fell on the lurid yellow cover of *Rubble on the Rails* and memory came flooding back—the perfidy revealed in those worn pages, the horrible deeds that must be known now to the entire world.

At least, he thought, those deeds had meaning only to those who knew Famke was with him: Dr. Beachly, of course, and the nurses who had found her, perhaps Rideaux the mortician . . . Overall, her presence here had been well concealed, as Edouard had wished. Or perhaps as *she* had engineered? There were so many lungers downslope that she was probably forgotten there by now, and if her purposes were nefarious she could accomplish much more by remaining anonymous.

Why, Edouard reasoned with belated understanding, there could be no other reason for Famke's appearance on his doorstep, with her farfetched story of a lost brother and a special relationship to his painting—no other reason than that she was scheming to make *him*, Edouard Versailles, a victim of the Dynamite Gang. Hermes reported she had done exactly this to a fellow called Stokes, whose fancy had built a medieval tower in Austin,

Nevada, which she robbed and destroyed; and then there was the owner of the Grand Hotel in Boulder, Colorado, who had seen his business literally go up in smoke while Famke entertained him at a house of ill-conceived pleasure. She must have done the same to this Goodhouse of Prophet City (or, in *Rubble on the Rails*, Elder Greathope of Bountiful)—of course—it made much more sense than her tale of a Mormon marriage and a patriarch's cruelty, for he could imagine no one being cruel to Famke. What he could imagine was the beautiful crystal palace, his father's labor of love, blown into shivers and scattered over the hillside, all the way down to the new hospital. But, no—there would be no new hospital anymore, for surely the Rubblers would destroy that as well.

These thoughts were chilling. Edouard ran up the stairs, once again shaking the house to its foundation. He did not bother to knock at Famke's door but simply grabbed the knob. He found it, naturally, locked.

This one time, this one time only, Edouard behaved like a man of violence. With his elbow he shattered the door's largest pane. "Miss Summerfield!" he called through the hole as he did so, ignoring the blood now dripping from his wrist. "I have a matter of some urgency to discuss."

Famke did not reply, but Life's Importance materialized at his side, holding a basket of keys. Silently she held one out to him, and he fit it into the lock. Life's Importance also tried to give him a black-bordered handkerchief to use as a bandage, but he ignored it. The door was opening.

Edouard stepped through the interior curtain into the sick woman's sanctuary. And there, as he might have expected, he found no Famke; only an unmade bed.

A mixture of anger and fear made Edouard bold. He placed his hand upon the mattress, beneath the crumpled quilt, and tried to gauge its warmth. He left a streak of blood on the sheet but could not tell how recently Famke had lain there.

Moving more slowly now, filled with a sense of dawning realization, he opened the door to the water closet. Of course it was empty, and the shining flush toilet gleamed innocently back at him. He noticed a drop of blood on the seat and touched it with the index finger of his uninjured hand. Dry.

"She is gone," he said wonderingly.

Life's Importance bobbed her head like the dutiful servant she'd been trained to be. "Gone," she agreed.

• ◆ •

Edouard organized a search party to comb the woods and the village, looking for Famke and her gang; but he did not expect them to find much, and in fact they did not. After swarming among the beehives and behind the cathouse, through the trees and into the rock fissures of the greening hillside, they found not so much as a lock of red hair or a scrap of the white nightgown that had been all she might have to wear—though, of course, her gang would have brought her some decent clothing, perhaps a fine silk dress like the one she'd had on when he first saw her.

Edouard himself did not join the search party. The long walk through the damp and dark had brought on a cough in earnest, and he took to his bed feeling hopeless. Famke was gone and his home, perhaps, condemned. He thought back over the last half-year, even unto yesterday, and he blamed himself.

He rang and told Precious Flower to send for Ancient Jade. "Really, I suppose I should thank her for bringing the book to my attention," he said, coughing feebly, though he did not believe Precious Flower understood his allusion for a moment. "And I have a responsibility to the woman, after taking her from the one profession she knew."

Precious Flower gave him the same bob of the head that he'd got from Life's Importance, but she had to tell him the third maid was gone. A search of the house confirmed it. No one could say exactly where she was, but the next morning, when the posse looking for Famke reported that a Celestial in a gray costume had boarded the train at Harmsway, Edouard considered the mystery solved. The train was headed for San Francisco; Ancient Jade must be returning not only to her old line of work but to the place she had practiced it as well.

"You might advertise for her," suggested Rideaux the mortician, who found in the three Chinese maids a mysterious fascination.

"I might," Edouard granted; but, exhausted by his emotions, not the least of which were disappointment in Famke and the fear of a future soon to be attenuated by disease, he could not compose so much as a single sentence fit for print.

Chapter 50

· · · · ·

The depredations of time have always something in them to employ the fancy,
or lead to musing on subjects which, withdrawing the mind from objects of
sense, seem to give it new dignity: but here I was treading on live ashes.

MARY WOLLSTONECRAFT,
LETTER FROM DENMARK

It was as if a fire had swept through Immaculate Heart, Birgit thought as
she stood in the empty office, gazing out a last time at the flowering elder
tree in the girls' exercise yard. Orphans, nuns, beds, the past—all had
been gobbled up. Of course this was not true; it was merely that all the
people were gone, and their chattels as well. Immaculate Heart as Birgit
knew it was no more: So complete was the destruction wrought by her own
hands.

The scandal around herself and Famke—a scandal founded on anonymous and unproven rumors—had brought new attention to the infamous
Immaculate chest. Too many orphans had died of it, and no lesser person-
age than the Queen herself had insisted on moving the surviving children to
the new *Børnehjem*—where no doubt they would be rebaptized as Lutherans
within the month—and dispersing the nuns to convents with more salubrious reputations. So the history of Immaculate Heart, founded in 1373,
came to an inglorious end. The building had sold to a merchant who dealt
in rare stamps; he would use the cells and dormitories as sorting rooms.
The sisters were assigned to farflung convents in Odense, Skagen, and the
northernmost reaches of Norway. They would take their coughs with
them. Only Birgit remained, to clean the building alone in an act of
penance.

It was her own idea, one which the bishop approved heartily. "God smiles
upon the truly penitent," he promised her. "The lost lamb, the prodigal son."

As she blew on a diamond-shaped pane and wiped it with her sleeve, Birgit thought again that there had been something not quite right in the bishop's words to her. Yet she was too tired to think what it might be; she merely checked the windows one last time for dust and fly specks, then left the room where she had held sway such a brief time as Superior. For the last time, she locked the door with the ancient brass key.

Outside, in the weak sunshine on the doorstep, with her bedroll and her Bible tucked beneath her arms, Birgit hesitated. She was not quite ready to leave. And no one was waiting for her; she was not expected to finish the cleaning for another day at least, and she was not particularly welcome at Handmaids of the Precious Blood, the tiny convent that the bishop had ordered to house her while she awaited passage to Tröndheim. The Handmaids were dedicated to prayer and did not take kindly to liars and cheats.

In short, for the next twenty-four hours, Birgit could go anywhere. She could do anything.

She turned and, with sudden purpose, unlocked the heavy front door again. Her shoes, ground down from years of wear, made a vague clomping noise on the hard floors, and when she got to the inner courtyard once used by the girls, she unlaced those shoes and set them on the lip of the stair, with her stockings rolled neatly inside.

Barefoot, she started toward the elder tree. *This is where everything started*, she thought, though of course that was wrong, too. The elder tree, the day of the soapmaking, had been simply a warning that Birgit should not let the girl have her heart; and Birgit had paid it no attention. Perhaps if she had listened, if she had punished Famke as the other nuns thought she should, none of this would have happened. Famke would have shed her wildness, might still be at Herr Skatkammer's house—no, with the farmer in Dragør—and she, Birgit, would still be parceling out equal measures of impersonal Catholic love to dozens of coughing orphans. It was all Birgit's fault.

These thoughts flitted through her mind in a few seconds, the time it took to cross the courtyard and grasp the elder's lowest limb in her hands. A flock of early butterflies flurried up and resettled as she gave a tentative tug on the branch. Near the trunk, Birgit thought she could see shadowy scorchmarks from that long-ago fire; but the branch held nonetheless, and she hoisted herself upward. Her arms were strong, if tired from the hard la-

bor of cleaning, and she managed to get high enough to swing a leg up. She
sat, then stood; she could nearly see into the empty second-floor rooms.
She grabbed another limb and climbed higher, till she could see the
rooftops first of Immaculate Heart and then of larger Copenhagen, all the
way to Nyhavn. She almost thought she could discern a fuzzy gray hint of
Sweden, which was very close here; though of course she could not see
Norway, much less the dark northern reaches of Tröndheim, a city so distant that a letter would take over a week to travel there from Copenhagen.
If in fact the bishop and the Handmaids of the Precious Blood sent Birgit's
mail on. If in fact Viggo wrote from America. If there was ever news worthy
of sending . . .

Birgit bounced on her elder branch, wondering if she might risk pushing up to the next one. If she fell from this height, she would break her
skull, her spine, at the very least an arm or a leg. But she might also see
Sweden.

•   •   •

Much to his own surprise, within days Edouard's cough improved and
then vanished, leaving him with no symptom but that old abstracted
ache in the chest and no conclusion but that he'd been suffering from nothing worse than a cold. This ache, he realized, he would have to live with; and
indeed it was only what other healthy mortals bore. Sooner than he might
have liked, he was on his feet again.

While he lay in his sickbed, Edouard had had time to mull over the events
of the winter and spring and to reread Hermes's novel. He concluded that his
house was not so likely to shiver to bits after all. Wasn't Famke known as the
Gallant Robber Baroness? And hadn't she protected a wealthy widow's house
in Santa Fé from sure destruction, by convincing the boys that those who had
lost their loved ones should not lose their homes as well? Surely such a
woman, however perfidious—and Edouard still felt that she was this—
would show mercy to the man who had lodged her, cured her, even (he allowed the thought, however unmedical) pleasured her after a fashion.

It was time for Edouard to rejoin the world. But the sad fact was that the
world did not welcome him. The hospital's three towers were just days from
opening their doors, and during the months in which Edouard had been oc-

cupied with Famke, the doctors and nurses had grown used to making decisions without him. It was almost, but not quite, as if they had sneaked the
hospital out from under his nose. Similarly, under the auspices of Precious
Flower and Life's Importance and the butler, Wong, the house was running
itself, and the grooms and gardeners were equally capable. For the first time
since he'd been inspired to found the Institute for Phthisis, Edouard felt
aimless.

"Surely there is something that needs doing?" he protested to Beachly.

The doctor scratched his bald spot, glad at least that Versailles was no
longer trying to force his crackpot "cure" on the medical staff. "Well," he said,
"the reception room wall still needs a painting."

Thus Edouard was finally forced to confront the memory that had been
nibbling away at him like a small phantom left after its greater sister had
been exorcised. *Hygeia*, Goddess of Health. Was any part of the picture sal-
vageable, or should Edouard order another from a reputable dealer? He
supposed he would have to look.

He could not quite face the painting alone, however, and he summoned
one of the maids to unlock the door. He did not care which one might
come, for he was displeased with them both now: They had watched
Famke's progress with the canvas and had done nothing to warn him so that
he might have prepared a more politic critique for her—though of course it
was for the best that Famke had left, as he might now hope his beautiful
glass house would be spared.

Mankind's hopes are fragile glass . . .

Edouard walked in and saw the curtains sagging, the sun beating
through the walls to illuminate the easel. Everything was as it had been
when last he spoke to Famke, when he told her the painting needed polish.

That is, the room was just as it had been, but the enormous easel was
empty. Edouard looked around the room's few furnishings, inspected
Famke's art supplies, and even checked behind those limp curtains before
shouting out, "Life's Importance!"

It was Precious Flower who was waiting down the hall, but she didn't
bother to correct him. She came scurrying from her hiding place and looked
at him unblinking, ready for instructions.

"Where is that painting?" he asked, his own voice ringing loud in his
ears.

Slowly, Precious Flower turned to the easel, and she saw, too, that it held nothing. Or almost nothing: *Hygeia's* gilded frame still sat hugely on it, bumping the ceiling, reaching toward a wall. During his search, Edouard had stepped right through without noticing.

Precious Flower tottered over to stand behind the empty frame, as if the painting might be of her. She waved her hands before her face. "Paint gone," she said.

Chapter 51

· · · · ·

We have regarded John [Chinaman] as a sort of overgrown boy, a kind of cushiony creature. You can thrust your finger anywhere into his character. You withdraw it, and he retains no print of it, any more than the water into which you plunge your hand. Within that apparently yielding characterlessness is a spine of heathen iron, and tough as the worst of it. A bridge made of such material would last the world out.

BENJ. F. TAYLOR,
BETWEEN THE GATES

When Edouard dismissed her from the glass house several days earlier, Ancient Jade had felt a cold, stony anger creeping over her for perhaps the first time in her life. She who had been raised to have no feelings, to obey her parents and eventually the mother-in-law and husband she had never had, then to do exactly as her uncouth customers demanded—she was almost blind with rage now, and she cursed Edouard for paying the missionaries to take her out of her crib, for curing her (or so he thought) of both the syphilis and the opium addiction that might have ended her life sooner. For now what was she to do?

She tried to imagine what it was like to be Edouard, to have this power over other people. And then it occurred to her that, in a limited way, she did have that power: She could bequeath him the same helpless feeling he had given her.

Just before sunrise, she climbed the stairs to Famke's room and turned the gaslight on just bright enough to see.

A hand on her shoulder shook Famke out of a long dream in which she was taking a bath in a tubful of her own blood, and it was the most relaxing, refreshing bath ever. She knew that she would never cough again, that she was just about to achieve her heart's desire; the lovely, shimmering feeling had just begun—and then, that hand.

"You. You," Ancient Jade was whispering in her ear—for once, not using the honorific "Missy" that Famke had come to expect. "You wake up now."

Famke groaned and rolled onto her other side.

"You." Did Famke imagine it, or did Ancient Jade actually slap her? Yes, her cheek was tingling . . . "You wake up. Something important."

"What is it?" Famke demanded, sitting up with her hand to her cheek. It had better be important, she thought, or else it might be worth speaking to Edouard again—just think what he would do if he heard one of the maids had dared— Famke's thoughts changed course when she felt the blood in her body resettle, finding equilibrium after her change in position, expelling its excess. The feminine flow that had come upon her Down There during Edouard's critique had kept her sluggish and in bed, feeding her sulks and making her wish to punish Edouard for his opinion even more; it was diminished now, but it still ran from time to time and reminded her of the nastier side of health. The blood was bound to come out from one opening or another. And to think that some women suffered this revolting condition every month.

"Versailles knows everything," Ancient Jade said in surprisingly fluent English. "All you secrets."

"*Fanden!*" Famke's hand dropped to her lap. "How?"

"He read about you."

"Read about me?" Famke repeated, thinking of the small nameless mention that had appeared in the *New York Times* the day after she immigrated. *Not without a share of youth and beauty, although the beauty was high in the cheekbones.* Or perhaps it had been as the "flame-haired Atropos" of the silk enterprise . . .

"*Rubble on the Rails.* One book, you and Dynamite Gang. He took from me." Ancient Jade waited, and when Famke continued to look confused she continued, "You tell boys, 'Steal from these rich men. Burn houses.' They do everything you say. Versailles does not like this."

"Who wrote that book?" Famke asked as understanding began to dawn.

"Hermes." She pronounced it *Herms*, but Famke had no trouble understanding whom she meant.

So Harry Noble had written a book, and he had put her in it. When she thought back to their last conversation, she realized she should have expected as much.

This was annoying, yes, but not dire. She yawned and burrowed deeper into the pillow.

"None of it is true," she said. "I never met any Dynamite Gang, but I did meet Hermes. He is a liar."

"He write different. Anyway, this is what Versailles believe," Ancient Jade said. She sounded smug, certain that she had a window into Edouard's convictions. "He write to man from yellow paper. WANTED, with you face."

It took Famke only a few seconds to understand: Edouard had written to Heber. The blood rushed around her body again and spread itself somewhere beneath her.

Ancient Jade poked Famke in the arm to get her attention. "I not finish this book," she said. "What happen at the end?"

"How should I know?" Famke said, and she swung her legs over the edge of the bed. She could hardly bother with the maid now. If Heber had gone to the trouble of distributing those posters, he must want her back so badly he would be here on the next train. "I need to leave right away, so you had better fetch me the dress I arrived in. The purple one. You must know where it is."

Ancient Jade did not respond. She just stared at the woman in the bed, her brown button eyes unblinking, her mind working very fast.

"Do you know where the plum silk dress is?" Famke asked.

Ancient Jade came to her decision. She tossed Famke the bedroom key and said, "I not maid here anymore. You find you own clothes."

And while Famke was too taken aback to speak, Ancient Jade hobbled out, collected her bundle in the hallway, and kissed her singsong sisters good-bye.

. . .

The dark house—with Edouard sleeping off his laudanum and milk—was impossible for Famke to navigate. The maids had the advantage of their invisibility; they were accustomed to walking in the shadows, locating rooms in the dark. But she had been almost exclusively confined to her room, and when she ventured elsewhere there had always been someone else to take her arm and help her along. She had no idea now where she might find clothes and shoes and money; she wasn't even certain of finding the front door. She wandered, candle in hand, looking for the plum silk dress—for any dress, really, as she needed to vanish before these blue hours turned gray. She was somewhat reassured to look through the glass of Edouard's office and see him deep in slumber beneath the gas globes; but he would not slumber forever.

As she went, she thrust her hands into the depths of armchairs and sofas, got down on her knees and felt behind chests and potted plants. She found two nickels and a penny this way; the maids were too conscientious, or too thrifty, to leave anything more lying about. Well, there were ways of getting money, so long as one had the right clothes with which to move through the world. Only this cotton nightdress was not the garment for it.

Eventually Famke remembered the system of steam heating that had kept the house so pleasant even on the long winter nights. Feeling resourceful and independent, she found a pipe in the ceiling and began tracing it downward. Her months as a maid in Skatkammer's magnificent house had taught her that the laundry room was most likely to be found near the boiler, where wet clothes and linens would dry most quickly. Perhaps the silk dress was there; perhaps something else, equally good.

She was right. She found the laundry in the cellar, in a hot room that smelled of mothballs, and there was indeed an assortment of clothing hung upon the drying lines. The trouble was that all those garments belonged to the maids: three gray tunics, three gray sets of trousers, six black stockings with tiny, attenuated feet. White cloths that Famke deduced must be for binding the feet, to give them the support that their slippers would not.

Famke chewed her lip and coughed to get the smell of camphor out of her throat. She had been hoping that if she could not locate the purple dress she could at least find some of Edouard's clothing, which would hang on her frame but would take her out of town; failing that, one of Miss Pym's uniforms. This was almost the worst that could happen, but it couldn't be helped. She would escape in the costume of a Chinese maid, a former hundred-men's-wife.

With a pair of scissors she found by the washtub, Famke cut her nightgown into a chemise. The skirt would make a good set of feminine cloths— how vexing that she had to think of such things *now*—or then again, for that purpose there were the maids' foot bindings, already cut. She tied on the trousers, buttoned up the tunic, and wrapped the nightgown's skirt around her head, to disguise her hair. She would keep her eyes lowered; perhaps she could find a hat. In any case, no one was likely to look close enough to see that this Chinese maid had blue eyes and an uncommon height, or that she was wearing felt bedroom slippers instead of proper shoes. To most Americans, Chinese were just Chinese.

She followed the pipes upstairs again to the back door, and she was on the threshold when she pulled herself up short. She could not leave now. Not without what she had come for those many months ago. *Had we but world enough and time . . .*

Famke climbed back up to the infirmary wing and used the scissors to jimmy the lock on her studio door. *This parting, darling . . .*

She opened up the scissors and ran one blade around the four sides of *Hygeia*, then rolled the stiff canvas into a cylinder.

. . . would be no crime. She tied the nymph up with a lock of hair she cut from the top of her head, where it was longest.

Now she could go. With eleven cents jingling in her borrowed pants pocket and a ruined oil in her hand, she sped out into the early morning, where the honeybees were already dipping into the last of the daffodils and the first of the violets.

.   .   .

After a long, foot-blistering walk downmountain, Famke skirted Edouard's fine new hospital and limped toward the lights of the town with a strong sense of possibility. She would find transportation somehow, find a way to San Francisco; for of course that was where she was heading, where she should have gone long ago.

But in the middle of the village's main street, she came to a halt. She had been on the point of entering the Springs Hotel, where the stage stop was housed, when she spotted a neatly calligraphed sign in the window. It declared, No UNACCOMPANIED BLACKS OR CELESTIALS.

Famke looked down at her costume in disgust. Of course no driver for a line traveled by ladies and gentlemen would give a seat to a Chinese without a white employer of some sort. And of course Famke could not reveal that she was white herself, for then, in this costume, she would be ridiculously easy for Edouard to trace. He had probably notified the hotel staff already—and they alone out of all Hygiene would recognize her, for it was in their parlor, waiting for a stage, that she had collapsed and been sent to the Death Hospital.

Famke turned around. On the other side of the street, in the window of a general mercantile, she saw another sign:

Due to risk of contagion,
municipal regulations strictly forbid spitting in public.
Carry your expectorations with you.
Pocket crachoirs *available inside.*

Taking this as a kind of portent, Famke reached into her trouser pocket. She found nothing but the eleven cents from the glass house. No tinderbox, no yellow pouch. No means of moving forward.

It was barely morning, and the clean streets were still shadowed. Famke wandered until she found a little park where she could sit with *Hygeia* tightly rolled, feeling lonelier than she had since the long, still days in Copenhagen after Albert had left. Now she was even poorer than she had been then, and there was no Sister Birgit to call on. Her months in bed made it impossible for her to trek the many miles to Harmsway, let alone do it in now-threadbare slippers; so she would have to pay for a ride in a wagon. Her limbs felt heavier and slower with each second. Soon she would turn to stone.

How stupid she had been. A lifetime of bad decisions had brought her lower and lower, when all she had wanted in the world was to recapture that dreamy feeling of perfect love, of being looked at and truly, completely seen. She felt another drop of blood leaking out of her Down There, and she realized she was in an impossible situation.

Just then an opportunity came along. It came hunching, halting, stopping occasionally to spit into a brass box that Famke concluded must be one of the advertised pocket *crachoirs*. A man of middle age, out to take the healthful airs. He had the Round Tower eyes and graveyard cough of the terminal lunger.

He stopped dead when he saw Famke on her bench; even with the wide hat on, she looked like no ordinary Celestial to him. He shuffled up to Famke, and she realized he could be thinking only one thing of her, sitting alone in this deserted park so close to the nighttime. She willed herself not to run away.

He spat once more for good measure before he spoke. "Sister," he said in the most polite of voices, "do you have your own room?"

. . .

Mercifully, prices were inflated in that remote region, where Edouard had driven all public women away. Famke was able to get ten dollars merely by retreating into the trees and disrobing for this man, who did not even mind the feminine flow that she wiped away as she removed her underthings. He touched her with moist, cadaverous fingers, and Famke shivered; he pinched a nipple and combed through her tuft of private hair. But he was unable to do more, even when he persuaded her—at the price of ten dollars more—to put her own hand into his pants and touch him. He was as wet and feverish Down There as Famke had ever been; and he was so sick that, strangely, she did not feel at all wrong for touching him, no more than she had ever felt for touching herself.

"It's no use," he gasped at last, flaunting municipal ordinance and spitting red-green into the dirt.

"It is the opium," Famke said wisely, helping him with his handkerchief. "It is good for the lungs but bad for letting down the juices."

Without asking her what she meant, her client said, "Strike that posture once more. With your fingers in the air."

And so, naked, Famke posed as Nimue again.

Chapter 52

. . . . .

After she telegraphed her aunt, Myrtice spent some days in bed, recovering from her journey. Since she had been expecting and then disappointed, she'd found herself tiring easily; her feet swelled at the slightest exertion, which had made that trek across the West in search of Viggo—that is, Ursula—a most painful enterprise. Now that she had found him, what a relief it was to lie down in this simple little room (with a convenience under the bed for someone else to empty), to put her feet on the pillow, and to feel the throbbing in them grow gradually weaker, until it no longer eclipsed the pulse of her heart. Viggo had given her a cool-ing camphor rub for her head, and she found it worked just as beautifully on the feet.

And yet she found it impossible to relax into sleep. It was not only that farmwife habits told her it was sinful to lie in bed in the daylight, and it was not just that she was glad to have found Viggo. She was also worried about him, for he looked utterly dreadful, hollow eyed and pinch faced, as if suf-fering from some internal agony. Of course he would not tell her what it was, and Myrtice did not pry. But even as her feet began to recover, Myrtice's spirits oscillated between joy at the progress she had made on her quest and a distress she thought could hardly be less acute than Viggo's, for all that it was inspired by sympathy with him. When she thought of him, she felt a tingling in her belly and limbs that completely prevented her from relaxing as she needed. She had to get up and use the convenience almost as often as when she'd been in a condition; her nerves were that worked up.

One gray evening Señora Garcia came knocking on Myrtice's door, and then it was time to marvel at the achievements of modern technology. Within a very few days, Sariah had received and replied to Myrtice's telegram in kind—no doubt at considerable expense, but they must not mind that now. Against all expectation, Sariah had information of her own:

Yr news recd. Urs. in Hygiene, Calif. See Edward Versailles there.
Heber ill Ft. Yuma infirmary.
    S.

Myrtice was up and dressed in a matter of seconds; indeed, she had never completely undressed, merely unbuttoned her bodice and loosened her stays. She slid her feet back into the shoes and felt them begin to throb again. But bravely she thumped downstairs and sent word that Viggo should meet her in the parlor.

From the looks of it, he had spent the days in bed, too, though just as sleeplessly as Myrtice. He had not bothered to shave or comb his hair. Myrtice was touched that he came to her so quickly, and her eyes were bright when she showed him the telegram.

"We must leave tonight," Viggo said. "Can you say where this Hygiene is?"

Myrtice had brought down her copy of *The Pacific Tourist* and showed him the description. "We take the rails to Harmsway and change there to a stage. We might could be there in five days."

Señor Garcia said helpfully, "There is a train south at nine-thirty. But I will have to charge you for the night's lodging."

"Nå, that is not matter," said Viggo; he, too, had become spendthrift in what he also felt must be the last phase of the search. "It is best if we leave at once."

"I'll pack my bag," Myrtice offered, hobbling toward the staircase.

"Mine is ready," said Viggo.

Neither one of them commented on Heber's new predicament. In fact, they had hardly taken it into account; they were both so glad to be leaving

Santa Fé. Myrtice looked happily forward to the long trip with Viggo in the second-class car, the soothing touch of his camphor on her forehead, the bitter taste of his arsenic on her tongue. Once they had caught up to Ursula and she had signed the annulment papers, Myrtice would at last be free of family duties. Then, with Viggo there for guidance, she could do whatever she wanted.

·   ·   ·

Famke had more cause than ever to be glad of her cure as she endured the journey northward in a third-class carriage. Crammed with her roll of canvas amid the lowest type of worker—broken miners, farmhands, prostitutes, immigrants, non-whites—she had shrunk as close to the window as she could and gulped down the air whistling through its poorly insulated seams, heavy and cindered though that air was, and much as it made her cough. Thankfully, by now she was sure it was just a healthy cough, clearing everyday debris from the lungs; Edouard had given her health enough to go on with.

Famke's fellow-passengers, however, reeked of garlic, perspiration, and emanations she did not like to think about; most of them also had the hollow, desperate gaze of the unhealthy and unemployed, the very expression she would not allow herself to wear. No, she might be traveling among such people, but she refused to be one of them. Once she arrived in San Francisco she would find her future: With each turn of the wheels beneath her, she was more certain than ever that Albert would be there. So she banished thoughts of the glass house and its luxuries from her mind and focused resolutely on him, Albert, until she no longer even dreamed of anyone or anyplace else when she dozed. The scrape of the wheels said *Sanfrancisco. Sanfrancisco.* The steam engine chugged *Castle. Castle.*

In the morning of the second day, she stepped into the chaos of a boomtown in early summer, a flood of sounds and smells and faces. Tarry black pavement burned through the ragged bedroom slippers as Famke gulped down more fetid air and held on to *Hygeia* and tried to get her bearings amidst heavy traffic. Everywhere she looked, she saw something in motion. Even where the carriages and wagons and omnibuses jammed up against each other at a standstill, the horses' ears flicked, their drivers jumped up and shouted at each other, the animals' urine hissed into the street and rose up again as a cloud.

For a moment, the third-class passengers surrounded her again. They seemed to be in their element here and to know at last what they must do; they streamed around Famke and joined the river of humanity rushing downhill, weaving among the vehicles, eyes fixed on some point far ahead, beyond the factories' and canneries' puffing smokestacks.

Famke decided it was best to do as she had always done and start with the proper costume. This impersonation of a Celestial had grown distasteful, and she could accomplish her goals much more quickly if she were dressed as a white person—man or woman, it did not matter much. She still had almost ten dollars left from the man back in Hygiene; it was surely enough for a good suit of clothes.

She found a street of shops and strolled down it, looking in the windows and debating whether her new costume should be masculine or feminine. A man would command fast answers; yet Famke thought it would be best if the first time Albert saw her again she were dressed as a girl. Now that she had breasts again, she longed to display them. In the window of one ladies' outfitter she saw a blue-sprigged frock, readymade, that looked as if it might do; so she stepped inside, savoring the tinkle of a genteel brass bell.

The woman at the counter looked up from a pile of linens and gave Famke a cold stare. "Service entrance is round back," she said slowly, as if speaking to an imbecile, and she pointed a finger on which a misting of black hairs showed to the knuckle. There was a more pronounced sprinkle on her upper lip. "If you're delivering that package, you'll need to do it there."

"I'm not a servant," Famke said, clutching *Hygeia* tight. "I am here to buy a dress for myself."

The woman looked close and saw that Famke was in fact not the Celestial that her attire announced her to be. Nonetheless, the combination of blue eyes, gray tunic, and paper-white skin indicated that nothing good might be afoot, and she shooed Famke out of her store.

"But my own clothes were stolen!" Famke protested.

"Try down the street. There's a branch of the Methodist Ladies' Mission eight blocks away."

"I have money—I need only the proper—"

But she had tried the clerk's patience too far, and the door slammed in her face with a clash of the little brass bell.

It was the same everywhere in that district: No store wanted to assist in transforming a Chinese servant into a white woman of uncertain identity. The city was large and established enough that a number of clerks considered themselves too refined to cater to prostitutes, and that was all they imagined Famke could be. Thus it was not until she wandered into Bush Street, a district with a fair number of theaters and performance halls, that Famke found a shopkeeper willing to help her.

Hearing her story, the woman's well-lined face settled into an expression of willing sympathy, and Famke nearly wept in relief.

"Isn't that just shameful!" her benefactress exclaimed. "Celestials robbing a lady of her clothes! A body reads about such things every day, but without expecting it ever to happen to oneself. Now, how much do you have to spend?"

For three dollars Famke bought a black-and-white plaid skirt, and the rest of her money was good for a pair of simple shoes, a lawn blouse, and the cheapest gloves and stockings and straw hat in that very cheap place. She even bought a set of stays, though Albert did not like them, because she had seen no white woman in the streets going without. She did not have enough to pay for the corset, but the woman was willing to come down in price, and even threw in a ten-cent box of handkerchiefs for free.

"You look like a regular girl now," she said, pulling a handful of pins from her own topknot and arranging Famke's hair for her. "There's a lovely color to your cheeks. And you'll remember this place—Mrs. Iovino's, near the Thalia Festival House."

"I will remember," Famke vowed; she was so grateful that she really thought she might do more business here, as long as she remained in San Francisco.

"I'll even dispose of those nasty old clothes for you," Mrs. Iovino volunteered, and Famke was glad to leave them to her.

A few hours after Famke left, when the secondhand dealer made his weekly visit, Mrs. Iovino offered him the Celestial costume. He was so impressed with the quality of the materials that it was no trouble to get twice the price of a corset.

. . .

Two bits lookee, four bits feelee, eight bits fuckee . . . Bundle in hand, Ancient Jade tottered into Hygiene, wondering what she would do from now on to support herself. The walk that had taken Famke an hour had required the better part of the morning from her, even though she had traveled not by the road but as the crow might fly, straight through the trees. She was forced to pause frequently to rest her feet. During one of those pauses, Ancient Jade had looked down at the broken, sweaty stumps the Chinese called lotus blossoms, and she wished that if her feet had to be deformed, they might have been made into hooves, like the zebras'—or perhaps like the deer's, for weren't those cloven? These tiny feet had made her valuable to the slave traders who'd bought her from her widowed mother (who had pretended to Ancient Jade and the neighbors that she was traveling to Golden Mountain to be married), but they made real travel impossible. It was small wonder she'd spent six years trapped in that crib, calling, *Two bits lookee, four bits feelee . . .*

Ancient Jade gathered up her determination and looked around for something to do. She saw the sign at the Springs Hotel: No Unaccompanied Blacks or Celestials, and it caused her to shake with another wave of anger. It was perhaps that anger that, all afternoon, made her seem sullen and intractable even to the low rooming houses and laundries that might have been willing to hire a crippled Chinese girl-of-all-work without references; and thus, when the sun went down, Ancient Jade found herself without a roof or a means of employment.

There was a sign posted in the little park as well—No Vagrants—but Ancient Jade was not sure what that word might mean, and in all that afternoon she had not seen a single man of the law. Perhaps Edouard Versailles had not found time to hire any such men, as the village would not be officially settled until the hospital admitted its first patients. So Ancient Jade sat on that bench, straight-backed and holding her bundle, until the twilight faded and black night swallowed the park. There were globes for gas light, but Versailles had not ordered them lit as yet, either.

She had not come to the park by accident; Ancient Jade allowed as little room for chance in her life as possible. She was here because during her search that afternoon she had heard, thanks to long habits of invisibility that made men speak freely around her, that this park was actually a den of prostitution.

"The sweetest, whitest flesh you've ever seen, and completely healthy," one sunken-chested man had whispered to another. "Like a Greek statue she is . . . Twenty dollars to touch, ten to look."

That was forty times what Ancient Jade used to earn in her crib, and she hadn't been allowed to keep any of that. Reluctant as she was to whore again, this seemed like the best business prospect she would have here. She thought she might earn enough to rent a bed in a house for Chinese cooks and launderers; she could tell them she worked nights at the hospital. This was, of course, if the girls who already worked in the park would let her buy part of their business.

The night stretched longer, and there were no other girls. Just Ancient Jade, sitting on her shadowed bench, so much a part of the shadows herself that when the first customer arrived he almost looked right through her and returned home in disappointment. But, sensing his approach, Ancient Jade turned on her old professional smile, the smile that had been beaten into her; and it lit a path straight to her feet.

"Ten for look, twenty for touch," she said. She made no other offers, calculating that if this man wanted something more he could damn well ask for it. She was also willing to come down in price, as the schedule she had heard was obviously for a white woman's services.

But this man did not argue; he saved his breath for the difficult business of breathing itself. He simply took out his purse and fished from it two heavy, beautiful golden coins. Ancient Jade smiled again, and this time the smile melted her clothes away. In the moonlight, her flesh was sweet and white, too.

Chapter 53

. . . . .

The street floors of the great avenues form one continuous exposition of all that art and science can produce. A pauper could enter these clothing stores and in a moment step out a prince, to the eye at least. [. . .] I could never have imagined women in whom beauty and charm are more general than in these.

GUILLERMO PRIETO,
A JOURNEY TO THE UNITED STATES

Feeling free of some horrible prison—though her movements were much more restricted in these clothes—Famke set out to find the city's painters. She had *Hygeia* rolled up in one hand, nothing in the other; for she had nothing else in the world. Yet with new clothes had come new hope, and she expected to find Albert momentarily. Perhaps she would turn a corner and run right into him; San Francisco seemed the kind of place where that could happen, and she was just hot and tired and feverish enough to believe that it would.

Then she stopped short, forcing the foot traffic to curl around her with a few curses and jolts of the shoulder. She ran quickly through the checklist of symptoms that Edouard had impressed upon her: *Feverish*. Yes, but anyone who had spent a day and a half locked up in a third-class car would feel feverish. And under those conditions, anyone's lungs would feel raw as well. No, she thought, and began to walk again, she would be better once she had some rest. Hygeia Springs *had* cured her, and she was going to have a long, happy life. With Albert.

She remembered the eleven cents she'd found among the cushions, tucked furtively into her stays at Mrs. Iovino's, and she stopped at a tea house for a glass of fizzy water and some information about art. She sat where the prettiest waitress would serve her and asked, "Have you modeled for the painters?"

The girl blushed as pink as her dainty bodice and, after a little more teasing and prodding, told Famke about the Old Supreme Court House on Montgomery Street. It was full of artists sharing studio space where once lawyers and judges had tried to impose some sense of order. Or, if Famke merely wanted to look at paintings, there were galleries in Woodward Gardens and at the San Francisco Art Association on Pine Street. The waitress also recommended a place called the Bohemian Club, where artists congregated with writers, actors, and their "misses." It developed that this last category embraced not failed works but the girls most intimate with the artists—girls of whom Famke had read long ago—and thus it was there that she made her first destination. The waitress drew her a map on a teahouse menu.

Famke strode into the Club bravely, with six cents remaining in her pocket and the colors in her skirt already beginning to run together from her body's humidity. She was immediately lost in a forest of plaster castings and gold-painted props, where paintings and drawings were as thick on the walls as scales on a flounder's belly. In the midst of this artistic clutter stood men and women deep in conversation, laughing and gulping at their wine with a determination to be merry, to live artistic lives.

"I am looking for Albert Castle," she announced.

If she had anticipated an immediate response, she was disappointed; the name appeared to be unfamiliar, or at least to excite no interest. The giddy chatter continued.

Famke felt a rush of weakness and realized she had not had a thing to eat in over two days. "Albert Castle," she repeated, less loudly, and looked for a chair in which to collapse. Finding nothing, she leaned against the wall and willed her ribs to expand beyond the corset, so the spinning and buzzing in her head would stop.

"Meess?" A voice with a dimly familiar accent hissed somewhere around her collarbone. "You are unwell?"

Famke looked down onto a brown head soaked with macassar oil, the smell of which rolled upward. "It is hot in here," she said; finding better words, a compelling story, seemed like too much trouble.

"You are perhaps 'ungry?"

"Yes," she said with relief, hoping this would mean food was about to materialize.

It did not. "You are looking for work?"

"I am looking," she said, "for Albert Castle."

At last, the man waved at a girl with a plate of tired-looking sandwiches; with a chivalrous gesture, he handed over a nickel and tucked a ham-and-cheese into Famke's hand. She tried not to tear at it too savagely or to think what she might owe this man for his gift. She did not want work; she wanted Albert. For now, she ate, getting crumbs all over her new gloves and wishing her benefactor had thought to buy her something to drink as well.

"I am an arteestic *entrepreneur*," he said, with that accent that she now identified as something like Edouard's: French, but perhaps from a different part of the country. "I stage a variety of spectacles to please the eye. Arteestic young girls such as yourself—"

"I am not looking for work," she interrupted. The sandwich now gone, she untied the tress around *Hygeia* and unfurled the canvas. It fell over the length of her and across a few feet of floor; she saw the thickly painted areas had cracked. "I am looking for a man who paints this way. See, there is his signature—the castle in that corner. A. C. Albert Castle. Do you know him?"

The little man studied the long picture carefully, looking from *Hygeia* to Famke and back again, then bending down to peer through his spectacles at Albert's castle. "As a signature," he pronounced at last, "it is fine. Yet as a painting, I may say—"

"Oh!" Famke began rolling the canvas together. She was not going to listen to another unpleasant word about *Hygeia*. "I did not ask for a review. I asked for the painter."

Strengthened by the sandwich, she left the little man and dove into the crowd, boldly cutting into one conversation after another, asking after Albert. She met with sketchy success: A few men said his name sounded familiar and had been uttered recently in San Francisco, but no one could recall actually having met him.

"He is tall and thin," Famke said, as if through description she could will him into being. "He has green eyes like a frog. He paints enormous pictures."

But none of this information meant anything to the members of the Bohemian Club. "Are you a model?" asked one man after another, measuring her hair, height, and bone structure with their eyes. "Or an artist?" the occasional woman added, clutching a shabby purse or a half-empty glass and blinking fiercely up at her.

Famke stamped her feet impatiently. "I am looking for Albert Castle."

.   .   .

F amke enjoyed no more success at the Old Supreme Court House than she'd found with the Bohemians.

"Not a Castle among us," declared a hirsute young man on the ground floor.

Famke recognized the feeble pun, but she continued to stare him down until he agreed to take her through the building. They knocked on locked doors and walked freely through open ones, inspecting canvases covered with fruit and flowers or decorously draped women; they spoke to artists in spattered smocks and models who cleaned their toenails when not required to pose. Their answers were always variations on a few themes:

"Never heard of him."

"The name sounds familiar, but . . ."

"Did he ever work in Colorado?"

"Try the Bohemian Club."

Famke refused dozens of visiting cards offered by men who hoped to awaken her to her own potential as a model. She had no interest in posing for anyone but Albert, and she did not trust these avid young men in their beehive of art. The hirsute fellow was becoming what Sariah used to call "overfamiliar" with her, and she even thought she felt his hand on her waist as they climbed their third set of stairs. She ran the rest of the way up and stood panting at the top.

"Keep soughing like that," said her escort, "and you'll sail away on the last of your own wind."

Famke leaned against the wall. She was tired and itched to be free of the corset, and she'd never realized how heavy a roll of painted canvas could be till she tried carrying *Hygeia* around for a day. She thought incidentally that poor *Hygeia* was no worse than the ugly French-style paintings she'd seen today; it was rude of these so-called artists to pucker up their noses and smile at it. She also wished she'd had the foresight to ask for a second sandwich. "This is not the last of my wind," she said stubbornly, and she led the march down the hall.

"Never heard of him."

"The name sounds somewhat familiar, but . . ."

Eventually they exhausted the possibilities at the Old Supreme Court House. The sun began to sink, and Famke's guide said he must return home to his wife. He pressed his card upon her and told her that, really, the painting she carried was not so bad. If she would ever like to pose for another, or learn some artistic techniques herself, she had only to call on him.

As he disappeared into the moil of the street, Famke at last weighed up the ugly facts. Sometime during the afternoon her last coins had disappeared, and she literally had not even two cents to rub together; all she owned in the world was the clothing on her back and the painting in her hand. She had nowhere to spend the night, and she was cold now and hungry again. It was time to contrive something.

She could not do here what she had done her last night in Hygiene; not only was it shameful, but it was too dangerous in this unknown place—and besides, there was a chance that Albert would hear of it. So she began to pick her way back toward Mrs. Iovino's store, where earlier in the day she had noticed several pawnshops doing a brisk trade. The gas lamps glowed gently, lighting her path, and at the end of the street, the Thalia Festival House was lit like a red rose, with the letters on its poster bills glinting golden dewdrops. But Famke did not need to go that far; only Acropolis Pawn was still open, and she was its last customer.

One final time she unrolled *Hygeia* and looked at the lines she had labored over, the delicate details, the whole truth of a woman's body. After a brief discussion, she accepted six dollars (this for the canvas that had once fetched seven hundred!) and stuffed the limp greenbacks down into the tight corners of her corset, where they felt hot and dirty.

"I will be back to redeem her," she vowed, looking again at the painting that had filled so many hours of her life.

"Sure you will, sister," said the pawnkeeper, a second-generation Greek with a waxed moustache. "Just you keep hold of that ticket." He twirled thoughtfully at one sharp point of hair, wondering where best to display the enormous, ragged thing.

Chapter 54

· · · · ·

The San Francisco Art Association is a delusive title. Rambling through their
rooms last week one would have noticed [. . .] contusions in black-and-blue,
and ravings in yellow ochre; tropical horrors and dropsical Niagaras; several
degrees of poisoned pup and some freaks in cattle. There were some paint
which resembled flowers, and some still-life which resembled paint; some con-
valescent landscape, and some hopelessly incurable architecture.

THE WASP

Famke plunged into the San Francisco art world with both feet and her
whole heart, clutching at anyone who might guide her toward Albert.
At city prices, her six dollars lasted precisely three days, and even then
she felt herself suffering from poor diet and a burst of unaccustomed physical activity, as she walked from the Bohemian Club to the Supreme Court
House, from one gallery to another, attending public auctions of what those
in the know called buckeyes and potboilers—in other words, hackwork—
and looking for solid clues that did not appear. First she obtained a list of
professional models from the Bohemian Club and visited them one by one.
None of them knew Albert, either, though again a few called the name familiar. She allowed a tall New Yorker to serve as her guide for a day, riding
the famous electrical cable cars up and down nauseous hills until it became
clear he was leading her about for his own amusement, not for her benefit.
She wasted another day trying to get into the classrooms at the San
Francisco Art Association, where she thought for some reason Albert
might be either teaching or taking classes.

Famke could not give up the conviction that he was here somewhere. So
she continued to dig and prod and try to survive until she had exhausted
every possibility.

One possibility came in the person of Miss Hortense Dart, an English
lady artist who had come to this liberated city in order to take lessons and

who was known for painting the fantastic castles of popular fairy tales. A spotty model mentioned those castles to Famke in a way that convinced her they were worth a try, though she was aware of grasping at straws and trying to turn them to gold.

Miss Dart's studio was at the top of a five-story building near the Woodward Gardens, where she caught all the sunshine that could squeeze its way through San Francisco's clouds. She was cleaning brushes when Famke came to call, and the smell of turpentine poured hot and sharp out of her open door. Peering in, Famke saw a short, fleshy woman of about thirty-five, with once-dark hair and pale eyes above a rumpled smock; the smock's neck was distorted by a goiter the size of a goose egg. After one look, Famke knew Albert would have nothing to do with this woman, however gifted and modern she might be. But Famke was tired, and Miss Dart offered quite calmly, as if hectic redheads presented themselves on her doorstep every day, "You look as if you could do with some tea. Shall I make a pot, Miss—?"

"Summer." It seemed too much effort to say the last syllable. "And a cup of tea would be very nice."

Famke sank down onto a hard chair. She thought now that the studio was really quite pleasant, small but clean, though with none of the clutter she had come to associate with artists' dens. A Japanese screen stretched over the darkest corner of the room, and Famke wondered if it hid a bed that must be as chaste and spare as a nun's—but a good deal more comfortable than the cot on which she herself lay at night, gritty-eyed from scheming and from the somnolent eruptions of the models with whom she shared a rundown room. Models, she had discovered, were no better than miners in a flophouse.

"Here you are." Miss Dart put a hot cup in Famke's hand and pulled up a chair for herself. The liquid in her own cup looked even darker than Famke's. "I like a really strong brew," she explained, blowing into the cup to cool it. "I hope you weren't wanting sugar or milk—"

Famke shook her head.

"They say we shouldn't drink milk anyway, as it passes on the tuberculosis."

Both women sipped. The tea tasted remarkably like Lydia E. Pinkham's Vegetable Compound; or perhaps it was the turpentine in the air that made Famke think so.

"Now," Miss Dart said briskly, when she gauged Famke's spirits to have strengthened, "what did you say I might do for you?"

Once again Famke uttered the name that had become an incantation. "I have looked all over," she added helplessly, anticipating another defeat, "and no one knows him. But I heard that you paint castles . . ."

"Oh, yes," said Miss Dart, "I have met him."

Famke stared at her—the pale eyes, the salt-and-pepper hair, the hideous goiter. She thought she must have misunderstood. "Are you sure?"

Miss Dart set her cup down in its saucer and put the saucer on a little table littered with paint tubes. "A tall man," she said thoughtfully, "with light hair and green eyes? Who repeats the words one says to him?"

Astonished, Famke gulped her tea and scalded her throat. Her breath came fast and hot, burning her lips. "Where is he?" she croaked.

A veil of discretion fell over Miss Dart's face. "Forgive me, young lady, but why do you ask?"

The more Famke looked at this poor, ugly woman, the more far-fetched became the notion that she and Albert were somehow connected. And now she, Famke, was being called upon to explain herself. Which story should she tell? Should she portray Albert as deserting husband or feckless brother?

"He used to paint me," she said, and her hands shook so that she nearly overturned her cup of faux Pinkham's. She noticed that the cup was a Flora Danica lily, and that started a flood of tears.

"My dear Miss Summer!" Now Miss Dart was kneeling with both Famke's hands in hers, chafing the rough thin fingers with her oily ones. "What can be the matter? Do you need money? Has he—forgive my frankness, but are you in a condition?"

Famke laughed through her tears. "No, no, nothing of that sort!" In fact, her courses had ended, leaving her with a clean feeling as if she were all new Down There. She did need money, but this was hardly the moment to admit it. "I only want to—" Now the tears set off a spate of hiccoughs, which turned to real coughs, and she accepted a rainbow-stained rag with gratitude. "I only want him to see me!"

Miss Dart had remained kneeling at Famke's feet, brushing the dirt off her hem. "To do that, Miss Summer, you must place yourself in a position to be seen."

"That is what I am trying." Famke blew her nose noisily. It seemed so obvious, but there was hardly any point in saying so to Miss Dart, who was now rummaging through a chest of drawers and scattering papers all over her sunny floor.

"Here we are." Miss Dart returned and thrust a scrap at Famke.

It was a pencilled bit of Albert's signature, the "A" turret and the "C" fortress. And there was a small but significant deviation from the usual: A window had been cut in the turret, and a woman's head appeared there; her hair tumbled over the sill and nearly to the ground.

Famke breathed very carefully. It was all so delicate that a sigh would have erased the lines.

"I met him only once, when he was attempting to draw the Seal Rocks," said Miss Dart, "none too successfully. It looked a great *pile* of rocks, really, with no seals at all. But I identified myself as an artist as well, and I showed him my sketches—no better than his, I confess; I do much nicer things with buildings and the human form—and we had quite a conversation about signatures. He drew me this as an example—Albert Castle, you see," she said, pointing out the letters as if Famke had not chased them all around the puzzle of the West. "And that is Rapunzel inside, with a ladder of her hair to allow her lover to visit within the palace of art. Quite a pretty conceit, don't you think? It inspired me," she added shyly, and poked another handful of paper at Famke, "to work on my own signature. Hortensia is a flower, and my last name—well, you see for yourself."

Famke held Albert's little square above the others, which drifted across her lap like dirty snow. Miss Dart had done the obvious: a large and fluffy blossom pierced with an arrow. The "H" was found in the intersection of stem, leaf, and dart, and the "D" was of course the bow from which the arrow had sprung.

Famke wondered if lady artists, like their male counterparts, were generally much given to disquisitions on technique and philosophy, for Miss Dart was providing one now. ". . . the artist's place within the work as well as the work's within the life the artist," she was saying, sitting on the floor with her arms clasped about her knees; "it has been woefully neglected. Mr. Castle made me see that, and he made me see castles themselves differently too, and the heroines I place in them. I have embarked, as you see, on a

series of paintings based on the old stories . . . The Goose Girl . . . Briar
Rose . . ."

Famke thought that if this were what it meant to be a woman artist, she
was just as glad that she had failed. She gazed at Albert's tiny Rapunzel,
imagining her with red hair, as Miss Dart's voice faded in and out of her
awareness.

At last she heard the Englishwoman's fruity voice saying, ". . . looking for
a model, and if you are accustomed to posing, you would be—"

"I do not pose for painters," Famke interrupted. "Except Albert. Can you
tell me where to find him?"

At that, Miss Dart looked crestfallen, and she stood to reach for her cold
teacup. "I do not know," she said, and in those four syllables Famke detected
a longing akin to her own. "I believe he is still in the city."

Miss Dart sipped her tea and then, politely but firmly, asked for the return of Albert's signature.

⋅   ⋅   ⋅

For the first time since her master had taken to his bed, Frøken Grubbe
ascended the stairs with reluctance. "Asking for you, he is, and he don't
look pleased," the housemaid, Vida, had reported with obvious glee. Frøken
Grubbe reflected with something as close to sadness as she allowed herself
to feel, that although she took no real pains to be liked among the staff, neither did it gratify her to be so disliked. And now it appeared that the man
she had saved from the flames, whom she had nursed back to a semblance
of health and the first pink patches of new skin—this man was displeased
with her.

"You sent for me?" she asked, standing at the bedside and reminding herself to relax her spine so that she might look the image of the loving care she
did in fact personify. The smell of burnt flesh was gone, replaced with the
bracing scents of alcohol and liniment.

"Grubbe," he barked, with his old failure to observe any sort of social
grace, "I want to know why that nun has not come round. Mother Birgit.
She did me one favor, and I need another."

Frøken Grubbe bowed her head. "If there is some service you need performed, I will be happy to do it." She, who had done everything for him—

from bandages to chamberpot, reading aloud to transcribing accounts, had thought his manner was warmer to her of late.

"I want Birgit," the man in the bed said stubbornly. "I hear you've kept her from coming back."

"It is said," Frøken Grubbe ventured slowly—for by whom were these things said other than herself?—"that, as Mother Superior, Birgit allowed improper behavior among the orphans and novices . . ." She coughed delicately, hoping to convey much through the small explosive sound; but the man who collected Japanese prints found nothing shocking in her insinuation.

"That doesn't affect me," he said brusquely. "You send for her directly."

She thought out her next words carefully. "Mother Birgit is no longer in this life," she said.

At those words, Herr Skatkammer seemed to shrink, nearly vanishing among the snowy sheets. It was a long moment before he said, "Send up that fat housemaid, then."

◆   ◆   ◆

So here was a clue and a kind of proof, a kind of hope, at last: Albert *was* in San Francisco. Famke reasoned that if he was not generally to be found among the city's artists, there was a natural next place to look. The time had clearly come to discover the bagnios and boardinghouses of San Francisco, to seek for Albert's art in the types of places that had most recently been known to sponsor it. She had seen nothing in the galleries here that impressed her, anyway; perhaps true art lay in the whorehouses these days.

Famke made new inquiries at the Old Court House, and she learned that there were something like three hundred known establishments of carnal business within the city. It was a crippling discovery, for even the lowest bagnio in the fearsome Barbary Coast district cost money, and if she were to be safe there she would require masculine clothes. But her money was gone. With so many trained painters about, there was no market for the refurbishments that had carried her through Colorado; and after the humiliation of *Hygeia* (now in the Greek pawnshop window, with a swathe of whitewash slapped over the ruddy triangle Down There), she knew she would get no commissions as a painter. It was out of the question to work as a maid, as she needed more money than a servant could command, and her days must be free for the search. To work for other artists seemed a betrayal of everything she'd had with Albert and, more importantly, of her long journey toward him. And yet this was all she knew how to do well: to stand still, to impersonate a figure from the world of the imagination.

And thus, she resigned herself to the one path open to her.

Chapter 55

Gorgeous decoration is characteristic of San Francisco; the people pay high prices for the necessities of life, so velvet and gilt work is thrown into the bargain.

FRANK MARRYAT,
MOUNTAINS AND MOLEHILLS;
OR, RECOLLECTIONS OF A BURNT JOURNAL

Paris is really as near San Francisco as New York [. . .] Perhaps in no other American city would the ladies invoice so high per head as in San Francisco, when they go out to the opera, or to party, or ball. Their point lace is deeper, their moire antique stiffer, their skirts a trifle longer, their corsage an inch lower, their diamonds more brilliant,—and more of them,—than the cosmopolite is like to find elsewhere.

SAMUEL BOWLES,
OUR NEW WEST

Mid-May 1886 was a mad season for San Francisco, with a play or a concert on each corner. Virtually every gentleman, and some few ladies, who lived in or visited the city during that month eventually came to the Thalia Festival House on Bush Street, in the heart of a labyrinth of hills and avenues and warehouses. Streetlamps glowed over walls blanketed in red poster bills; there were no illustrations, but yellow letters masquerading as gold leapt off the page and burrowed into minds and hearts of even the most rushed passersby, awaking a passion for art.

Professor Charles Martin du Garde
presents
A Night of *Tableaux Vivants,*
or, The Living Waxworks
featuring ARTISTIC *enactments from renowned works*

of painting and sculpture
among them, Rubens, Renoir, the Pre-Raphaelite Brotherhood
~and the breathtaking Winged Victory~
8:00 of the evening
~two dollars~

And so, urgent as their business in town was, Viggo and Myrtice paused before the red walls and glass doors and considered.

"Two dollars," Myrtice said. "That's forty miles' train fare each."

"But we are not taking a train," said Viggo. "We are in San Francisco, waiting for Edouard Versailles." He took four silver dollars from his pocket, and he and Myrtice looked at them: Liberty's face on one side and the eagle on the other.

Both Viggo and Myrtice felt the time was ripe to glean some enjoyment from life. Upon arriving in Hygiene, they had been dismayed to learn that they'd missed Edouard Versailles by a mere four hours—this despite having hired a private carriage at Harmsway and scaled impatiently over the wall of Versailles's estate. The foreign maid with the sad round mouth regarded them suspiciously and pressed her lips together, but they agreed her words had the ring of truth: Famke had disappeared, and Versailles was not home.

Myrtice fell to the ground in a fit of tears—which in the end had saved the day, for the mournful maid had taken pity on her and told her where to find the master.

"Hotel called Palace," she said, "five floor. Fireproof."

And so Viggo and Myrtice had come to San Francisco and camped in the marble lobby of the Palace Hotel for as long as they could, while men in frock coats and top hats made frequent and enthusiastic use of shiny brass spittoons nearby. It was said there were a thousand rooms in the Palace, and Myrtice and Viggo scrutinized every person who might be going into or coming out of one. When the staff finally shooed them into the street, they left their names and swore to come back the next day. When they did, they missed Versailles by only ten minutes, or so a disdainful clerk explained. They were not allowed to sit in the lobby again, and both were burned standing outside in a day of unusual sunshine.

Now here was the Thalia in its crimson glory, seducing them with the promise of a deeper glimpse of the world in which Viggo, at least, had been seeing Famke during the long months of the search. Art in Mæka, in the city that the Celestials called Golden Mountain.

"What is a tableaux vivants?" asked Myrtice, conscious of mispronouncing the words.

"It is artistic," Viggo said firmly, though he was no more certain of the meaning than she was; the word highlighted in majuscule letters reassured him. "There will be a place to sit. Shall we go in?"

Myrtice thought yet again that Viggo was the nicest, most considerate man, certainly not what she'd expect Ursula's brother to be like. Tableaux vivants must be something educational. And Myrtice's skin was now beautifully clear, so really she should not feel at all self-conscious as she stepped into first a foyer and then a concert hall full of handsome men and women, all of them (so it seemed) in silk, with opera glasses and gloves. Walking in there was like walking into fairyland. Everyone was covered in jewels, and the gaslight glittered off their diamonds and threw patterns of illumination on faces and walls, dancing like fairy lights through the smoke from their cigars. The odors of their various perfumes were a blessed relief after the rotten reek of a city in early summer.

Myrtice and Viggo took seats toward the back, perhaps fifty feet from the red-curtained stage, at the top of the room where the heat of gaslight and excited art lovers' bodies was strongest. She reminded him to remove his hat, and he reminded her to hold on to her purse. She was doing that anyway, but she liked that he thought enough of her to pay these little attentions. Indeed, she fancied that, away from Utah, he had begun seeing her in a different light: if not as desirable, at least as a woman. The rest would surely follow.

Shortly after they settled themselves, she saw a man, even more resplendent than the others, strolling onto the stage. His hair was dark and well oiled, gleaming in the light, and countless diamond stickpins studded the lapels on his simple black suit.

"Ladees and gentlemen," he boomed, in a voice calculated to quiet every one of them. "I am your host, Charles Martin du Garde, and eet is my fondest pleasure to welcome you to the most unforgettable night of your lives. I bring you ze art treasures of Europe, displayed here in unique fashion, as you have never seen them before or since . . ."

His voice droned on until Myrtice found herself blinking sleepily. She scarcely noticed when the glittering man finished talking and left the stage, but she snapped to attention when the red curtains peeled apart. For there, directly in front of her, stood a naked woman.

Charles Martin du Garde's voice came from backstage. "*The Little Fur*, by Peter Paul Rubens," he said.

Out in the audience, heads began to nod as if in recognition. The diamonds' light played over the woman's arms and stomach and legs, over her pale brown hair, over the fur she had draped from one shoulder to swoop behind her back and settle around her hips, just above the place a woman grew fur of her own. Myrtice blushed at the very thought of such things, but she was too awake now to look away. She certainly would not look at Viggo.

Du Garde went on explaining the beauties of the painting and its significance in the history of art, but it was clear no one heard what he was saying. Every ounce of energy in the room was fixed on that shameless pink flesh, flesh that didn't even move to cover itself. Perhaps, thought Myrtice, she is not alive at all—but then a breeze whispered through the hall, and the woman's hair stirred. The hairs on her fur stirred, too, and they released a sudden flurry of white moths—an unexpected event that provoked laughter throughout the room. The girl in the fur sneezed.

At that moment, the curtain closed again, much more swiftly than it had opened. Everyone started to chatter excitedly. Myrtice could not make out a word, and she and Viggo said nothing. She wondered if he were as hot with embarrassment as she; certainly his face was red, and he stared forward as if he could not bear to meet her eyes.

When the drapes parted again, there was another nude woman. This one had her back to the audience, and all they could see of her figure was that expanse of flesh, quite broad—as broad as Myrtice's—ending in an insolent cleft where she sat. A large Negro maid held the long blond hair off to the right, as if to make sure no one could overlook that place where her back divided; there was also a small bronze Cupid lifting up a glass in which the people of the audience could see the naked woman's face and neck. Her plump red lips were smiling.

"*Venus at her Mirror*," said du Garde's voice. "Painted between 1613 and 1615, this large picture ees rightly considered one of Rubens's masterworks . . ."

When du Garde was finished with that one, he described another; there were no more moths, and the living canvases began to succeed one another so rapidly that their spell did not break between partings of the curtain. The audience was enchanted.

Myrtice could hardly bear to look, and yet look she must. It became clear that all of the "works" were composed of women, and all of them in some stage of undress: chalky white statues and bright rosy oil paintings, even a few works of bronze and gold—how did Charles Martin du Garde make the women look like metal?

"*The Three Graces*, by Antonio Canova, 1814. This marble sculpture is a most winsome rendition of a popular *thème*. Note ze sweet elegance with which Aglaia, Goddess of Splendor, whispers her secrets to Euphrosyne, Goddess of Rejoicing—or ees she about to bestow a sororal kiss upon the cheek? Handmaidens to Venus, the Goddess of Love, these three daughters of Jupiter . . .

"Salt cellar, by Benvenuto Cellini. Cellini, a goldsmith, fashioned this intricate cellar on a mythological conceit between 1540 and 1544. The figures are Neptune, God of the Sea, and the Earth Goddess . . ."

That was a most remarkable work indeed. The gold bedazzled the gaze, and Myrtice stared as if mesmerized. It seemed the Earth Goddess was holding her breast in a gesture of abundance, contrasting with the god's spiky trident. Yes, a *male* figure, nude but for a small drape in the lap—and then Myrtice blinked, and she realized that he, too, was impersonated by a woman. Here in the realm of art, one could not trust one's eyes at all, even in the most basic matters of perception.

◆　◆　◆

Near the front of the room, Edouard sat with his hat in his lap and his hand on a fiery red watch fob. As was his habit in moments of distress, he worried away at the fob—while at the same time feeling irritated that, long after he'd expressed a desire for such a thing, Life's Importance had produced a rope of Famke's hair, and Wong had used it to replace the worn-out one. Edouard was most uncomfortable. How could all these spectators, some of them ladies, allow themselves to be assaulted with the sight of so much flesh? Even if it were in the name of art, this display was obscene. After all, these were not really works of paint and stone or even wax, but actual women undraped upon the stage, and there was no purpose for their deshabille other than the audience's entertainment. Yes, it was appalling. Edouard blamed this Charles Martin du Garde—whose accent was quite obviously as sham as his art. What must people think of the French now? Particularly as so many of the unlucky artists were of that nation. He himself had been lured by the promise of seeing the world's masterpieces life size; but here was no *Mona Lisa*, no *Infanta*, no *Liberty Enlightening the People*, and those figures were not likely to appear among this bunch.

"*Etude de nu*, by Paul Gauguin. A simple tableau of an unclothed seamstress was painted during the artist's exile in Copenhagen, Denmark . . .

"*Bathers*, by William-Adolphe Bouguereau. This splendid picture, completed only two years prior to the present date . . ."

Two years ago, Edouard had still been experimenting with electricity while workmen cleared the land for his hospital. Precious Flower had been recovering from the disease she'd picked up in her horrible crib. The magnificent old lion, centerpiece of his father's menagerie, had still been alive. And he had not heard of Famke Ursula Summerfield Goodhouse or of the painting that had brought her to him; and, he told himself as the red drapes parted yet again, he had been happy.

While du Garde extolled the beauties of yet another full-bodied woman in a bath, Edouard admitted that this trip to San Francisco had been a mistake. He had found nothing worth bringing to Hygiene: Few artists painted canvases large enough for his needs, for one matter; and for another, most of those pictures were either military in subject or, like these women on stage, utterly unsuited to a hospital, even one that prescribed frequent immersion for its patients. He had become so depressed he did not even look at the mail that the two remaining maids dutifully forwarded from Hygiene. Wong the butler, who had accompanied his master on this trip but naturally was not allowed in auction rooms, galleries, or performance halls, made no bones about the fact that he was at his wits' end.

"You buy something," he said. "Plenty good paint here."

But even under this duress, Edouard could not bring himself to buy; and after interviewing all the major gallery owners and calling upon the best-known artists in the city, he was preparing to leave empty-handed. Yes, he decided as he looked at the large blonde woman caught climbing into a tub, in this very moment he was giving up; tomorrow he would go home.

He could always move a potted palm or two from the glass house down to the hospital; they would make a striking show against that troublesome blank wall.

So the unfortunate whim that had led him here to the living waxworks had brought an unexpected benefit. Edouard had made a decision: Clearly, it was most appropriate that he depart as soon as possible, both from the Thalia Festival House and from San Francisco itself.

Edouard peered down the row of men to his right and left, all of them in thrall to what they had convinced themselves was art. He could not squeeze past without disturbing them and drawing unpleasant attention to himself; he would have to bide his time, wait for an auspicious moment. So he shrank down in his seat, pulling his collar up nearly to his chin and veiling his eyes with thick lashes.

◆   ◆   ◆

"And now," trumpeted the voice of Charles Martin du Garde, "ze work that has inspired admiration for more than two thousand years, ze single most perfect female form ever captured in stone."

The audience leaned forward. This was du Garde's most famous representation, and they were hot for the viewing; but the professor refused to satisfy them just yet. He left his listeners to stare at red velvet folds undulating in the current of their breath while he exposed the history of the piece they were about to view.

"In 1863, a French archaeologist unearthed over one hundred pieces of marble on the Greek island of Samothrace. At ze great Louvre museum, he was able to assemble those bits of stone into the figure you are about to see here. Posed as if to adorn the prow of a *grand* stone ship, zis magnificent statue once stood on the cliffs overlooking Samothrace Harbor—although, *triste*, her arms and head disappeared so long ago that we have no record to show what they were. Instead, we must gaze and imagine what might have been, as I give you . . ." He paused, allowing them and himself to savor this moment. ". . . Winged Victory."

At last, the curtains parted, the gaslights dimmed, and the audience vented a collective gasp.

There was utter silence as the diamonds reflected upon a young woman's breasts and hips and legs. Hers was in fact a nearly perfect form: perhaps a shade too slender for the current tastes, but exquisitely proportioned. There was something to say, too, for the aesthetic pleasure of seeing the skeleton beneath the flesh clearly. Victory was veiled in a sort of shift, but it was so thin and clinging that the outlines of nipples and the deep stop of a navel were clearly visible, before the veiling thickened slightly over what appeared to be a private region completely bare of private hairs. So arresting was this vision that one scarcely saw the arms were stumped before a pair of massive, ragged wings, and the lack of a head hardly registered. A shape this lovely had no need for a face—indeed, some might say its beauty was heightened by the sense of what was not there. One could not but imagine the act of violence that had robbed Victory of her laurels, and one treasured her the more for her fragility.

In the stage wings, Du Garde parted the red velvet backdrop and watched his creation weave her silken spell over the audience, as she had done this week running. To be sure, a few among the audience appeared to be alarmed, as if this were the most outrageous sight of the evening; these, it was clear, must be parsons and schoolmarms who had wandered in by mistake. Far more were staring outright, trying to catch the flutter of ribs that would prove *this* statue, at least, was alive; and feeling somehow triumphant when the chest stayed still, as if they had willed a creature of stone into being. How, they wondered, was it possible to produce a woman with no arms or head? And how was it possible for such a woman to be so beautiful?

Eventually, those who were properly susceptible to beauty stopped asking themselves how it had come to be and merely let it hold them in in its spell.

Regrettably, not everyone present was such an elevated soul; for, suddenly, the tide of attention turned. Down toward the front, a man dressed in black had got to his feet and was stumbling toward the aisle, floundering on knees and hats and angry whispers. He tripped and nearly fell before catching himself on a stout woman's shoulder. A whiskery man stood up and began taking him severely to task.

The stout woman shrieked out at the audience—"That man—*assaulted* me!"

"Patience, my friends!" Du Garde's voice quavered, as if the disturbance beyond the footlights put him in dread of an outright riot. The stage wings were filling with models eager to see the spectacle among the seats. "There is one final representation of the evening, the most *magnifique* of them all . . ."

The man in black began to rush, stumbling over more legs and feet, nearly falling into a lap or two but keeping his hands in the air. A watch fell from his pocket and swung like a pendulum on a reddish rope.

"Friends, friends!" called du Garde. "There is more to come!"

A wave of outrage against the man in black swept through the audience. The artful spell was broken; they began to move, and the diamond sparkle swept crazily over faces and shoulders and coiffures as they became suddenly aware of what the beauty before them consisted of: Everyone was conscious once more of plain nakedness, even unto what each of them had under his or her clothes.

"I've been touched, too!" exclaimed another woman. Some ladies and gentlemen got to their feet and followed the masher toward the door.

As if this were their cue, du Garde's curtains swished shut—but not before one or two of the spectators saw, faint but distinct, the swell of Victory's breasts as she took a most definite, mortal breath.

Chapter 56

. . . . .

It is an odd thing, but everyone who disappears is said to be seen in San Francisco. It must be a delightful city, and possess all the attractions of the next world.

Oscar Wilde

With shaking hands, Famke pulled the black bag off her head and took a deep gulp of air. If she had had the capacity for irony, she would have recognized it here: She had never felt so vulnerable in her life as when she posed as the statue called Winged Victory. In front of hundreds of eyes, she was blind in her hood, naked but for her paint; if the audience decided to storm the stage, she would be completely at their mercy.

Du Garde saw her standing still when she should not be, the white chalk misting off the greasepaint base on her skin. "Ursie Summer!" He grabbed the hood from her hands and gave her a push. He did not bother with the French accent when he was alone with his models. "Don't stand there— prepare for the finale!"

Too dizzy to do anything but obey, Famke ran backstage, shedding the cardboard wings as she went. She seized a fingertip between her teeth and peeled away the long black gloves as well. Once she had thought it was so clever, the way they faded into the darkness when the stage was lit dim, making her disguise as the shattered statue complete. The hood did the same—but, she vowed to herself, she would never wear it again. It was too terrifying when the audience went mad.

"Quickly!" du Garde hissed. The other girls were arranging the few props necessary for the last tableau: some blocks of papier mâché, some white paste jewels, a cardboard mask or two. "Ursie, that audience won't wait on you all night."

Hastily she rubbed more paint onto her arms, where the gloves had been, and smeared her face with it, then dusted herself with powdered chalk for the proper sheen. She made herself cough a good long time, so she would not have to cough later. She cast an appraising eye over the papier mâché lumps and made a few adjustments here and there. Then, shaking out her hair, which was startlingly red against the white paint, and pulling the damp chemise away from her body for a more floating effect, she stumbled back onstage and assumed her pose.

When she raised her arms in the air and froze, du Garde ceased complaining. He did have an eye for beauty, and out of all the handsome girls in his employ, Ursie Summer was the master of the trade: She knew just how to engage the onlooker's eye, how much to display, what to conceal in order to keep the audience both titillated and intrigued. It was almost as if she were a painter or sculptor herself. The other girls' tableaux were sometimes called vulgar, sometimes offended San Francisco's churchgoing ladies (who had little appreciation for art anyway); but if Famke's scenes disturbed their viewers, it was because she tapped into a part of their being that felt primal, dangerous. She was the wild part of themselves distilled into one static image.

So accomplished was she that du Garde had allowed her to serve as his collaborator, and this final scene, bringing together all of the girls, had been her inspiration. Thus far it had proved popular both with critics, who admired the technical skill it showcased, and with casual viewers, who enjoyed the spectrum of feminine charms—alabaster, golden, fleshly pink—it displayed. The audience never failed to be astonished to find that on a given evening they had watched only nine women, not half a hundred. Each viewer came away with a new respect for the manipulations of art.

Now the other girls fell in before Famke, and du Garde returned to his megaphone. "Ladies and gentlemen," he said in what he hoped was a commanding—yet soothing—tone, "I give you one final spectacle: *Evening of the Muses, in a Castle of Ice.*"

The stagehand pulled the curtain, and there they were: gleaming here, glittering there, nine females arrayed in poses surprisingly familiar to certain habitués of the western demimonde. Their like was found in Boulder, in Santa Fé, in towns that even Famke had not yet visited; and tonight there were several men who recognized the picture before du Garde launched into his final description, as written by Famke: "This notable composition, featuring the classical demigoddesses of drama, dance, and so forth, is rapidly gaining a *réputation* throughout America . . ."

Alas for the maestro, his audience did not fall silent; the buzzing that the earlier fracas had started, continued now, drowning out du Garde's speech about the young artist's significance to contemporary culture. The painter's name vanished in the room's apian murmurs; and as to the somewhat rigid composition itself, and the impressive feminine talent it displayed—the finer points of even these wonders melted away, and there was only naked flesh, raw and material.

Then came the moment at which, each night, du Garde moved among the girls and, just when the audience expected the poses to be broken, affirmed their fixity by contrast with his own motion. Tonight he stepped hesitantly, and his trepidation communicated itself to the models.

Famke sensed the place was ready to erupt. So she did what she had never, in all her nights at the Thalia, allowed herself to do: She blinked.

Now the scene came into focus—the eight girls spread before her with the attributes of the Muses, in the positions in which Albert had painted one coop of soiled doves after another: The skinny girl of *The Little Fur*, the golden ones who posed as Bernini's bronzes and Cellini's salt cellar, the pink Renoir and Ingres and Crane girls, all now holding their flutes and pens and masks, both laughing and tragic. All beginning to look a little nervous. The light glowing and sparkling in the paste crystals, the hair blowing in the audience's brisk wind. Famke's shift slapping her legs like a wet wing until the lyre at her feet—for she was Terpsichore, Muse of the dance—toppled over.

This tableau vivant was the most effective advertisement she could think of. It was her WANTED poster, her announcement in the newspapers, the equivalent of a gleaming sign on the side of a building saying, *Albert, I am here. Come quickly.* It was Famke's masterwork, and it was beginning to crumple. She fixed the girls with a stern eye, to freeze them in place.

While du Garde took his bows and the girls remained more or less still, the mood in the room continued to swell. People were speaking out loud now, and there was a sense of tension drawing them toward the stage. Famke heard them speculate: Which one had been Winged Victory? She heard men getting to their feet and stepping forward. Some few, mostly ladies, took the opportunity to step back, toward the doors and sanctimonious, thick-swathed freedom; but the majority wafted irresistibly up. Nothing would do but that they should make their experience of art physical, feel the warmth of real flesh where they saw cold metal and stone, force the illusory two dimensions of famous pictures to assume the third, most vital, dimension.

Famke blinked again, and her eyes swivelled outward, beyond the footlights, where there was nothing she could see but a diffused sparkle from so many diamonds dipping toward her. The glare pricked her eyes and blinded her again. She sneezed. Then she coughed.

• • •

At the glass outer doors of the Thalia Festival House, Edouard heard the audience begin to swarm. He was aware that a few souls had followed him out of the auditorium—and for this he was grateful, as they confounded both his accusers and the gentlemen who sprang to defend them—but he did not realize that, simply by leaving his seat, he had broken the artists' enchantment. Neither did he apprehend, as Famke and Charles Martin du Garde were starting to do, that because of him the spectators wanted to handle the painted girls. Edouard merely wanted to leave. He felt ill and in need of a bath; for hygienic reasons, it was also high time to let his juices down.

But Thalia's doors, he discovered, were locked. He shook the handles and rattled the panes in their frames.

Presently, a red-coated usher came running, straightening a bit of braid coming loose from one sleeve. "We have to lock 'em, sir, or the riffraff come in. This program is of a very delicate nature."

"Open this door," Edouard demanded with an air of tragedy. He thought he saw the riffraff now, in the darkness beyond the glass—dirty faces, many of them yellow, black, and red—thrusting forward just as the Winged Victory had seemed to do. In the theater, he had thought she might topple into his lap; now he feared the famous San Francisco hoodlums and jayhawkers would set upon him and cover him with filth. Surreptitiously he adjusted the congestion in his trousers. More men and women assembled behind him, the usher fumbled with a ring of keys, and Edouard stroked his watch fob's silky thickness.

"Sir? I beg pardon?" The voice came from behind him and was exquisitely deferential. Blushing to a shade he could not explain, except to hope that his trouserly manipulation had not been witnessed, Edouard turned halfway round and gave the man his ear.

But the next voice to address him was a woman's.

"We noticed you've a rope of red hair there," she said in the accent of the American South. "My companion, Mr. Viggo, and I. We were wondering if you know—"

"We wonder," said the man's voice again, "if you are Mr. Edouard Versailles."

At that moment, the key turned in the lock, and with a triumphant smile the usher held the door open.

＊　＊　＊

The girls onstage were starting to betray their humanity. They made little movements, minute softenings of their poses that drew them slightly farther from the edge of the stage. After that first cough, Famke tried to remain steadfast, but the scratching in her lungs would not be denied—it was as if a whole flock of butterflies had hatched in there at once and begun to flutter about. At last she dropped her arms and doubled over in a fit of hacking.

When Famke broke her pose, she affected every person in the room. The other girls allowed themselves to uncurl and flee the stage. Du Garde melted away, glad to let his star model crest this wave of public aggression—though he thought he might scold her for it later, if all turned out well; it would not do to give her too heady a sense of her own power. The audience, however, froze solid, too awestruck to budge. They had just realized what a gift it was, this ability to hold still and create illusion. A sudden quiet seized the room, a quiet in which Famke's ticklish breath rasped like a struck match.

And that was call enough for one viewer: One man in all that crowd managed to find his feet again and step forward. He shouldered the others aside and walked to the stage, where he gazed up at Victory. She looked very tall to him. He looked rather short to her. The recognition was complete.

"Famke," he said simply, holding his arms out. "Darling."

That night the audience of the Thalia Festival House saw a brilliant light break out over the face of the chief Muse, the Winged Victory, the most perfect example of feminine flesh San Francisco had ever seen. It started with her smile. It grew as she ran a few steps forward, to the lip of the stage, and launched herself into the air.

For several seconds she seemed to float above the footlights, as if she still wore Victory's wings; a trick of the stage set made her appear momentarily to be made of the footlights' gas flames. When she began to fall, she did so slowly. First her chemise unfurled itself, streaming away from her waist and past her ankles; as she fell, she fell into that filmy garment, and it pressed so close to her body as to become invisible. The audience saw that underneath it all, she was very naked indeed.

And then Albert caught her; and he who used to sprint through the streets to relieve tension, now sailed through the amphitheater, with Famke in his arms cleaving the sea of faceless bodies in two to let them pass.

.6.

WINGED VICTORY

I went half mad with beauty on that day.
WILLIAM MORRIS,
"THE DEFENSE OF GUINEVERE"

Chapter 57

*San Francisco is a mad city—a city inhabited for the most part by perfectly
insane people whose women are of a remarkable beauty.*

RUDYARD KIPLING,
"HOW I GOT TO SAN FRANCISCO AND TOOK TEA WITH
THE NATIVES THERE," IN *THE PIONEER*, ALLAHABAD

When they were alone together, in a spendthrift cab, Famke could
not wait to begin telling Albert a version of her long journey
toward him: the places she had looked, the methods she had
used, the marvels she had contrived. She was so eager to do this that she
forgot about kissing; but Albert did not forget.

He kissed her. It was just a gentle brush of lips on lips, but it quickened
Famke's heart until there was no room in her chest for anything but its
hard, fast thumping. She could not catch her breath—but breath was
hardly necessary at this important moment. She would breathe later.

"Darling," Albert said, and his voice seemed unsteady, "you are alive."

Famke giggled—how silly everything was, in the great wonder of their
finding each other. She had always known he must be looking for her, and
now he spoke like a man who had prayed for a miracle and, against all expectation, received it. She said, "Both of us are alive."

"But I thought—"

"No, wait." She put a finger on his lips and settled back into the curve of
his arm, quite drunk with happiness. "You shall tell your story from the beginning, and I shall tell you mine."

"But first," Albert said practically, "you must tell me where you live. We'll
collect your things and you can come to my lodgings."

"I have no things to collect," she said, as the wheels rolled onward. "My
only dress and shoes are at the theater, and I won't go back for them." She

did not mention the cheap room she shared with three other girls or the men's clothes in which, as funds allowed, she had begun to visit the city's parlorhouses; such things did not deserve attention when she was with Albert. He had given her his jacket to wear, and he did not seem to mind that she was coating it, and the upholstery, with chalk and greasepaint. It was all she needed in the world. "All the money I own is in that dress pocket and is much less than a dollar. I could not even pay to see the living wax-works—is that not funny?"

Albert kissed her again, for he could think of nothing to say that would measure up to that overwhelming revelation; and again there did not seem to be air enough in the carriage for all she needed to breathe. She opened the carriage window to gulp down the dark night air. It was scented with the loose green balls their horse had just dropped, but it smelled sweet and nourishing to Famke, for she was breathing it with Albert, and he was giv-ing the driver his address; she was going to Second Street with him.

"Tell your fortune, madam?" called a gypsy-woman, and Famke declined happily.

Once her lungs were working on their own again, she leaned her head against the reassuring hardness of Albert's shoulder and began her story. How much she had to tell him—how pleased he would be with her. "In Boulder, I met a woman named Ma Medlock. Her daughter had just died, and you had painted a picture of the Muses—"

But this was not what Albert wanted to talk about, or not yet. "Darling," he interrupted, with a faraway cast in his eye, "I must ask you. Up on the stage—I did not recognize you until the end, when you were Nimue. It was astonishing—even marvelous, quite different from the other girls. Tell me how you achieve the effect."

Famke wiggled until she could look him in the face again. His dear face. He was saying such lovely, admiring things to her. "What effect do you mean?" she asked, though she did have some idea.

He touched her where the jacket gapped above her breastbone, where she wore nothing but paint and powder. Then his hand, stained gray and brown with his own old paint, slid down to where the filmy shift bunched in her lap. "The *artistic* effect," he explained. "The one whereby you appear to be—well, darling, you know the word is code for appearing without clothes. You appear to be completely naked—I can see you don't wear a body stocking, like the other girls—and yet there is no natural covering over your privates. It is, as you once said, as if a cloud is passing over . . ."

"Oh, that." She giggled; this, too, was silly, and yet perfect, that he wanted to discuss her hair Down There after a year apart. "I barber it away. I learned from watching you and your beard. Then I put a little white clay into the—the—"

"Crevasse," he supplied. The word came out as a croak.

"—yes, and then it is quite smooth. It looks better than the body stocking, don't you agree? More like a real painting or a statue."

"Yes," he said, and lifted her chin so her lips would meet his, "it looks like a real painting."

After a little while, she said, "I did not know 'artistic' meant 'naked.'"

When the cab stopped at Albert's rooming house, both of them were suddenly awkward. Famke even felt shy—she who had not hesitated when Albert pulled his buggy into the farmyard and invited her to live with him; she who had married Heber and lived with Edouard and still kept searching for Albert. Somehow the fact of having sought and found, the awareness that this was the end of that adventure, made this homecoming different from the others. *The cottager returns after a long journey . . .* Her heart began to skip, the clay Down There to slide a bit. She made a great business of gathering his coat around herself and bunching the shift so she would not trip going down the carriage step and up the rooming house stairs. (Albert paid the driver handsomely, but she could not be expected to notice that.) She read the sign in a grimy ground-floor window: ROOMS AND BEDS TO LET: 25, 50, 75 CENTS. The house was something less than Fru Strand's had been, but somewhere inside was Albert's bedroom and studio, so to Famke it looked like a palace. She floated down the narrow, empty hallway, hardly registering the reek of cabbage that linked it to all the other drab places she had lived.

Albert unlocked his door and led her in and turned up the gas that even simple rooms enjoyed in this wonderful city. At last he could really look at her, knowing full well who she was. Famke, standing in the gaslight, shrugging out of his coat but with her arms still trapped in it: the Winged Victory of Samothrace. Then she freed herself of the coat and reached up to adjust the gas jet, and she was Nimue again.

"Darling," Albert murmured, and he dropped to his knees.

He had intended to take her hands in his and cover them with kisses—
a romantic gesture, one appropriate to the moment—but in his new position his face was level with what would have been her lap, if she were sitting
down, and that was so fascinating that for a moment all he could do was
look. Through the thin shift he saw that the soft white clay was pulling
away from her cleft, exposing a faint line of moist pink within the marble
whiteness. It was the most tender, arousing sight Albert had ever seen. He
pressed his lips to it through the gauzy fabric.

Famke, too, wanted to make a dramatic gesture. She seized the shift's
low neckline and ripped it, pulled it up and ripped some more, until it fell
open and then slid away from her shoulders. She was naked.

Albert dug out the clinging clay and kissed her again, just where he was,
on her bare skin. Famke could not help thinking of Edouard Versailles and
his pig-snouted galvanic device. She was astonished to find that, soon,
Albert was performing much the same procedure on her; only he used his
mouth rather than a mysterious current in the wall. His tongue in place of
Edouard's knobby node. It was strange, but not unpleasant; and then it was
wonderful.

"*Fanden*," she breathed, clutching Albert's hair in greedy fingers.

She did not notice that his hair had thinned in the past year, but her gesture reminded him of the unhappy fact, and he pulled away from her.
"Would you like a bath?" he asked.

If Famke was disappointed, she tried not to show it. She reasoned that
he was only thinking of her comfort, and it was true that she had not had a
real bath since she'd left Hygiene. "You are right," she said, looking down at
her white body, rosy where Albert's mouth had been; his face now wore
some of the whiteness. "I will dirty your bed if I get in it this way."

"Dirty . . . ," he repeated with some dubiety, wiping at his lips with a
handkerchief. But the opportunity to make love to an alabaster statue was
one Albert knew he would not soon find again; all the urgency of his
desire returned, and he pulled her, tinted as she was, on top of the narrow bed. They proceeded to ruin his landlady's Log Cabin quilt and his
own best trousers and shirt. Albert declared the experience divinely
worthwhile—and even if her pleasure did not exactly approach his, Famke
at least was gratified that he should be willing to sacrifice such a good suit
to their love.

. . .

Spent and satisfied, Albert dug in his coat pocket for a cheroot and a match, and he began to smoke and tell her his story. By now he wore almost as much white paint as she; they looked like two half-glazed porcelain statuettes. Even the base of the cheroot was soon ringed in white, and while he spoke, it grew a long white ash at the tip.

He said that he had been looking for Famke in every town he had visited and in every face he had painted. He might not have known as much at the time, but it was none the less true for all that.

Famke wriggled to scratch herself discreetly Down There, where Albert's motions against the bare skin had created some irritation. "But why didn't you *look* for me?" she asked practically. "In Denmark, for example."

"Because, darling"—he seemed surprised, and released a cloud of fragrant smoke over her face— "I thought you had died."

Famke gasped and struggled in his arms. "Died! Why—" She broke off, overcome by an eerie feeling that she *had* died, and that what had happened tonight was merely a dream. And when had she died? In Utah, when she felt the worms gnawing at the soft tissue of her lungs? Or in Hygiene, when she felt Nimue burn and freeze her, burn and freeze . . .

"Why did you think that?" she asked, curling back into him again.

Albert tapped his cheroot to rid it of ash. "Well, darling, it was the letter. The one your employer sent me." He quoted: "'The person of what you write is no longer in this life.' Her English wasn't much good, but I thought the meaning clear enough."

Famke broke in, "My employer?"

"I wrote to you at Mrs. Strand's, but the reply came from this other woman. Grub, I believe her name was—"

"Grubbe." So, Famke thought, Fru Strand's nephew had forwarded the letter as promised—but too late. Famke had already left Herr Skatkammer and Denmark, and Albert, who had at last received his reply in New York, believed she was dead. He gave up on her and moved on to other models, out in the West.

"But they weren't you, darling," he said into her ear as she lay still rigid with the shock of her own death. "They weren't you. They could not hold a candle." He did not say that it was only that very night, after seeing the extravagant representation of his greatest work, that he had realized fully the extent of his need for her; for as he told the story, he became more and more convinced that he had in fact spent the last months on a romantic quest to regain some elusive essence of her.

Now Albert confessed to her what she already knew, describing his months among the prostitutes. Famke did not comment, for she no longer cared much that Albert had painted the *Ludere*, or even if he had more than painted Mag; of course he would not do it anymore. This had been his way of grieving, and she must not mind anything that had happened while he thought she was dead. She pinched herself hard on the thigh and was reassured to feel the sharp pain that tied her to this world.

She was alarmed, however, at his next words: "I say brothels, but I should say butcher shops—for they butchered my paintings there."

He explained that in November he had experienced a crisis of artistic inspiration and had decided to revisit some of the pictures he had made in the summer. "Almost every one of them had been cut and pasted together differently, darling—almost every one! Can you imagine that someone would do such a thing to a work of art!"

"Did the ladies tell you who had done it?" Famke asked in a very small voice.

"I did not identify myself, and they did not know me," he said, much to Famke's relief. "The inhabitants in those places change so rapidly; I saw new girls everywhere, with their faces and features painted crudely over the ones I had done so carefully. Given that, I promise you I did not linger to chat with the madams who had allowed the—well, I believe I shall call it vandalism."

Famke took a few deep, slow breaths.

Mercifully unaware of her distress, Albert lit another cheroot and told her what had happened to the painting he now called *Nimue, a Nymph Enchanting*. The captain to whom he had traded the picture had been traveling with a mistress who had always wanted her portrait done—"just like a society lady"—and Albert had seen a chance to earn money for his start in America. He agreed to paint over the frame and alter the central figure: Slender Nimue had become a thick-waisted blonde.

The blood puddled in Famke's veins. "Did she have brown eyes? And a mole on her cheek?"

"Yes, she did." Albert twisted his head to look at her. By a trick of the gaslight his eyes were bright green and particularly amphibious. "How did you know?"

"Because that painting sold again." Famke pulled away from him and began to fray the sheet. She itched fiercely all over. "To a man here in California—his name is Edouard Versailles. I went to see him because I thought I could find a clue there . . . It is where I lived the past five months."

Now the fate of *Nimue* hardly registered to Albert; he was caught by another name. "You know Edouard Versailles?" he asked excitedly.

Chapter 58

. . . . .

The ladies of San Francisco are noted for the excessively scant style of their costumes.

SAMUEL PHILLIPS DAY,
LIFE AND SOCIETY IN AMERICA

The next morning, while Albert went out to buy her a new dress and shoes, Famke washed the last bit of paint off herself. She let her skin dry in the air while she emptied the meager contents of his clothes press into a carpetbag.

The two of them were going to Hygiene. Hygeia Springs. Albert wanted it badly, and why had she chased him across the globe if not to follow his wishes and further his dreams?

"He is as rich as Croesus—that's a very rich man—and has hundreds of blank walls to cover. If you could introduce me . . ." Remembering her old gesture, he had framed her face in his hands and kissed her on the nose; after that she could refuse him nothing, even though she was uncomfortably sure both that Edouard would sneer at Albert's paintings and that he would be cold to her. She could no more tell Albert these things than she could slap him. And in any event, Albert said he'd kept a few pieces from the winter's work, and that he had returned to his earlier more painstaking methods: Perhaps there would be something there to appeal to Edouard Versailles and ensure a welcome for both Famke and Albert.

With a faint glimmer of hope, she hunted around the bare little room until she found a stack of pictures under the bed. She pulled them out into the gaslight, and her heart sank. One oil depicted a heap of sardines; the other showed the same sardines neatly stacked in a basket held by a grim Chinaman. There were two sketches of boats on the Bay and one of a cor-

ner of Albert's room. What had become of Nimue, or even of the regimented Muses? These were the dullest pictures Famke had known him ever
to make, and not one of them featured even a hint of her. Looking at them,
she got the sensation that a heavy stone was settling somewhere in her belly.
But after a moment's contemplation, she packed the pictures up in a slender
portfolio. Albert must have samples to display, if he were to present himself
as a professional artist. And she must do her part; she would have to make
a good introduction, give Albert every slim chance of succeeding. Again,
why else had she chased him around half the world?

"This is Albert Castle," she practiced out loud. "My brother, the painter,
who grew up with a family in England." She had told that lie so many times
that it should feel natural to her by now, and yet she was certain that
Edouard would detect a stiffness and artificiality in her voice. *This is the
painter of dead fish.* Still, she had to keep the story alive; she could hardly expect Edouard to believe her innocent of involvement with the Dynamite
Gang—for Albert had promised to clear her of all suspicion—if she were
confessing to other lies. Running the town as he did, he might clap her in a
hoosegow for his suspicions, and then what would become of her, and of
Albert?

Once the portfolio was packed and set on the bed with the carpetbag,
everything was done. The day was foggy and Famke realized she was
chilled, so she draped a sheet around herself; her torn chemise was good for
nothing but the ashcan. She wondered what color the dress Albert would
buy might be and wished that it could be blue or green. Blue or green silk.

That wish made her think somewhat wistfully of Heber and his plans to
put the future of the Mormons in threads—but no, she would not think of
him now, or of Sariah or Myrtice or Sister Birgit, or anyone but herself and
Albert. *Their* future was about to begin, and the only piece of the past that
interested her now was hanging in a Greek pawnshop.

While the traffic roiled and smoked beneath her, Famke stood in the
window, watching for Albert and daydreaming about the new paintings for
which she might pose. Certainly there would be no more sardines; she
would make sure of it. Once again they would take up mythological subjects: mermaids, perhaps, if Albert wanted to continue painting scales and
fishtails . . . Or then again, when she was working for Charles Martin du
Garde, she had thought of a tableau that would mingle Mormon, Catholic,

and classical mythologies in a way that would certainly be novel and striking. In her mind's picture, a young woman awakened on a bed of clouds to
find three creatures before her: an old man, a young man, and a bird that
might be either dove or California seagull. The woman, like Paris, was to
choose among three deities—for a husband. Whichever she selected, she
would be God's wife, and a flock of ghostly women in warrior helmets
waited to dress her for the wedding in a glimmering frock woven of diamonds and pearls. Of course, the waking woman was completely nude, except where the clouds twined lovingly between her legs. Famke thought she
might call this *The First Bride*. Professor du Garde had refused to mount the
tableau, fearing that the police would shut down the Thalia if he presented
a scene that was not already to be found somewhere out in the world; but
perhaps if she described it in the right detail, Albert would paint it. It had
so many of the elements he liked.

Albert. Famke realized she had slid her fingers Down There, where fric-
tion had left a red rash; and she withdrew them with a feeling of impatience. It was nearly ten o'clock—what was taking him so long? Was he
dawdling, when their whole future and a thousand paintings were waiting
to be born? Still thinking of *The First Bride*, she lay down on the cot and essayed a few poses, trying to imagine which would please Albert best, and
which would show most compellingly under his brush. Her breasts must
show to advantage, and her nose, and the hair on her head. But there could
be no emphasis on that other thatch. Which, *Fanden*, was becoming most
uncomfortable as the shaved hairs pushed inexorably against the chafed
skin, trying to grow. It was all but impossible to lie still.

Suddenly she felt she could not wait a moment longer: She would begin
the picture herself. She got up, opened Albert's bag again, and found a
sketchpad and a pencil. With careful, faint lines, she began to sketch out her
idea. She drew the woman, the clouds, and the bird, leaving the men and
the crowd of Valkyries till later. Albert could certainly fill those in; it was
most important to her to get the central figure right. Famke sketched her
with long limbs and a bow-shaped mouth, open as if to speak.

Famke stopped and studied this woman with a critical eye. She looked
perhaps too much like a modern girl, a splendid American-Bohemian who
would just as soon gulp down a whiskey or swear—loudly. Famke thought
this over, then began sketching an antique fullness in the waist and body.

Meanwhile, she began to consider new titles: *The Bride Awakens to Judgment.* *The Judgment of Eve. Choosing a Master.* Somehow none of these seemed right.

When the doorknob rattled, Famke ripped out her sketch—*The Bride's Prelude?*—and folded it into her fist. She had learned from *Hygeia:* She would not show her work until it was perfect, and there was still much to do.

"Darling!" Albert did not notice her movement, but he appeared most excited to see her. "I brought you a frock—though I'd much rather keep you as you are, in that fetching drapery." As Famke took the parcel from him and went to work on the string, he added, "You should have seen how the clerk stared when I chose women's clothing."

The dress was of coarse cotton and a little too large, but Albert had remembered gloves and stockings and a hat. Famke put them all on and decided she looked good enough, given how she had left Hygiene. At least, she thought, the clothes were blue, even if it was a washed-out color that did not suit her complexion at all. She was in fact surprised he had chosen something so pallid; perhaps he thought it respectable.

"Very fine," Albert said when she showed him.

"I hope you did not spend too much on all of it." She tugged at the waist in an attempt to make it stay up.

"Not too much. And I was happy to do it."

"Then—" She hesitated, unsure how to tell him what she felt he would want to know. "I hope you might give me six dollars more." She explained about the Greek store and what she had to redeem there.

Albert shuddered. "Really, darling, a pawnshop—how sordid." Then the rest of her speech sank in and he asked, "But you say this is the original *Nimue?* Are you certain?"

"Quite certain," Famke said, taking pleasure in his excitement. He need never know that she was the artist who had applied the last layer of paint; and if he did not like her version of herself, he could always strip it away, along with the layer that was the captain's mistress. She would not mind. She would be glad to see the real Nimue, the real Famke, again.

They took a carriage to Acropolis Pawn—but found *Hygeia* no longer on view. The Greek told them it had sold that very morning.

"There's a living waxwork just like it at the theater down the street, miss," he said, sharpening his moustache; he was much more deferential to Famke now that Albert stood beside her. "I could not keep that painting to myself. Without a frame, even, I sold it for thirty-seven dollars, and the gentleman which bought it had a bargain. But I see you are really fond of this painting," he said craftily. "If you like, I can get you one just the same. Painted all new. One just like that waxwork."

"No," said Famke. She was too disappointed to argue or ask more questions. "It would *not* be the same."

"Don't fret, darling." Albert twined her fingers in his. "I can make a new Nimue, one who looks as she should—like you. Just one commission from Versailles, or two, will set me up with supplies for a year. Let's go to Hygiene now and defend your innocence."

Famke followed him out to the carriage, climbed up onto the high seat, and leaned against the slender portfolio case. If only she were not so tired; if only Albert had allowed her to sleep a little last night, rather than repeatedly demonstrating his joy in finding her again. She stifled a yawn that came out as a mewling sound.

Albert put his hand in his pocket, reaching for a cheroot and a lucifer, then he broke out in a bright smile that showed all his nearly-white teeth. "Here's something to cheer your spirits," he said as the wheels spun their way toward the harbor. He pulled out a silver object, so shiny that at first all Famke saw was a flash of light on Albert's palm. "I'd nearly forgotten—it's the twin to our old tinderbox," he said. "See, the Three Graces—just as we found them in the ruins. I bought this one in Boulder, Colorado. We may not have Nimue back, but we have it."

The light spanked off a backward Grace's bottom. Famke said, with a sense of wonder wakened again, "It is the *same* box."

Albert did not seem to find much of the extraordinary in this coincidence, did not even question how such a thing could be. "You see," he said, "in the end everything is exactly where it belongs."

There was much more that Famke could have told him, but she decided it was hardly worth the effort now. "Yes, I suppose so," she said merely, and looked out the window for a last glimpse of the city.

Chapter 59

· · · · ·

If a man cannot stay at home, traveling in a Pullman palace car is the most
like staying there of anything in the world.

BENJ. F. TAYLOR, BETWEEN THE GATES

A California train is a human museum.

BENJ. F. TAYLOR, BETWEEN THE GATES

Edouard was unaware that he was soon to have visitors; and if he had
known, he would have declared himself uninterested. He wanted
only to walk through his own front door, to let the invisible servants
take his hat and coat and luggage, give him a warm drink, and leave him in
peace. He was worn out with cities and with art. He longed for his quiet office with its specimen jars and anatomical drawings, and for the deep peace
of the Taj Mahal. But instead here he was, trapped in one corner of a
Southern Pacific palace car with the Mormon widow Myrtice Goodhouse
Black and the man she had introduced as Mr. Viggo, Ursula's brother.

Edouard had naturally been suspicious when these two presented themselves to him. For weeks he had been convinced that his patient had made
up her brother from whole cloth; and yet it was impossible now to believe
that this open-faced, gentle-mannered Dane was anything else—for he
was too polite to be a member of the Dynamite Gang, too uncomplicated
to paint better than second-rate art. Pangs of remorse beset Edouard
again as he remembered his suspicions. Thus when Mr. Viggo and Mrs.
Black explained their errand, Edouard had felt honor bound to buy them
tickets to Hygeia Springs so they could collect Ophelia's—no, Ursula
Summerfield's—few belongings; though really, he thought now, it had been
Ursula who took advantage of him, living in his house all those months and
profiting from his waters and electricity. Edouard felt very much as if someone owed him a favor. Yet it was he who had responded to the Wanted
poster, he who had started the machinery of quest and fulfillment in

motion, and now he must see it through. He would let Ursula's brother and former employer come to Hygeia to collect the contents of her pocket and see what they, who felt they knew her much better than he did, might make of the assorted dingy scraps.

But what maddening people. They had dithered so long about the travel arrangements and assembling box suppers that it was late afternoon before the four of them managed to climb onto a train. The woman would not stop hinting at her physical discomfort and fatigue, yet she refused any easement; the car's other occupants, all well dressed, most of them reading newspapers, books, and magazines, occasionally glanced at her with annoyance. And Albert Viggo—Edouard remembered that Ursula had called her brother Albert, though that first name seemed at odds with his last—smelled so strongly of the chemicals used for corpses that Edouard had to keep the window closest to them open, despite the ash and cinders that flew in.

The wheels roared and the train rocked side to side. Several people dozed, including an infant in a nurse's arms and a man in a green suit who had climbed on at the last minute. There was a woman who looked something like Ursula up ahead, but when she turned her face toward the light it became plain that she was several years older and did not have anything like Ursula's refined facial architecture. Edouard decided to nap.

The train pulled into Fresno City and out again—halfway home. Some miles later, as they were gathering speed, Myrtice cried out in pain. A cinder had flown into her eye.

The Dane, who had been sitting next to Edouard and politely respecting his wish for silence, took down his black bag and opened it. Edouard saw there were no canvases, sketchbooks, or brushes inside, only bottles of those noxious fluids and a few worn scraps of clothing.

"You have given up painting, Mr. Viggo?" Indeed, the man's hands, rummaging among his effects, did not look at all as Edouard imagined an artist's hands would. Surely the stiffened scars would impede the more delicate movements of the brush. Edouard might suspect Viggo to be as much a fraud as his sister—if he hadn't had the evidence of that disastrous painting to prove the man existed.

The man in question fished out a ragged handkerchief and gave it to Myrtice. "I will paint again," he said, "if there is another death."

Edouard found that declaration highly peculiar. But artists were known for unusual behavior and odd aesthetics—second-rate artists perhaps more so than others. Edouard thought incidentally that Albert Viggo looked as if he would make a good sailor or farmer.

Albert Viggo. A. V. But Ursula had given him a different last name—

"I am curious about something . . . ," Edouard began.

The other man's attention was on Myrtice, who was dabbing at her eye; she would not allow him to search for the cinder. "No, no," she said, pulling the lid out by the lashes and sliding the cloth underneath in a savage operation particularly exasperating to Edouard, "I can manage."

Without showing a trace of annoyance, Viggo turned to Edouard. "You have a question? Is it about Ursula?"

Edouard spoke stiffly: "No, Mr. Viggo." He had in fact made a point of saying as little about Ursula as possible. "I wish to ask about your work. It occurs to me to wonder why you sign your canvases with a—"

He was not able to finish his question. There was a sudden roar, followed by an earsplitting shriek as the brakeman gave a mighty pull. Everything was flung forward. Myrtice landed in Viggo's lap. The black bag hit the back of Edouard's seat, and several bottles broke, soaking his coat and filling the car with overwhelming odors. Screams started up around them; the baby howled.

"What has happened?" cried Myrtice. She clung to Viggo's neck.

Still the machine ground forward, wailing like a dying animal. Now its lament was punctuated with a loud twanging sound. Edouard struggled to tear the coat off his back—the chemicals were burning his skin—while Viggo said calmly, "I believe the rails is going apart."

It was true. The metal rails split and the train rushed forward, burying its nose in the dirt. The rear cars rushed to catch up. They knocked against the engine and then, with surprising grace, tipped slowly onto one side.

When it was over, Edouard lay in a jumble of limbs with Albert Viggo and Myrtice Goodhouse Black. His face was pressed against the window frame, and Viggo had fallen halfway out. Myrtice was crying. "What happened?" she asked again, and then repeated the question hysterically: "What happened what happened what happened what—"

Far away, someone said: "The Dynamite Gang."

In the confusion it occurred to Edouard to wonder, irrelevantly, whether the death Mr. Viggo was waiting for might be his sister's.

Chapter 60

· · · · ·

Nobody will ever, by pencil or brush or pen, fairly render the beauty of the mysterious, undefined, undefinable chaparral.

HELEN HUNT JACKSON, "CALIFORNIA," IN
GLIMPSES OF THREE COASTS

The new Hygeia Springs Institute for Phthisis was now open. Tides of the sick were washing up the mountain, and each train that pulled into nearby Harmsway delivered a new wave bound for the healing waters and fresh air. Famke and Albert stepped off to find that stagecoaches going up the mountain were so in demand that it would be necessary to spend a night in a cramped hotel room.

Albert first chafed at the delay and then decided it gave him an opportunity. He took her in his arms. *Darling, Famke, I—*

As if she heard his unspoken words, she turned her face to his for a kiss; but it was just a kiss like countless others they had exchanged, and she began to move against him until the only words he could say aloud were "Hold still." Then it was he who moved against her, and he kept the unspoken sentence on his lips. But even at the most intimate moment, he could not bring himself to say it. Words might break the new spell he'd fallen under. He thought then of the Winged Victory; and instantly he shuddered and spent, painting Famke's womb in a way that was itself most satisfying to him.

When Albert slid off her, Famke decided it would be safe to move. She rolled as far from Albert as she could and, feeling thwarted herself, did her best . . . *The cottager comes home to find his roof is missing, and he must climb up on top* . . . but somehow it was not enough. The shimmering sense of longing still persisted, though it was not so pleasant now. She wanted that other feeling, the one that Heber and Edouard knew how to give even without the little stories she told herself. She lay stiff all night, listening to Albert's snores and dodging the limbs that flailed during his dreams. She thought about *The Bride's Prelude* until she was thoroughly sick of it and concluded there was no point mentioning the idea to Albert or anyone. *Just a silly woman,* she thought. *She would probably choose the bird.*

The next morning, the Paradise Hotel lounge was full of hollow-eyed consumptives waiting for stagecoaches, coughing into pocket *crachoirs* and maddening the hotel staff with requests for cold compresses and draughts of now-famous Hygiene water. Famke and Albert claimed a settee at the far side of the room, as far from the patients as possible. Famke tried to nap, while Albert took out an old journal called *The Germ*, which declared itself to contain writings of the Pre-Raphaelite Brotherhood.

"Darling, wake up. I have been thinking of my next painting," Albert said, thumbing through the pages. "I'd like to do something with wings—an angel, I think. Listen to this poem:

> The blessed damozel leaned out
> From the gold bar of Heaven;
> Her eyes were deeper than the depth
> Of waters stilled at even.

'Deeper than the depth'—isn't that pretty? And doesn't it just describe your eyes?"

Famke accepted the compliment, nice as it was, with less grace than she might have done if she'd slept. She imagined those words painted around a picture frame, which would of course be gilded—just like the gold bar of Heaven. She had a flash of inspiration. "Maybe I could be leaning out of the picture. You know, over the golden bar."

Albert thought this over, mouth pursed in a gesture that reminded her of Myrtice. "I don't see how it could be done," he said finally. "A frame is the painting's limit. But listen to the conclusion:

> And the souls mounting up to God
> Went by her like thin flames.

That has some possibilities, doesn't it?"

"Maybe you should write poems," Famke said. She decided she was tired of discussing art and picked up a copy of *Frank Leslie's* to look at the fashion sketches.

They arrived in Hygiene that evening, to find the hospital's triple towers lit like beacons and the main street awash with patients. Many of these were too weak to walk and had to be lifted into buggies; nurses had come with wheeling chairs to collect others. Famke saw Miss Pym, or someone who looked very like her, hauling away a man with a beard a bit like Heber's but the skeletal body of one of Edouard's anatomical drawings. Some of the worst cases were spitting on the streets, despite an abundance of signs that warned them not to: Everywhere she looked, Famke saw disgusting puddles of red and green and yellow. The sight made her start to cough, if only to avoid being ill there and then herself; and the smell of so many sick people sank deeper into her body.

"We must go directly to Mr. Versailles's house," she said. "Leave your bag at a hotel and bring the portfolio." She thought of her tranquil white bedroom at Edouard's house, the faded Flower Garden quilt under which she had spent so many restful starry nights. But of course Edouard would not let her sleep there again.

Steering Famke through the chaos toward a likely-looking hostelry, Albert could not have been more pleased. It was as if all their desires were coinciding, and in coincidence were finding perfection. She would win him an opportunity with this Edouard Versailles; these thousands of wealthy patients and their families would see his work; many would commission final portraits by which to remember the dead: The future would be secure. He had never, in the two days that he had loved her, felt closer to Famke.

She cut into his thoughts: "When we get close to the house, we must mind the zebras." To Albert these were words from a dream. "They can be quite fierce."

*   *   *

In the tumult, neither Famke nor Albert noticed a few shaggy mountain men, independent miners and hunters, who had come down from their cabins and now stood looking as confused as if they had wandered into a foreign land on a high holy day. They had heard there were now public women in town, but they had not expected any of this. Neither did Famke see the Asian woman clad in yellow silk and spangles stepping up to greet them, or hear the woman say, "Ten dollar for a look, twenty for a touch . . ." It was doubtful she would have recognized the hundred-men's-wife anyway; but to some, this was already the new meaning of Hygiene.

* * *

The Southern Pacific derailment caused a day's delay while the tracks were repaired and the wrecked train hauled away. There were several injuries and one death, and the conductors announced that only the wounded would be removed to Ringsburg, the next town, and lodged there. It took a considerable bribe from Edouard to procure transportation and hotel rooms for himself and Wong and the other two, both of whom looked disapproving about the bribe but accepted the benefits. They all slept tolerably well, and Edouard decided to ask no further questions about Viggo's artwork.

The next morning, when Myrtice and Viggo met Edouard in the hotel's private lounge, they found the mid-California papers were full of the event. "Dynamite Gang's Revenge!" trumpeted the first headline Myrtice saw. She read the article with excitement that increased when she spotted a familiar name.

> In a letter mailed to this office, persons claiming to be members of the Dynamite Gang took responsibility for the act. In their missive, the Gang protests a recent Dime Novel and financial success authored by the celebrated correspondent known as Hermes. Rubble on the Rails, they aver, is a misrepresentation of their constituents and goals: In politics and philosophy they are anarchists, enraged by the exploitation and careless mutilation of workers in the West's many mines. No women are involved with the group, who announce that they traced the novelist, in the manner of Pinkerton detectives, to that very train. "Let him experience an incident firsthand," the letter concludes. . . .

"That man was right," she said aloud. "We have been victims of the Dynamite Gang." She was aware that her voice sounded its most schoolmarmish, but to herself she admitted there was something exhilarating in the whole situation. She had met a man with a pen powerful enough to make him a target for political desperadoes; she had been attacked by a band of criminals more famous than the James Gang; and she had survived. Two men had taken care of her, and she had slept in her own room in the most luxurious hotel she had ever seen. She could be—she *was*—the heroine of a thrilling narrative.

Viggo murmured politely, nursing a badly scraped cheek, but Edouard hardly heard her. He was reading another item.

The Methodist Women's Mission at long last succeeded in their crusade to close down San Francisco's Thalia Festival House, after a visit from police determined that the spectacle recently mounted there was indeed corrupt of morals and obscene of intent. This, noted one lady-errant, was accomplished despite the disappearance of the programme's chief star, the handsome redhead known as Ursie Summer, who did not perform on the night the police came calling. The other girls have registered a protest, clamoring that if they are arrested, the exotic Miss Summer must be as well; but few who witnessed her portrayals of masterworks such as the Winged Victory of Samothrace can truly regret that Ursie is to escape unscathed. We may hope that this bird has flown south to weather the storm. . . .

My God, thought Edouard, wondering he could not have recognized her. *She is on her way to Hygeia.* He rang for a clerk and demanded to know when the track repairs would be finished.

"It is a matter of hours, they say, sir." The clerk rushed away as soon as he could; that man in black had the light of madness in his eye.

Edouard tore out the page and folded it into his pocket, feeling it was somehow evidence that must be preserved. His nerves chafed until he remembered the bottle of laudanum, mercifully intact, in his trunk; then he summoned Wong and got a blessed measure of relief. In his suspended state, the clock hands did not move so slowly, or rather he did not heed them; and soon enough came the siren-call of a new train whistle.

•   •   •

The zebras were merely hoofbeats and an effect of broken moonbeams among the trees, running away as Famke and Albert took the trip over the high stone fence and into Edouard's sanctuary. The tiny exotic deer family rustled in the undergrowth, and the same cool light gleamed on their tusks as they, too, fled.

The animals led the way up the riding-road. Famke and Albert trudged after them in silence; they needed all their strength to pull nourishment from the thin mountain air, and Famke, at least, needed some time in which to think. Of new paintings, perhaps, and even more of what she might expect to find at the great glass house on the hill. Of how she might explain her relationship with Albert to Edouard; a relationship for which she was hard pressed to find words. Her brother, lover, mentor— the man stumbling along beside her, plucking at her skirt so she might guide him.

"We should be able to see the house by now," Famke said after a few hundred yards, but in the cloaking darkness it did not seem to exist. Perhaps Edouard's wish had been granted and the world immediately around him had become invisible.

In a few moments the Taj Mahal came into view; or rather, two Tajs, for it seemed the original had twinned itself in the moonlight. At first Famke was confused—the twin seemed to have replaced Edouard's glass house— but then she realized it was merely that the big house was dark, and its darkness had made it a looking-glass. Moonlight and alabaster showed in the shiny surface, and it was all but impossible to tell the difference between the actual mausoleum and its reflection.

But why is the house dark? Famke wondered. *It has never been so before.*

"Is that Versailles's house?" asked Albert. He spoke like a sleepwalker, for the deeper they got into the woods, the stranger this place seemed to him. He even felt like a stranger to himself: The scene in the street had nearly convinced him that illness was the norm and good health a mysterious aberration; stepping into Edouard Versailles's private domain was like drifting into a collective fever dream.

"No, it is for Mr. Versailles's parents. They died of the lungs." Famke found she was having trouble with her own breath. The hot tinny taste of blood sat on her tongue, but she thought that must be an illusion—as much an illusion as the reflected tomb. She had been cured. She wondered where the servants were, and if anyone would bring her a draught of the hissing water.

"And that sound?"

Famke stopped to listen; there was a half-roar, half-wail coming from the forest where Versailles kept his collection of big cats. "I think it must be a panther."

Not knowing that the panther lived in a house, too, Albert drew even closer to her, as if he were nervous. "Hansel and Gretel," he said, trying to laugh at himself. Then the moon drifted behind a cloud, and there was only one dim white fantasy on the hillside after all.

"Come," said Famke, pulling briskly away from him, "I know the way inside."

She walked toward the vanished reflection with her arms outstretched and soon found a glass wall slick with dew, then the cold iron-lace door with its countless panes. The moon came out again just long enough for her to see her own ghostly figure reflected in myriad before she turned the knob and entered.

"I don't suppose the man is at home," Albert said, more and more unnerved.

"I am certain he is not." Famke groped toward the gas controls.

To Albert it was as if a sudden sun rose within a primeval landscape—the green palms and tree ferns towering toward the ceiling, the ropes of white-flowered vines that poured forth scent as soon as light touched their petals. Famke merely saw that now the looking glass was reversed; the walls reflected what was inside the house, and that was as it should be.

"Perhaps we should go," Albert suggested.

But now that she was here, Famke was no more willing to leave than she was to don a Mormon union suit and go to Catholic mass. A new determination seized her. "I do not know where Mr. Versailles is, or his servants. But somewhere in this house, there is a purple silk dress that belongs to me. There are some papers, too, that I would like to have, and the lucifer matches from the royal tinderbox." That box was in her hand now, hot and hard, and she planned to fill it again with matches—if only to prevent it from being used like those other little metal boxes in patients' pockets.

"Darling," Albert said with palpable unease—for he had just seen a specimen jar containing a rubbery seven-month fetus, floating over the warped hall table—"I am sure Mr. Versailles will return your property—if we don't anger him by poking around where we should not be. Let us come back in the morning. We have a nice room in the hotel . . ."

But Famke had already disappeared down the hallway toward Edouard's office. *There is something in this world that is mine,* she thought as she opened the sanctuary door; for although she'd so recently been glad to come away with Albert penniless and clad only in clay, she had since discovered that, in fact, there were reasons to claim what was once hers. One of the pigeon-holes in Edouard's enormous desk had to hold the old yellow pocket, and she felt an urge to review its contents, to retrace, for herself, the path that had brought her here.

The first object her eyes fell on was the galvanic device, sitting by the bottled hand on Edouard's desk in its tailored leather case, solid and full of promise. She ignored it as she searched the overstuffed nooks and desk drawers, shoving aside charts, letters, and drawings that—even though medical in nature—neglected to depict the thatch Down There. No doubt a male artist, or perhaps a proper lady-artist like Miss Dart. Impatient, she balled one of the charts up and tossed it into the air.

"Darling!" Albert followed her inside, alarmed at seeing her worked into such a state. "We have no right to rifle through the man's belongings, even if you do think he has something of yours. We should go. I don't like the way this house lights up—if a guard comes along, he might take us for trespassers and shoot."

"There are no guards or guns. And everyone on this land knows me." But Famke stopped her search: She had found the tattered pocket, and now she reached in and opened it.

How pitiful they looked, these documents that had led her halfway across the world and over a continent. The Dragør sketch was just a dirty scrap of paper now, the words on the back faded until only memory could read them: *lovely* . . . The newspaper and magazine clippings were nearly as bad, and several of them had fallen into mere fragments. The matchheads were completely clean of phosphorus and would not light anything. The one item that retained any of its original clarity was one she had not put there: a large and much-mended paper, of a brighter yellow than the buttery cloth pocket, on which the enormous word WANTED stood out like an alarm.

"What is that?" Albert asked behind her, and Famke crumpled the poster convulsively. "Darling, is it supposed to be you? *What is that paper?*"

Famke looked around, coughing distractedly. She stuffed all the pages into her bodice and glared at Albert. *Had we but world enough* . . . of course there was world enough for her and Albert—there was more than enough world, really—and as to time, it had served only to rub away the last recognizable bits of the most important artwork he had ever done and to leave her with the feeling that, in fact, she had roamed all over the world just to end up . . . a mere blot on a limp page.

Albert was looking at her with a decidedly odd expression, one that at this moment she simply could not understand.

In fact, her gesture had reminded him of what he had seen the fair but frail do time and again while bidding good-bye their customers. It was vulgar . . . but not unpleasing. He slid his arms around Famke's waist and pulled her to him, savoring the rustle of paper in a woman's bosom. Famke was no winged angel, he thought as he bent to kiss her. She was a girl of the earth, and her body radiated heat. Her lips burned under his. *Darling, marry me*, he thought of saying; and the thought fanned his ardor.

At first Famke struggled a little, thinking he had grabbed her in order to retrieve the handbill. Soon, however, she realized that he was merely what the nuns would call prurient and the prostitutes would call gay, and she was in for another celebration of their reunion. At that thought, she really did break away.

As she backed into the desk, Albert gazed at her with wounded eyes as big as the towers of Hygeia Springs Institute. Then Famke felt guilty. Memories of the past years unfurled through her mind—her months as model, wife, patchwork painter, patient. Why had she done all that if it were not for love of Albert? Loving him had always meant acceding to his wishes . . . An image popped into her head: once again, her idea for *Eve's Judgment*, or *The Bride's Prelude*. Eve was making her choice.

As she thought about the picture—which she decided she would paint after all, but not for Albert; she would keep it to herself for a good long while—her heart began to pound against the thin tissue of her lungs, sending the blood reeling through her body. She was aware of days' worth of congestion Down There, where the rash still prickled. And as she looked up into Albert's round eyes, she thought that perhaps it was time to show him something that even the *Ludere*, apparently, had not. Yes, she would show him something; he would see. More than a gray graphite smudge. It was high time to let some fluids down.

Breathless, she picked up Edouard's heavy electrical machine, and the rush of blood increased. She coughed and spat, surreptitiously, into a palm tree.

"There is a better place than this room," she said, and smiled a bedazzling smile of clean white teeth and red cheeks. "And there is also something special. Come with me."

Chapter 61

. . . . .

Surely if these scenes are beyond the powers of the artist, no discredit can follow when the writer's pen fails to attain to the full measure of their grandeur and beauty.

Stanley Wood,
Over the Range to the Golden Gate

Famke knew of nowhere but her old sickroom for tapping into the electrical current, and she was just as glad. As she and Albert climbed the shivering stair, the twining vines filtered the lamplight in Edouard's office to a dim oceanic glow. It all but vanished in that pristine room where bed and basins and bleached wood shone softly under the open sky, the full round moon and glittering stars. By their light Famke unpacked the machine and arranged it on the faded counterpane, the galvanic nodes and wires winding through Grandmother's Flower Garden.

"What is that?" Albert asked; but he hardly cared. The machine was ugly and modern, entirely wrong in this ethereal setting that the artist in Albert considered one of the most exciting places on earth.

Famke was exciting, too. She undressed him and turned so he could unbutton her bodice. When she shrugged it to the floor, all the papers inside—clippings, picture, poster—fluttered to join it; but neither she nor he had an eye for papers now. Famke stepped out of her skirt and petticoat, shoes and knickers, stockings and camisole. She radiated heat, but Albert thought he was the one with a fever. Without being asked, she raised her arms in Nimue's *presto* pose, and Albert fell upon her, kissing and tugging and arranging her to perfection.

Famke allowed all of this while inclining gradually toward the bed. Albert was drawn along in her wake. A little distance from the wires and nodes, she lay down and he lay on top of her, and that was when he entered her first. But he found this was not quite what he wanted. His face cast shadows over hers, and he had to see her clearly.

"Let me look," he whispered. He rolled onto his back and pushed Famke upward, so the moon was a silver circle behind her head and the stars spread out behind her like wings. *Diana*, he thought. *Mary. Magdalene.* She was even more dazzling now than onstage: *Victory*. His thin lips parted to repeat the names out loud, along with perhaps the other words that had fluttered through his mind these past days.

This was precisely what Famke had waited for. He looked like a happy frog, just as on the first day she had seen him. She gazed down and said, "Do not move." A luminous bead of sweat dropped from her brow to Albert's.

She clambered off as gracefully as she could and reached for the galvanic invention. "Just one moment," she whispered. She left the heavy node where it was and took the fanged end of its cord to the wall, remembering that the inlet was somewhere near the water closet. In a very short time she found what she wanted; the metal teeth slid into the steel rib of the house, and Famke took satisfaction in seeing a blue spark born just before the plug gobbled it up. She turned the switch on the machine, and the node coughed, then began to hum.

Albert lay waiting on the faded Flower Garden, arrowing as if to pierce the moon. He was remembering an afternoon long ago during the Danish idyll, when Famke sat atop him and braced her arms against the ceiling, and he had begun the only real work he had ever finished. He did not look at Famke now until she climbed atop him once more, and she leaned forward until her hair fell about his face, blinding him in the darkness of a fragrant grotto. *Lizzie Siddal Rossetti*, he was thinking when she kissed him. *Euphemia Ruskin Millais . . . Famke . . .*

Famke pressed the node to herself, and herself to him.

It was an uneasy sensation, that of the woman upon him, around him, not only moving herself but also vellicating from some mysterious source deep within. At first it shocked Albert back into the moment, the room, the sense that he was an intruder in a strange man's house—and then it produced a swell of feeling so overwhelming that he forgot everything else. He stiffened again and surrendered to the enigmatic pleasures of science.

Holding him tight with hidden muscles, Famke looked down into Albert's eyes and felt puzzled. *He is hardly doing anything. Why does he simply lie there—like one of his own dead fish?* She bounced against him and the device; jerked, wriggled, and realized, *I know how to fix his paintings!*

Famke stopped moving, and the electric hum was loud in the room. When Albert twitched, she put a hand on his chest to quiet him. She thought of those painted sardines and of cottagers coming home, of train trips all over the West. *They need* . . . What was the word? The one used for music and machinery . . . *rhythm.*

Almost unconsciously, she began to move again, but more slowly now. She thought that even a dead fish might coil around its neighbor, and the bodies could intertwine—not like Albert's regimented Muses but like the tinderbox's Graces—for the visual needed to have the same transformative thrust and vibration as the wheels of a train or the snout of a galvanic invention, and that rhythm should change as the feelings changed. In her mind she rearranged all his paintings again—she saw that she *had* butchered them before, but now she might make them better—or create new paintings, even outside the bounds of Muse or Valkyrie . . .

She looked up and caught her own reflection in the glass wall. She tossed her head and she was Calafia, Gunnlod, Nimue; she was other women whose names Albert had never spoken. She rocked back and forth against the galvanic node, and she was the painter of *Hygeia*, with a vision to make greater pictures. In mounting excitement, she looked into her own blue eyes and then through them, beyond the glass. And thus, after three days and nights in which Albert had toyed with her wildness, only to leave it unsatisfied, Famke's crisis began. Electric rhythm cast its spell, and her juices came down.

As this happened, Famke shuddered and gasped, her face twisting into a mask. Albert had never seen such a thing before. It was alarming—disgusting. "Darling"—he shuddered, too—"really!" But she did not seem to hear.

"Famke!" He reached up and grabbed her by the ribs, to shake that strange pulsing out of her. But that only made her begin to cough.

It was all too much for Albert. He squirmed out from under her, letting her fall where she might. "The Devil!" he cried, staring as Famke continued to shudder and hack, spraying one wall with a fine red mist. The old impulse to dash overtook him.

Albert ran for the door, hardly pausing to grab at his clothes on the way.

When he was gone, Famke collected herself slowly. She had landed on the floor and felt a bruise beginning to form on her hip; but that was only a little pain, and did not bother her any more than the pain that had reignited in her lungs. Albert was gone, no doubt to hurtle down the road and release that awful tension that kept him from doing his best work. And yet, she thought as she straightened up and shuffled through scattered papers toward the still-humming galvanic device, she was not sorry. She did not miss him. He might run all the way back to the hotel and fetch his carpet-bag and take the next stage downmountain. He was welcome to go.

She looked fondly down at the snouted machine, now radiating waves of heat as it chugged its magic into the empty air. This, perhaps, could be called hers, and she would take it with her wherever she chose to go next.

Famke turned, admiring her reflection in the glass panes, and grabbed the galvanic device by the tail. She wanted to make a grand gesture, and Edouard had never warned her against this particular one. Still watching herself, she yanked hard on the snaky cord, to pull the stout plug from the wall.

It was anchored fast. She dug in her heels and pulled again, much harder, and was pleased to see blue and orange sparks pouring from the wall as the machine gave way to her will.

◆　◆　◆

It was an astonishing sight, viewed from the forest below. First the shower of light within the room, crackling stars born when the cord separated from the stubborn plug. Then flames, as the carpet of thin paper and cloth gave itself greedily over to consumption. A luminous white body hopping up and down to stamp the fire, throwing a quilt to smother it.

From outside it was clear that Grandmother's Flower Garden swept the fire downward through the floor, where it wrapped itself around a steam pipe and began to lick at dry palm fronds and a faded armoire. Water played its part, too, as the sparks continued to pour from the steel rib and Famke ran to fill a bedpan from the sink. Thinking to douse the conflagration at its source, she flung the water toward the hemorrhaging outlet. But this angered the sparks; they crackled and jumped toward the ceiling, the mattress, the canvas shades. Then everything was on fire.

A false dawn came up over the landscape. Smoke was already on the wind; in the cat house, a tiger and a panther screamed that they could smell it. The family of tusked deer streaked by, heading for higher ground. The zebras snorted and reared in place; one dashed himself against the stone wall, and the other ran into the stable, where she kicked down a stall door and huddled against one of Edouard's black horses, which were out of their minds with terror. The baby zebra was too young to know she should run; she stood among the pine trees and trembled.

Viggo, Myrtice, and Edouard walked right past her as they came through the forest, so close they might have run their fingers through her mane. They scarcely noticed her, however. At first they were delighted at the sight of the immense glass domes lit up like an Oriental lantern, illuminating the hillside—it was a marvel to Viggo and Myrtice, a glimpse of home to Edouard—and then alarmed when the light became too bright and they knew this was not the gentle lumens of the gas jets but the start of a fierce inferno. They saw a naked figure, a woman, beating her fists helplessly against the heavy glass, then bent over and coughing.

Edouard began to run toward it, his lovely house, and then he stopped, as a fearful conviction occurred to him. He recognized Famke, his greatest achievement, prey to the lungs once more.

Throw a stone, he thought. *Break the glass; set her free.* It was what she herself should have done; but she was obviously too overcome to think of it. *Where are all the servants?* Wong was back in the village with their bags, but the singsong sisters should have been protecting his home; perhaps they had gone to join Ancient Jade. Edouard searched the ground for rocks that might be big enough to do some good, and he came as close to the house as he dared. Every stone he threw fell short.

Viggo put his arms around Myrtice's waist and neck and held her in place. The protective gesture was wholly instinctual; he had eyes and mind only for Famke, whom he was seeing in the flesh for the first time in six years. She was lovely, with the smoke swirling around her and her red hair outshining the flames. And she was terrible; for it was clear what her fate, and the fate of any who tried to save her, would be. Nonetheless Viggo thrust Myrtice aside and ran past Edouard, nearly up to the house itself.

Before he could reach it, the inevitable occurred. A tongue of flame found its way to the mouth of a gas pipe, and fire flew into the house's inmost structure, consuming gas till there was nothing left within but flame. The infection could not be contained; it fevered the steel ribs, it bled through the jets into the rooms, it swelled against the sealed glass, and finally it burst.

For a moment, it was beautiful.

All who witnessed the house's destruction would remember it the rest of their lives. The memory would come to their minds when they thought of God or Satan, of the sublime or the supernatural. For in the instant that the house exploded, it shot its light forth in shivers of glass, sparkling brighter than diamonds, eclipsing the stars and the moon, sweeping through the air with a whistle that for a moment drowned the crackle of the flames. They speared a bird or two and showered the earth with deadly hail.

Edouard ran to press himself against the far side of the Taj Mahal, hoping its walls would shield him. He cursed his own cowardliness and even, in the space of a heartbeat, sent up a prayer that he might change.

Viggo's heart was still bent on rescue. When he saw a body sail from the house into the trees, he turned as if he might catch it in his arms. Thus the flying slivers lodged in his back and shaved away a patch of scalp; forever after, he would look as if he had been in a savage massacre, but he would live.

Myrtice, stopped among the trees, was safest. The net of needles and leaves above her caught the glass, and only the big shards fell through; one of them neatly severed the little zebra's jugular, and the animal quietly sank to its knees. Myrtice wept for it as she had done for her own lost baby—until she saw that Viggo was injured, and then she could not stop herself from rushing to him. Without a thought for the danger, she ran out into the glass storm, and this time it was her arm that encircled him, her handkerchief that stanched his blood.

In a very few moments, the glass panes were spent. But the implacable flames continued to gobble up the air, swallowing the very house itself. Soon the floors and furniture collapsed, and the fire spread over the ground in an orange blanket. Edouard fled the Taj Mahal while, with the glitter still piercing his back, Viggo abandoned Myrtice to run after the body he had seen flying.

By now people were arriving from the village, the nurses and doctors and families of the sick, anyone able-bodied enough to fight a fire or tend the injured. They had broken down the gate and came with wagons and barrels of water, horses, medical supplies.

"Halloo?" they shouted through the trees. "Mr. Versles? Survivors? Anyone?"

But Viggo and Myrtice, Edouard, and even Albert—he had escaped the house, though without time to dress himself, and in his terror he had abandoned clothes and portfolio inside—were too busy to answer. Already they were searching the woods for Famke, shaking bushes and sometimes shouting, each according to his strength and feelings for her.

"Famke, it is Viggo! I—" But even after all these miles, he could think of no more to say.

"All is forgiven," called Myrtice when he fell silent; she voiced it rather quietly, however, as she thought—unworthily—of what Famke's disappearance might mean to her.

Edouard had only one thing to say, and it cost no small effort: "*Hygeia* was a beautiful painting!"

The fire snapped close behind them.

In his nakedness, Albert was moving slowly, almost paralyzed with fear that glass would shred his skin and fire would catch him in a fatal clinch. He called, "Wherever you are, darling, don't move! Do not move!"

As he would discover, there was no way for Famke to move, for she was lying in pieces on the ground. When she landed, a thick glass sword had plunged through her chest, pinning her to the earth. More glass had cut away one foot and most of her fingers; fragments of her bones showed orange in the firelight. Part of an ear was missing, and the tip of her nose, and almost all the once-flaming, wild locks of hair.

When the searchers first came upon her, all together, they drew up short, struck dumb by the picture before them. No one knew how to look upon it. Famke's eyes were open and glazed, plainly sightless; yet there was a rasp coming from her chest that said she must still be alive.

Bravely, Viggo seized the glass sword. The old scar tissue protected his fingers as he first pulled, but soon his blood mingled with hers. Myrtice cried out then and tried to swathe his hands with her petticoat. Seeing this, Albert realized how very naked he was, and he covered himself with both of his hands. He was ashamed in front of the others, especially Edouard Versailles. But Edouard did not notice Albert's nakedness or Famke's; he knew the ground's softness meant it was soaked in blood, and he knelt to take Famke's pulse.

Famke was beyond caring about any of this. When her lungs were free of their burden, they released a wild, tired sigh. *It is too bad*, she thought dimly; *just when I was ready to begin my life.*

A great bubble of blood formed through the hole in her breast and hovered there, growing hard and dark. The artist in Famke might have liked to see that, but her eyes remained fixed on the great sea of sky, and her red lips slowly stiffened, wordless. The three men and Myrtice watched to see if they would close entirely.

And thus Famke Sommerfugl, a girl of good family, departed from the earth.

EPILOGUE

·····

She is the West's greatest artifact.
"ART NOTES,"
SAN FRANCISCO CHRONICLE

We laid her out most beautifully," remembered Albert. His expression was blank behind the smoked lenses, but he put a hand on the glass coffin in what the widow thought a tender, though somewhat horrible, caress. She fancied that his face and figure stood out against the stone walls like some medieval church figure of death, with black holes for eyes.

From the next room came the sound of groaning and cracking wood, as the Chinese workers pried away the sides of the enormous crate. With the reverberations, the blue-gowned, white-skinned, rubber-limbed corpse shuddered in her tube of glass. Her lashes fluttered as if she were about to blink, and the widow felt faint.

"She was fully embalmed," elaborated the man from the widow's own country. He, too, put a hand on the glass, and with the most delicate sympathy for what he knew must be the widow's horror, he explained that every ounce of Famke's blood had been replaced with formaldehyde, and the best quality arsenic was used. The blood drained for embalming Famke was now rusty red dust in an urn that sat atop the tombs in the Taj Mahal. In consultation with the Institute's experienced morticians, Viggo himself had directed the procedure. "But as you see"—he indicated his gnarled paw, grotesque beside the blind man's delicately gloved one— "after the glass storm, my hands were in no condition to do the fine work. They are good only for rough labor now."

"Then who is it who put her in this—this bottle?" the widow asked. Her eyes met his severely, with the look she would use to scold a servant or impose a penance.

There was a long silence, as if the men were waiting for something. And in the end it came: One of the draperies at the back of the room twitched, then undulated, and a dark man in mourner's black stepped from what turned out to be not a window recess but a small sitting area. This, she realized, must be Edouard Versailles, the art collector and amateur doctor himself.

Without introduction, he said to her, "The idea of the bottle came at the funeral. We all agreed she was too lovely to put in the ground, and we pulled her from the coffin." He stood gazing quietly down at the glass tube without touching it. The widow thought it odd that he did not look at her; but then, she realized, he had seen enough from behind his drapery.

"Monsieur Versailles has a collection of specimens in jars," Albert said. "They demonstrate that the body may last in alcohol for ten years, even twenty. I stitched her together myself," he added proudly, "though it was no easy job. I shaped a fingertip into her nose."

"My finger." Viggo showed her the stump with a modest air. "I had sliced it off in pulling the glass sword."

Against her will, but drawn by overpowering fascination, the widow bent to peer at that nose in profile. When she looked closely, it was indeed misshapen; but the stitches were nearly invisible, concealed with some sort of clay.

"The foot is her own," Albert elaborated, "but the fingers are of a girl, a lung patient, who died in the stagecoach before reaching Hygiene's hospital. Monsieur Versailles thought of it, and the family was willing."

Edouard Versailles felt compelled to tell part of the story. Once Famke was dead, he explained, he had realized he did not loathe or even fear her: He—as he confessed in a dispassionate voice, oddly divorced from the setting—he loved her. As he held her body against his, he knew that Hermes's story had been lies, that she had done no wrong but had been the angel in each house she had graced. That night, for the first time, he wept for someone other than his parents.

He visited the Anteroom the next day—there was clearly no reason to bring Famke there, so she occupied a suite at the Springs Hotel—and begged the dead patient's parents for use of her hands. Famke's corpse must be perfect for the final viewing, as her body had been in life; he would pay any price to gaze on it in its youthful glory. In this way, the Thomas family from Vestal, New York, were able to assuage their own grief with a first-class Grand Tour of Europe. And when Edouard offered a reward for tresses of bright red hair that might be stitched into a wig, Hygeia Springs was fairly flooded with boxes and bags of the stuff. He selected the truest reds and paid each contributor as promised; several of the fair but frail retired on the proceeds and became schoolteachers, then wives.

His story ended there, as if he expected the widow to make some comment—perhaps to approve of the prostitutes' moral advancement. But for the moment she would say nothing.

Viggo and Albert explained that several other great things had come to pass:

Myrtice mailed a copy of the death certificate to the federal agents, who had Heber Goodhouse released and returned to his family. With rest and Sariah's concentrated care, he regained much of his health and began to dream of ways for improving the life cycle of Chinese silkworms. After years of innovative husbandry, he succeeded in breeding a hardy new strain that he christened the Sommerfugl. It entered the Mormon record books as a miracle, and Prophet was renamed Heber City.

Viggo, meanwhile, kept the promise to Myrtice that Heber had first made three years earlier: After a small wedding in Hygeia Springs, he fathered the first of what would prove to be many offspring. Myrtice loved her husband very much, and to secure his affections she agreed to give up the eating of arsenic and to remain in Hygiene as housekeeper of the massive new residence Edouard was erecting of native stone.

To build this new house and the gallery-fortress nearby, Edouard filled in a horrible fissure that the fire had opened in the red earth. Very few were privileged to know exactly what the new house concealed, and the men told the widow about it in whispers while Edouard made feeble demurrals. Where one huge steel rib of the old palace had thrust into the earth, a spring gushed forth; and in those bubbling waters gleamed a golden dust that suggested there must be a mother lode in the rocks of Hygeia Springs. Edouard confessed that the very thought of this still caused him to wake at many a midnight, heart pounding, fearful of what it might portend for the future. The Dynamite Gang could easily find Hygeia's mountain; what might they do if they discovered the riches it contained?

The butler, Wong, hired a team of his countrymen good with shovels and pipe, and they cleverly converted the spring to a steady source of household water, with a filter to catch the gold dust. That dust was his to dispose of as he pleased. He used it to fund the fulfillment of a longtime aspiration, a wood-frame hotel he designed and named the Celestial, and he settled into a life of prosperous hostelery. Viggo was the manager-in-name who gave a respectable front to the business. The stone walls pressed the gold back into the ground, and it lay there unsuspected even by the three singsong sisters who helped direct the hotel.

Albert lived a long while in the Celestial, where he had a special suite of rooms designed along the lines of the old house, with plate glass walls for abundant light. In that airy studio he experienced a bout of intense inspiration and painted the six canvases that were to earn him Edouard's lasting affection and, in the dark years to come, his protection: *Immaculate Heart, Pearl of Great Price, Slim Princess, Angel in the House, Belle Dame Sans Merci, Winged Victory*. The paintings were based, naturally, on what Albert knew of Famke and what he could learn from the others who had known her. The series of masterworks was completed in one frenetic year by virtue of frequent visits to the glass coffin then housed in the Celestial's Royal Suite. These paintings might have pleased Edouard but would not, Albert came to know, win him much fame in the world beyond Hygeia. Even the most narcissistic of artists must realize eventually when his talents are on the wane; and Albert's waned very quickly. His renewed passion for precise detail and observation could not be satisfied, and his lines grew sloppy as he lost control of what an artist must value most: his vision. For Albert had begun to see things that were not there—faces, fingers, fish tails; mouths that laughed at him, snakes that hissed forth sparks. These images intruded on the careful painterly compositions in his mind and on his canvas. Most people thought he was going mad.

Edouard, however, called in a raft of specialists from Chicago, New York, and Paris. These learned men theorized that in the explosion, tiny splinters of glass—invisible, impalpable, insensible—had wormed into Albert's brain and infected those parts directly concerned with vision, or perhaps with inspiration. Maybe they flew up his nose or swam down his ears; more likely they pierced his skin and entered his bloodstream, forced through veins and arteries by the implacable pump of his heart, until they found harbor in his skull.

"Imagine your head as a cave," suggested one surgeon. "The glass shards have stuck to your bones and may even be growing there in the manner of stalactites . . ."

"Or ice," said Albert.

"Yes, or ice."

In the end, everywhere Albert looked, he saw nothing but Famke's face. The greatest torture was that no single image would stay before his eyes long enough to be painted; and so, since he could not have his mind's eyes removed, he took up the dark glasses and shut out exterior images. He moved to a smaller and more manageable room in the Celestial, paid for by Edouard; and although he could no longer see the paintings amid the crowd of pictures in his mind, he visited the new gallery-castle on every month's first Monday. Occasionally he climbed up to the house to share a beer with Edouard and exchange tales of the past, or to enter the Taj Mahal, cup the urn of Famke's blood in his hands, and know what it was to hold the out-pourings of another person's whole heart.

"I would like to see this urn," the widow said on that winter afternoon, years after the grand explosion. "I would like to hold it in my hands also." She was imagining it shaped not as a heart but as a face, the face of a little girl who had suckled her life's sole guardian away and still had the strength to wail and demand; the face of the woman who had held sway on the wall of a room that the widow's husband, Jørgen Skatkammer, had built espe-cially to house the vast, intricate, ugly painting that she now knew the model had painted herself.

"But first we must look again at the picture," she said; and thus it was she who led the way into the next room, to see the thing tilted in the gilt frame that her husband had commissioned to bear the inscription:

> *Himlen sortner, Storme brage!*
> *Visse Time du er kommen.*
> *Hvad de gav de tog tilbage.*
> *Evig bortsvandt Helligdommen.*

The sky is darkening, roar the gale! / Fatal hour, you have come. / What they gave they took away. / Forever ruined, sacred thing.

Seeing it here, the widow felt an unexpected surge of relief: The painting had at last been laid to rest, and with it the most painful part of her conscience. While it hung on her own wall, that face, that hair, that figure had reminded her every day of her life how she had failed to protect the most precious soul in her care, how the girl herself had fallen beyond her reach. And yet it was the ugliness in that painted face which, ironically, had inspired Jørgen Skatkammer to give up his foolish dream of spring love and write to a convent in the distant reaches of Norway with an offer of marriage: Hygeia's coarse features had secured Mother Birgit a kind of life she had never even thought to dream about, a life of comfort and what passed in most circles for love.

Thus each person who was intimate witness to the spectacle of Famke Ursula Summerfield Goodhouse's life, who felt its beauty and its dangers firsthand, would spin out the remainder of his or her days. From time to time, they would all cough and suffer exaggerated fevers; but these were slight prices to pay for more than the usual measure of happiness.

While those four looked at the painting in its cracked wooden shell, the ash-white corpse slowly settled into stillness in the dark room next door. In repose, she no longer seemed boneless; her hair and her lips even lost their unnatural flame, and she looked like a normal girl—one with broken pearls for eyes and a deep streak of gold in her veins. The widow glanced back at her as she and Viggo, Edouard Versailles and the blind Albert Castle closed the door on the painting that had at last found its home.

Birgit let out a deep breath. "It is terrible, what happens to the body."

"That is true," Albert agreed, "but is it not just as wonderful what art can do?"

ACKNOWLEDGMENTS

I am grateful for the historical and/or medical expertise, sagacious critical opinions, and inventive support of a number of people: Maarj and Buster Darraugh, Robert Alter, John Vernon, Lynne Landwehr, Frederick Aldama, Josh Russell, Jennifer Beachey, Julie Anderson, Sadie Iovino, Paul Keats, Josephine Park, Kathryn Rummell, Mary Armstrong, Joanne Ruggles and her models Doña and Susan, Siouxie Lee, Stanley Walens, Salaam Quintanilla, Brian and Cynthia Donnelly, Lael Gold, Karin Sanders, C. Puff, Grant Mudge, Miriam Cokal, the great spirit of Grendel, my former colleagues at California Polytechnic University, and my new ones at Virginia Commonwealth University. I am especially indebted to my dear friends Leslie Hayes, who read the earliest version, and Tom Fahy, who read the latest (several times); both gave me exactly what I needed, and I would be reduced to graphite smudges without them. I would be even worse, of course, without the good offices of my agent, Liv Blumer, and her partner, Bill; or of Fred Ramey, Greg Michalson, Caitlin Hamilton Summie, and the rest of Unbridled Books. I thank you all very much.

I extend my gratitude, also, to every reader; and for those who may wonder at my choice of subject matter, I quote again here the words on the title page of Lydia E. Pinkham's pamphlet on female complaints and ailments:

This little book treats of delicate subjects, and has been sent to you only by request. It is not intended for indiscriminate reading, but for your own private information.